"Boggards! Coming out of the tom

Mirian spun and saw about two do.

from the tomb. Four in the front were blinking in the others fanned out as a large, hunched mottled-brown boggard pointed them forward.

They weren't alone.

More boggards erupted from the forest on their right, croaking war cries as they spotted Mirian's little group. Suddenly she was face to face with two of them, trading blows. The moment one went down another was there to take its place.

The next one dropped with its brain-pan half melted by a lance of green acid from Ivrian's wand, but those behind showed no sign of stopping. In moments, Mirian and Jekka were in the thick of it, broad forms on every side thrusting at them with wicked barbed spears, all the while gnashing pointed teeth.

She sent another down in a welter of blood, heard a male cry of pain.

"Help!" Venthan called. "Lord Tradan's been hit!"

There was no time to worry about that. Mirian knocked a spear aside with her free arm and slashed another foe across the leg. It dropped, warbling.

There were too damned many of them . . .

THE PATHFINDER TALES LIBRARY

THE PATHFINDER TALES LIBRARY

THROUGH THE GATE IN THE SEA

Howard Andrew Jones

A TOM DOHERTY ASSOCIATES BOOK

New York

This is a work of fiction. All of the characters, organizations, and events portrayed in this novel are either products of the author's imagination or are used fictitiously.

PATHFINDER TALES: THROUGH THE GATE IN THE SEA

Copyright © 2017 by Paizo Inc.

Maps by Crystal Frasier and Rob Lazzaretti

A Tor Book
Published by Tom Doherty Associates
175 Fifth Avenue
New York, NY 10010

www.tor-forge.com

The Library of Congress Catalog-in-Publication Data is available upon request.

ISBN 978-0-7653-8438-6 (trade paperback)
ISBN 978-0-7653-8439-3 (e-book)

Our books may be purchased in bulk for promotional, educational, or business use. Please contact your local bookseller or the Macmillan Corporate and Premium Sales Department at 1-800-221-7945, extension 5442, or by e-mail at MacmillanSpecialMarkets@macmillan.com.

First Edition: February 2017

Printed in the United States of America

0   9   8   7   6   5   4   3   2   1

To the memory of Kris Ghosh, M.D. (1969–2015), father, chef, surgeon, traveler, and brother in all but blood.

Inner Sea Region

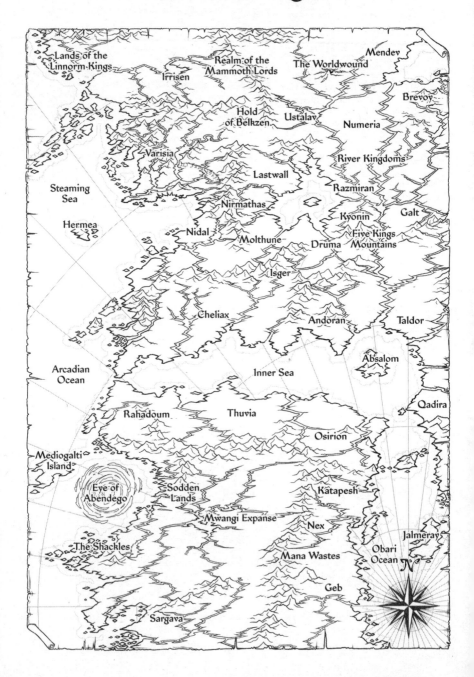

Sargava

1

TREASURE IN THE DEEP

MIRIAN

As the *Daughter of the Mist* slipped lightlessly past Smuggler's Shiv that night, Mirian Raas would have laid bets some mangy vessel had sails spread nearby, either coasting in or heading out from the berths that tongued from the rocky shore. While the band of pirates known as the Free Captains was oath-bound to keep hands off Sargavan shipping, approaching the famed haven of cutthroats, privateers, and murderers was tempting fate.

Mirian had no choice. A nighttime drop, with all its inherent risks, was still safer in these waters than anchoring near the Shiv in broad daylight, when she would be seen by thousands of curious and covetous observers.

She stood in the high, narrow prow of the swift little caravel, leaning without thinking into every roll of her ship as she searched the darkness. The brightest gleam rose from the distant lanterns of roisterers lairing in Smuggler's Shiv. Mirian glanced up at the scudding clouds. She was cautiously satisfied. As long as they continued to cover the silvery arc of moon, the *Daughter* had a reasonable chance of slipping in and out without being seen.

Mirian wasn't averse to danger, but she abhorred risking her people. Sending her crew into the shrouds in this darkness increased the odds someone would plant a foot wrong and plunge to the deck, or into the black waves. She was reasonably certain her old hands could manage well, but as she turned away she felt another pang of guilt for gambling their lives on this venture.

She walked aft to the narrow quarterdeck, nodding at two of the hands as she passed, and stopped at the wheel to consult with their passenger, who waited beside Rendak, the *Daughter's* first mate.

Though Rendak was fit and compactly muscular, his belly usually sagged just a little. Even in the dim light, Mirian could see he was sucking in his gut. Rendak held himself a little straighter than usual, too, though his height couldn't approach that of their passenger and guide, the druid Djenba.

The woman lingered on his left, a slim figure redolent of sandalwood and coconut. Her husky contralto carried softly to Mirian. "We'll be there soon, Captain."

"How soon?" Rendak asked smoothly. With Djenba, he took any word as an opening for conversation. Divorced twice, widowed once, Rendak was hardly a romantic, but Djenba had him acting like a lovestruck youth.

"It's hard to say." Djenba spoke every word like a drawn-out sigh, detached and languid. "The animals I speak with are hardly exact." A gull on the rail screeched piercingly, then launched itself into the night. "Soon enough. I think you'll need to veer to the right a little."

"Starboard," Rendak corrected, good-humoredly, then shifted the wheel under calloused hands.

"Yes, starboard." Djenba patted one of his thick forearms. "Thank you."

Mirian was certain Djenba knew damned well to say starboard, since the famous druid had consulted with sea captains and sailors for at least a decade. Even Sargavan nobles called upon Djenba at her ramshackle oceanside mansion when they wished word of the sea, or came with coin to have her bless newly commissioned vessels. The druid's renown—and beauty—could land her just about any man she wanted, so why toy with Rendak? Mirian had a hard time gauging her.

Djenba was a fixture of the coast, true, but that didn't make her trustworthy. Reefs and currents were fixtures of the Sargavan coast as well, and they could be treacherous even when well marked on the charts. Djenba had agreed readily enough to help Mirian's expedition, though she'd refused to name a fee. She'd simply said Mirian would owe her a favor.

Mirian had chewed over the meaning of that phrase ever since, and she gnawed on it some more as Rendak exchanged a grin with the woman. Was Djenba simply playing with him, or was she honestly interested in the older man? Having never really caught on to the art of flirting, Mirian was a poor judge.

She couldn't help sounding a little clipped as she said, "I'll tell Jekka to ready for the drop."

"I'll keep her on course," Rendak declared with confidence. Of course he would—he was the first mate. But then, Mirian knew the words were really meant for Djenba.

Mirian strode off, feeling the wooden deck roll under her bare feet. She couldn't shake a sense of disquiet about the druid. Mirian would only be too glad when they put her ashore.

She opened the door to her stern cabin.

Once inside, there was just enough room to walk upright, so long as she ducked every now and then under the framing timbers. She knew the cabin well enough to have managed it in the pitch dark, but she had no need. Dull lights glowed on the table just to her right, shielded from outside view by draped and shuttered windows. Straight ahead lay her tidy bunk, under the small stern gallery windows. To her left, her well-organized desk was a blocky shadow built into the bulkhead.

She stepped to the right, where her blood brother Jekka sat at the narrow table, his long, scaled hands tracing the characters on a black metal cone the size of a small gourd. On the table beside the robed lizard man sat two of the hand-sized glow stones they were going to carry overboard with them, doubling now as night lamps.

Jekka glanced up at her, his long, dark tongue flicking out from his snout. He was slim and almost monkish-looking now that he'd taken to wearing an off-white robe. The hood hung shapeless below his wide shoulders.

His forked tongue-flick judged much more than scent. He'd told Mirian that tasting the air enabled him to read moods and gather information a human understood through facial expressions. He was getting better at comprehending body language without it, but more subtle readings still eluded him.

"I thought you had every line memorized," Mirian said.

"I do." Jekka pushed back the black metal cone, fingers brushing across the tiny, precise lizardfolk script beside a sapphire gem embedded into the reflective metal. "It's still easier to think about the words when they rest beneath my fingers. Is it time for our drop?"

"Nearly so."

While Jekka's mannerisms were a challenge to read sometimes, there was no missing his eagerness. The yellow-golden eyes above his narrow snout practically glowed, and not just because they were more reflective than her own. "Do you think there'll be a message for us when we return home?"

"Probably not at night."

He objected with a polite head inclination. "It might have arrived late in the afternoon, right as we left."

"It's possible. Don't get your hopes up, though. There may be nothing. I don't know if my sister's husband is going to have any information." Or if Tradan would even want to share it, but Mirian didn't want to explain *that* to Jekka. Mirian had rarely spoken to either her half sister Charlyn or her husband, and neither had attended her father's funeral. Who could say how they would welcome a letter from a half-native relation, when they were blue-blooded aristocrats?

"I understand," Jekka answered.

She didn't think he truly could. The differences between human society and that of Jekka's own were too great. But then, Jekka had virtually no society left, apart from interactions with his cousin Kalina. She was likely burning oil right now at the Sargavan Pathfinder Society lodge, where she'd been welcomed to search through a small collection of lizardfolk book cones. Neither Mirian, Jekka, nor Kalina thought it likely those cones would tell them anything helpful regarding the whereabouts of other surviving lizardfolk from the Karshnaar clan, which was why Jekka was so desirous to hear something from Mirian's brother-in-law.

Tradan was one of those rich men who thought themselves experts in fields they only dabbled in. His particular interest was antiquities, which had led him to Mirian and Charlyn's father years before. In addition to Charlyn's hand, Tradan had acquired a number of Raas family artifacts, among them several ancient charts that might contain information on a small landmass off the coat of Sargava described on Jekka's book cones. The island of Kutnaar existed on no modern maps, but one of the three cones Jekka had been studying discussed Kutnaar's lizardfolk metropolis in some detail, down to the layout of its port and glittering central dome. Was the island fictitious? Had it sunk? Or might the old mapmakers have had access to knowledge long since lost and unknown to modern explorers?

The soonest Tradan could possibly have sent a return message was three days ago, assuming he'd been inclined to respond at all. Both Jekka and Kalina had practically lived upon the Raas family porch since that time, frightening any passersby by springing up to see if they'd brought letters or packages.

"We'll have to worry about packages later," Mirian told him. "It's time."

"Very well, my sister."

Jekka set the cone aside and stood to shrug out of the robe. Draped over his powerful, green-and-white-scaled chest hung

a necklace of turquoise stones and a circular medallion personally awarded to him by the Custodian of Sargava. Apart from the
robe, his only garment was a long loincloth, similarly belted with
turquoise stones.

Mirian wore tight-fitting, calf-length breeches and nearly all
the swim gear she required. She pulled off her loose blouse to
reveal a muscular midriff and a dark halter, then lifted a belt from a
chair back—one that held both her knife and wand—and buckled
it around her waist just above the sword belt she already wore.

The wand was one-third of a legacy passed down through
generations of family salvagers. The other two-thirds she wore on
her ring fingers. One dark band granted her the ability to breathe
beneath the waves, the other the ability to move in water as freely
as in air. When Mirian swam, she experienced no resistance or
counterpressure, no matter the depth.

The second ring's twin, once her great-great-grandfather's, was
her objective this night. It lay somewhere in the murk below. Her
friend Ivrian had fumbled and dropped the ring while rescuing
Mirian from drowning. She didn't hold that against the young
man. On the contrary, she was grateful to Ivrian for rescuing not
only her, but her second mate Gombe as well. But she had no
intentions of letting the valuable magical bauble lie in the muck
forever. It wasn't just an expensive and useful tool; it was a unique
one, handed down through her family for generations.

Mirian reached down to grab her haversack. She didn't expect
to find anything below apart from the missing ring, but there was
always a chance they'd spot something else worth recovering.

She and Jekka took up the glow stones, dimming them with a
word before slipping them into pouches they draped about their
necks. She waited a final moment while Jekka grabbed his staff,
then stepped with him out onto the deck.

The wind was up, and Miriam breathed in the ever-present
salt spray on its breath.

Djenba quietly instructed Rendak to slow, so he ordered the crew to slack the sails. A few minutes later Djenba told him to halt and, as the rest of the sails were hauled in, word was quietly sent forward to drop anchor. Gombe trotted over to report the act complete. He grinned at Jekka.

Rendak cleared his throat, and then affected a formal tone: "Captain, are you sure you don't want me and Gombe down there with you?"

Normally he just called her Mirian. She supposed the title was for Djenba's benefit. "Jekka and Djenba and I will handle it." In truth, she *did* want Rendak and Gombe with her, but she also wanted the ship to be safe. "It should be a quick trip. You ready, Jekka?"

"I am, my sister. Gombe, you will guard my medal?" He took it from his neck, wrapped the red ribbon about it, and passed it to his friend.

Gombe smiled. "With my life, Jekka."

"I thank you," Jekka said with a head bow. Gombe was always quick with a joke, but he had enough sense not to tease Jekka about a point of pride.

Mirian turned to the druid. "Priestess Djenba?"

The woman cast down her robe and there was a soft gasp from some of the crew nearby.

The priestess cut a shapely silhouette, trim and toned, her figure curving against fabric so wispy it left only a few patches of skin to the imagination.

"I am ready now," she said, and stepped to the ladder. "My form will change once I'm in the water. Don't be afraid. Once we are near the place, I will speak with the sea life there and learn where your ring's to be found." Without further preamble, Djenba plunged over the side in a perfect dive.

"Damn," Gombe whispered. "Can we travel with her more often?"

Mirian was surprised by a little surge of envy—not for the attention of the crew, but for the excellence of the woman's dive.

Mirian checked to make sure the straps were tight over each of her sheathes. Her tightly kinked hair was too short to drape into her eyes, but she ran a hand back through it in an effort to settle her thoughts. Determined not to be outdone, she took a running leap and flung herself over the rail, parting the waves with barely a ripple.

The water was deliciously cool. The salt was a familiar discomfort to her eyes, one she blinked away. She delayed a moment to allow the magic of her rings to flower. A dull radiance shone about her neck as shimmering yellow gills appeared to filter water into air, and a similar glow rose as transparent fins took shape over her feet and formed luminous, tapering flukes from wrist to elbow.

Jekka dropped in beside her, light from his glow stone reflecting off the sharpened point projecting from his staff.

The water was inky black, and Mirian whispered her glow stone to life. It lit the area before them in a white cone.

The illumination startled a school of sleepy surgeonfish, which darted off into the darkness with a flash of blue scales.

A small whirlpool floated a few feet out, and it took Mirian a moment to realize it must be Djenba in her elemental form. The druid's swirling form kept pace as Mirian kicked down. Jekka was quick to follow, propelled by long legs; slim, clawed feet that served as natural flippers; and a powerful tail.

It was not as dark below the water as above. They passed a school of small fish with blue glowing bellies and foreheads. A radiant eel swam only a few yards out, a rippling rainbow that might have been a warning or a mating enticement.

Twenty, thirty, forty feet they dropped, passing motes of silt and tiny fish. Still they descended farther, and Mirian felt the weight of the water above even as the ring protected her from its effects.

The whirlpool that was Djenba darted swiftly away. The ring might be nearby, but it was still a vast span of seabed, even assuming Ivrian was roughly accurate about where he'd been when he lost it.

Mirian swam on, eyeing the darkness and wondering how she'd be able to spot the ring on her own. The druid was their only hope, and, she reckoned, a slim one. She didn't imagine sea creatures would have paid much notice to something dropping from the surface, let alone remember it for very long.

Suddenly there was a flicker of movement in the lemony light she shined below, and she tensed in alarm. A tentacle?

No, it was only kelp. A forest of the stuff. They were approaching the bottom. Ocean charts had shown her a few shallow ridges in this area, but she hadn't dared hope the ring might lie in the midst of one.

The druid's swirling spout appeared on her right for a moment, then vanished once more. Was she seeking creatures with whom to speak, or could she do that in elemental form? Mirian hadn't asked. She glanced at Jekka. He could hold his breath for long minutes, but she knew he was reaching his halfway point, so she was surprised when he suddenly darted off to the right. He had no time for wasted movement or energy. Strange. If Jekka had seen something threatening, he should have signaled her. That's what he'd been taught to d—but then, he was still new to all this.

She would have instantly turned to investigate if she weren't intent on following the druid. She kicked after Djenba.

Mirian saw the claw only moments before the enormous crab reached up from the kelp to snap at her. She swung away and the thing scuttled after, the clack of its pincer rattling her ears. The monster could easily have cut her leg in half.

As the crab launched itself at her, she arched over it with a dancer's grace. The creature reached for her again and pivoted sharply to follow. Frowning, she lifted her wand, concentrated as she kicked away, then sent a burst of green glowing energy from the weapon's tip and into the waving plant life beside it.

The thing stopped short at the sudden flash of light. Then, apparently deciding to pursue easier game, it trundled off into the jungle of marine foliage.

Mirian searched the darkness and the kelp again with her light, then discovered the waterspout spinning beside her.

As soon as the light touched her changed form, Djenba sped on past the kelp. She sent up a cloud of silt as she dropped toward a rocky downslope.

Mirian frowned, virtually blinded, and held her breath while the disturbance subsided. A moment later she saw the ring of black metal wobbling slowly up amid Djenba's swirling shape, and she smiled despite herself.

It seemed intrusive to just reach in and pluck the ring from the water that was for all intents and purposes part of the druid's body, so she was glad when Djenba sent the ring drifting toward her.

Mirian caught it in her palm, shone the glow stone upon it, and grinned in relief.

The druid had done it. This was the ring worn by her father, and her grandfather before him, and her Ijo-blooded great-great-grandfather before even that—an ebon band with a faintly traced wave pattern angling to the right, identical to the one on her own finger.

She smiled in gratitude, then carefully set the ring in one of her belt pockets.

The druid spun a little slower, then started up.

From her left came a flurry of motion and Mirian turned to find Jekka swimming for her in a direct line.

He looked worried, with wide eyes and raised frill. He hung in the water beside her, pointing with one hand in the direction he'd come from, and motioning her toward him with the other. He hadn't yet mastered all of the signs her salvagers used for communicating underwater.

He shouted into her ear, his words dull and characterless in the water.

"Shipwreck!"

Then he swished toward the surface in an explosion of kicking feet and swinging tail, his great lungs finally hungry for air.

She tempered her own reaction with awareness of his inexperience. It was always interesting to see a wreck, but often there was little enough to recover. Her family had made their living salvaging shipwrecks for generations. All manner of vessels littered the ocean floor of Desperation Bay. Jekka had none of that experience or tradition to draw upon.

Wand tight in her hand, she swam in the direction her blood brother had pointed, her glow stone lighting her way.

The wreck lay only a few hundred feet on, close enough that she wondered how she'd missed it. The gloom, she thought, or the crab's attack.

She mouthed a prayer to Desna that Jekka could see farther underwater than she could, for he had found a fine treasure indeed.

A long sleek ship sat upright upon the ocean floor, its black flanks only lightly polluted by barnacles and moss. That in itself was astonishing, given that sea life quickly rendered a wreck almost unrecognizable. Yet the ship's condition was the least of the surprises here.

Mirian swam along the vessel's immense length, her eyes taking in the high prow and bowsprit, the intricacy of the lizard faces shaped into its rail . . .

From this alone, she knew without question this was no modern vessel. It must have rested here on the bottom for thousands of years, somehow uncorrupted by time.

A ship of the ancient lizardfolk.

2

THE BLACK SHIP

MIRIAN

As she played the glow stone over the hull, Mirian imagined the vessel surging along the waves in its glory days, full canvas spread from the trio of towering masts, the dragon-shaped prow rising and falling with the ocean current.

And then she was once more staring at a sunken hulk.

She was swimming slowly toward the bow, wand at the ready, when Jekka joined her. She gave him the hand sign for caution. There was no telling what might be using the wreck as its home.

The figurehead was even more lovely than she'd supposed, carved with that minute detail she'd seen on many lizardfolk objects. Upon closer inspection, Mirian recognized it as a stylized rendition of one of her least favorite creatures: a sea drake. She scowled at the thing. One of the monsters had stalked her when she was a child, and another had chased her expedition through the tunnels of a lizardfolk city before killing her friend Ivrian's mother.

Her hand tightened around the wand and she came perilously close to blasting the serpentine image into floating chunks.

But she had better sense. Provided they could get the figurehead free, they'd probably get a tidy sum for it from some collector. As a member of the Pathfinder Society, she knew not to let personal feeling interfere with a historical find.

Mirian drifted away from the figurehead and back along the narrow bow, light from her glow stone glinting off something half hidden in scum. She swam closer to investigate.

A lumpy object was set into the ship's side six feet below the rail and about the same distance from the bowsprit, in the approximate place that Osirian mariners painted eyes on their ships.

Often she wore gloves on salvage runs, but having anticipated recovering nothing more than a ring down here, she'd dived without them. She reached to touch the object gingerly with her left hand, wiping fingers through grime to reveal a large violet jewel.

At that her eyebrows rose. If this were a real gem, it could easily be worth thousands of gold sails.

Realizing she'd been focused single-mindedly upon her discovery, she checked behind, above, and around her. Her father had taught her not to be so intent you forgot your surroundings. *Nearly everything under the water is a predator,* he'd told her, *and some of them are larger than you.*

She saw Jekka's light still playing farther back. Time to confer. She swam over to him and the lizard man's slit pupils contracted in her light beam. She shined the light at her hand so he could see her signal to surface.

His tongue extended, as it sometimes did when he was thoughtful or uncertain, but he followed as she kicked up, and in a few moments they were drifting in the darkness under the stars. Mirian's instinctive sense of direction told her the *Daughter of the Mist* lay to her left, but she couldn't see it, or even hear the lap of the ocean against its side.

"Isn't it amazing, my sister?" Jekka asked. "A ship of my people!"

"It *is* amazing. I'd give a lot to know what they painted on the hull to preserve it so well. But there are two things, my brother. Listen well."

Sometimes, when she spoke with the lizard man, Mirian found herself unintentionally adopting his formal diction. She supposed she was learning some of his habits, just as he learned some of hers.

"You have my attention," he answered.

"You must *always* signal me. And be watching for me, under-water. Don't dart off like that."

He nodded, an exaggerated bob on that long neck.

"We have to watch for each other," she went on, "because there may be something watching us."

"So you have said. Forgive me, Sister."

"No harm done—yet. Don't forget, you need to swim back to the ship and report in. Tell Rendak what we've found and borrow his air bottle."

"I don't need it."

"You damned well do. You can't keep popping up and down the whole time. I want to go inside the hull and look around, and I want someone to back me up. You could get trapped in the hull and drown."

"I don't need it," he repeated stubbornly.

"You promised to defer to me in salvaging. Are you going back on your word?"

He hissed. "You shame me, Sister. Very well. But how am I to watch you if you're going alone to the wreck?"

"You're going to come back quickly. And I'm going to continue my inspection on the outside." Not the safest option, admittedly, but Mirian was an old hand at this, and the seas seemed pretty calm at this drop.

"I will do these things."

"Thank the druid while you're there," she continued, "and apologize to her for the delay. Tell Rendak to turn four points to starboard and come a half mile before dropping anchor. And when he asks if he or Gombe should drop, tell him I'll let them know when we're done scouting."

"I will remember," Jekka assured her.

She was fairly certain he would. The lizard man had an amazing ability to retain oral information and repeat it word for word. Habits, like those of salvaging routines, however, were different from rote memorization.

"Get it done and come find me. I'm as eager as you to see what lies aboard."

Then she raised a hand in farewell and dove below.

On her return trip to the wreck, she wondered what would have happened if she'd descended for the ring alone, or with Rendak or Gombe. Nothing, probably. She'd chosen Jekka in part because he needed to get used to what a salvaging run was like, but also because he'd been so excited to become a salvager. She guessed that was because he now saw the crew as part of his extended clan and wished to contribute to its well-being.

While she waited for Jekka, she carefully surveyed the ship's perimeter, familiarizing herself with the length and breadth of the vessel and searching for telltale warning signs that something large and unpleasant lurked within. Ocean predators weren't especially noted for their intellects. If there were anything nasty living here, there'd likely be discarded carcasses nearby, each crawling with bottom-feeders.

She saw no such indications. That didn't rule out the possibility of more intelligent creatures like aquatic ogres or sea devils lairing there, but she saw no sign of tracks or prints along the rail or upon any of the closed cabin doors leading into the bowels of the ship.

Mirian almost missed the large gash at the vessel's stern, in the shadow of the hull. She studied the damaged wood and realized she was probably looking at the ship's death wound. Most likely the ship had struck a reef.

After a careful examination, Mirian had a pretty clear picture of the ship. It was half again as long as a typical three-master, but perhaps a third shallower across the beam. The decks were high and rose steeply at the prow. Probably there were a good three decks below, and back of the quarterdeck were two more above.

Two masts were forward and a mizzenmast stood broken off almost to the deck, right through the wheelhouse itself.

Mirian was looking at the wheel when Jekka finally rejoined her. He took hold of the wheel with one hand to steady himself. Straps of a haversack crossed his chest.

Jekka had slid an object used by the other salvagers in her crew into a side pocket of his haversack. The magic item was colloquially known as an air bottle, and once someone learned the trick of using one, it was possible to spend long hours below the water. Her grandfather had invested in two for the family's help, and hit upon the idea of a tube to affix to the bottle so the fragile object could be kept in a padded back satchel.

The tube worked much better if you had lips to close around it—something Jekka lacked. When he'd first attempted to use it, he couldn't pull air without water coming in as well, unless he jammed the tube so far down his throat he nearly gagged. She understood why he didn't want to repeat the experience, but he'd have to adapt if he was going to be a salvager.

A cool current buffeted Mirian as she examined a peculiar column rising beside the wheel. At first glance, it looked like another mast had been sheared off, but that made no sense. That would have placed it off-center from the rest of the vessel.

She scraped at a layer of blue algae. Instead of a broken mast, she uncovered a diagonal plate resembling a display in an expensive jewelry shop. An array of gems was set into its black metal. She scrubbed harder, exposing tiny symbols incised beside each jewel.

Jekka leaned close, running his scaly fingers over the letters.

The writing certainly resembled the same language Mirian had seen on the lizardfolk book cones, but she knew many languages looked similar to the uninitiated. She pointed to the symbols and then back at Jekka.

The lizard man nodded vigorously and touched a set of characters. "No wind!" he shouted, air bubbling out of his mouth.

He put his fingers beside a flat, violet stone, and it took him three attempts before she could understand him through the water: "Opener of the way."

Jekka paused to suck in the tube, then pulled it out, coughing more air bubbles.

There were four more gems with inscriptions. Mirian spread her hands apart in a silent question.

Clearly perplexed, the lizard man shook his head.

She traced the multifaceted ruby he'd told her meant "no wind." It looked like it might turn in its pitted housing.

Interesting. Slowly, carefully, she set her fingers on the gem and tried moving it clockwise. It didn't budge. When she twisted in the other direction, the gem lit from within.

Mirian looked to Jekka for explanation, but he merely shrugged.

She made a second twist and the deck shook beneath them. Clouds of silt billowed up, and from somewhere below came a loud scraping noise. It wasn't until she looked to port and turned her beam there that she noticed the landscape moving . . .

No, the ship was! Mirian let out a colorful oath and quickly twisted the jewel all the way to the right so that it returned to its original setting. It ceased glowing and the ship slowed.

She looked at Jekka as if to say, *What the hell was that?*

The lizard man stared back at her, reptilian eyes blinking.

This was a major find, but there was no way they'd pry any of the gems out of here. "No wind" apparently meant the ship could be set in motion magically when there was no breeze. She marveled at that, wondering whether a skilled enough magic-worker could remove it from the ship and install it on another. Like, say, the *Daughter of the Mist*, or that behemoth Ivrian was so set on building.

She pointed to an opening into darkness and directed her glow stone onto a barnacle-encrusted ladder. Apparently only the hull had the special protective coating.

Jekka tapped his chest and pointed into the hold, letting her know he intended to lead, then brandished his own glow stone.

She almost objected, then decided he was at least communicating this time, and remembered he was both an experienced warrior and excited to be searching a ship made by his own people. She allowed him to swim in front, staying a few feet back from the swish of his whiplike tale.

Most of the hold's contents had shifted to starboard. Her light played over brown and green weeds dusted by occasional splotches of red and blue. They obscured the hold's contents in a soft, furry blanket.

Jekka floated above it all, shining his own light on something to the right, then pointed at a long segmented worm with pincers. Mirian's father had always called them rot worms, though to Mirian they looked more like oversized centipedes. Their bite was deadly poisonous and they tended to be aggressive when disturbed, so she moved quickly.

The arm-length creature shifted away at Jekka's spear thrust, rearing up and stirring the water with its legs. Mirian cut it in half with her cutlass. It floated apart, wriggling in its death throes.

Jekka brushed it out of the way and shined his light on the patch of growth where the rot worm had been hidden. It didn't seem to have any nest mates.

She floated on with Jekka, imagining the hold moving with robed lizardfolk, perhaps lashing down that stack of crates over there, or walking on through the narrow archway into the next chamber.

Jekka stopped beside three large chests resting against the hull, each rotten with age. As Mirian played her light over the area, tiny crustaceans swam frantically for darkness. Little silver fish flashed away in alarm.

Mirian signaled Jekka to keep watch and he turned from her to survey their surroundings.

She had never seen a lizardfolk chest before, but the one directly before her proved little different from those built by humans, save that the lock mechanism was inset along the top right. That in itself was of interest. She made a mental note to record the information in her Pathfinder journal.

Normally, she would have simply smashed open a chest this old and rotten, but it was such an odd, rare find she wanted to handle it with care.

The bronze lock was green with corrosion and looked as though it had been designed to accommodate a cylindrical mechanism rather than a key—far beyond her lock-picking abilities, but there were other ways. She removed a small pry bar from her pack and set to work on the hinges.

The tool's teeth sank easily into the rotten wood, and in moments both hinges were floating free. After that, the lid came up easily. Mirian drifted back as she lifted it. There was no telling what might come crawling out.

Nothing did.

She again swam closer, her light settling on a rotted wooden frame inside the chest that kept a dozen blue cylindrical bottles upright and separate. Five were broken along their necks, but the others, though empty, looked intact—more tube than jar, with a peculiar fluted opening at the top.

Mirian played the light over the inside, then carefully lifted one of the vessels free and drew it closer it for examination.

Jekka drifted beside her. His long, forked tongue flicked with excitement.

She looked at him questioningly.

His head cocked in interest and he mimed drinking with it.

Mirian handed it to him to examine, then signed for him to put it in his pack. They could spend months clearing this wreck. It was probably time to fetch Rendak and Gombe.

Desna had truly blessed them. The wreck was a fantastic find. There was no telling what sort of oddities might be left aboard, let alone their value and historical significance. As a salvager, she depended upon scavenging sites like this. But as a Pathfinder, she was dedicated to uncovering the secrets of Golarion's past to preserve and disseminate knowledge. If the magical wind mechanism built into this ship could be understood and replicated, it might very well change the future of sea travel.

Jekka pointed to the chest next to the one they'd opened. He clearly wanted to see what was inside.

She decided to humor him and signaled for him to guard once more.

The hinges on the second chest were even more worn, and yielded with no resistance.

Within stood twelve rows of sculpted lizardfolk heads fashioned from a thin metal alloy and inlaid with jewels. Each eye socket was set with amber stones, the figures themselves rich with the minute symbols of Jekka's people.

The sight so thrilled her blood brother that his frill rose, and Mirian had to remind him to keep watch, though she did acquiesce to setting all two dozen of the sculptures within her pack.

The haversacks they wore had been gifts from Ivrian's mother, and were ensorcelled to contain more space on the inside than was apparent without. All of the sculptures fit easily without altering the haversack's weight in the slightest, another wonderful feature.

Jekka signed to indicate they should open the third chest, but she shook her head and pointed to the surface. Then she looked back to the chests and smiled, trying to reassure him they'd come back for all of it.

Mirian led the way out. Jekka trailed some length after, seemingly reluctant to leave.

Sooner than expected she found the anchor chain and, looming above, the dark bowline of the *Daughter of the Mist*.

Her hands closed on the familiar rungs of the ladder built into the vessel's side. She felt the magical gills fade the moment she thrust her head above the water and breathed deeply of the crisp salty air.

All was silhouettes and shadows against the lesser darkness of the sky, but she thought she made out Gombe's lean outline near the ladder. She grinned at him as she stepped forward, slinging her bag off her shoulder.

"You won't believe what we've found," she told him.

A man with a sword stepped around Gombe, the point of the weapon at the first mate's throat. "I'm all ears."

3
UNEXPECTED ALLIES
MIRIAN

Mirian Raas," said the deep, cultured voice at the back end of the sword. "Well, this is most unexpected."

Mirian peered into the darkness, saw a crowd of figures on her deck as Gombe was pushed away. "I'm sorry," he said, only to be brutally cuffed.

The unfamiliar voice spoke on. "Why, just yesterday I was saying to my mate how much I'd like to meet you, and here Desna has thrust us together."

The stranger might have been in the mood for play, but Mirian's voice was deadly serious. "Where's the rest of my crew?"

He laughed shortly. "Dear lady, you're a commander after my own heart, devoted to the safety of her people. Fear not." The sword gave a little flourish and came to rest pointed at her breast. "They're unharmed. As is your lovely passenger. I'm a gentleman, and have no interest in inflicting bodily harm upon anyone so long as we come to a financial arrangement."

Mirian searched the sky beyond the looming figure and saw a tall-masted ship alongside her own with grappling lines attached. She let out a low oath. Maybe Ivrian was right and they *did* need a bigger ship. One with a trained crew of fighters she could keep aboard.

She forced a steely politeness. "What sort of arrangement do you have in mind?"

"To begin with, one that isn't conducted with weapons in hand. It's distasteful. Second, one conducted under lighted conditions.

There's no need for us to keep to the shadows. So. First, I'd like you to slip off that weapons belt and make no move to withdraw the wand I've read so much about."

Read about? Of course. Ivrian and his damned pamphlet. Local bookstalls been selling his account of their adventures for the last few months.

So far she'd heard no sound of Jekka surfacing behind her, and her questioner made no mention of awaiting him. Probably Rendak had said as little as necessary.

"With whom am I speaking?"

"Forgive me." Again the sword dipped. "I'm Meric Ensara, Captain of the *Marvel*. Now, please, divest yourself of weapons so I may sheathe my own and we can get down to business."

"And my crew will be unharmed?" Mirian asked.

"So long as they prove reasonable they'll be safe, I assure you."

"Where are they now?"

"In the hold."

"I'd like to speak with them."

Ensara sighed, but his reply was tempered with unctuous patience. "But of course, dear lady. First, though, the weapons. Sarken, light her, please."

There was the clatter of a metal lantern shade being pulled open, and suddenly she found herself completely illuminated. Some man behind Ensara let out a wolf whistle and Ensara snarled: "Belay that!"

Mirian would have given much to know where Jekka was, or to have a chance to draw a weapon, but she did as bade and unbuckled her sword belt. It thumped to the deck.

"Now the belt with your wand, if you please," Ensara instructed.

"You're very polite," Mirian said dryly. But she followed his instructions carefully and undid the belt with her knife, the wand, and utility pouches, hoping against hope that the priceless ring she'd just recovered would somehow remain undiscovered.

"Sarken, take the wand."

"Yes, Cap'n," said a thick, gruff voice, and the lantern drew close. A muscular arm reached out from the darkness behind it and she relinquished the belt to a hairy fist.

"Now then," the captain said, sounding more relaxed. "I'll sheathe my weapon and we can talk in your quarters. Lads, keep your eyes sharp. There might be some other entrepreneurs out there tonight."

"Aye, Cap'n," Sarken's deep voice answered.

"If you don't mind, Captain," Mirian said, "you promised me a word with my crew. I want to verify their well-being."

She finally got a good look at Ensara as he took the lantern from his first mate and broadened its cast. A dark man in the prime of life, well tanned, but likely a native of some Inner Sea port. His clothes were fading finery, a billowy white silk shirt with lace about collar and sleeves, dark crimson breeches with stains along one knee, black calf-high boots a little scuffed. His mustache and goatee were trimmed to perfection, though. He was rakishly handsome and seemed to know it, for he flashed her a cocky smile, as if to say, *I'm easy on the eyes, don't you think?* But what he really said was: "Of course. Follow me."

"I know the way to my own hold, Captain," she said coolly, and brushed past him and the pair of men posted at the stepladder. They parted only at the last minute, and she was soon descending into darkness.

"Oh," she heard Ensara call in irritation, "pass this down to her."

And she looked back to see a lantern dangled from one of the pirates above.

"Don't attempt anything clever, Mirian," Ensara said. "Sarken, go down and lend an ear."

By the lantern light, Mirian saw the whole of her crew: Caligan the sailmaster, lanky Melvane the carpenter, and the rest of the dozen. In their forefront stood an embarrassed-looking Gombe and an angry Rendak.

She heard Sarken clomp down the stairs behind her.

Rendak mouthed the name "Jekka" and then, in the sign language employed by salvagers to communicate underwater, indicated something hidden. Jekka, at least, was still at large.

"They popped up out of nowhere," Gombe said. "I think they must have had a spellcaster."

"My brother," Sarken said gruffly behind them. Mirian ignored him.

"I'm sorry—" Gombe began.

"You're all right?" Mirian cut in.

"Aye," Rendak answered. He was glaring at Sarken over Mirian's shoulder.

"Where's the druid?"

"I don't know," Gombe answered.

But Sarken answered. "The captain confined her to your cabin, Captain Raas. He's a gentleman, he is. He's never done a lady no harm."

"That's gratifying to hear."

"No matter how fine she looks," Sarken went on, and there was no missing the insinuation in his tone. She guessed Sarken's view on the matter of women might differ from his captain's.

"I've seen enough." Mirian turned on her heel. She wanted to test Sarken's reaction time. He proved a burly man with a square face and short black hair. And he wasn't that fast, for he stumbled to get out of her way.

Good.

She started up the steps, Sarken trailing, and this time she tried numbering the pirates appointed to her ship. Two men at the stairs. Four forward. As she rejoined Ensara, she saw he'd posted another at the bow.

Ensara doffed his hat to her. "You see, as promised. Unharmed. Now, as to that conversation."

"Of course. Might I have my belt back?"

His eyes briefly considered her waist. "Sarken, the belt. Minus the knife, of course."

Sarken had left it on the deck and, miracle of miracles, no one seemed to have opened any of its pouches. The mate unsheathed her knife and scrutinized it as she buckled the belt.

"An old blade," Sarken remarked. "Not real balanced."

"It's for underwater use," she explained, wondering why she bothered. The weapon was specially treated with an anti-rusting agent.

"Your cabin, Mirian."

"Captain," she corrected.

"My pardon." He bowed his head to her. "I've already confined the druid there for her own comfort."

Ensara opened the door and gestured for Mirian to enter.

The cabin proved empty, a fact that set a mild oath to Ensara's lips. He advanced into the room, ducking under the beams and stepping around the hanging lamp before spinning on Mirian.

Not long ago the *Daughter* had been invaded by different pirates, who'd ransacked the quarters and wrecked much of the furniture. Ensara seemed to have done none of that. Even her Pathfinder journal lay upon the desk exactly where she'd left it. Whatever he was, exactly, Ensara was no common thug.

"Where is she?" the man demanded.

"How should I know?"

He frowned. "I asked you not to be clever."

"I'm not being clever."

His voice was tight. "Is there a hiding place? A hidden panel?"

"I keep a bottle of my father's whiskey in a hidey spot. But unless she's squeezed into one of the bunk drawers, my guess is she just crawled out through the porthole." Mirian pointed.

"That tiny thing?" Ensara objected. "There's no way she'd have been able to squeeze through it."

"She's the Druid of Eleder," Mirian said. "Some say she can walk on water. Who's to say she didn't just turn into a seagull and fly out?"

Ensara took off his hat and tossed it in disgust toward the chart table. "Of course." It landed with a dull thud.

"You must not be from around here, or you'd have heard of her."

"One hears all sorts of things. And one doubts." Ensara pulled out a chair and gestured to it.

She sat down, a little surprised by his courtesy, and then he took a seat at the table's head, placed the lantern beside his brimmed, feathered hat, and ran his fingers through his dark hair.

"For instance," he said, "I assumed that little booklet I bought last week was a trifle, but I was assured there really was a salvager named Mirian Raas, and she really could breathe underwater. And here I find myself sitting in her cabin. I'm just disappointed you don't have your lizard man with you."

"I didn't invite you aboard," Mirian said.

"No. But times being what they are, a man must do what he has to do to stay alive. So, Captain, I'm going to turn you loose in a long boat, and take the *Daughter*."

"You're *what*?"

"It should fetch a fine price—"

"It's not for sale!"

"Come, come. The book told how you're building a bigger, better ship. And your first mate even backed up the story—said your lizard man was in charge of its construction."

Rendak must have lied to give her crew any advantage he could.

"And everyone knows that you came back from your jungle trip with a basket of jewels, so surely the loss of this vessel will be no real hardship."

"My father built the *Daughter*," Mirian said. "And I'm not exactly rolling in money."

The pirate waved his hand dismissively. "I'm sorry, but that's what has to happen. I regret, as well, that I must take your crew."

"*What?*"

"There's a market for well-trained sailors in any number of navies."

She felt her nostrils flare, and her hands shaped naturally into fists. "You're pressing them into service?"

"I do have to make a profit." Ensara sounded almost apologetic. "There are places where you'd fetch a fine price as well, but that wouldn't be gentlemanly."

"None of this is particularly gentlemanly."

"I beg to differ. It could be far, far less gentlemanly, as I'm sure you know."

"You do know the Free Captains take a dim view of the piracy of Sargavan ships, don't you?"

Ensara cleared his throat. "You're a special circumstance."

"I am?"

"There's a bounty on the *Daughter* and her crew. And you, if truth be told."

"What bounty? Who put it out?"

"I'm not sure of that," he admitted. "But I know the purse is held on the Shiv."

Who would put out a bounty for her? But there was no time to worry about that. She needed to get Ensara thinking about other money sources. "I can provide you with something better."

"Better than money?" Ensara cocked an eyebrow and grinned.

She ignored the implication. "Better than the *Daughter* and her crew. Do you know why we dropped here?"

"Your mate said you were looking for treasure. Something about a lost ship."

"Exactly. And you won't believe what we've located aboard her. It's the find of a lifetime, Ensara."

His eyebrows rose in wry amusement. "Go on."

"You don't need to resort to petty thievery. It's going to take me weeks, possibly months, to explore this ship."

"What kind of ship is it?"

"It's from the days of the lizardfolk."

"The lizardfolk had ships?" he said in disbelief. He must truly be from far afield. Most colonials, even the aristocracy, referred to the lizardfolk by the derogatory term "frillbacks." Sooner or later the slang slipped into their speech even if they didn't mean to use it.

"They made ships more advanced than anything afloat today."

A smirk slowly spread over his face. "At best, lizardfolk can carve canoes with outrunners."

She shook her head. "On my father's name." She nodded to the woodcarving of her younger self and her father that hung on the bulkhead wall near his head.

He glanced briefly at it before turning up a hand. "Suppose I believe you. How can that help me?"

"Look where we're anchored. We'll have to clean the wreck out while in full sight of *any* ship headed in or out of Smuggler's Shiv. We could stand protection, especially if there's a bounty on us. We can't do it in one night, or even a chain of nights. It's going to take a while."

Ensara stroked his beard. She had his attention, at least. "What would my percentage be?"

"Thirty."

"Thirty? That hardly seems worth my time."

"We'll be doing all the work. All you have to do is float there and look menacing."

"Seventy," Ensara said. "For us. Thirty for you."

She shook her head. "Not only will we be doing the salvaging, we'll be fencing the goods. This is antiquarian stuff, and I know the people in Eleder who'll pay for it. I can get a far higher profit from legitimate dealers in Eleder than you would dumping it on the markets at the Shiv where people won't know what to make of half of it anyway."

He mulled this over. "How much money to you think we're talking?"

"Fortunes. There are secrets down there that could remake the way we sail."

He snorted. "On a rotting ship?

"The ship isn't rotting. The hull's virtually intact. Big long planks, black as pitch and cleaner than many a ship floating right now in Desperation Bay. That alone is probably worth a fortune, if we can figure out how it was done."

He looked skeptical, but she pressed on. "And the hold's stuffed with chests brimming with weird lizardfolk artifacts."

His eyes locked with hers. "Sixty-forty. I'll be running risk, Mirian."

"Captain Raas to you. Remember that."

He actually flushed. "My apologies. If your diving really will take days, my crew and I will be challenged. Repeatedly. Possibly by more than one ship at a time."

"We're the specialists. You'll just be hired muscle."

"Good hired muscle."

"Are you? I've never heard of you. Sixty-forty is as low as I'm willing to go."

He stared at her, then burst into laughter. "Or you'll go with the other plan, the one where I sell your ship and your crew into slavery?" He laughed again and slapped his knee.

She forced calm into her voice. "You'd be passing up a tremendous opportunity. No one else in these waters can recover this stuff. And this crew you're getting ready to sell off is trained to salvage. These are specialists."

Ensara drummed his fingers on the table. "The crew and I prefer swifter returns on out investments."

"Good things come to those who wait."

His look was sly. "How do I even know what's down there?"

"Look in my pack. You'll see a whole parcel of gem-encrusted sculptures. You'd think that the first thing you'd want to do would be to pry out the stones, but they're actually more valuable to collectors if you leave them in."

Ensara stared at her, then got up, wordless, and pushed open the cabin door. "Sarken, bring me her pack!"

"Right away, Cap'n."

In moments he had it open on the chart table and was turning one of the sculptures over in his hand, so that a trio of rubies winked in the light. He traced his fingers along the symbols, then looked over to Mirian. "What does it say?"

"I don't know. But I'd be willing to bet some graybeard will be ecstatic about finding out. That's just what I found in one chest, in one compartment of the hold."

"The rest could be full of rotten linen," Ensara pointed out.

"Could be. But you forget the value of the ship itself, and its weird construction. If you don't believe me, you can borrow one of my salvager's air bottles and—"

"And get myself drowned for my efforts? No thank you. But I'll be taking a look. I have a wizard aboard my ship and we keep a small supply of water breathing potions to hand. I want you to take us down so we can look this ship over. Before we make any kind of final arrangements."

She tried to eye him without guile.

"Or don't you like the sound of that?"

She liked the sound of that very much. She'd hoped to lure him overboard, but she didn't want Ensara to know it. "A deep dive's no simple thing for the untrained," she warned him. "There're dangers down there. And it's a night dive. Do you have lights? Do your men know how to fight underwater?"

"You let us worry about all of that. You just show us this treasure ship."

"If that's what you want."

4
THE THING IN THE HOLD
MIRIAN

Ensara led the way to the *Daughter*'s side. With him came a half-dozen pirates, chief among them the mate Sarken and what looked to be a man stretched out a bit after he was pulled from the same mold. Ensara introduced the latter as his wizard, Kavel, who was thinner and taller than Sarken but otherwise shared his same beady eyes and blunt nose. *My brother*, Sarken had said.

"You'll be wanting to take off your boots," Mirian pointed out to the captain, who smiled good-naturedly as some of his men laughed.

"And do you have anything to see by?" she asked.

"I'll manage something," Kavel answered. His voice was even more gravelly than Sarken's.

Mirian meant to press home her expertise to make herself more valuable. And to make them a little nervous. "It's more dangerous down there than it looks. I almost ran straight into a giant crab in the seaweed. In the depths, things might look placid, then something can spring out at you. It's like the jungle, except creatures can pop out from every direction. It can take a while to get used to looking six ways."

"It's not our first venture overside," Ensara said, "but the warning is appreciated."

"I never dive without weapons," Mirian said.

Ensara wagged a finger at her. "You'll have plenty of protection below, Captain Raas."

"If we wander into a nest of rot worms down there," Mirian said, "you'll want every sword you can lay hands on."

"A rot worm?" Ensara asked.

"A sort of undersea centipede that loves to forage among fungus and mold and disintegrating wood. They're poisonous."

"I see." Ensara frowned. "Well, you'll have to tell us where to look for them. I'll warn you again not to try anything clever, as we have you outnumbered. And Kavel has other magic at his command. Speaking of which—Kavel, the potions."

One by one the wizard handed over five red bottles, and Ensara and his team pulled free the corks. The captain's nose wrinkled as he lifted his bottle to his nose. "Smells like seaweed. Couldn't you have made it a little more appetizing, Kavel?"

"The important thing is that it works, Captain." Kavel tipped the stem to his lips and she watched his hairy larynx bob.

"Down the hatch then," the captain said, and as he drank, the rest of his team followed suit. "Tosten, you're in charge. Overside, lads. Captain Raas, lead the way."

She touched the dulled glow stone still hanging about her neck and lit it with a soft word before anyone could ask what she was doing. "All right then. Follow me."

And over she went.

She couldn't be sure where Jekka had gone and it had occurred to her that something very bad might have happened to him.

More likely, though, he'd had some inkling of what was going on and waited for an opportunity to move in and protect his adopted sister and ship. She wished there was a way for her to signal that the wizard Kavel was most dangerous. Then it occurred to her that there was.

After the men splashed in, Mirian played the glow stone over them as they blinked away the stinging salt and rubbed their eyes. She settled the light upon Kavel the longest. If Jekka were watching, he had to have seen the emphasis she placed upon the wizard.

But she didn't leave it on him for long before turning and swimming slowly down. Since she wasn't moving at her magically enhanced speed, and she'd asked Ivrian to leave details about her equipment vague, the pirates couldn't know one of her rings provided her a distinct advantage: that she could move freely underwater, even at great depths.

Really, all she had to do was get them below and disoriented in the darkness. She wouldn't need any help ditching them if it weren't for that thrice-damned wizard, who surely knew offensive spells.

There was another hope: that the druid had remained, waiting to assist, or to at least take vengeance against men who'd dared to hold her prisoner. But Mirian had no idea what the druid was capable of, or really, how she might feel about the pirates. With her ability to slip in and out of elemental form, the druid might very well have moved on for Eleder and left Mirian and the crew to their fates. After all, Djenba hadn't been paid anything but the promise of a return favor.

Mirian couldn't predict what Jekka would do, either. He was a skilled and experienced warrior, but he didn't think the same way as a human. What she hoped was that he'd follow and use any distractions as an opportunity to pick off the pirates to sow further confusion.

The safest bet was to carry on as though she had only herself to depend upon.

And so she led them down and farther down into the darkness. They followed in a clump, Ensara and Kavel near the front. Kavel conjured an eerie white beam from an amulet he held in one hand, lighting the area immediately before him and his captain. Mirian supposed that might be as good a signal as any to Jekka to indicate the best target.

She swam on and on and still there was no sign of her blood brother, only the glowing denizens of the deep water. A few yards off her right side swam a whole flotilla of pink-and-blue jellyfish, and farther on a school of pineapple fish, the patches along their jaws glowing an eerie white, like pupil-less eyes. By day they looked far less fierce, their scales being of the same shape and color as unripe pineapple skins.

Mirian reached the ridge of the seafloor at last, her light playing along the gently undulating fronds of seaweed. She'd never before hoped to run across a giant crustacean, but she did this time. Where was that damned crab, or its cousin? Really, that's all she needed, and so she kicked along the bed of fronds, eyes sharp. It was a dangerous game she played, for if one of the beasts should surprise her, it might very well snip her in half.

Yet the crab was gone and no other seemed anywhere close. Without really meaning to, she arrived within sight of the lizard-folk shipwreck.

She glanced over her shoulder.

Ensara's divers had spread out only a little. They tended to hover close to Kavel's light.

Mirian swam slowly forward to the hull, playing her light along it so Ensara could see the perfectly preserved black planks, barely affected by any coating of mold or fungus.

He was close enough that the expression on his face was perfectly clear, and it was so genuinely curious she briefly considered changing her course of action. If they were to drop here repeatedly, they might very well need some kind of guard.

But then she thought of Ensara's casual willingness to sell her men into slavery and take her ship. He was no prospective business partner and his men seemed even less civilized.

She swam up the side, waving Ensara and his crew to follow. She moved on up over the prow, where she pretended to examine the figurehead before Kavel drifted on with the light.

Mirian kicked on without approaching the wheelhouse. There should be any number of distractions down in the hold, and she didn't want them seeing the control panel.

Except that the control panel might just be the finest way out of this mess, now that she'd led them here. She mouthed a curse that would have earned a slap from her mother. This was the find of a lifetime—a discovery that could benefit not just her crew, but Sargava and maybe the entire world. Yet because of the pirates, she would have to abandon it.

Mirian stopped at the hold and motioned her companions forward. Ensara and Kavel preceded her, swimming awkwardly. She hesitated, and Sarken pushed her ahead into the gangway. She shot him a dark look and he grinned at her.

She went inside, still swimming at normal speed. She caught up to Ensara in the hold, already considering the contents of the two chests they'd opened. One empty, one with the strange bottles.

He grinned at her and mouthed something she couldn't make out. He took in the surroundings, then stuck out his hand, beaming at her. Apparently he was satisfied and wanted to shake on the deal.

But that wasn't what she wanted at all, and perhaps the gods sensed it, for at that very moment a tentacle writhed out of the dark opening into the next hold and seized one of the pirates around the head, jerking him into inky blackness.

Even as the other pirates whirled in horror and reached for swords, more tentacles lashed out.

Mirian was never sure quite why she did it, but she grabbed Ensara's arm, still hanging there as he turned, slack-jawed in horror. She pulled him off-balance so that the tentacle missed him by a handspan.

And then she turned and swam for it.

She'd held back while leading the pirates. Now she moved at full speed, her magical ring leaving her unhampered by the resistance that slowed and tugged at everyone else, forcing them to fight through the weight of water and its currents and eddies. She dimmed her glow stone as she hit the stairs, pushing past Sarken.

She heard the dull sound of shouts, saw the orange glow of a spell behind her, and then she was up the gangway and out.

And very near the quarterdeck and the wheel and the strange control panel beside it.

She slowed herself by grabbing the pedestal beside the wheel, then activated her glow stone and shined it on the panel. She spun the "no wind" gem to life. The old ship shook.

She spotted Sarken rising at the top of the stairs, saw the snarl on his face even as the ancient vessel shot forward on its last voyage, rumbling and shaking across the seafloor, a cloud of silt rising behind her like the train of a wedding gown.

Mirian shot toward the surface.

Pirates be damned, and the priceless shipwreck with them.

She and Jekka had been incredibly lucky the squid or devilfish or whatever the hell that thing was hadn't come out after them when they went into the hold, or that they hadn't probed into the next chamber where it laired. She almost pitied Ensara, and then she remembered how he'd meant to steal her ship and sell her crew into slavery, and told herself she didn't care.

She surfaced in the darkness and spotted the glow from a light high on Ensara's ship.

The last time she'd faced off against pirates, a few months back, she'd had her wand. This time it was undersea along with Sarken, probably lost forever. There'd be no blasting Ensara's ship open as she'd done with that Chelish privateer.

No matter. She'd been incredibly lucky when it came down to it. She hated the loss of the wand, hated the loss of the shipwreck, but she was free, and her crew's freedom would follow shortly.

She sped on toward the side of the *Daughter* and was closing on the ladder when she saw a flash beside the ship—just a wink. A glow stone had come on, then off, revealing Jekka floating below the ladder. He held the stone and stared right at her.

They surfaced quietly together, and the lizard man pushed the air tube from his mouth.

"The pirate sentries on the *Daughter* are done," Jekka reported. He tended to confuse words like *finish*, *killed*, and *complete*. "I was coming to look for you."

"Is the crew all right?"

"Yes. They stand post where the pirates were. Easy to manage once you led their leaders away. Clever, my sister. I knew what you intended then."

She nodded, letting him think she'd had a more complex plan. "What about the watch on Ensara's ship?"

"They've called over once."

She hadn't gotten a terrifically good look at the enemy vessel, but she hadn't seen any ballistae or shipboard weapons. "Any sign of the druid?"

"I am here," a quiet voice said beside them, and suddenly she was, boiling out of the depths in a swirl of water, regal and strange.

"Where've you been?" Mirian asked. What she'd meant was why hadn't the priestess helped them, and the priestess seemed to sense that.

"I don't take lives," she said, "unless it's something I mean to eat."

"Can you work a spell that won't take life, to help us get away?"

"I might."

"I'm going to cut their anchor line," Mirian said. "If my brother will swing out his scythe. I know you can bless a ship with current, Djenba. Can you set Ensara's ship spinning away to give us time to unfurl sails?"

She knew this was within the druid's power. She'd witnessed her send forth powerful blasts of wind as vessels launched.

"I can do you this favor," Djenba decided. "It would be a long swim back to Eleder."

Of course. "Right. Jekka?"

She sensed reluctance on her blood brother's part, but he moved nimble fingers over the surface of the staff and its spear-point retracted. He quickly flipped it on its other end and another press of inlaid sigils conjured up the long scythe blade. She'd studied both blades a few times and determined they were fashioned from some high-grade steel. The lizardfolk had once been incredibly advanced.

"All right," she said. "Get up there and get ready."

"Rendak is prepared to cut grappling lines as soon as he gets the signal," Jekka said.

"All right. I'll be back any second." Mirian dropped below once more.

For a brief moment as she followed the outline of her ship's hull, she thought about the men trapped on that ancient wreck rumbling along the ocean bottom, the tentacled horror grasping for them, and felt another twinge of remorse.

She put it from her mind as she traced the hull of the other ship with gloved fingers and found her way to its cable.

As always, the freedom her ring provided made working underwater easy. Between that and the sharpness of Jekka's blade, the cable was soon parted.

Immediately she darted away, Jekka's scythed staff carried before her, and in moments she was slipping up the ladder of the *Daughter*. In the darkness, she heard Gombe whisper that Mirian was back, and then the chunk of lines being severed, the slap of waves on the *Marvel*'s hull. As she hurried to the quarterdeck she saw the pirate ship spinning away as figures ran back and forth along its deck, calling to the crew they thought still stood watch on the *Daughter*.

Rendak shouted her crew into action, but they were already unfurling sails, and the priestess sent a blast of wind into them before they were fully sheeted home. The ship surged ahead and Rendak bellowed at the sailors to get the lines secured.

"Everyone's really all right?" Mirian asked, breathless.

Rendak, at the wheel, glanced at her. "Aye, we are. Rutting pirates. How'd you ditch the whole lot of them?"

"A story for another time," Mirian answered grimly. "We had a hell of a find, too."

Jekka had come up on her left and she looked at him. "I'm sorry, Jekka. I don't think we can get back to the ship again. There was something on it."

"What kind of thing?"

"I'm not entirely sure." Mirian fought down a shiver. "But it seemed hungry."

"Don't worry, Sister. I am certain your brother-in-marriage will have answers for us."

Jekka was so damned hopeful about that spoiled rich man that Mirian didn't have the heart to nay-say him again. He'd have to learn that disappointment on his own.

But it turned out she didn't have to do so at all, because once they'd finally docked and secured the ship and made their way to their home on the hill, a packet from her brother-in-law was waiting for her. Tradan had found the map.

5

DRAGON TEARS
IVRIAN

Another thrilling adventure was passed, but I'd played no part, for I'd been ashore contemplating deck plans. Rest assured I was far from bored, for I had a fine mansion, select wines, and the company of the charming Jeneta, warrior-priestess of Iomedae.

Once I learned my friends had been in mortal danger, I all but smote my breast, wishing I might have been there to protect them! All I could do was pledge to shield them from any travails that followed. So it was that the morning after their return I found myself trundling across the streets of the old city, rocking over ancient stones in an allegedly luxurious carriage in the company of Mirian, Jekka, and my dear friend Kalina.

—From *The City in the Mist*

Kalina sat forward on the cushion, her long-fingered hand to the carriage door curtain so she might peer at each street they passed. In contrast, Jekka was motionless across from her, all but his snout hidden by the hood of his robe. If the carriage hadn't been jarring them over the rutted road every few feet, Ivrian might have assumed he slept.

The lizard woman was smaller than Jekka, with a shorter snout and duller coloring, but it was her manner that differentiated her more. Even after a month among her human friends, her curiosity about their customs hadn't ebbed. "What a long beard that man has," she said brightly, and Ivrian smiled to himself without bothering to look. "How long does it take to grow a beard, Ivrian? Can you grow one?"

"I could," Ivrian answered. "They're not really in fashion right now."

"That's strange," Kalina said. She whipped her head around on a disturbingly flexible neck to consider Ivrian. "There are a lot of men with beards." She looked out the window again. "There's another."

"Probably sailors," Mirian said. "Beards never go out of fashion for sailors and pirates."

"Oh," Kalina said. And then she was off on a different topic as something else caught her attention. "What a strange house."

Ivrian grinned at Mirian across from him, but she was lost in her own thoughts. He noted that she'd taken more time with her hair, and even applied light rouge to her rich dark skin and brightened her lips.

As pretty a picture as she made, for some reason she sat hunched, her arms crossed.

"What's wrong?" he asked her. "You look darling."

Mirian's eyes flicked up like dagger points. Her voice, though, was calm as she uncrossed her arms. "Thank you, Ivrian."

He leaned forward. "I've made some preliminary notes about your adventure, but I've a few questions."

Mirian cut him off, sharply. "I don't want you writing this one."

He gaped. "You're joking. You and Jekka single-handedly took on a band of bloodthirsty pirates. It'll be a shorter pamphlet, of course, but it will sell like—"

"They weren't actually bloodthirsty," Mirian corrected. "I'm the one who left them under the sea with the monster."

At Ivrian's disbelieving stare she explained further.

"I keep thinking back to their captain, and how he was ready to shake on the deal."

"You would have been foolish to trust him," Jekka said.

Mirian shook her head. "If we'd stayed to dive there, we *would* have needed a guard, just like I told him. And who better to guard us from pirates but another pirate?"

"You regret the ending of them?" Jekka asked.

"It doesn't feel right. I think I might have been able to work with Ensara."

"Even after he'd threatened to sell your ship and crew?" Ivrian asked.

"You should have seen that wreck, Ivrian." Mirian sounded almost breathless. "It was the find of a lifetime. I've half a mind to seek it out again."

"Why don't we?" Kalina asked. She pushed back from the window and blinked large eyes at them as she settled into the seat beside Ivrian.

"There's no telling where it stopped." Mirian shook her head. "It probably went straight off the ridge and into the depths. I should have tried to work with them. When that devilfish attacked, I took advantage of the situation. But if I'd stayed—"

"You might have been killed, my sister," Jekka said. "And it would have been complicated when you returned with Ensara and he found I had finished his sentries."

Mirian nodded. There was no missing the sense of Jekka's statement. The pirate captain might have killed every sailor on the *Daughter* once he realized his own crew members had been slain.

And if Mirian could be convinced of the sense of this observation, it might be Ivrian could gradually bring her around. It really was too good of a story to keep silent about. The first short book, *Daughter of the Mist*, was in its fourth printing after just two months and was garnering a great deal of attention, not to mention a steady supply of money. It had transformed them all into minor celebrities in Eleder. A second tale, however short, could only improve matters.

But he could see he'd have to wait before he pressed that argument again. Maybe, though, this was a good time to raise another matter. "If you had a larger ship, you would have been harder to attack."

She didn't like that topic either. Mirian seemed especially cross this morning. "And what will we pay a bigger crew with? I know you've got money, but won't you just be throwing it down a hole? The *Daughter*'s paid off and we know how to earn enough to keep her afloat. In good years, I mean."

Why wouldn't she listen to him about that? "I've told you I can build a bigger ship, whatever you need. And the way things are going, I might be able to finance it with my account of our adventures." He couldn't help himself. "And the more new adventures people have to read, the better they'll all sell."

"Not going to happen," Mirian said.

He couldn't tell if she was reacting to the ship or story idea, and kicked himself a little for pressing the latter. He'd known he should wait. Aware that Kalina was staring at him intently, he decided to focus on what he thought to be the simpler argument. Probably the lizard woman would later pepper him with questions about human social customs.

"What about this price someone's put out on the *Daughter*? We're bound to be attacked again. We need to be able to defend ourselves."

"Ensara might have been lying." Mirian didn't sound like she believed the idea herself. She was arguing for the sake of argument now. "There might be no bounty."

"My new ship will have weapon placements. We can fight off all comers, or outrun them. And won't we need a larger ship to search for the lost island on that map? We'll be heading into the deeps instead of seeking near the coast."

Mirian's lips turned down. "Let's not get false hopes raised. These charts are clearly wrong. Jekka knows that."

Jekka held the cylinder that had arrived via courier from Port Freedom the previous night. He tapped it with two long, green fingers.

"But you said the Pathfinders could help us," Kalina said. "That there might be an island, just in a different place."

"Might." Mirian gentled her tone while speaking to the lizard woman. "Do you know how our maps are made?"

"Ivrian told me," Kalina said quickly. There was no missing the speculative look Mirian shot him, as if to suggest that she was waiting to see what Ivrian had gotten wrong. She really was in a foul mood today.

Kalina appeared oblivious to the tension. "Intrepid humans sail out and draw careful pictures of what they see while the ship is sailing, and then take those pictures to a mapmaker, who combines them with others, and they turn it into a big map."

"It's a little more complicated than that," Mirian said. "There's the matter of accounting for navigational fixes to calculate exact distances when you're constructing the chart, making depth soundings . . ." Mirian paused, seemed to consider her audience, then started over, speaking more slowly. "You have to remember that not all of the . . . pictures . . . are equal. It really depends upon how carefully distances are judged by the individuals making the charts. Not all of the navigators are equally skilled. Sometimes the graybeard in charge combines the most likely features into a finished version and adds a few artistic flourishes." She paused briefly for effect. "Accurate charts are a lot rarer than you think."

"Oh, yes." Kalina's head bobbed. "That's what Ivrian said."

Ivrian thought that might win him a few points, but Mirian didn't even look at him. "Now that Desperation Bay's been settled for so long," she continued, "good, basic charts are easy to come by. That wasn't the case when that old chart was drawn."

"But there might be an island," Jekka said. "Just like this old map shows. Just off a nearby coast. If someone had drawn it wrong in the long ago."

There was no missing the hope in his voice, or the question there, even if he didn't phrase it like one.

"Or the island might have sunk," Ivrian suggested, and instantly regretted it as all three of his friends turned to look at him. He couldn't see Jekka's eyes, hidden as they were by the hood, and Kalina's expression was hard to gauge, but even one of the lizardfolk could have deciphered the message in Mirian's narrow-eyed glare. These two were hoping against hope that they weren't the last of their clan, that somewhere out there across the vast blue other members yet lived. They'd risked their lives, and Jekka's brother—Kalina's mate—had lost his, searching for information about where others of their kind had traveled. Ivrian's own mother had perished in the same expedition, along with Mirian's brother and other friends and allies.

And he'd just casually pointed out to the lizardfolk how unlikely their hopes were to come true. "Even if it's gone, there's still that other lead, isn't there?" he said swiftly. "The city mentioned on the book cones near Port Freedom?"

Mirian ignored his question and looked pointedly away, turning her head between the lizardfolk. "There are no tales of a sunken island in Desperation Bay. None. If this lost island of Kutnaar had been where this old chart shows, there'd be folk legends all over Desperation Bay. Some old chart maker probably made a mistake and put it in the wrong place. If we look at the collection of charts in the Pathfinder lodge, we might just spot an island off some coastline that looks like this one." Her finger waggled as she pointed to Jekka's cylinder.

Now who was raising false hopes? Ivrian wondered. If there really were an island of lizardfolk anywhere nearby, wouldn't people know about it?

He frowned to himself, supposing the same truth held for the lizardfolk city that the old book cones located near Port Freedom. As much as he wished it otherwise, his friends probably sought in vain.

Looking over at Kalina's profile, he felt an onrush of pity. "It might be that the island is much smaller than is shown," he suggested. "Sometimes it's not just location but scale that the mapmakers got wrong."

With that suggestion Mirian was finally in agreement, and she nodded slowly. "Don't give up yet."

The carriage finally rumbled to a stop.

They'd arrived at the Pathfinder lodge. Eager to have the uncomfortable moment over, Ivrian threw open the door to be greeted by a warm breeze bearing the sweet floral scent of mallow flowers. The lodge stood on a hill overlooking the wharves of Eleder's main harbor. Ivrian turned to offer his hand to the ladies—women, he self-corrected, then corrected himself again, for there was no reason Kalina couldn't be considered a lady. He spotted two sloops of Sargava's small navy floating at anchor, their bare masts rising like pruned trees.

Kalina hopped from the carriage, eager as always to get the lay of the land, her scaled, green feet covered in long leather sandals.

Mirian's brown eyes fixed him with a hard look, the message therein either *shut the hell up*, or *think before you speak*. Maybe both. Ivrian sighed a little and bowed his head to her as Jekka followed, his staff in one hand and cylinder in the other. Unlike his cousin, he hadn't taken to wearing human footgear.

Ivrian told his driver to pull around and see to the animals, then trailed all three of his friends, reminding himself to be more circumspect.

They'd been let out beneath a wide wooden awning that extended over the flagstone driveway, flanked by well-trimmed mallow bushes, bright with brilliant cupped red blossoms. Wide stairs led up to the main entrance. As they climbed, Ivrian saw some men gathered about a large cart being loaded from the door downhill that led into the lodge's basement level. Amongst the crates and gilt wooden chests was something that resembled a coffin with bronze fittings.

Ivrian couldn't help staring at the handsome man supervising the loading. He was tall and tanned, and wore his casual travel clothes like royal raiment. Ivrian would have given a lot to know who he was and where he was going, and if Mirian weren't already irritated with him he would have begged an introduction. He just about had to be another Pathfinder. Maybe he wouldn't be as interesting as he looked, but Ivrian regretted not being able to find out.

A black-clad doorman, probably half-native Mwangi from the lighter tone of his sepia skin, advanced to ask for identification. Mirian pulled the slim, silvery-blue wayfinder from her belt pouch and showed it to the man. Ivrian had only been allowed a glimpse of it once before, and he barely caught sight of the palm-sized object this time.

The tool's presentation was really only a formality, for Mirian was well enough known in Sargavan Pathfinder circles. The guard nodded politely, and Mirian repocketed her wayfinder, then followed after the guard. He led them to two towering teak doors and opened one with a bow.

They stepped through the threshold into a high, vaulted room. The wooden floorboards beneath worn but elegant rugs creaked faintly as Mirian headed within. From the right came a burst of laughter and Ivrian turned to find a dark-paneled sitting room with a bar.

Mirian led them past a mixed group of natives and colonials talking about the best route through the Bandu Hills. Ivrian tried to listen in, but the strangers fell silent to stare at Jekka and Kalina. Or possibly, he realized, they stared at Mirian, or even him. It wasn't as though anyone had ever suggested he wear a sack over his head, after all, and he surely knew how to dress.

Mirian's course took them beyond several archways and tall, closed doors before she headed left through a columned archway into a huge room with high, narrow windows that looked directly over the blue-green waters of the bay. He caught his breath, not at the magnificent view, but at the great library that surrounded him. The entire south and west walls were taken up with long rows of shelves. Arranged among them were squared-off slots holding scrolls, skulls, and strange bits of architecture. The majority of the space, however, was given over to leather-spined hardback books. Ivrian's heart leapt the way only a true bibliophile's could. Here, he knew, were treasures accumulated over lifetimes.

It would probably require a lifetime or more to become familiar with everything stored here. What wonders were hidden behind the tooled leather covers? What mysteries did they speak of, and what secrets were revealed therein? It could be that the lovely shelf of red leather tomes was the autobiography of a pirate queen. And that imposing brown book with gold leaf decoration could be the tale of an expedition into the Mwangi Expanse, handwritten by its lone survivor.

Mirian noted his look and smiled at him. She even sounded a little like her usual self. "Thrilling, isn't it?"

"Oh, yes," he said. Kalina and Jekka were speaking quietly to one another and he noted the former's hand sweeping toward the ceiling.

Both lizardfolk were studying an immense, snakelike skeleton hung by wires to the right of three chandeliers dangling over the chamber's center.

"You have access to all this and you actually leave?" Ivrian asked.

Mirian laughed good-naturedly.

For all its size, only a handful of people were inside the great library. Two sat alone at tables arranged on either side of the main aisle, older men who looked up from their work to stare at the newcomers. The only other occupant apart from themselves was a bent old woman close beside the south wall studying a book she held in the crook of her arm.

Mirian patted one of the empty tables. "You three stay here while I go find what we need." She strode away.

His first inclination was to amuse himself studying book titles. Jekka, though, had opened the cylinder he carried and was unrolling the map on the table top. Ivrian had brought his carriage around to pick them up that morning, so he'd only heard a description of the map. Curious, he joined his reptilian friends, watching as Jekka placed the cylinder's closing cap and a leather-bound tome to hold down either end of the map.

Mirian's brother-in-law Tradan hadn't sent the original, but a copy.

"Who made this?" he asked. It looked like a slapdash affair. Clearly the mouth of the Oubinga River was in the wrong place, and the Bandu Hills looked more like mountains. There was no sign of Eleder, either, but that made sense, owing to the original map's antiquity. The city of his birth might not even have existed when the original was drawn.

Strangest of all was the small island just a few leagues east of the squiggle that was probably Smuggler's Shiv. Under it, in crabbed cursive letters, he could just make out the word "Kutnaar."

"You see," Jekka said, tapping the island. "This is it. This is where some of our people went."

Ivrian nodded. There was no disputing the fact that the map showed an island there. Just as there was no disputing that there was no island there now, as Ivrian was pretty sure he and Gombe had traveled through that space a few months ago with some Ijo sailors.

"Who drew this?" Ivrian asked again. He wondered how many of the map's inaccuracies were the result of the copying itself.

Jekka bent over the map, as if staring longer at it would clarify matters for him. "Some human."

Clearly the artist wasn't a topic of any great interest for the lizard man.

Kalina was holding a smaller rectangle of paper that had slipped out of the package. Ivrian stepped closer and immediately recognized it for a letter, at the same time seeing that Kalina held it upside down. The lizard woman couldn't read Taldane, but like all the lizardfolk Ivrian had met (an admittedly small number), she seemed to have an innate artistic sensibility. She was probably admiring the characters.

"What does that say?" he asked. "Is that from Mirian's brother-in-law?"

"Yes," Kalina answered. "I think that's what he's called."

"Do you mind if I look at it?"

"No, not at all," Kalina answered, but didn't hand it over. Ivrian reminded himself there were still any number of gaps in their ability to communicate.

"I hoped you could hand it to me so I could read it."

"Oh, of course." Kalina gave the paper to him, then swung up her head to consider their surroundings. "These books are not so durable as our own. And human writing is not so pretty. But I like this place."

Ivrian nodded distractedly and focused on the letter.

Dearest Mirian,

I hope that the years have been good to you. We were, naturally, very sorry to hear of your father's death. I can't claim we were on good terms anymore, but do believe me that we are both sorry for your loss. We were even sadder to learn of Kellic and regret, again, that we could not attend the ceremony for his remembrance.

As to the matter of those items, there was indeed a very old map to which I had taken quite a fancy. It is currently framed upon my wall. It's very fragile, alas, but you can feel free to visit and look at it yourself at any time.

I have had my assistant make a copy of it for you, and I think he made a fair job of getting down all the important bits. I know it doesn't look like much without the colors, but don't think badly of it. These old mapmakers just seemed to make things up where they couldn't find things.

There is an island named "Kutnaar" on the map, where there's no island at all now. I'm not sure what good that will do, but it is something.

I do hope you will find time to visit us. Charlyn would be delighted to talk with you. We've read a garbled version of your recent adventure and would love to hear details without all the gaudy sensationalism.

Ivrian looked up from the letter for a moment, smirking. Garbled? Well, he supposed he had poured a little purple into his prose. And judging from Tradan's dry, formal style, the fellow was likely to have thought Ivrian's flourishes gaudy. But you had to give the people what they wanted.

He returned his attention to Tradan's words.

You may be interested to know that I looked into the coordinates you said you'd found on the lizardfolk book cones and discovered some ruins right where you said they'd be, no more than a few hours south of my own home. Most are long since looted, but I'm taking my time exploring the rest. I can read just a little of the lizard-folk glyphs, and there's a big bloke they've got statues of, everywhere, named Reklanit, or something to that effect. If the natives were more industrious, we'd be much further along, but they refuse to work during the heat of the day, or within an hour of twilight, and by the gods, the jungle grows fast. If we delay at all, it seems like any of the chopping we've done to clear away a site has been for naught because the plants just grow right back!

If you have time to visit, there are some beautiful pieces of artwork you might find of interest. The ancient frillbacks certainly loved their bright colors, didn't they?

Ivrian groaned a little. The writer was so breezily, unconsciously racist. The letter was signed by Tradan ven Goleman with an elaborate flourish and even the family crest stamped from a sigil ring. He was old Sargavan nobility, all right, although he honestly seemed a little warmer than some.

Ivrian looked away from the paper and glanced to where Jekka seemed to ritualistically be circling his fingers over the image of the island.

What must it be like, he wondered, to be one of the last of your people? Not for the first time he wondered if Kalina and Jekka had considered mating, or if Kalina had to observe a mourning period for her dead husband, Heltan. But even if they were to mate, there'd be the problem of who any of *their* offspring would breed with.

How strange to think that only a few months ago Jekka had frightened him. Now, he pitied him and Kalina both.

"Do you mind if I look at that part of the map?" Ivrian said gently.

"Which part?" Jekka cocked his head.

"The part you keep blocking with your hands."

"Of course." Jekka withdrew green fingers.

Ivrian peered more closely at the island, north and west of the jagged little islet he guessed for Smuggler's Shiv. Beside Kutnaar was an even smaller figure, slightly smudged by Jekka's rubbing. He leaned in for a closer look. Finally he decided he recognized what the image was supposed to represent. "This looks like a crying dragon."

Kalina pressed beside him and leaned forward over the table. He'd been in close proximity to the lizardfolk many times. Even in stultifying heat, after days of hard travel, neither had a particularly strong scent. The most noticeable fragrance upon Kalina was the floral-scented soap used on her robe. "I don't see it," she said.

He tapped the paper. "Right here. A dragon covering its face with its talons and it's bent over."

Jekka looked without blinking. "My people don't do that when we cry."

"It's sort of a stagey way to show grief," Ivrian explained, then added, "And sometimes you're wracked with so much sorrow you *want* to hide your face, so it's not always just about the stage."

"The stage," Jekka repeated. He seemed unfamiliar with the word. Kalina cocked her head at him.

"I'm going to have to take you both to see a play." He wondered what the locals would think of that! "There's one going on next week scripted by my friend Neider, based on a great Ailson Kindler book."

Jekka's hiss seemed drawn out and dismissive. "Is that the place you write for, where people go and mime scenes from history?"

"Not just history, cousin," Kalina said. "Adventure, and tales to instruct the young."

"I have no interest," Jekka said.

"Ailson Kindler writes the most amazing adventure stories," Ivrian said. But before he could continue, a deep, affable voice interrupted him.

"Well, well, well. You must be the Lord Ivrian and the lizard-folk scholars I've heard so much about."

Ivrian turned to find a stout, handsome man of late middle years walking down the aisle. His well-tailored blue robes were all but silent as he moved over the deep carpet. His skin was brown, and smooth rather than weathered, his dark brown beard going to gray.

"Are you a pirate?" Kalina asked.

The stranger laughed. "No."

Kalina looked to Ivrian for clarification, and he realized she must be thinking still about his comments regarding beard styles. More importantly, the stranger was advancing toward the map. That wouldn't do. Ivrian pushed the anchoring book aside, as if by accident. The map rolled in upon itself.

"Sir, I'm afraid this is a private matter—"

"It's all right, Ivrian."

Mirian returned with a small stack of particularly wide books that she set on the table before making a little bow.

The stranger returned this with a smile and then, as Mirian presented her hand, brushed it gently with his broad lips.

"This," Mirian said, "is Venture-Captain Finze Bellaugh, who runs the Pathfinder Lodge in Eleder. Captain, may I present Lord Ivrian Galanor, my brother, Jekka Eran Sulotai sar Karshnaar, and our cousin Kalina Shevek Oletai sar Karshnaar. She's the one to whom your assistant loaned out some book cones last month."

"But of course." The venture-captain bowed once to them all, and Ivrian, flushing a little, quickly returned a formal bow of his own. Jekka imitated the gesture with fluid grace while Kalina watched.

Mirian's entire manner had suddenly grown more relaxed than Ivrian had seen in weeks. "I didn't think you'd be free!" she said.

"I'm not." Bellaugh winked. "But how could I miss the chance to see you? Or to meet these new friends of yours?" He considered Jekka. "So this is the warrior priest," he said, then looked to Kalina. "And the deadly hunter. Mirian writes that you have an exhaustive record of lizardfolk legends and histories. I'd love to have one of our scribes sit down with you and record them."

"My sister flatters me," Jekka said. "It was my brother who was chronicler of our people. With his death, much of our past vanished. But why do you humans want to hear any of it?"

The venture-captain patted the paunch beneath his robe. "The goal of Pathfinders everywhere is to preserve knowledge so that it might be remembered and studied by future generations."

There was a prideful, rehearsed quality to his words, but then Ivrian supposed Bellaugh had said something similar many times.

"I should like us to be remembered," Jekka said. "But I would hate to think our legends would be used to profit humans, who made boots from the hatchlings of my people."

Bellaugh's large, tufted eyebrows rose at that. "I assure you," he said gravely, "Pathfinders preserve knowledge for the future. For any scholars. Regardless of race or species."

"Are there lizardfolk Pathfinders?" Kalina asked.

"Not that I'm aware of," Bellaugh admitted. "But if you're asking because you'd like to be one—"

"She is merely curious," Jekka said.

"I am always curious," Kalina affirmed. "Can lizardfolk become Pathfinders? What would they do if they were? Can they find lost things and look at them?"

Bellaugh looked to Mirian, then back to the lizard woman, whose small frill had risen along her neck and head. This usually indicated aggression or caution, but Ivrian had learned it also could indicate exceptional interest.

"That's almost exactly what we do," Bellaugh said with great dignity. "And we find a way to bring those things back so others can see and learn from them."

"Oh, yes. Mirian has shown me her drawings. I cannot do that."

"You don't have to be an artist," Bellaugh said. He opened his mouth as if to expound further on the duties of Pathfinders, but Mirian interrupted him.

"Perhaps we can talk about that another time."

"Oh, of course." Bellaugh patted his belly once more, then turned to Ivrian. "I read your account with great interest, Lord Galanor, although Mirian wrote me that the actual adventure took place on the Kaava peninsula, not in the Laughing Jungle, and that there were many incidents glossed over or left from it. Would you be interested in writing an accurate account for our official annals? I could arrange a small fee. For Jekka or Kalina too, of course."

"I'd be honored." Ivrian nodded politely. Bellaugh moved in powerful circles, no matter his known association with adventurers and rogues. And what an honor it would be to have writing preserved by the Pathfinders! It would give him a kind of literary immortality he'd dreamed about . . . although he'd rather have it for the stories he invented.

Bellaugh cleared his throat. "Now, if it's not too much trouble, perhaps you might show me that chart of yours."

Ivrian glanced to Mirian for confirmation, saw her slight nod. "Of course."

Ivrian unrolled the paper once more, setting the book on its far side so that the map lay flat.

"That's the island," Mirian said, pointing.

"A dragon's tear," Bellaugh said softly, his voice tinged with honest surprise. He looked up surreptitiously, taking in the rest of the people in the room.

"A *what*?" Ivrian asked. Bellaugh didn't answer. Ivrian glanced at Mirian and saw her dark eyes were riveted on the venture-captain.

"Allow me to invite you to my private study room," Bellaugh said. "Gather up your things."

He stepped away and Ivrian worked quickly to give the map a tight roll so it would slide into the case. Bellaugh was already moving with some haste, and Ivrian almost forgot the letter, which he now handed to Jekka.

Jekka and Kalina followed the venture-captain; Ivrian fell in step behind Mirian. "What's this all about?"

She shook her head quickly so that he wasn't sure whether she didn't know, or just didn't want to talk about it in public.

They reached the lobby and climbed stone stairs to a higher level with polished parquet floors to pass beyond a bored pikeman in scale armor. Beyond him was a wide hall and two oak doors that opened onto a small chamber with a wide harbor window. A bouquet of sweet pipe smoke lingered in the air, perhaps soaked up by two heavy couches facing each other across an old oak table weighted down by a weathered stone head.

Bellaugh stepped around the table and stood before one of the two inner doorways. "Go ahead and close the door, Mirian."

This she did while the venture-captain waved Ivrian forward. "Let's see the map again. Kalina, weigh down the edges with those books. That's good."

"What's a dragon's tear?" Ivrian asked.

Bellaugh smiled thinly. "I can't be sure that it is one. But . . ." He waited for Kalina to step back from the map. He pointed to the smudged image near the island of Kutnaar. "Look at the pose. Look at the dragon's profile, to the left. Clearly this chart is a copy. Have you seen the original?"

"No," Mirian answered, then corrected herself. "Well, maybe. But I don't recall—"

"You must look at the original. If whoever drew this copied it exactly, it may just be a fanciful image. And of course, it's smudged a bit."

Jekka hissed, faintly. "I didn't know it was important."

The lack of response was maddening to Ivrian. "What," he asked again, "is a dragon's tear?"

Bellaugh crossed his arms and tapped his elbow with his other hand. "A dragon's tear is a magical artifact of tremendous power. Wizards in ancient times could level mountains with them. Or sink islands."

Ivrian winced inwardly. Might that be the explanation of Kutnaar's absence from modern maps?

"Let's hope that's not what happened here," Mirian said. "Why would there be a dragon's tear drawn on the map?"

Bellaugh shrugged his large shoulders. "I can't say."

He looked as though he was about to say something though, for his mouth was opening when Kalina interrupted with a question of her own. "What does one of these tears look like?"

Bellaugh drew himself up as if he were in a lecture hall. "A true one is teardrop-shaped, and looks like it's made of fine clay or marble." Bellaugh lifted one hand, fingers pointing upward, then met it with his other, thumb pointing down. "It's about the size to be cupped in a hand. And each is said to be a reservoir of great arcane energy—not necessarily destructive energy. Powerful sorcerers sometimes used them to achieve amazing feats. Like opening gates to other planes of existence. They're priceless, as you might imagine."

"You've seen one?" Ivrian asked.

"I've not had the honor. I've held a duplicate. There were always some whispers that they were lizardfolk creations or some sort of artifacts made by an ancient race of dragons, although most people wanted to say they'd been crafted by the Azlanti. Maybe it really was the lizardfolk." Bellaugh turned to Jekka. "Are there any legends of such things among your people?"

Jekka watched Bellaugh for a long time. "My brother is dead," he said finally. "He might have known. But this is a crying dragon shown on the image. Not lizardfolk."

"That is a—well, somewhat poor icon—of the symbol shown among ancient documents for one of the tears. It might mean that there was a tear upon this place."

"Have you read anything about the island of Kutnaar? We were going to search through the map files and historical records for any mention of it."

Bellaugh looked at all of them then and moved toward one of the other doorways. "Give me a moment. Please. Take a seat. All of you."

While his friends lowered themselves onto the furniture, Ivrian leaned to get a better look at the man's destination and saw a room cluttered and crowded with books and knickknacks. Under one pile was a desk. He strongly doubted anyone could locate anything quickly in such a place, but Bellaugh returned a moment later. He blew dust off the old red-leather tome and placed it gently on the table beside the map as he settled into the couch. Ivrian sat down beside Mirian, across from the older man.

Bellaugh opened the old book with great care, supporting the spine with his right hand. "Jekka, Kalina, you might be interested in this. It's a history of the pre-human days in the region, at least what we Pathfinders know of it. It's highly fragmentary, of course. It would be wonderful to get your thoughts on the text. I'm sure you might know more than you're even aware of."

"I can't read your human language," Kalina said.

As Bellaugh turned pages, he stopped after a few dozen and rested his finger just above the old browned paper, where deep black lines were etched in a precise, slanting hand.

Kalina leaned inappropriately close to the venture-captain. "Do those symbols speak of Kutnaar?"

Bellaugh was untroubled by the invasion of his personal space. "They do indeed." The venture-captain cleared his throat, put his finger to a line and peered with his chin up though his eyes were rolled down. "I'll translate on the go, as they say. 'For many years, the human tides swept in against the lizardfolk, battling over and again, and the savages . . .'" Here he looked up. "I'm afraid that means natives of the region. Our forefathers were not always so enlightened. Ahem. '. . . and the savages fought and killed them and drove them on. Some claim the lizardfolk were actually far advanced, with great magical abilities, and I myself have looked upon ruins in the jungles said to be from the lizard days. There are strange glyphs everywhere, and many of them show lizardfolk in positions of power, so I am inclined to believe the locals, even though they are prone to exaggeration if they think it will please me. What tales these glyphs could tell if only I could read them!'"

"Who wrote this?" Mirian asked.

"Tyrvale of Taldor, originally. This is copied over from him. Now here's the important bit I was looking for. 'The most interesting of all these legends is that of the dread lizard king, Reklaniss.'"

Ivrian saw Mirian start violently, and give Jekka a significant look. The lizardfolk cocked his head to one side, as he often did when curious.

Ivrian recalled the letter. "That's similar to the name of the lizard king in that city Lord ven Goleman found."

"Tradan ven Goleman?" Bellaugh arched an eyebrow.

"Yes," Mirian answered. "I gave him some coordinates to look into south of Port Freedom, and there's a small ruin there. Apparently one dedicated to someone he named Reklanit. It was mentioned on the same book cone as the island of Kutnaar, which is supposed to be this Reklaniss's colony. Do you suppose they're the same king?"

"It may be." Bellaugh looked back at the text and read aloud. "'It is said that he fought back against the tide of humans for many years, and that he perfected a life-sustaining elixir. Many were his sorceries, and he killed or enslaved countless ancient tribes. Yet still the humans were too strong for him. He sent his people to safety through a gate in the sea to an island named Kutnaar, then closed off his people from the rest of the world so they could be safe from humans.'"

Bellaugh broke off, though he continued to read silently to himself. "I think that's it," he said after a moment. "Now he's writing about the human natives again." The venture-captain cleared his throat and looked up. "Is anyone else thirsty? I can call for wine, or brandy."

"I always welcome the gift of wine," Jekka answered.

"I know not what this means," Kalina said. "How can you have a gate in the sea?" She didn't flick her tongue nearly as often as Jekka, but she did so now.

Mirian looked to Bellaugh, now leaning into the corridor. He'd pulled a little brass bell from his robe and rang it. From down the hall a steward came running, and Bellaugh softly conferred with him.

"Finze said that the dragon's tear could be used to open gates to other realms," Mirian said.

Ivrian had heard of other planes of existence but never really spent much time thinking about them, because they seemed chiefly the concern of priests. "You're saying this ancient wizard-king sent his people on to paradise or the Plane of Water or something?"

"Not necessarily," Mirian answered. "And if he did build a gate, he probably wouldn't build it to any place like those."

Bellaugh shut the door behind him and answered, eyes glinting with eagerness. "There are said to be pocket dimensions and planes of existence parallel to our own. Truly powerful magic-users can access them."

While Ivrian considered that, Bellaugh nodded to Jekka. "I'm having some refreshments brought round."

"Do you think," Mirian asked Bellaugh slowly, "that there's a gate over there, northeast of Smuggler's Shiv?" She pointed to the map and the icon of the weeping dragon that was located right on top of the Lizard Kings—a reef chain that had been carved into towering likenesses of lizardfolk by Jekka's ancient forebears.

"It certainly sounds like there used to be. Surely it's not there now or we'd have heard of it, wouldn't we? People would be slipping through all the time. But then, that old quote from Tyrvale said the lizardfolk were sealed off behind the gate. So it's probably closed."

"Then we must open it again," Jekka said.

"That's liable to be difficult." Bellaugh opened his arms and shrugged, as if embarrassed. "I'm sorry to say it. If this Reklaniss used a tear to close the gate, you'll probably need one to open it. And those are in very short supply."

"What if he made the gate with the tear, but you need something else to get there?" Jekka asked.

Bellaugh patted his belly once more. "I suppose that's possible . . . If I were you I'd get down to this jungle city and poke around. You can read inscriptions to see if there are any clues about it on the buildings there."

Jekka bowed formally. "I thank you, Venture-Captain. You have done us a great kindness."

"Not at all, not at all."

"You don't understand," Kalina said with great sincerity. "We shall return the favor, and give you whatever information we have that interests you, though I don't think it can help anyone as much as you have helped us."

"You never know." He tapped the book. "I doubt old Tyrvale ever imagined he'd be aiding lizardfolk searching for their lost people when he wrote the text. Although, if you're in the mood for favors . . ." He smiled at Jekka and Kalina, who simply stared back.

Bellaugh apparently hadn't had enough experience with lizardfolk to know they were vague on any number of social cues.

"You need to finish the sentence," Mirian suggested.

"My pardon. I by no means wish to impose. But I'd be quite interested in getting some help translating some lizardfolk book cones we have in storage here, and if possible, getting a translation of those you have in your possession. I know you've been looking over them, Kalina. Do both of you read your language?"

"Yes," the lizardfolk answered in unison.

"Well then—perhaps one of you could remain here while the other journeys? Surely Mirian doesn't need you both."

Ivrian rather expected she might. Jekka's coloring flared across his skinlike facial scales, bright blues and yellows, mostly, with hints of red. For all that he'd spent months around the lizardfolk, Ivrian still didn't know how to interpret all of the color shifts.

Kalina and Jekka faced each other and exchanged rapid-fire vocalizations. It sounded something like warbling intermixed with growls, rather like low-pitched birds.

"What are they saying?" Bellaugh asked Mirian quietly.

"I've no idea."

"You don't really need them both, do you?" he asked. "This ruin isn't too far from Port Freedom, and Tradan surely has manpower to spare if he's already looking into it."

Mirian looked displeased, though it didn't show in her answer. "It's really up to them."

As one, Ivrian, Mirian, and the venture-captain turned to watch the lizardfolk argue. The two neither moved their hands nor shifted stances. Only their necks and heads drifted from time to time.

They reached some kind of accord. Eerily, both turned to face the others at once.

"It is decided," Kalina said. "I will stay."

"You don't have to," Mirian said. "You can return the favor at a later time."

"Indeed," Bellaugh said, hastily. "I was really only jesting."

He hadn't been—Ivrian could tell that much. In his eagerness to latch on to more information for his lodge, Bellaugh had pressed harder than he'd possibly intended and regretted it, or at least regretted upsetting Mirian, for whom he seemed to harbor some honest affection.

"No, I will remain." Kalina bobbed her head. "I would first like to finish reading the lizardfolk books you have here, in case they can be used in our search."

"Of course." Bellaugh nodded.

"Will the wheeled box be available each day to take me from Mirian's home to here?"

"My dear," Bellaugh said with an expansive gesture, "I will make comfortable quarters for you here. Consider it your home away from home."

"Also," Kalina said, "can you teach me to read the human letters?"

"Well, there are many . . ." Bellaugh's voice trailed off as he confronted the lizard woman. Despite the lack of facial muscles, her expression somehow denoted eagerness. "What I mean to say is, that can definitely be arranged."

"And I should like to hear more about being a Pathfinder," Kalina added.

Bellaugh laughed. "Whatever you like."

Ivrian thought Bellaugh lucky he hadn't promised that to Jekka, because the lizard man would have sucked down bottle after bottle of his finest wine without showing the slightest sign of inebriation.

"You three will be fine without me for a while," Kalina said. "You managed well without me once."

Mirian frowned and Ivrian grimaced at the memory of Kalina's death, which numbered right up there among his least favorite recollections. Though her body had been preserved by Jeneta, priestess of Iomedae, there'd still been no guarantee her spirit would be strong enough to return to the physical world. It had been a grueling few days waiting to find out.

"We'll be in touch as soon as we return." Mirian glanced at Ivrian. "How about you? You up for another venture? This one you can write up."

Ivrian laughed. "You think you can keep me away? I'll look forward to meeting your half sister."

Jekka, who had been silent up until then, cocked his head to one side. "I have been wondering, Mirian. Is your sister my half sister as well? You name Kalina your cousin."

"That's up to her," Mirian said. "It's bad enough they have a native woman in the family. Charlyn never really accepted our father remarrying, in part because my mother is native. I'm not sure what they'll think when they find out I adopted two lizard-folk. Ivrian didn't put that in his book."

He hadn't—just as Ivrian had left other specifics private, he'd merely declared that Mirian and Jekka had pledged a lifelong bond of friendship. He chuckled, remembering how Tradan had referred to him in his letter. "What will they think when they learn you're friends with a gaudy pamphlet writer?"

Mirian smirked. "This might be fun."

6

THE NEXT BOTTLE

ENSARA

Ensara sat alone with his drink on the balcony, wishing the raucous music below was either softer or more tuneful. He despised it almost as much as the sound of the boasting sailors and the forced laughter of the prostitutes.

One of the latter drifted forward in the swirl of her flounced skirt. Mevrana.

"Why the long face, Meric?" she asked with a smile.

He gulped another swig of rum. "I hate this place."

She sat down beside him and put a dimpled chin on one manicured hand. "So leave it."

"And go where?"

She smiled and put her other hand over his. "Seems to me you ought to feel a little more celebratory. From what I hear, you and Sarken were lucky to get away with your lives."

Ensara withdrew his hand, suppressing an inward shudder, and poured himself another drink of rum from the half-empty bottle.

"What was it?"

"Dramen said it was probably a devilfish, but all we ever saw were the tentacles."

He didn't want to talk about it, but the words started whirling up out of him anyway. "Snatched up Kavel and dragged him off. We could hear him screaming even through the water. And then there was all this blackness. Ink, Dramen said. There was no way to get him free. It was all we could do to get out alive. We almost didn't."

"But here you are."

"Aye. Me and Sarken and Dramen." Three out of the six who'd dived with Mirian.

He looked down over the balcony rail to the lower level. He could hear the women oohing and ahing. Sarken was going on again about how he'd show that salvager what-for if he ever caught her. How he'd personally kill Mirian Raas because she was a double-crossing witch.

"I wish he'd shut his damned mouth," Ensara muttered, and took another drink.

Mevrana reached for his hand and swirled her fingers along the hair there. "You want to go in back? Take your mind off your troubles?"

He shook his head.

"You know I can get you thinking about something else," she said with a winsome smile. "Or stop you from thinking at all for a good long while." She pushed the bottle away. "And it will be a lot more fun than *this*."

He drank.

She pouted. "You're really broken up about it."

He shrugged, distractedly reached for her hair with one hand. She smiled as he toyed with its ends. And unbidden, that dark, curling hair of Mirian Raas's came to his mind.

"So are you really going to hunt down this salvager?" she said softly. "They say she all but sank Kradok's ship a few months back. Killed him with that wand Sarken's waving around."

"Is he doing that again?" Ensara didn't even want to look.

"So are you going after her?"

"No. I've got better things to do."

"Do you?"

"The way I figure it, we kind of had it coming, you know?" He met the woman's eyes. "We ambushed her ship, took her prisoner.

We had her outnumbered but she took us down. All's fair in love, war, and cards, right?"

"That's what they say."

"But what do you do when you sit down for a play and someone's just better than you? Honestly better? Do you get up and kick the chair? Or do you reach over and shake their hand and tell them they did good?"

"I think you like her."

Ensara stared down at his glass.

Mevrana laughed, suddenly a little shrill. "She handed you your ass, and you liked it."

"It's just . . . I respect her, you know?"

"Oh, I understand." Chair legs scraped in protest as she stood. "You get over your pirate queen, you know where I am." She smiled sourly and sashayed off.

He listened as she took the stairs down to the main level.

There was a time when he'd liked crashing in with a grin and a swagger, watching the women come running. They went to him because he was a captain, which meant he'd have money and gave them status and bragging rights. They'd smile and laugh at his jokes and moan loud when he took them to the back rooms.

Somehow it had all gone sour as lime.

What he really wanted was to go back to the ship, but it felt like a prison now. He had to earn some money; the crew was getting restless. And that jackass Sarken had them all worked up about getting vengeance. What he should probably do is arrange for Sarken to get himself killed, but Ensara wasn't really interested in that, either.

He poured himself another drink and swirled it around in his glass. He stared at the empty chair, tried to imagine what it would be like to have Mirian Raas sitting across from him. They could talk about the sea and the stars, about life on the waves, and places they'd been. He could give her back the wand and apologize.

What would she say?

He still wondered about that moment right before she darted off. She'd pulled him out of the way. He'd said as much to Sarken. Maybe she hadn't known the thing was there and she really had wanted a deal. Surely with that beast lurking around the corner she would have seemed more leery.

Or maybe she was just treacherous and sneaky. That part didn't matter so much. *He* was treacherous and sneaky.

Ensara emptied the glass.

What mattered was that she had pulled him out of the way before turning to flee. And that made her interesting.

He toasted her imagined presence across from him. "Here's to a better meeting," he said softly.

The conversation below lulled. Ensara didn't bother looking to see who had entered. He reached for the bottle, poured the last drink, and thought about downing it.

But then he heard his name, and the low sound of a woman's voice, then Sarken's answer: "What do you want with the captain?"

"A business proposition," the woman replied. She sounded haughty, confident.

"He might already be up to some business if he's moved off the balcony," Sarken said, and there was a roar of laughter.

Ensara climbed to his feet, surprised by how uneven his stance was. He didn't actually feel drunk. He leaned against the rail and looked down, then tipped his hat.

He didn't recognize the willowy woman with the dark hair and expensive clothes, nor the well-dressed, grim-looking man at her side.

He put a bit of a growl into his voice. "What's all this, Sarken?"

"Captain!" Sarken brightened and gestured to the two strangers. "This lady here, she's looking for you. Says something about business."

He felt the woman's eyes seek his own. She had that unmistakable air of nobility one usually didn't find on folk at Smuggler's Shiv.

What the hell. "Send her up."

He saw them divert around the bar and pass out of sight, Sarken trailing. Ensara really wasn't in a mood to deal with Sarken, but he might need him on hand. The woman's bodyguard could be trouble. And who knew what either really wanted?

He could hear the creak of their feet on the stairs, the patter of Sarken asking questions and the woman's curt responses, though he couldn't make out what was said.

Could be they needed to hire him for something, and by Gozreh, his ship needed money. Ensara quickly whipped off his hat, fluffed its feather, then reset it before inspecting his collar and sleeves. A bit frayed, and that wine stain had never come off the left cuff. He didn't look his best, but then even slumming he looked a cut above the usual riffraff of the Shiv.

It didn't take much to affect that old confident grin. When Sarken guided the woman and her guard to his table, he had one hand thrown over the back of a nearby chair. He touched the tip of his hat to her.

She was older than he first thought. Still attractive, shapely under her emerald dress, but sort of sour-looking, really. Pale. Even featured, with dark eyes and long black hair. And she was wearing long white gloves, like a woman might at the opera. That in itself was a damned strange thing. It could get a little chill in Sargava, some nights, but it wasn't cold this evening.

No, there was something odd there, just as there was something peculiar about the woman's companion in his plain black suit with waistcoat, all made from the finest materials. Like someone had told him to avoid notice by wearing dark clothes, but he had too much money to do it properly.

He would have stood out in any case, for he was as tall as Sarken, and broader besides, as though he spent all his spare moments climbing ropes to build up his shoulders.

"Cap'n, these two wanted to see you."

"Much obliged, Sarken," he answered with a grin. "I'm Captain Meric Ensara, of the *Marvel*. But I gather you know that."

"I do," the woman said curtly.

"You can join me if you like," Ensara told her. "But I don't recommend what I've been drinking."

"Then why are you drinking it?"

If she'd smiled he would have assumed she was flirting, but on inspection he wasn't sure she had ever smiled. It was a question reflecting mild curiosity.

"Because I had nothing better to do until you came along," he said with a grin.

Still no smile. The bodyguard pulled out a chair for her and she sank down across from him, sitting prim and proper, back straight.

Sarken swaggered over to stand behind Ensara.

"I," the woman said, "am Lady Rajana Rotaine. I understand you recently encountered the salvager Mirian Raas."

"Word gets around, m'lady." He eyed her, trying to decide what her origin point was. Not Sargava, clearly. "How can I help you?"

There. He was being gentlemanly, but not deferential.

"I have it on good authority that an item of hers may have come into your possession. If you would be so kind, I should very much like to examine it."

Not really phrased like a question, he thought. More like a polite command.

"I'm always pleased to oblige a lady, m'lady. But before I do, how did you hear, and why do you want it?"

"I have friends who keep me well informed of the goings-on here in Smuggler's Shiv."

Vague as the answer was, it satisfied Ensara. For it wasn't as though anyone on the crew had kept their encounter with the sea monster secret over the last few days. Especially not Sarken.

"As for why I want it, if it meets my specifications, I may offer monetary compensation."

Ensara was pretty certain he must be drunk then, because he realized he wasn't thinking very clearly. He needed money, and this woman smelled of it. Yet he wasn't really sure he wanted to give up Mirian's wand. He wanted to turn it over to Mirian instead, maybe send it in a package. An opening gesture, like.

"I've got it right here," Sarken said. "How much is it worth?"

Then there was that problem. Ensara looked over his shoulder at his first mate. Sarken had claimed the wand from the start, saying it was his in payment for the loss of his brother.

"If it was really hers," Rajana said, "I might be very generous. And I might have other financial incentives as well. A simple examination will inform me."

"Oh, it's hers." Sarken's lip curled. "That bitch handed it over to me herself."

The guard beside the woman flinched as Sarken whipped up the wand. The man watched, tensely, as Sarken advanced and slapped the thing down in front of his mistress.

Rajana stared at it a moment, eyeing the smooth, pearl white finish and the small emerald bands that circled its tips.

Then, with seeming infinite care, she used the last two fingers of her right hand to pull the glove from her left. And here Ensara noticed something else peculiar—the other fingers and thumb of the gloved right hand stood out stiffly.

Her left hand, though, seemed perfectly fine. Pale, well formed. Uncalloused, he saw clearly, as she lifted the wand.

"I am a practitioner of magic," she told them. "Don't be alarmed, for I mean you no harm. I will examine the wand, and if I find it belongs to Mirian Raas—"

"You bet it does," Sarken cut in.

She ignored him. "—then we will discuss payment."

Ensara nodded, and then, to cover his own indecisiveness, reached for the bottle. It was empty. "Sarken, get us another bottle, will you? Some good bourbon. The lady might get thirsty."

"Sure. You mind if I have a bolt, Cap'n?"

"Help yourself."

Sarken trotted off.

As the woman muttered under her breath, her eyes seemed to take on a reddish glow. Was it Ensara's imagination, or were the shadows thickening in the room?

"Oh yes." The woman finally smiled. It might have been a pretty smile if there was any prettiness in the soul behind those dark eyes. "This is hers. How much do you want for it?"

"How much are you offering?" Sarken asked. Ensara had been so intent upon the woman's spellwork he hadn't even heard him return.

The first mate uncorked the bottle and poured a drink for the captain before noisily swirling some whiskey into a glass for himself.

"Are you authorizing him to negotiate for you, Captain?" Rajana asked.

"It's my wand, now," Sarken asserted.

Ensara ignored him. "What do you want it for, m'lady?"

"Are you trying to be difficult, Captain, or merely better informed?" She tapped her chin with one red-stained nail. "I don't think you're as drunk as you pretend."

Ensara grunted and took a drink of surprisingly smooth bourbon, then set his glass upon the table and waited.

"Mirian Raas killed my sister with this very wand," Rajana said. "And nearly killed me as well."

By the gods. So maybe the whole pamphlet had been true. Of course, the woman in the pamphlet had been a countess, and her name hadn't been Rajana, but . . . Ensara couldn't keep his eyes from sliding over to the remaining, gloved hand.

Rajana frowned. "I see you're familiar with that laughable fairy tale penned by Galanor's twit of a son."

"He didn't use your real name," Ensara guessed.

"He left out many crucial details and embellished others. My sister was a beauty, but she was even more of a half-wit than Ivrian Galanor. But Mirian Raas did slice off much of my right hand."

"Gods!" Sarken said, and leaned closer. As if the woman were going to give him a look. She glared instead, then shifted her attention back to Ensara.

"Are you acquainted with the workings of magic, Captain?"

"My brother was a wizard," Sarken said. "A water wizard."

"He served me well for three years," Ensara said. "May Pharasma guide him home."

The woman seemed unmoved. "Some practitioners," she continued, as though lecturing to an intellectually stilted youngster, "are able to look in on people from far away."

"Like a peeper," Sarken suggested.

Those thin lips shaped themselves into a frown. "The problem," Rajana went on, "is that unless one knows the subject well, one has to rely on looking in on them with something they owned. A piece of hair. A personal belonging."

A finger. Ensara smiled thinly at his own wit.

"I observed her lizard man several times while I was in possession of his staff. But I no longer have it. You're acquainted with Mirian Raas's reptilian guard?"

"I can't say as I've met him, no." Ensara found himself wondering if there'd be another pamphlet coming out soon featuring his encounter with Mirian Raas, and what it would say about him.

And then he began to wonder what this woman meant to do with an object with which she could spy on Mirian Raas.

But Rajana was already telling him—something about spying on Mirian and listening to what she planned.

"And why would you do that?" he asked.

She gave him a whithering look and gestured with her muti-lated hand. "Why do you *think*, Captain? But it's not my only reason. I also have friends who've learned certain rumors about the elusive Miss Raas and that idiot Galanor."

Friends, Ensara thought, must mean "spies." He doubted Rajana had any real friends.

"The Custodian has further plans for them," she continued. "He's hoping to lure them into service to search for additional treasures."

"So you want the wand so you can learn where those treasures are?"

"I will pay you a flat fee of fifteen thousand crowns for that wand. And I'll pay you a further five thousand to transport me wherever it is she plans to go."

Sarken grinned, revealing square, gapped teeth. He leaned against the table and stared at the woman. "If there's any killing to be done to her, I want to be in on it."

"I think that can be arranged," Rajana said coolly. "So long as it's nothing clever. Nothing melodramatic, you understand. Just dead."

Ensara didn't like the sound of any of this. "I'm a businessman, not an assassin."

One of her slim eyebrows cocked at him. "Yet you were willing to take up the hunt for her. I'm the one that fronted that bounty offer on her and her ship."

Of course she was. "That's still different," Ensara protested. "I wasn't planning on killing anyone who didn't resist."

"You can count on her resisting," the woman said. "What do you want, Captain?

Sarken looked momentarily troubled himself, and then his expression cleared. He slapped Ensara on the shoulder.

"He wants us a cut of the treasure, your ladyship."

That wasn't what Ensara had been thinking at all. He'd been trying to puzzle a way through the whole nasty arrangement.

But the woman smiled, genuinely this time. She really was quite striking.

"I begin to see that you're more than you seem, Captain. Let's speak clearly, then. If it turns out that Mirian Raas is on another treasure hunt, the important thing to me is that what she's after never gets into the Custodian's hands. If you and your men are actively involved in helping me acquire it, I suggest an equitable split."

"What's that mean?" Sarken asked.

She lifted her left hand and wagged a finger at Ensara. "I appreciate how you have your subordinate raise the most challenging questions. It makes you seem more approachable. You don't need to play games with me, though, Captain. I am what I appear to be."

"I think you're far more dangerous than you seem."

"How very astute of you. I begin to think the same of you. By an equitable split, I imagine you will receive between fifty and seventy percent, depending upon how involved you are in the actual recovery of the treasure, how much risk we find ourselves under, and how much personal risk I myself face in the course of the escapade."

"And whether or not we put the screws to the bitch, right, m'lady?" Sarken asked.

"I'm not interested in that," the woman answered without even considering Sarken. She seemed done with him. "I just want her dead."

Ensara blinked.

"So do we have an arrangement, Captain? Fifteen thousand up front, and then a variable percentage of the treasure?"

"Perhaps a contract is in order," Ensara said, stalling for time. He didn't think she'd like a contract.

But damned if that didn't make her smile again. "To be honored in what court, Captain?"

"I just want everything clear between us."

"And how much treasure are we talking about?" Sarken asked.

"I was under the impression you only cared about killing her." Rajana looked sideways at the mate.

"I didn't say I wasn't interested in gold, Lady."

"I can't very well determine the sort of treasure until I've been able to observe Mirian Raas at length. Which is why," she continued, "I need to purchase the wand first. I'm prepared to pay you this evening."

"You're walking around this crap hole with that much coin on you?" Sarken asked.

"Of course not. I can arrange to have it sent your way. My man will bring it to your ship and exchange it for the wand. Then we'll commence with the rest come morning. Do we have an agreement?"

Ensara tried to marshal his thoughts. This wasn't at all what he wanted to happen to Mirian Raas. And he sure as hell didn't want this woman spying on her, although the thought of being able to look in on her was a little titillating. Which embarrassed him, because he knew a gentleman wouldn't be thinking such things—or maybe, he thought, the difference was that a gentleman wouldn't act on such impulses—

"Captain?" Rajana prompted. "I've made a fair and reasonable offer."

"The captain's just weighing his options," Sarken said, clapping Ensara on the shoulder. "For instance, who's to say how much a wand like this is really worth?"

"I am," she answered. "It's worth no more than five thousand, based on the spellwork involved. Less, if the magic hasn't been recharged recently. I'm offering you three times that, to avoid the tedious business of haggling." She leaned forward, looking him in the eye. "I'm sure you're used to people trying to run gambits on you, Captain. I am not. I am a noblewoman of Cheliax—Galanor got that much right. My pledge is my bond, and I follow the laws of my people."

"The captain's a man of his word as well," Sarken noted.

"And a cautious one. What is it you want that you haven't heard, Captain?"

Ensara shook his head. "I'm always suspicious of a deal that sounds too good to be true."

"Ah, well, you see, it may not be as easy as it sounds. There are liable to be unexpected challenges. Mirian Raas is clever, deadly, and surrounded by professionals loyal to her."

"So I learned."

"To your detriment, I hear. Come, Captain. Do we have a deal, or not?"

"I suppose we do," he said, though he wasn't sure why. He felt trapped into saying it, what with Sarken looking on, and the guard glaring at him and the woman eyeing him like a vampire sizing up her next victim. He wondered if she might really *be* a vampire, given the dark hair and pale complexion, but surely if she were, Ivrian Galanor's booklet would have worked that into the story. Besides, couldn't vampires heal themselves by sucking more blood? If so, then she wouldn't have missing fingers.

He was too drunk for this. His thoughts kept drifting idly into the wrong channels instead of staying on tack. He rubbed his forehead, not feeling particularly clear on anything. He was aware that the woman was rising, so stood himself, quickly, as it was improper to remain seated when a lady rose. He even tipped his hat.

This time she offered her hand to him. The left one. Automatically, he put his lips to the back of it. Lilacs, he thought. She smelled of lilacs.

"This has been an unexpected pleasure, Captain. My man will arrive at your ship in another hour to make the arranged trade, and then I shall see you in the half hour after dawn so that we can make final arrangements."

"Charmed," Ensara said. He felt he should have said something more, but that was all he had left in him.

As the woman turned and left with her guard preceding her, Ensara managed to find his chair, even as Sarken's elbow dug into his side.

"Damn, I think she's got the hots for you, Cap'n. And she's not bad looking, either, for an older lady. She's got class, you know?"

Ensara grunted.

"Now about the wand. I knew it was worth something, but I didn't realize it was worth so much. How much of a cut do you want to give me of that?"

"Sarken, piss off."

"What?" The thick eyebrows rose on that heavy skull.

"Go away." Ensara took back the bottle, listened to it gurgle as he poured the dark bourbon into his glass.

"We've got to get back to the ship and wait for the guy with the money!" He lowered his voice. "We're talking about thousands and thousands of crowns here, and the chance to put Mirian Raas good and under, and probably get you laid by that fine piece that just walked out of here. What's your rutting problem?"

Ensara quaffed another drink. "Just handle it yourself, Sarken. I don't give a damn."

Frowning, muttering under his breath, Sarken left him there.

When the bottle was empty, he ordered another.

7

RIVER OF BLADES

MIRIAN

The *Daughter of the Mist* dropped anchor that evening at one of the so-called "ocean piers" on the outskirts of Port Freedom. Due to the shallow anchorage near the city itself, the harbor mostly consisted of a series of dismasted hulks a quarter league off shore, linked by walkways. Some sailors never even bothered leaving the hulks for the city, for over the years an astonishing assortment of storefronts, inns, brothels, restaurants, taverns, and merchant stalls had been erected upon them or floated nearby.

Only flat-bottomed barges could navigate the maze of sandbars that led to Port Freedom itself. A virtual fleet of them was for hire, controlled by the infamous Rivermen's Guild, and Mirian studied the vessels idly as hands lowered the ship's gangway. Dozens were rowing from the mainland to reprovision nearby ships, their decks stacked high with fruits, cages of live animals, and barrels of water or grog. Others were poling their way toward the city invisible behind the sandbars, heavy with passengers, luggage, crates, and the occasional oddity, like what looked to be an expensive racing horse.

Rendak shook his head as Mirian checked the placement of her gear a final time. "I still don't like this," he groused, then ran a hand back through his thinning hair.

"You'll be fine."

He sighed at her. "It's not me I'm worried about."

Gombe had come up behind him. "It should be. Every time she leaves us, we run into pirates."

That earned Gombe a scowl, which he studiously ignored. "What Rendak really means is that you should take us with you."

"I'm going to be gone for an overnight, possibly two. I'll send word if it's two," she added, before Rendak could suggest the obvious. "Don't let more than three of the crew off the ship at once."

Rendak grunted. "They'd rather get fleeced by familiar faces in Eleder."

Mirian hoped he was right, but knew the crew was liable to get bored, and enticed by the thought of new sights. "Try to keep them from doing anything too stupid, will you?"

And with that she glanced to her shore party: Ivrian, Jekka, and Jeneta, the young priestess of Iomedae who'd joined them in Crown's End near the end of their last venture and seemed inclined to continue her association.

Mirian didn't mind having a healer along, though she still missed superstitious, crotchety old Tokello. Jeneta was almost her complete opposite, full of a deep-seated faith that lent her dignity beyond her years. Tokello had been blocky and plain, to be charitable, while slim Jeneta, with her natural grace and pert features, tended to draw stares.

Yet it wasn't Jeneta who drew attention as the four of them crossed the gangplank to the hulk where they'd anchored. Their fellow travelers and merchants were clearly curious about a lizard man. Jekka wore his beige belted robe, hood down, and carried a staff. It granted him a more civilized aspect, true, but there was no mistaking his alien appearance. Even in such a cosmopolitan location as this busy harbor, lizardfolk were a rare sight.

From the fronting ship they passed on through a series of connected vessels, arriving finally at a rickety dock lined with passenger barges. Those intended primarily for cargo were either pulled straight up to ships or rowed into the northern side of the docks. Here a long line of merchants, travelers, sailors, and even some scholars and pilgrims wandered along the line of docked boats, sizing them up.

The sailors who manned the transport vessels were a blend of tribes and colonials and mixed races, and this being their living, different groups put flare into their presentation. One set of men at the oarlocks wore the same white-and-blue striped shirts. Another band was garbed in yellow and wore black kerchiefs.

To a one, though, the steersmen wore traditional tall rounded hats, and they were a boisterous, smiling bunch, calling to pass-ersby with practiced patter. They complimented and promised smooth rides and juggled, danced, or even played flutes or beat tambourines.

"Is it always like this?" Ivrian asked Mirian.

"You should see it in the morning. It's even wilder as the first passengers disembark." She passed by the blue-and-white sailors, no matter the fine singing of their steersmen, because the crew looked sullen, and headed for an older man who'd pinned a colorful parrot pin to his tall black hat.

"Mirian Raas?"

She turned to find a steersman in a yellow shirt doffing his hat to her. "Are you Mirian Raas?"

"I am."

He made an awkward bow. "Your brother-in-law paid your fee already, Miss Raas." His accent was broad and rolling. "If you will follow me?"

Interesting. She'd sent word ahead, but Mirian was a little surprised it had gotten to Tradan so quickly. She supposed it was just possible, and she shook her head a little as she tried to imagine the expense of hiring one of the barges to wait for several hours. With tides and currents, after all, it was impossible to thoroughly predict when a ship might arrive, even on as short and as well-known a route as the run from Eleder to Port Freedom.

But then, Tradan had money, old money, in a straight line from the original Chelish colonists.

The steersman glanced nervously at her and then at Jekka. She wondered why the man should be nervous, then realized there was probably a further tip for him if he ensured delivery and could report he'd given a pleasing voyage.

"Lead on," Mirian told him, and they followed the fellow to a long, lean barge with a high prow crewed by eight rowers.

"I hope you haven't had to wait for us too long?" Mirian stepped down into the boat and then eyed the gesture of the steersman, whose sweeping arm suggested she walk the raised path to the front passenger compartment. It was shielded by a brown canvas awning. As she motioned her people ahead of her, the crew watched each of them somewhat warily, their eyes fastening with special care upon Jekka.

"It's all in the line of duty," the steersman answered, then unhitched the line and jumped to the boat. "There are fruits and drinks up front for you, courtesy of your brother-in-law. We'll have you through the maze in three-quarters of an hour, less if the gods are kind. Put your backs into it!" This last was directed at the rowers, who bent to their oars.

Mirian followed him past the rowers and the line of storage cabinets that separated the front compartment, then dropped into the shaded space up front. Clean, cushioned seats were built into the sides, and three wicker baskets were arranged in a line on the deck.

Jeneta opened the first with a glad cry, and Jekka was already lifting a bottle of wine.

They pulled away from the dock and headed across open water for the sandbar-strewn opening to the river and the head-high reeds that grew jungle-thick along the banks. Ivrian watched neither the view nor the baskets, peering instead toward the rowers.

"What is it?" Mirian asked him softly. Ivrian could be self-involved and flighty, but in his best moments he was observant and thoughtful, and when the chips were down he had proved himself one of the bravest, most dependable souls she'd ever met. When she saw that look in his eye, she was inclined to trust it.

"Something's not right," he said, pretending a smile toward the steersman, who faced them from aft, grinning. "Isn't the steersman pouring it on a bit thick?" he asked as he turned his head.

He was right. Mirian, still smiling absently, set her hand to Jeneta's as she was readying to peel a banana. The priestess frowned as Mirian forced her wrist down, then opened her mouth as though in challenge. Ivrian, still watching Mirian, made a soft shshing noise.

Jekka lowered the wine bottle he'd been studying and set it back in the wicker basket.

The thought of cold wine down her throat sounded wonderful. Probably she and Ivrian were both being paranoid. Probably.

"What is it, my sister?" Jekka asked softly.

"Maybe nothing," was her bland answer through a vague smile and nod as the steersman, operating the rudder in the aft, glanced over at them.

The rest of the rowers heaved the oars with their backs to the passengers. Only one man sat forward of them, the pilot, sunk into a seat just shy of the prow, his black headscarf just visible above a storage cabinet that separated him from Mirian and her crew.

"Please," the steersman called, "avail yourselves of all the food you want! Don't let it go to waste."

That cinched it. Mirian nodded and waved a hand, then turned from him. To Jekka she said, "Watch them."

She bent as though to tighten her bootlace. Seabirds called to one another, white specks in the evening light. She pitched her voice low enough that it would not carry far over the creak of the oarlocks and the slap of waves against the boat: "Be on your guard."

Now that she considered the situation, it didn't make sense that her brother-in-law would hire a boat to wait for them, not when there was never a shortage of them; not when there was no real predicting when the *Daughter* would turn up.

And then there was the look of the sailors themselves and their way with the oars. Their oar movements weren't well synchronized, and the pilot never called any directions to the steersman.

It might be that some new Rivermen's Guild company had just started up and hired a load of cheap, inexperienced rowers to man its boats. And it might be that they offered cheaper rates, which was why her brother-in-law had hired them.

But it might be something else. Here in the bay they were in little danger, for there were any number of nearby boats and ships. But they were closing on the maze of channels that led to Port Freedom, and it struck her suddenly that it would be a fine place for an ambush. Especially if some or all of her people were sickened, poisoned, or rendered unconscious by doctored food and drink. She wondered if Ivrian had noticed any or all of these things, or if he just had an innate sense. Whatever it was, she was thankful he'd put her on the alert.

When they closed on the lane of reeds, there were two other nearby boats in their particular channel, one some thirty feet wide, crammed with passengers unhappily fanning themselves with their hands while the sun beat down. Little gray marsh birds and long-legged storks moved among the reeds, and unseen insects buzzed at them.

The steersman grinned to her and called out in a friendly tone.

"Miss Raas, they told me you were Mwangi, but they didn't say what tribe. Bas'o, I think? Or Mulaa?"

"Bas'o." *They who?*

"And what interestin' travelin' company you have. They didn't say you'd have a lizard man with you."

That was strange, because she'd specifically mentioned to her brother-in-law that Jekka would be along. He was their whole point in coming.

"Which 'they' is it you mean?" she asked with a smile.

The steersman's grin widened. "The folk at the shipping company, ma'am."

"Are you a new outfit?" Ivrian asked.

"Why yes. I'm an old hand myself, but a lot of the crew are new. There's always folks wantin' to get into the business side of things. Steady work for those willing to put in the time."

The boat headed deeper into the lane, lagging farther and farther behind the nearer vessels. The steersman called every now and then to keep his crew together, but he seemed more concerned with his passengers.

"Ma'am, all this food and drink was sent along special-like, and I'm to make sure you enjoy it. I'll like as not be getting a tip if you report satisfaction with your journey."

"We're not thirsty," Mirian said, "just eager to make port."

They veered into an opening in the reeds. "Ah," the steersman said, "the shortcut I've been looking for."

Mirian tensed. Damn stupid Ensara for taking her wand. She wondered if she'd be able to hire the druid to find it on the ocean bottom once they were through with all this.

She'd loaned Ivrian its double months ago and he'd since offered to return it. But he'd actually proved to have a greater knack with wands than she'd ever had. He preferred to keep it tucked in an inside pocket of his vest, and she saw his hand slipping there even now.

Jekka's expression was always hard to read, but once he'd relinquished the wine his eyes hadn't left the rowers. Jekka met her eyes and gave a small nod.

The steersman said a word Mirian didn't recognize, and the rowers let go of the oars and turned, reaching under their benches. They rose holding short spears with broad leaf-shaped blades.

"I want the steersman alive," Mirian hissed.

Jekka was first in motion, springing with inhuman dexterity to land on the bulwark of the rowers' section. He sidestepped a solid thrust at his thigh and took off a man's head with his staff's scythe blade. Scarlet blood sprayed wide and painted the nearby marsh grass.

A rower to Jekka's left dropped his spear, screaming as an emerald acid bolt from Ivrian's wand caught him in the chest, then threw himself overboard.

She left Ivrian and Jekka to deal with the folk behind and spun to confront the man in the prow only to discover there was not one man there but three—the storage cabinet between the pilot's seat and the passenger compartment had swung open and two sweaty men were rising with short spears.

Jeneta threw herself to one side as a spearpoint struck her seat, drawing her longsword.

Mirian snapped a spear shaft in half with her cutlass, veered from a thrust from another warrior. As he pulled his weapon away, Mirian caught his spear just above the point and shoved the weapon toward him. He stumbled against the side of the boat and tripped backward into the water.

His fall shook the boat, which was a good thing, since the pilot had raised a blowpipe. Mirian felt the air of the dart as it missed her.

She lunged, took the pilot through the chest. While he gagged and clutched at the red stain on his yellow shirt, she turned to find the remaining spearman thrusting at her.

Jeneta knocked his spear up and away, leaving him open for Mirian, who plunged her sword deep through his chest. He sank to his knees, gurgling, as she finished him with a blow to the neck.

"Make sure they're down!" Mirian spun to take in the rest.

What might have seemed a simple ambush hadn't gone well for their enemies. Jekka had cut through three of the rowers and Ivrian had dropped two with the wand while Jeneta advanced on another, sword blazing with holy light.

This resistance was far more than the steersman must have anticipated. As Mirian moved forward, she saw his eyes, wide with surprise, lock on to her before he turned and threw himself into the water. He landed with a splash and swam for a nearby reed bank.

"Jekka," Mirian cried, "get him—alive!"

The lizard man leapt out with a longer stride than a human might have managed, striking the water at the same time he brought his staff down, clublike, on the escaping steersman.

"What about them?" Ivrian pointed with his sword toward the rowers who'd dived overboard, and now swam for the reeds.

"Let them go." Mirian scanned the battle's aftermath. The dead men she briefly inspected before telling Ivrian to heave them overboard.

Jekka returned with the limp form of the steersmen and Mirian helped drag the body onto the boat, afraid for a moment that Jekka hadn't been careful enough and that the fellow was already dead.

No—he was breathing. He'd just taken a good smack to the head.

"All right," Mirian told the others. "Here's the fun part. We get to row. Ivrian, you can steer. Jekka, tie our prisoner with one of the dock lines. Come on, Jeneta."

Once the prisoner was secure, she and the priestess bent to the oars. Mirian was in fine shape, but she didn't train with heavy weapons the way a priestess did. It wasn't long before her hands and shoulders ached with strain.

After a half mile, they heard chatter from another boat passing beyond a screen of reeds. Good. So they weren't completely lost. They ground their oars into the muddy river bottom.

A blister had risen on Mirian's left hand. For some reason that struck her as more irritating than the attack.

She leaned over the imprisoned steersman Jekka had laid down in the passenger area. She saw that the lizard man had tied the fellow a little tightly, with ropes around his chest and arms and wrists. He lay motionless apart from the rise and fall of his chest. Unconscious, or shamming?

"Jekka, let me borrow your staff."

Her blood brother handed it over, and then she posted him as a lookout.

"Who do you work for?" she asked. There wasn't an answer, so Mirian nudged him with the staff. "I'm pretty sure you're awake. Let me explain something. I'm a little . . . annoyed. I've got a whole lot of rowing ahead of me. A bunch of strangers just tried to kill me. I can toss you overboard with or without the ropes on. You just give me some answers, and I'll cut the ropes. Then you'll go over the side alive, and you can fend for yourself however you want. That's your best deal."

The steersman's eyelids flicked open as she podded him again.

"Don't," he said. "It's not—"

"Just talk."

The steersman did, and much of his broad coastal accent fell away. "We were supposed to make sure you drank the wine, which would put you to sleep. If that didn't work we were supposed to subdue you."

"Why?"

"There was a man, he told me all about you. He paid me to take some of his men and wait for you."

"What kind of man?"

"I think he was Mzali—he referred a couple of times to 'Holy Walkena.' You know about the Mzali?"

"I know," Mirian answered. What she didn't know was why anyone from Mzali would have it in for her. The nation of Mzali was no friend to Sargava, and labeled any colonials or their allies—or, indeed, any foreigners whatsoever—as occupiers. Walkena, their leader, had allegedly been restored to life by ancient prophecy. But then, a lot of people said a lot of things to make their rule sound more legitimate. "They mention why they wanted us?"

"I asked, but they weren't really talkative."

"What did they say?"

He licked dry lips and looked at her through wide eyes. "Their leader—he just said, 'It is Walkena's word.'"

"And that was good enough for you?"

"They were scary." The steersman sounded defensive.

"As scary as us?"

His eyes flicked up to her and over toward where Jekka stood in the prow. "You're scarier than you looked at first."

"How much did they pay you?"

"Er . . . fifty crowns."

"You were willing to kill us for fifty crowns?" She felt her eyebrows rise.

"It was take the fifty crowns and lead you into the swamp, or get stabbed and thrown in the swamp. Their promise."

"I see. All right, Jekka, cut him loose. Give over the crowns, and swim for it."

"From out here?"

"You want my sympathy?"

"No . . ."

Jekka took his staff, flipped it about to get the proper blade, then deftly sliced the man free before putting the spearpoint to his chest. "My sister wants the gold."

"Sister?" he asked.

"The crowns." Mirian wriggled her fingers. "Reach for them slow."

With great care, the steersman loosed a bag at his waist, and set it on the boat planks. Jekka lurched forward and jabbed it so that coins leaked out.

"How nice," Mirian said. "Looks like we get your blood money. And you get a swim. Jekka?"

But the steersman had already dashed for the side of the boat. Jekka slammed him across the backside with his staff and the fellow howled as he dropped into the water.

Jeneta cackled.

"Why, Jekka," Ivrian said, "I do believe you've developed a sense of humor."

They went back to the oars, Jekka relieving Mirian. Ivrian resumed his post at the rudder. After the steersman thought himself far enough off to be safe, he resurfaced and cursed them, telling them the Mzali would get them, and that he'd be glad, and that Mirian's mother was a lizard-humper.

"Where's a crocodile when you need one?" Ivrian asked.

"What warned you about them, Ivrian?" Mirian asked.

"Something about the steersman. And the way the rowers didn't look at us. They weren't like bored workmen. They were on the alert and pretending not to be."

Mirian nodded. "Well, good job catching that."

"Any thoughts on why the Mzali want us?"

Mirian shook her head. She hoped this didn't mean that Tradan and her sister had been hurt. It was odd to go from rarely thinking about them to being concerned about their welfare. Would they care if she were in danger?

When they hit the main channel they encountered a line of boats. So protective was the Rivermen's Guild of the monopoly it held on shipping that Mirian's group was challenged almost immediately by the steersmen manning other boats, demanding they show their papers and permits to operate their craft.

Their rowing at least was over when crew members from other boats climbed on to theirs to guide it in, but the confusion and skepticism over their tale took them the rest of the evening to sort through at the rivermen's guild house. Ivrian's status as a lord had little to no effect. The rivermen were chiefly concerned that Mirian and her group had stolen the boat or even murdered its original crew.

In the end, she greased palms with most of the blood money from the steersman, gave testimony and an address where they would be staying, and left.

Port Freedom sprawled in an eclectic blend of architectural models, from Chelish influences, to the thatched roofs of Ijo make, to mud-and-wattle buildings scattered down shadowy side streets. It spread out well back of the great nest of spindly quays that were its lifeblood. It prospered in its way, but there was no true "old town" as one could find in Eleder or even Crown Point. The settlement seemed built up from whatever had rolled through.

It was crowded even in midafternoon, when Sargavans often withdrew from the tropical sun. Mirian knew her way around well enough to have chosen from several decent inns, but instead hired a carriage for her weary group and ordered it out toward her brother-in-law's estate.

The route led them east of the city along a rutted road. Moss draped the limbs of the towering live oaks, hanging like green waterfalls. The air was rich with the scent of rotting vegetation.

Most people seemed content to ride in silence, but Ivrian, as usual, came up with questions. "When's the last time you saw your sister, Mirian?"

"Probably when I was thirteen."

"How do you get along?"

"We'll find out," Mirian said, and Ivrian must have heard something in her voice that made him decide not to press further.

It seemed a long, long time ago. Tradan had been in Eleder on business, and Charlyn had come to take Mirian shopping in

Eleder's central district. Charlyn was the daughter of Mirian's father and his first wife, the Lady Tanara, who'd been scandalized that the man she'd divorced had married a native woman.

Charlyn had been stiff and uncomfortable, and had tried to mask her reaction, but throughout the day the shopkeepers had assumed Mirian was a servant being outfitted by her mistress, and Charlyn had grown increasingly embarrassed at having to explain at every place they stopped. Given Mirian's lack of interest in dresses to start with and the uncomfortable atmosphere, she'd been only too glad when Charlyn had given up and taken her home.

She stared out at the darkness as their two-horse cart rolled on, wondering how Charlyn must have felt about that day. She would probably have been in her late twenties then, about Mirian's age now. Had she honestly been trying to reach out to her little sister? To mend fences with her father?

Charlyn might surely have handled matters better, but she'd at least made an attempt at forging a connection, something Mirian had avoided over the course of three journeys through Port Freedom. Charlyn hadn't tried since, though. The most she'd managed at Kellic's funeral was a letter.

The sun was low by the time the little cart turned down a lane dense with trees and their thick shadows. They advanced only a few yards before stopping at a closed gate fashioned of vertical metal bars. Two men stepped into view. One opened the shutters of a lantern and demanded to know the driver's business. Both were stern-looking Kalabuta tribesmen dressed in matched pants and white shirts, though they wore traditional sandals.

The cart driver pointed immediately toward his passengers and explained who they were.

"Mistress Raas," the elder of the guardsmen said, relaxing the hold on his sheathed longsword. "You've been expected." He turned to the other guard. "Ohano, you stay here. I'll escort them to the house."

"Yes, Captain."

Captain? How large of a guard force did her brother-in-law have in place?

"I'm glad you made it safely, Mistress Raas," the stout, powerfully built man told her soberly. "Things have been a little more lively around here lately."

"Why?"

The captain glanced back at her.

"I'm really not sure," he said.

Mirian gritted her teeth. She knew a lie when she heard one.

8

REUNION

IVRIAN

Ivrian had expected an aging manor with fading paint and vines worked into its greening stone, but what he found instead was a meticulously maintained home, the bright yellow siding of its second floor shining in the light of countless lanterns. He couldn't spot a single line of creepers or mold among the mix of gray and red native stone of the ground floor.

He had ample time to study the building and its grounds as they moved down the long straight drive under hanging willows. There was even a working fountain in the turnaround, one with a statue of a Kalabuta warrior in its center, spear raised heaven-ward—treeward, actually, for the boughs of majestic live oaks shaded the entire courtyard.

The captain dropped down before the cart drew to a full stop. He jogged for the entrance, there met by another armed figure who quickly moved into the house.

The cart rolled to a halt and servants hurried forth—two Kalabuta, a graying one in starched colonial dress and white gloves, and a woman a little younger than Jeneta. They asked to help with any baggage and Mirian somewhat stiffly gave them permission. She seemed preoccupied and far more formal than usual, managing a great amount of dignity despite bloodstained travel pants and soiled shirt.

As Mirian and Ivrian stepped down, the captain cleared his throat.

"No weapons inside the house, I'm afraid, Mistress Raas."

"I'd prefer to hold on to my sword," Mirian said. "We were attacked on our way from the ship."

Ivrian's eyebrows rose. It wasn't like Mirian to be so rude. They were in a guarded compound now, one hardly dangerous.

"Attacked by whom?" the captain asked.

"Agents of Mzali."

The captain's frown deepened. He opened his mouth as though to comment, then closed it at the creaking sound of sandaled footsteps.

Ivrian's first thought upon looking at Tradan ven Goleman was that he was an old man, but he then realized the lord's skin was deeply seamed from a thick tan. His hair was blond going to gray, cut short and feathered back. He wore loose white pants and a light blue shirt with the sleeves rolled to the elbows, and as the lord descended the steps, Ivrian saw his narrow feet were tucked into the same sort of sandals the natives wore. When he smiled, flashing even teeth, Tradan proved good-looking in a lean, weathered way. He was devoid of ornament save for a signet ring on his left hand and the brown cord of a necklace just visible at his collar.

"Sister! I'm delighted to see you once more." He took Mirian's hand and bowed, pressing his lips to her fingers. "My, how you've grown! But of course it's been years since I last saw you. And did I hear that you'd met with some manner of misfortune? Are you all right?"

"We're fine."

"I do believe you're taller than I am! You must get that from your mother's side, for Charlyn just comes to my nose."

Mirian's cool manner melted only a little before his genuine warmth. "I hope you'll forgive the state of our dress," Mirian told him. "We were assaulted on a riverboat by men who pretended to have been sent by you."

"Gods! And your people are well?" He glanced at her entourage.

"We got through."

To Ivrian's mind they'd kicked ass, but he kept his thoughts to himself. Many traditional colonials frowned upon any suggestion of self-aggrandizement.

"Good to hear. Captain, you'd best put the men on alert."

"Of course, m'lord. The guests bear weapons—"

"Oh, they can carry them."

Ivrian thought Tradan's laugh sounded nervous. It stopped abruptly as he faced Mirian once more.

"I don't blame you at all for wanting to hold on to them, especially after that experience. I've held dinner for you. If you're up to it, I'd hear the details. But please, introduce me to your colleagues. You must be Jekka."

He offered his hand to the lizard man and Jekka considered it briefly before clasping his fingers and allowing his arm to be shaken.

"I've never met one of the lizardfolk before. I very much hope you'll have time for a longer visit. I've found much of great interest. Great interest. You do read your language?"

"I do," Jekka said.

"Good, good. And you're well versed in the iconography of your people, I hope?"

"My brother was the true expert," Jekka answered. "But he is dead."

"I'm very sorry to hear that. I read a somewhat fanciful account of your expedition and I wasn't sure how many of the events were actually true."

Again with the fanciful? Ivrian bristled a little, then decided that was probably fair.

"Most of it was true," Jekka said.

"That's terrible. Simply terrible."

Ivrian offered his hand. "Lord ven Goleman, I'm Lord Galanor." He tried his best to grin. "Author of said account."

"Oh." Tradan managed to recover his smile before his expression fell too far. "Yes, of course. An entertaining romp, but if I may be so bold, you may wish to tone things down. You'll have everyone thinking that jungle digs and archaeological matters are routinely dangerous and that every find leads to hoards of gold. It'll be the end of any real knowledge recovered from such places, for treasure hunters and the romantic will dig things up to right and left and generally make a mess." He shook his head. "I've seen it before. In any case, welcome to Stanton Manor! We have room for you all in the main house. Am I to understand you came with no servants?" He failed to conceal his astonishment. "Do you have any following?"

"None," Mirian answered. "We're used to fending for ourselves."

"I see." Tradan sounded a little bemused. "Well, come along. There's plenty for all."

Ivrian fell in step beside Jeneta, who rolled her eyes at him.

Ivrian couldn't help fastening on Tradan's words about his book. He debated telling the lord that he'd actually left a few of the most sensational moments out of the account—but it really didn't seem the time.

Beyond the thick old doors they entered a high cool hall, paneled in dark wood and decorated with hunting trophies. A bright chandelier fashioned from curving horns and other large animal bones hung from the dark recesses of the ceiling. Beyond the wide entrance, an arching stair with a carven balustrade rose toward a dark second floor. Beside it, a long hallway plunged spear-straight through the mansion, with wide doorways to right and left. As Tradan spoke quietly to Mirian, gesturing to the surroundings, another serving girl came running to whisper at one side of the chief servant's graying head. Bertram cleared his throat. "Dinner is ready, m'lord."

That was odd. Where was Mirian's sister? Mirian herself seemed to be looking for her, as if she expected her to pop up out of one of the shadows.

Tradan brought his hands together. "Ah. Excellent. Do send word for her ladyship. I'm sure the rest of you will want to have time to freshen up. Bertram, show them to their rooms."

"Of course, m'lord."

It was a pleasure to wash up and change into clean clothes, and Ivrian struggled not to ready himself too quickly, for it would be improper to demonstrate too much eagerness. Still, he was out in the hallway before the ladies and didn't want to enter before them, so was pretending to study a landscape painting by lamplight for the servant Bertram's benefit when Charlyn Raas emerged from the mansion's depths.

She was not so tall as Mirian, nor as dark, but there were more family similarities than Ivrian would have expected. She was a mature but handsome woman, perhaps in her late thirties or even early forties. The long, straight nose he'd always assumed was part of Mirian's Bas'o heritage was present upon Charlyn's oval face. Her lips were thinner, and her hair straight and dark rather than curly. There were a few fine lines about her wide brown eyes and mouth, but her skin was as flawless as Mirian's own, only a light olive complexion rather than umber.

Bertram cleared his throat. "The Lady ven Goleman."

"Honored, your ladyship," Ivrian said quickly. "I'm Lord Galanor."

She extended one tanned hand, on which a small ruby ring glinted darkly. "Charlyn ven Goleman. But then, I think you know that."

"Yes, m'lady."

"Charmed," she said as he kissed one perfumed hand and released it. "I enjoyed your adventure tale. I trust your journey here was less eventful than your expedition into the interior?"

Her voice was not at all like Mirian's. It was higher pitched, with a different inflection pattern. She, like Ivrian, had been brought up trying to use the shorter vowel sounds of their colonial forbears.

"I'm afraid, m'lady, that it was rather brimming with events, not all of them savory." His mouth twisted in memory of the look on his attacker's face when he'd blasted his chest.

Hers was a lovely smile. "Perhaps you can regale me with the story over dinner."

"I'm not sure the story would make for good dinner conversation."

"Then I'll trust you to edit it down."

Ivrian thought for a moment, then bowed his head. "M'lady, we had a dangerous adventure, but arrived safely."

She laughed becomingly. "Now you've gone and removed all the fun from it. Tell me, m'lord, did my half sister bring her lizard man?"

Did she think being a lizard was Jekka's profession? "He's in the dining room now with your husband."

"Oh. Gods. I hope he's patient."

Ivrian blinked, wondering at the insult. Jekka was so quiet he could hardly be said to challenge anyone's patience.

"The poor fellow won't know what to do once Tradan starts gassing on," Charlyn continued. "He's just fascinated with these new ruins. But I'm afraid his interest has brought on some adventures of its own. I'm sure you've noticed our guard?"

Ah—so she was chattering because she was nervous. "It would have been hard to miss," Ivrian said quickly.

"Good. I hope anyone who's thinking about attacking will feel the same. We've always maintained a pool of guards, of course, but Tradan's doubled their number."

The others returned at last, Mirian in the lead. Jeneta trailed, still fussing with the hem of a blue dress.

It felt as though time had suspended its forward momentum, for Mirian and Charlyn stood staring at one another, Mirian in her plain white dress, belted with a scarlet sash that lent her a swashbuckling air—Charlyn in her evening gown. The elder sister seemed a smaller, paler, more stately reflection of the younger.

"Mirian," Charlyn said formally. "How good to see you."

"Charlyn. It is a pleasure."

Ivrian couldn't recall a time when he'd heard Mirian sound more stilted.

"How long has it been?" Ivrian prompted cheerfully.

"More than ten years." Charlyn continued to face her sister even as she addressed Ivrian. "Ever since I tried to take little Mirian for a shopping trip in Eleder. I'm afraid it didn't go very well. Everyone assumed she was my maid."

"I didn't help matters." Mirian glanced at Ivrian. "I was sullen and resentful."

"You just seemed very quiet." Charlyn smiled gamely. "You've grown into a lovely woman."

Mirian nodded politely. "You remain one."

"Thank you, Mirian," Charlyn answered gravely. "I was just saying to Lord Galanor that we should probably join my husband and your lizard man for dinner or he's liable to talk the poor fellow's ears off. Come to think of it, do lizard men have ears?"

"They do—they just don't stick out like ours. His name's Jekka," Mirian continued, "and he's . . . actually my blood brother."

There was no disguising Charlyn's surprise. "Your blood brother?"

"We swore an oath," Mirian explained.

"I see." Charlyn cleared her throat. "I was very sorry to learn of our brother's death." She put the tiniest amount of inflection on the word "our" although it was perfectly clear she referred to poor Kellic, killed during their last mission. "I hope you received my letter?"

"It was very thoughtful," Mirian said, sounding strained. "Mother appreciated it very much."

Had she, really? It was the first Mirian had mentioned the letter, even though Ivrian had attended the quiet little ceremony at the private cemetery. There'd been no body to inter, owing to the fact Kellic's former lover had thrown it to the sharks after she'd killed him. Family and friends had gathered around the stone with his name while Mirian and her mother spoke a few words and Jeneta intoned formal prayers.

Charlyn motioned them forward and then walked slowly toward the closed doors. "I should have liked to have known Kellic," she said. "I regret that I never did. What was he like?"

Ivrian tried to anticipate Mirian's answer. Would she say that he was indecisive? Weak? That he'd made mistakes but tried to come through in the end? Ivrian had deliberately muddied the details about Kellic's deficits in his published account, mostly for the benefit of Mirian's mother.

"Complicated," Mirian said finally.

There was a small downturn along Charlyn's mouth. "We really shouldn't keep Tradan waiting much longer. Oh, and who's this?"

"Jeneta, a priestess of Iomedae."

The priestess, holding back the left side of her dress with one hand, stepped forward and curtsied. "It is wonderful to be a guest within your home, Lady ven Goleman."

"Thank you, Jeneta. It is our pleasure to have you here." Charlyn offered her arm to Ivrian, who took it as Bertram opened the door for them. They walked together into the dining room.

9

FACES OF THE DEAD

JEKKA

Humans spent a great deal of their time communicating through vocalizations. They seemed unable to understand the nuance of stance and color. Even his beloved Mirian was slow to pick up on the latter unless the physical movement was overt, akin to shouting in a loud room.

Instead, humans talked, and talked, and talked. Sometimes they communicated pertinent information while doing so. More often they simply indicated their emotional state, which tired Jekka. He had no interest in a running commentary on the feelings of those around him. One of the things that differentiated Mirian was that she kept such things to herself unless it was a ritual time, such as during the death ceremony for her brother.

Mirian's brother-in-law subscribed to a different philosophy. His talking was a continual stream, and it took concentration on Jekka's part before he finally divined the meaning behind all of the words. While Tradan chattered and showed him various tomes, books, and carved hunks of stone displayed along one wall of the room for eating, he communicated excitement. Also, he was alert, and nervous, but possibly happy as well. At least that's what he kept saying—how happy he was to have a true lizardfolk scholar beside him, for he himself was just a dabbler. It didn't matter that Jekka had already communicated he wasn't a scholar. Humans, Mirian had told him once, affected a practice called modesty wherein they pretended lesser competency than they actually possessed.

Jekka found modesty pointless, but Mirian explained other humans practiced its opposite, exaggeration, wherein they boasted of prowess they did not possess.

"As a result," she'd said, "some civilized people feel the need to act with modesty so they won't be seen as braggarts."

It was a little confusing, but Jekka got along among his human companions by listening more to general intent than specific words. After standing beside Tradan for some interminable minutes, during which Jekka was not invited to drink the sweet wine he smelled, he finally understood the man was pleased because he looked forward to Jekka translating lizardfolk writing he had found upon the temple to the south.

"This would please me," Jekka said, because he fully hoped these ruins would have something to do with the great wizard and the gate in the ocean. Might there really be an entire city of his people flourishing on the other side of some kind of magical barrier? Why, he, Heltan, and Kalina might have sailed within sight of the thing when they first traveled with Mirian and Ivrian. If only they had known . . .

Tradan moved on to express his pleasure in Jekka's interest and said something about gratitude and compensation, which held no interest for Jekka either. "There is something that concerns me," Jekka said instead.

"Oh?" Tradan's expression grew neutral.

"We were attacked on the boat."

"Yes—Mirian mentioned something about that. Were you in much danger?"

"We were almost poisoned," Jekka said.

"Gods! What do you mean?"

Jekka thought he'd been perfectly clear, but explained further. "They supplied us with food and drink and insisted we partake. Mirian advised against it."

"How do you know it was poisoned?"

"They suggested it when we questioned them," Jekka said.

The man looked puzzled, so Jekka realized more explanation was warranted. "In a remote section of the riverway, all of them attacked."

"By the gods. They attacked the women as well?"

"Why would they not?" What peculiar questions. Was he not being clear somehow?

"How many foes did you face?"

"Nine."

"Nine?" Tradan seemed either surprised or doubtful. Jekka had difficulty telling the difference. "How did you defeat them all?"

"Mirian and I are deadly warriors. Jeneta is a trained warrior-priestess of Iomedae. Ivrian is a competent warrior and mastered a dangerous magical stick. No, a wand," Jekka corrected, "that fires a terrible melting blast. Many of our foes were slain. Others dove off the boat. One we threw off once we had finished questioning him."

"Is Mirian really as dangerous as that dreck writer makes her out to be?"

Jekka wasn't sure what dreck was, but he knew what a writer did. "She is," Jekka said simply. "Our foes waited for us, and they were aware of your relationship to Mirian. And now I see that your own home is under guard. Are we in danger here?"

Tradan cleared his throat and Jekka heard the door open behind him. He tasted the air and knew before he turned that it was Mirian, along with Ivrian, Jeneta, the servant Bertram, and someone new.

The stranger was another human woman, one Ivrian must have known, for she clutched his arm.

"Jekka," Tradan said, "allow me to present my wife, Charlyn, sister to your, uh, sister. I'm not sure what that makes her to you," Tradan added with a laugh.

"Nothing," Jekka answered. "She is of your clan, not mine. But," he added after a moment, "if she wishes, she might be my friend." Not so long ago he would never have considered saying such a thing, or even thinking it, but he'd since learned that some humans, like Ivrian and Rendak, could truly be as close as clan. Humans called them friends. And he found himself hoping that Mirian's sister might be one of them, though he wasn't certain why.

Charlyn laughed as Ivrian brought her forward. "A friendly lizard man. Whoever would have thought. You have beautiful coloring, Jekka. I hope you don't think that rude of me."

Jekka didn't know what she meant by that, so he hissed lightly to gauge the air for her mood. Charlyn's eyebrows rose.

"Don't be alarmed." Ivrian leaned toward her ear. "Some of Jekka's senses are tied to his tongue. Probably, he didn't know what you meant."

Ivrian was intuitive that way, which Jekka liked. He bobbed his head in thanks for the explanation.

"I don't mind, if that is what you mean, sister to my sister. I understood your words as a compliment." Jekka thought quickly. How did one compliment a human? "Your coloring is also quite lovely."

He saw Mirian smile at him, which probably meant he'd done well.

"Please, won't you be seated?" Tradan indicated the chairs.

There followed much commentary from the humans on the decoration of the room and other such matters that Jekka ignored as he fished out the specially designed lizardfolk drinking glass from his shoulder pack. Once he set it on the table, both Tradan and his mate remarked on its worksmanship, and so Mirian explained its use to them while Jekka passed it down the table for them to consider

Finally, wine was served, and it was even more delicious than it had smelled. Also there was vegetable matter, presented in a wooden bowl.

"We were discussing the guards at the estate," he said after he drank deeply. "Is there any danger?"

"No." Tradan glanced quickly to his wife. "There's no real danger, I assure you. The natives can get so protective of a few acres of jungle. They've scared off some of my workers, and left little threats. I found a spear lodged on my front doorstep two days ago, and promptly doubled my guards." He patted his wife's hand. "There's no need to worry, my sweet."

But Charlyn didn't look convinced. Or she was angry. It was a very similar look.

"Were these attacks carried out by Mzali?" Mirian asked.

"I can't really say as I know!" Tradan let out a little laugh.

"Have there been any more aggressive attempts against you?" she asked him.

"No. No! We're perfectly safe. Nothing dangerous has happened to us at all. Now let me tell you about these ruins." He leaned forward. "They're gorgeous, Mirian. And they're only a few hours' hard travel from this very mansion. To think that they lay so close, but the jungle was so thick I never knew! Anyway, even someone far less well trained than you or I would be able to see that they're lizardfolk ruins. I have no idea why the natives would be so . . . agitated by our exploration of them. They hate lizardfolk just as much as they hate colonials, don't they?"

"That's what I'm told," Mirian answered.

"It stretches on for acres. Acres! And the murals. Jekka, you will be thrilled by all the murals. Your people were . . . ah . . . are great for murals. They are truly lovely."

"Thank you," Jekka said.

Even though Tradan repeated himself, Jekka learned that with each iteration there was a little more information to be gleaned. He forced himself to listen intently. With no one among the expedition members who could read much of the lizardfolk language—apart from Tradan, who said he recognized the meaning of crucial ideograms—they had no inkling about what sort of buildings they'd uncovered.

"Just think," Tradan went on, "there might be vast riches there. Wouldn't Baron Utilinus be happy with that?"

"I'm sure the find will add a great deal to our understanding of this region's history," Mirian said.

"Oh, undoubtedly!" Tradan laughed shortly. "Undoubtedly!"

The main course was one of the cooked cows the rich folk of Sargava seemed to enjoy. It was too well done for Jekka's taste, though he did appreciate the wine sauce along the side.

Afterward there was more talking. They looked at another version of the same map that interested the humans but differed in so few details Jekka was bored by it. Arrangements were discussed for their trip to the ruins in the morning. Tradan was all for leaving immediately following a hearty breakfast. After eating yesterday and this evening, Jekka didn't think he'd be likely to need a meal for at least another day, but he knew humans had different needs, so he left them to their planning and asked if he might be allowed to turn in.

They'd given him a very nice chamber with a bed in the upper story of the home. It was an old servant's room that they had readied for him. Mirian seemed a little irritated for some reason until Tradan said he knew lizardfolk preferred the heat and that the upper rooms were warmer.

And so he bade goodnight to his sister, his friends, and his allies and hosts, then went to the room, carefully folded his robe, and curled up on top of the bedcovers. He was asleep in moments.

And then suddenly he was awake. His hand went to the staff he always kept nearby, and he sat up in silence, head cocked attentively.

It was the deep dark of the night, an hour or two before dawn. Someone was moving quietly in the room below him, making a peculiar muffled, choking noise.

He stopped to slide on his robe and belt it, then eased from the chamber, his movement silent as a serpent's, even over the worn floorboards beside the stair.

He kept to the edge and rim of every step, alert for intruders. Were it his clan, he would have known just how many warriors waited without and how finely honed their abilities were. There was no guessing how good these guards were.

The steep back stair wound down and came out just beside the room where he'd heard the noise. He heard it still, a faint choking. A dim orange glow, as from a single candle, flickered under the door, which was partly open.

Jekka nimbly activated the spearpoint, which emerged with a soft click from its hidden housing at the end of his staff. He pushed wide the door and leveled the weapon.

He'd thought he would find an intruder with hands about someone's neck. Instead, he discovered Charlyn ven Goleman seated on a peculiar chair with crescent legs. She wore a white night dress and her hair hung in disarray. As her eyes widened, he saw they were red rimmed and her cheeks were wet.

She looked up at him and gasped.

A sign of human distress. Jekka quickly took in the rest of the room, including the window. There was a very small bed on the right with walled sides, but no one was hiding there, which left only the wardrobe. He dashed forward and threw it open.

Inside he found several racks of very tiny dresses, and shelves with towels. But no intruders.

"What are you doing?" Charlyn said in the same choking voice.

He whirled on her. "Were you under attack?"

"No!"

He stared at her, trying to piece it together, then his eyes wandered as he sought more clues. He spied numerous additional small articles on the shelves, including two small masks. No, he realized, plaster casts of small faces with closed eyes. Human younglings. This was a nest . . . but one that lacked nestlings. The clothes were unworn. The small bed was empty.

It came to him then. This was a mother who grieved.

Jekka ran fingers over the staff and the spear retracted. He saw Charlyn's eyes, in the dim light very much like Mirian's, and felt foolish. His frill ruffled and he knew that his skin color flushed, so he dropped to one knee and hung his head to be clear he presented no threat.

"I came to assist, not to harm. I heard noises and feared someone was in danger."

"It's . . . it's all right," Charlyn answered. Jekka wasn't sure why her voice was so hesitant. His posture and tone were clear.

"You must have exceptional hearing," she said.

"I do not think so."

Charlyn smiled weakly and leaned back in the chair, which tilted. Its peculiar construction enabled Charlyn to rock backward, then forward.

"Then I'm much louder than I thought. I'm sorry I woke you."

"You need not apologize. I frightened you."

"A little."

He thought that she lied and that he had frightened her greatly. "I apologize for that, sister to my sister. And I think I know what you do here. Is today a grieving day for your people?"

Her eyes watered further. "Every day is a grieving day."

His head came up. "The loss is recent."

She had ceased rocking and her head nodded slowly. She wiped at her face and hid her eyes. Some humans, he knew, did not like to show their grief.

"I have grieving days," he said. "I had two young ones, and they are lost to me." He rose slowly. His frill had settled, and he gestured gingerly to the little masks. "Forgive me. I am no judge of ages of small humans. How old were they?"

"Elliana was almost two. Geltrand died the day he was born." Again she choked back her words. "Only a few months ago."

Jekka could not hold off tasting the room, though he turned partly away, for he knew humans found his tongue repulsive.

The moisture in the air was obvious, as was the woman's raised temperature.

"It is hard to lose them," he said.

She nodded.

"Mirian wondered that you did not come to Kellic's service. Now I wonder why you did not tell her of this. It would have been about the same time."

"It's a private matter," she said.

"And I intrude," he said. "Again, I apologize. I do not know your customs."

A smile fluttered at her lips. "You're very kind, Jekka."

"Kind?" he repeated. He didn't think himself so.

"What happened to your children?" Charlyn asked softly

"There are humans," he said, "who prize the skin of young lizardfolk for the making of fabric. It is more pliable."

Her mouth formed a circle, but she made no noise apart from a sort of coughing gasp.

"It has been two years now," Jekka said, "and I think about them often. It felt good to track the men who did it, and to kill them, but the pain remains. To whom shall I pass my songs, sister to my sister? Who now is left to hear the tale of my people but the bearded man in Eleder, who will write it in his book for some scholar to learn when my people live as nothing but glyphs in the books of humans?"

For some reason this set the human's eyes watering the more, and she reached out for his hand.

This contact startled Jekka, but he allowed it. She squeezed his fingers.

"I'm so sorry," she said. "I didn't know."

"Were yours slain?" Jekka asked.

Charlyn shook her head quickly. "Fever claimed my daughter. The healer said it was nothing, but she went to sleep one night and never woke up. And then Geltrand . . . he was stillborn."

Jekka had never heard that term before, but he inferred its meaning, and as Charlyn released his hand he turned to consider the little masks. "These are imprints of their faces, so that you have a visual reminder."

"Yes."

"It is a fine idea," he said. "Perhaps you should save them only for grieving days."

"Do you grieve only on certain days?"

"It is the way of my people." Jekka gave his hand to her, palm first. "Press your hand to mine," he said, and she stopped rocking in the chair and stretched up to do so. "Press hard. Do you feel my pulse?"

"I do."

"We live. Those we have lost do not. I have lost so many that were I to give them reverence every day, my warmth would fade, my own blood would cease to pulse. I might have done as much without your sister."

"Mirian must be very special to you."

"When I had nothing left, she shared her name and blood with me. She gave me strength."

She lowered her hand slowly, then wiped her eyes. "You are nothing like I imagined, Jekka."

"Why not?"

She laughed. "Am I anything like you imagined?"

"I didn't know what I would think of you, but I like you."

"And I like you as well. Tell me. There is something almost . . . priestlike in the way you—"

He turned his head toward the doorway, for he'd heard another creak.

Charlyn fell silent. Then, whispering, she said, "It's an old house. It settles—"

But Jekka held up a hand to indicate she should remain silent, for he'd heard another faint creak while the woman talked. He reached down beside her and snuffed out the candle. "Stay quiet." He crept into the hall.

All was dark without. No colonial, he thought, would be wandering the house at night without a candle. It was not the way of those who lived in houses. And so he moved into the hallway, staying low, his own steps muffled by the rugs that the humans used to hide the floor planks.

The hall was long and straight. His eyes had already adjusted, and there was no missing the sound and odor of someone from the wild moving through a forward room. With the intruder came the fresh scent of blood.

Jekka cocked his head, moved across the hallway, and peered round the open doorway to see a shirtless human placing an object in the midst of the dining table, near a vase with a single rose. The object was the source of the blood, as well as the smell of dead flesh, and Jekka knew by scent it was the severed head of the guard captain.

The soft flick of Jekka's tongue had made virtually no sound, but the human whirled, a short, sharp knife in one hand.

Jekka advanced. His target swung out of the way and backed around the table. It was only then Jekka heard the scuff of a second pair of feet and slid to his left, near Tradan's bookcase treasures. He heard the passage of the sword through the air just past his arm. He swung the back end of the staff at his target.

He struck something soft, heard a muttered "oof" and a clatter as his assailant stumbled into a chair. From the sound, both chair and human had fallen to the floor, but he could spare that opponent no attention, for the first had leapt atop the heavy table and flung one of the chairs at Jekka's head.

He slid easily aside and drove his spear into the man's abdomen.

This elicited a scream of pain and further crashing as the attacker lost his balance and cracked his head on the floor. The chair smashed beside him and the jolting rolled the severed head off the table.

Calls of alarm echoed through the home.

The man beside the table lay dead or dying, but the other darted from the room, favoring his left leg.

Jekka tore after him, thrust the spear to trip him. He caught the intruder's legs so he sprawled into the hallway.

With instinct born of many hunts, Jekka leapt forward and drove his spear through his enemy's heart.

By then lights were shining farther down the passage and Mirian had appeared, dressed only in a robe but carrying her sword.

"What's happening out there?" Tradan's voice shouted. "Charlyn, where are you?"

"Enemies sent a message," Jekka reported to Mirian. "I say we send one back."

"What message did they send?"

"The guard captain's head."

There was more stomping about, and Ivrian, shirtless but sword bared, appeared in the hallway.

"And your idea?" Mirian asked Jekka.

Charlyn had crept out of the room where he'd told her to remain and stood poised behind Ivrian. And it occurred to him that humans of this house might not wish him to cut the heads from enemies and send them rolling out the door. Such an act might also make a larger stain than had already appeared on the carpet.

"Perhaps," he said, "it is enough of a message that the warriors they sent do not return."

10

WARNINGS FROM THE DARK

MIRIAN

Mirian had retreated with Tradan to his study, across the hall from the dining room. As she moved to open windows so she could close the shutters, she saw the lanterns blazing upon all the poles set beside the walkway from fountain to house to stable. As if the light alone would hold back the attacks.

While her brother-in-law paced, Mirian stood with arms crossed over her white nightgown. Her unsheathed sword leaned point-down against one of the display cases.

There'd been a knife impaled in the mercenary captain's head, almost incidentally jammed through a note that now lay crumpled and blood-smeared on Tradan's desk. Its message was plain enough. In bold, stark Taldane characters it read, *Leave the ruins or die.*

"I don't understand," Tradan mumbled again. "Those ruins have lain there for millennia. And they're clearly not Mzali. It's lizardfolk work."

"Well, those two dead men are Mzali, and there's something in the ruins they don't want us to have, or don't want disturbed. Why don't we start from the beginning, Tradan? Over dinner you said that it's hard to keep the workers from wandering away."

He nodded. The colonial looked haggard and older in the lantern light, his hair a little wild both from rising without seeing to it and because he kept raking it back with his fingers.

"Has it been difficult digging from the start," she asked, "or did you find something?"

"I just don't understand," Tradan continued. "We pay them quite reasonably, you know, and I provide them with food and water—"

"Tradan." Mirian put a snap in her voice and this time her brother-in-law seemed to see her again. He was, she understood, in a mild state of shock. She supposed this sort of violence, and in the sanctity of his home, wasn't just new, it was incredibly frightening.

"I think the first troubles began when we found the murals. Up until then the workers talked about eyes watching them from the jungle, but I paid no heed. They're full of superstitious nonsense like that."

"What's on the murals?"

"All sorts of things. Lizardfolk striking poses, like they're kings or queens. They probably are. Huge black ships—towers and buildings. And lots and lots of lizardfolk writing. I'm sure Jekka will be able to make out a lot more of it than I have, although I do have some—"

Desna grant me patience. He talked in circles. "Tradan," Mirian said, "what have you been able to read?"

He cleared his throat and shuffled papers about on his desk uncertainly, then finally raised one and bent closer to the light. "Here we go. You see, there's talk of this ruler. That's what these sigils mean—'great one' actually, but it means ruler."

"Named Reklaniss?" Mirian asked.

Tradan nodded enthusiastically. "Yes! And he sent out a ship and, if I understand correctly, built a city on an island, although the phrasing is odd."

"What's the phrasing?"

"Here, I've written it down." He came over to her side and ran a finger along the glyphs he'd painstakingly copied. She would say this for Tradan, he had a deft hand. Mirian had seen lizardfolk carvings before, and looking at Tradan's work and the precision of it she guessed he'd copied it exactly.

"You see, here." He tapped with his finger. "It says Reklaniss sent away a city with a gate upon the sea. And there is a bright star shining above the mural to guide the way. Interestingly, the lizardfolk don't call them stars, they call them tears. The tears of the goddess."

Mirian knew a sudden chill. "And did you share this with anyone?"

"Er . . . I read it aloud to my assistant," Tradan went on, "when I found it at the site."

"And after that is when people started disappearing? When the problems started?"

Tradan mulled that over for a moment, nodding. "You know, some of those natives I'd hired were about, clearing jungle away. Do you suppose some of them might be Mzali spies?"

"Or your assistant. Or they coerced one or the other into talking."

"Venthan's no spy. He's a good fellow."

"Your assistant? How long have you known him?"

"Four years now. And if the Mzali had paid him to spy on me, they must be able to see into the future. Besides, would the Mzali really work with a colonial?"

"They might, if it served their ends. And they might not have paid him," Mirian said. "They could simply have frightened him."

"I don't think so. You can judge for yourself when you meet him in the morning. But what's so important about this particular mural?"

"That star may be what's known by wizards as a dragon's tear. An ancient magical artifact created by lizardfolk."

"By the gods. They really were clever fellows, weren't they?"

"Yes," she said dryly. "If the Mzali have a sorcerer among them, they might think the ruins hold that tear. How many men do you have with you on the dig?"

"I started out with three assistants and a few dozen native laborers. I think we're down to about fourteen. And only Venthan stayed with me."

"How many of the workers do you trust?"

Tradan rubbed a hand along his hairline. "I can't say as I really trust any of them, now. I don't know them. I mean—they're just laborers."

"And your assistant?"

"I trust him, of course. He's a good chap."

"How about your guards?"

"Oh—now Captain N'bala and his men come highly recommended. Poor fellow. I hope Charlyn didn't see what had happened to him."

"I'm pretty sure she did."

"Barbarous! And think of the mess it made of the floor! Our dining table may be ruined now, not to mention the carpet where the poor captain's head rolled."

"Yes," Mirian said drolly. "Too bad about that."

His eyes flicked up and he was blinking rapidly. "Don't think me inhuman, Mirian. I sympathize with the poor captain and his family. But there are other practicalities to consider. The least of which is the impact this will have on my wife. She's already in a fragile state—how will she feel if there's blood all over the room where she eats? A person's dining room table should not remind them of an assault or violence. A home should be a place of safety."

"Fairly said," Mirian said. "What do you mean her 'fragile state'?"

"Ah. Perhaps I shouldn't have spoken."

She thought she understood. "Is she pregnant, Tradan?"

His face fell a little. "No, Mirian." All bluster was gone from him now. "She was. She lost the child only months ago and she hasn't come to grips with the poor little fellow's death. My son," he added simply. "Lost to us before birth, I'm afraid. Not like our daughter . . ."

"I'm so sorry, Tradan." Her anger began melting away. "No one ever told me. And you lost a daughter as well?"

"A fever carried her away three years ago. She wasn't quite two."

Mirian felt as though she had been gut-struck. "Desna have mercy. I had no idea."

Tradan smiled sourly. "If not for losing our son, Charlyn and I would otherwise have come to Kellic's funeral, you understand. It was just too much all at once."

Mirian nodded slowly. As she mulled over her changed understanding of both her extended family and the situation before her she found herself wishing she'd brought Gombe and Rendak along. It would be reassuring to have a few more people about whom she could really depend upon. "I think we'd best leave most of your guards here tomorrow, rather than have them escort us. For Charlyn's safety, and peace of mind."

"Don't you think that it's those of us who're going into the ruins who'll be in graver danger?"

"Undoubtedly. But I think we can watch out for ourselves. Charlyn can't. And let's not bother with a whole team of native workers. We'll just take your assistant for a look around."

"Are you certain that's the wisest course?"

"No," she admitted. "Tomorrow's going to be dangerous. I'm just hoping we can get in, find what we're looking for, and get out with having to wade through a sea of blood."

II

THE NEWCOMERS
IVRIAN

We arrived at last. I had thought the jungle city of Jekka's forebears from our last adventure had been a magnificent site. But it could not compare to the jungle-shrouded remnant of the city of Reklaniss that lay before us. There were acres of vine-choked walls, each covered in decaying but colorful murals.

Yet the outside was nothing as to the wonders, and horrors, we discovered once we made our way to the city's heart, and found what had been lying in wait for two thousand years . . .

—From *The City in the Mist*

After all the commotion, Ivrian returned to bed and tried to sleep. He felt a little guilty he hadn't been faster on the scene. Maybe he wasn't the seasoned adventurer he thought he'd become. Mirian had been out far more swiftly, and Jekka so alert he'd already dealt with the entire situation. Probably it was to be expected. Jekka was a creature of the wilds and Mirian had honed her survival skills for years, so it probably wasn't fair to hold himself up to the same expectations.

Despite those rational conclusions, he lay staring at the dark ceiling despairing of his own abilities and wondering whether a city-born aristocrat could ever truly be Mirian's equal. His mother had, but then Mother had wandered the wilds for years. He needed to be of better service to his friends *now*, not years from now.

Breakfast was a somber affair held in a drawing room, probably so there'd be no reminder of the conflict from the night before. Or bloodstains. Charlyn and Mirian seemed to have come to some sort of understanding, for they talked softly at a separate table, leaning in toward one another in a way that would have seemed unlikely just last night. Jekka and Tradan were looking over some notes and the lord said "by the gods" every now and then. He said it often enough that Ivrian supposed one could make a drinking game of it.

Jeneta sat near him, saying little but watching him with large dark eyes whenever she thought he wasn't looking. She tended to do that, which always made him a little uncomfortable. He liked her well enough, but frankly wished she'd stayed aboard the ship, or better, at the temple of Iomedae. If she was going to be a permanent member of the team, he hoped she'd learn not to stare at him like he was a specimen. He already knew he didn't really belong.

Near the end of breakfast they were joined by Tradan's assistant Venthan Krole, who'd ridden his horse in from Port Freedom. He was a handsome, somewhat fey young colonial in tailored jungle gear, complete with brimmed cap boasting a black feather. After expressing surprise and horror about last night's attack, he sat down at the little table Ivrian and Jeneta shared and fell to the breakfast repast with great relish.

Venthan finished his plate and set it aside, shaking his head sympathetically as Ivrian finished his full account of the previous night's events. The young man had an infectious energy and winning smile. "The Mzali are a beastly bunch. But then, they have a beastly leader. Do you believe those stories about him being an undying god?"

"I've seen some pretty strange things," Ivrian said, "but I know a little about exaggerating a story to make a point. Walkena's a figure-head the priests replace with a new child whenever he gets too old."

"Well, they're all monsters," Venthan said.

Jeneta chimed in with her own opinion. "Is it monstrous to want your own land?"

"Eh?" Venthan asked.

Jeneta briefly met Ivrian's eyes before turning on Venthan. "This was our land before you colonials came. How would you feel if we came north, landed on your shores, and drove you out?"

"But that's not how it worked," Venthan objected. "Your people didn't have civilizations, at least not as advanced as Chelish civilization. You needed us."

Ivrian groaned, but it was too late.

"*Needed* you?" Jeneta's voice rose in disgust. "Fah—we needed you the way a tree needs the dry rot! Are you honestly going to let him say these things, Ivrian?"

Venthan didn't wait for him to answer. "Are you honestly telling me you approve of the Mzali taking that man's head off and sneaking into Lord ven Goleman house last night?"

"No! But I'm saying the Mzali have a right to be angry."

"Are you angry?" Ivrian asked mildly. "You seem to enjoy the luxuries of Ch . . . Sargavan civilization. And Iomedae herself was Chelish."

"And so we *Mwangi* should be thankful for you taking our land?" Jeneta placed great emphasis upon the catchall word routinely used by aristocratic colonials to refer to any native, regardless of tribe. "Because my goddess started life as a white woman, she belongs to you?"

"I didn't say that," Ivrian countered.

Venthan joined in. "Lord ven Goleman is just saying that we brought benefits to you that many have enjoyed—"

Ivrian spoke from the side of his mouth: "You're not helping."

"Were we free to *choose* those," Jeneta said, "maybe we would have accepted them. But you came with a sword, not an offer."

"So," Venthan said, "you'd see all Sargavans killed in their sleep?"

"No!"

"Because that's what the Mzali want."

"That's not what I'm saying. Oh! Ivrian, do you actually agree with this oat-brained git?"

Venthan blinked in astonishment. He was likely unused to having insults directed at him.

"I understand what you're saying about land," Ivrian said gently. "Our forefathers arrived here and took what wasn't theirs. But do you think we should simply give it back and sail away? Where would we go?"

"I didn't say that. I just don't think that the Mzali are completely without—"

"They're demon-worshiping savages," Venthan insisted. "And I can't believe for a moment that a priestess would identify with their position. Especially not after they violated the sanctity of his lordship's home last night."

"They're not savages," Jeneta retorted. "And their civilization is every bit as ancient as the Chelaxians'. And they don't happen to worship demons!"

"They claim to worship a child-god who walks as the dead!"

"Can we agree to this?" Ivrian said quickly. "That what the Mzali do is savage, even if *they* are not?"

"I'm not even sure I can agree to that," Jeneta said stiffly. "Are you saying that the Chelish colonists never committed atrocities?"

"Our ancestors," Venthan said. "Not us."

"Oh, how thoroughly you refuted my point." Jeneta rose stiffly. "Your pardon. I must tend to my packing."

Venthan watched her departure in bewilderment. "Is she always like that?"

"You shouldn't have prodded her."

"Do you agree with her, m'lord, or are you just trying to stay on her good side? Or," Venthan continued with a sly smile, "are you interested in her for other reasons?"

"She's not my type."

"And what is your type?"

Stupid ass. Venthan was a good-looking man, and he knew it. Was he honestly flirting after he'd just insulted Ivrian's friend badly enough to drive her from the table? Ivrian wasn't used to thinking of Jeneta as a particularly close friend, but he'd been touched that she seemed to think so well of him, and he felt as though he'd let her down.

"Venthan," Ivrian said slowly, "be so kind as to treat my friends with more respect."

"Sorry, m'lord." Venthan's expression blanked.

Ivrian sighed. "I'm not pulling title on you. I'm asking you, one human being to another, to be a little kinder, all right?"

Venthan ran a hand through dark hair and studied Ivrian, then smiled tentatively. "All right, then. Is she really that important to you?"

"She's been there when it counted."

"Very good then. I think you'll find I'm cut from reliable cloth myself."

Ivrian nodded. Venthan had a year or two on him, but somehow Ivrian felt a little older. Had he himself sounded so naive only a few months ago, before that expedition into the jungle?

He supposed he had. Back then he'd believed all that nonsense in the adventure novels.

They rode out within the next hour on sturdy Kalabuta horses from Tradan's stable. The mounts were broad, powerful animals with high stamina. Their coloring tended toward gray and dun, their temperament stolid.

Mirian rode point with Tradan; Jekka, inexpert as he was with horses, rode in the middle, with Jeneta to assist, and Ivrian brought up the rear with Venthan, who kept trying to chat with him about plays and playwrights. Normally Ivrian would have welcomed the attention, but he still felt inadequate after having failed to assist last night, so he kept his replies short. Nothing, he told himself, was going to creep up on them from the flanks.

Trailing them all were a handful of wary guards.

After the first few miles from Tradan's mansion, they were forced to ride single-file along a newly cut jungle track. Monkeys called raucously down at them from high in the canopy. Other, larger animals moved through the bush without showing themselves, and Ivrian spotted a tree snake coiled around a limb overhead watching with placid, unreadable eyes.

It was the Mzali he searched for most, though he expected them to be the most difficult to spot. Theirs was a city many leagues east, one that had attacked Kalabuto no less than three times in the last few years. The Mzali were both persistent and capable—and as they'd recently made clear, deadly.

When Ivrian and his party emerged at last from jungle, it was with astonishing swiftness. One moment they were all but surrounded by greenery. The next they arrived at a small clearing, and here they left the horses and quartet of guards before advancing down the narrow path likewise carved out by machetes. As Tradan had said, the jungle was already fighting to reclaim its territory, reaching onto the trail with viny tendrils.

Just as Tradan announced they were nearly to the ruins themselves, there was a rumble from above. Rain seemed imminent. Jekka halted Mirian and crouched down beside something along the trail. Ivrian crept closer so he could hear their discussion.

"What kind of tracks?" Tradan asked.

Jekka pointed to a patch of mud beside a fern, then indicated a series of naked, archless footprints. They looked almost human. But no human who wore shoes had such widespread toes. And the toes were clawed. One of the prints even revealed webbing. Ivrian groaned. He was no tracking expert, but he knew what creature made those kind of prints.

"Boggards." Mirian said the name like a curse. As well she might, for the frog people had attacked them en masse in the Kaava jungles and even captured some of their team.

"There were four of them," Jekka relayed. "They walked by in the last two days."

"It's never easy, is it, Jekka?" Mirian asked.

"I think it was a hunting party." Jekka pointed to the tracks. "A spear butt."

"I hate those damned things," Ivrian said.

Jekka's head bobbed. "I share your sentiment. We shall end some together when next we see them."

12
THE DEAD KING
MIRIAN

The jungle had eaten the city. There was no wonder the buildings had gone unnoticed even lying less than a day's travel from Port Freedom—five feet out from the city's outskirts Mirian would never have known it was there. Trees and grasses had grown into its paving stones, and vines and creepers draped its walls.

Tradan's workers had cleared a narrow path through the low buildings on the outskirts, but already the greenery had thrust questing branches and creepers that she and Jekka cut with machetes as they advanced.

At first, all they could see of the city were scraps of walls, remarkable only in that the stones were fitted so well the greenery had been hard put to root into its mortarless seams. Tradan urged them on, saying there was little here to see, that the best ruins lay at the city's center. Mirian lamented there was once again no time to sketch anything she saw, and hoped she'd have a moment once they arrived at this courtyard Tradan kept speaking of.

It proved so overgrown with trees Mirian would have thought they were in the jungle once more if the trail hadn't loomed ahead. It stopped at last before a wall almost completely clear of plant growth. While Tradan jabbered in delight about how he'd had his men clear it as soon as he saw a spot of color, Mirian took in the art their labor had revealed.

There, bright green and yellow on the stone, was an immense mural of lizardfolk bowing to one of their kind in a throne with a high back and elaborately flared arms. In one palm he held a teardrop-shaped crystal.

The dragon's tear.

She grinned, then shook her head ruefully. If anything she'd seen lately deserved to be recorded for posterity, it was this image.

"Do you think the tear's inside that building?" Jekka asked.

Mirian doubted it. "Maybe."

The building itself was constructed from closely interlinked stones, like the rest of the walls fitted without mortar. If anything, the work seemed even more advanced than that they had found in the city beyond the pool of stars.

Mirian pushed through obscuring foliage into the shadowy recess of the temple's opening. A wide stone door stood within, hidden behind a layer of grime. Mirian pulled out a cloth and wiped it clean. Behind her Jekka chopped vines with a machete, holding them in one hand as he worked so they wouldn't fall on her.

After delicate scrubbing Mirian discovered the entire door was inlaid with geometrical whorls. In its center were twelve tiny lines of lizardfolk glyphs.

She stepped aside for Jekka to inspect them, her gaze flicking up to the vines, always alert for something within them or, Desna forbid, the vines themselves swaying hungrily to life. She knew Pathfinders who'd seen such things.

Mirian glanced back at the others. "Keep watch," she reminded Tradan, who was trying to crowd forward with Venthan. Ivrian at least was looking out into the jungle. Jeneta seemed poised half in between, one eye looking at the tomb, another toward the jungle, its leaves thick with rising mist as light rain began falling.

Jekka stared at the lizardfolk icons carved into stone, then read from them. "This is the tomb of Reklaniss. Master of gates, ruler of the six clans. Enter and marvel."

"We're being invited to enter?" Mirian had a hard time believing it.

"Yes."

"You're sure you read that right?"

"I'm certain."

"Human tombs usually offer curses," she said. "And extol the virtues of their occupants a little longer."

"Perhaps he didn't expect to be forgotten," Jekka speculated.

"Any idea how to open it?" Mirian hadn't seen any sort of door seal, handle, hinge, or lock.

Jekka stepped closer to the letters, than ran his finger along the whorls. "Please pass that fabric you were using."

The moment she did, he scrubbed one long spiral on the left from the inside out. "Ah. There is writing here. Probably on the other curling feature as well."

"What do you see?" Tradan asked behind them. "Is there anything interesting?"

"Watch our backs," Mirian said. "We have Mzali *and* boggards out there somewhere."

"Here's hoping they kill each other," Ivrian muttered.

"Ah, I see." Jekka finished scrubbing out the spiral directly on the other side of the words. "It is simple." So saying, he put a finger of either hand at the center of each whorl, then traced the patterns backward. Twelve times his fingers spun in widening circles, and when he removed his fingers at the last the whorls glowed a lovely violet. Mirian grabbed his arm and pulled him back as the other spirals in nearby stone lit up from within, one by one, and the stone door rumbled.

Jekka tensed at her touch—the lizardfolk weren't big on physical contact. She watched nervously as the door sank down, dislodging centuries, possibly millennia, of dirt and dried soil. The plant tendrils hanging from above shifted and swayed and a rain of beetles fell. Mirian brushed them from her shirt and shoulders, then froze in astonishment as singing rang from the darkness within.

Behind her, the rest of the humans in the expedition erupted in surprised commentary and she silenced them with a swift command.

Mirian's heart sped. Could there really be living lizardfolk within? She dropped hand to sword hilt and checked with Jekka, whose frill was up. He was just as startled as herself, then.

The voices warbled strange low and high notes with no discernible melody, as though the singers gasped out whatever sounds occurred to them, then held the notes as long as they could before taking another breath and starting anew.

"Are the Mzali in there?" Venthan asked.

She shook her head. Her heart still raced, but reason had reasserted itself and she understood what was happening. "Lizardfolk magic." They'd encountered something similar in the Kaava Lands. It had been just as creepy that time, too.

Mirian pulled a glow stone from her shoulder pouch and activated it with a word. Immediately, the yellow-gold light poured into a stone corridor stretching away to their left. The illumination reflected from a wall of glass built into the inner wall. It astonished her that the glass had endured so long; she assumed it must have some magical or alchemical protection to improve its durability.

She then considered the flawlessly laid stone flooring, mortarless like that outside. None looked obviously like pressure plates. Some of the ceiling stones were wet with moisture, and loose webbing hung in corners, though none seemed large enough to conceal anything monstrous. Poisonous, perhaps, but not monstrous.

While Jekka stepped forward to gingerly test the floor with the blunt end of his spear, she turned to face the others. "All right," she said softly. "Jeneta, you're to stay here on guard with Ivrian." If there were Mzali about, she didn't want them sneaking up from behind, and they'd left the guards and horses back at the little clearing where Tradan's work crew had erected a crude barracks and stable. She hadn't wanted to leave the horses untended, and they couldn't have brought them forward. "Tradan, Venthan—you're with us."

Jeneta frowned, but nodded. No doubt she wanted to see what was inside as badly as Mirian did, but Mirian had to hand it to the girl—young or not, she was a soldier. Iomedae's priestesses understood chain of command.

Tradan and his assistant, meanwhile, clamored like seagulls hunting for biscuit crumbs, so desperate were they to see the source of the singing. Mirian urged them to calm once more and looked to Jekka.

"It seems clear."

Mirian played her light over the glass case facing the doorway. Over three dozen pieces of glazed clay sat on shelves behind it. Each was shaped like human lips, painted a variety of shades of red. Most were closed. A few, though, were open, and the peculiar vocals still rang from them.

As Mirian watched, two of the open mouths sealed their lips and ceased singing. A final low note washed over them and then a petite mouth in the upper corner shut. An eerie silence closed over them.

"I expected sculptures of lizardfolk heads," Mirian said to Jekka. After all, that was what the noisemakers had looked like in the lizardfolk ruins they'd seen earlier in the year. "Why would Reklaniss display carvings of human lips?"

"I cannot say, Sister."

"They're fascinating!" Tradan beamed. "We should take these for study."

"I'm not sure we should," Mirian mused. "If there's anyone nearby, you can be sure they heard that singing. So let's keep moving. We're after more important things."

Tradan gaped. "For the sake of preservation, we must take these with us. You see my point, surely?"

Mirian glanced at Jekka, but he was already peering farther down the hall. To the right was a blank wall. There was only one way forward, left of the display case following the outer wall.

"If we have time. Later. You might want to turn on that glow stone I loaned you. Jekka, head a few more paces in. Carefully."

She trusted Jekka's wariness aboveground far more than beneath the water, but he was a veteran warrior, not an experienced salvager. So far he appeared to remember all the instructions she'd given him, and he was so capable it would be easy to forget to remind him of safety procedures. She didn't want to risk getting him injured or worse, and she reminded herself again that she'd have to keep a close watch on him. "Keep testing the floor plates, and watch the ceiling and walls."

"I remember," he said.

As he moved into it, tapping the floor with appropriate caution, she smiled and breathed in the scent of wet stone and must. Was there something wrong with her that those smells pleased her? That they suggested adventure and mystery?

She heard Venthan and Tradan whispering complaints behind her and resisted the impulse to hiss them silent. They sounded like children.

The light reflected from something shining ahead of them in the wall. Jekka peered into the darkness, then halted.

It was another display case, built into the outer wall. This one held four shelves of tiny wooden human figures. Shorts and shirts were suggested with bright splashes of blue and green paint.

Jekka passed his staff to Mirian, then put his hands near the glass and clapped twice, loudly. The figures sprang vigorously from foot to foot, shaking wildly.

"My father saw one of these, when he was a youngling. He spoke of it once."

"Gods!" Tradan said. "It's amazing!"

"An amusement for younglings. But they are well fashioned, don't you think?"

She would have loved to have sketched these figures, too. But, as seemed so often the case, there were more important things to worry about. When this was all over she'd have to return with a Pathfinder team.

The hallway reached a corner and turned, by Mirian's estimate still following the outer wall. Jekka investigated once more with proper caution, shining his own glow stone on floor and ceiling. But it was Mirian who spotted something in the dust of the floor.

She muttered a soft curse and knelt, holding up her hand so Venthan wouldn't advance past her.

"What is it?"

"Footprints. In the dust."

Prints were scattered in this hall ahead. Bare, amphibian feet, unarched. "Boggards," she said slowly. "There must be another way in."

Jekka returned, crouched beside her, and brought his face very close to the tracks. "Not within the last few days," he said, and she breathed a quiet sigh of relief. "But they aren't very old."

The prints trailed back and forth in the hallway ahead, almost as though the boggards had been inspecting the display cases alternating along either side.

They pressed ahead.

In a few more paces they reached a case containing four shelves of sculpted human noses. Some were painted pink or black or brown, approximating human skin tones, but others were blue, or painted in polka dots.

"Do you suppose they sniff?" Mirian asked.

As they advanced along the hall they witnessed more and more—a case of human ears, a case of overlarge human eyes of various colors. As they turned right once more, Mirian assumed they were again following along the outer wall. They reached first a display of carved faces, then entire heads, each standing on its neck and carved with eerie precision except for the hair, which was represented by squiggly lines carved into the scalp.

Soon they were heading north, and before much longer the corridor turned right once more. The hallways spiraled inward.

"It looks like the museum winds all the way around the inside," Tradan observed.

It seemed an obvious comment, but she didn't want to appear impolite. "Yes."

"Is that typical?" he asked.

"This is as new to me as it is to you."

"It's very interesting," Jekka said. "And strange."

"So this isn't typical of what you'd find in a lizardfolk tomb?" Tradan asked.

"I have never seen one," Jekka admitted.

"Why do you think they were so interested in human anatomy?" Venthan asked.

"Who can say? Apparently the designers found humans curious. Perhaps they studied their enemy to know them better."

The next case was stuffed with dark, rotting fabric squares, and in other cases nearby hung larger fabric samples that might once have been tunics or dresses.

Around the next corner, as they turned inward once more, was the longest and most disturbing of cases yet, stretching all the way to the end of the corridor.

Behind the glass, dried human bodies hung from wires, posed in different attitudes. One ran, another walked. A desiccated woman cradled an unstrung harp. A child stood on two legs, a second on one leg, and a man stood on his hands. There were dozens of dead—men, women, and children in a variety of poses. Some sat at tables or stood beside simple wooden farm implements. One set had even been set up to simulate the act of intercourse. Had she not been mortified by the display, Mirian would have felt more impressed that the bodies had been so thoroughly protected they had not succumbed to rot.

Venthan swore, and Tradan immediately reprimanded him before launching into a prayer to Pharasma.

Mirian's skin crawled, especially when she noticed the boggard tracks were thick in this hall. Apparently they liked looking at the dead people. "Jekka, please tell me you find this as unsettling as I do."

"I find it strange," Jekka said. "I understand why the boggards have not eaten the long-dead flesh. But why did my people preserve it?"

"It's disgusting," Venthan muttered.

"Savage," Tradan agreed.

Jekka's head swiveled to consider the two men before he looked into the darkness before them.

"You said the lizardfolk might have been studying humans," Mirian suggested.

"Yes. How do you say it, my sister?" Jekka's voice was low, solemn. "There has been little love between our people. First we hunted you. Now you hunt us."

As they wound carefully inward they found two items of interest. On their right stood a sealed archway. Further on, the corridor sloped down unevenly. The last several feet of floor, up to the corner and around it, had fallen in. It took little skill to see the telltale signs of footprints in the moist earth below the collapsed flooring, the scrabbling of claws on the stones nearby.

"Now we know how they got in."

Mirian glanced around the corner, saw another display case of human bodies. "Tradan, Venthan, stand watch here. Don't let your eyes rise from this hole."

Tradan cleared his throat. "Your pardon, Mirian. But I do have some expertise about these things."

What he meant was that he was a lord, and not a lackey to be used keeping watch. Tradan had spent a lifetime giving orders, not taking them.

This would have to be handled with delicacy. "I know, Tradan. But I need Jekka to read the door. And I need to be ready to help him if there's anything on the other side." She nodded once and stepped away before Tradan could object. "What's it say, Jekka?"

"'Behold now,'" Jekka read haltingly, "'the final works of Reklaniss, Opener of the Ways, and . . . most learned of . . . human studiers.' I do not know an elegant translation of the phrase, my sister. It means scholars and experts, with the word for lesser beings, and humans, and also suggests mastery. And subjugation."

Mirian grunted. "It's clear enough. Can you open it?"

"I believe so."

She glanced over her shoulder to ensure Tradan and Venthan really were watching the hole, then turned in time to see Jekka finish sweeping his fingers over the text set in the door. The lizardfolk lettering glowed faintly blue, and then the door rose slowly into the ceiling with a rumble of stone running against stone.

Mirian readied her cutlass. Jekka bent his knees, spear clasped tight.

Their light spilled upon a lizard man sitting upright in a throne with flared arms.

Jekka completely ignored every protocol and darted through the doorway toward him, his tongue testing the air.

"Jekka, be careful!"

She followed after, eyes roving over floor panels, ceiling, the floor to left and right. She gained a vague impression of a small rectangular chamber lined with shelves that supported dozens of strange objects, but otherwise empty of figures.

Jekka halted in silent regard, and Mirian, still watching her foot placement on the square stone tiles, drew up beside him.

The figure's skin was a dried-out husk under a rotted, black fabric robe, and the mold that coated him—or her, she couldn't tell—had turned it brown. Oddly, the room smelled only faintly of a sweet spice flavor.

"You should have been more careful," she said.

"It is not a place for traps, my sister. Or hazards. It is a sort of museum."

"But it's a tomb."

"One where secrets were to be shared, not hoarded. I think this is Reklaniss, but he does not hold the tear."

"What's in there?" Tradan called.

Damn the man. Did he have to be so loud?

She slipped out to remind her brother-in-law to quiet down.

By the time she returned, Jekka had stepped past the body and studied the shelves lining the far wall, each stuffed with sculptures. A few had small human figures in poses eerily similar to those in the hall outside, but many were models of the moon in its various phases.

"It seems like he was looking into the heavens in his last years." She turned to regard the body again, still a little astonished this temple wasn't guarded. She half expected that decayed corpse to lurch up and reach for them.

"This room is a little less disturbing, yes?" Jekka asked.

"Except for the body in the chair. It must have a preservative on it, or something would have done a better job eating through it by now."

"He," Jekka corrected. He bent down to a lower shelf, beside a row of black lizardfolk book cones. Mirian stepped away to investigate the distinctive glitter of jewelry along a low shelf.

Two large, flat onyx gems lay winking in the light of her glow lamp. They were cut with impossible precision, matching perfectly to one another. Yet they looked strangely familiar, and after a moment of reflection she realized why. They were reminiscent of the gems she'd seen set in the prow of the lizardfolk ship.

"Mirian," Jekka said, "these book cones may have what we need."

"What does it say?"

"It talks about Kutnaar," Jekka answered slowly. "The island he sealed from the humans. He used the power of the . . . the tear of the goddess, and protected it with a gate the humans could not open. He thought at first he could turn back the humans, and that his people were weaklings to despair, but as he aged, he wondered if there would be anyone left to look upon his marvels."

"Does it say anything about how to get there?"

Jekka's tongue slipped out. "One must have 'a ship that sees,'" he said. "I do not know what that means."

Mirian understood immediately. "The eyes in the prow. These gems here, Jekka. If we put them on the *Daughter*, we can find a way!"

"And the directions are here!" Jekka's frill rose against the back of his robe. "We can get through the gate!"

From outside came a strangled cry of alarm. "Boggards!" Venthan cried. "There's boggards in the tunnel!"

13

DEATH IN THE
HALL OF CORPSES

MIRIAN

A trained warrior would have told her numbers, armaments. Something useful. Tradan was a twit. Mirian slipped off her haversack. "Take what we need," she ordered Jekka, then dashed from the room.

In the corridor outside, Tradan and Venthan were backing away, swords drawn. She heard the slapping of boggard feet on flagstones to her right. Three of the vile creatures had crept from the crumbled rim of the hole, squat and toadlike, and two more were just behind them, their mouths open to reveal needle-sharp teeth. Their gray, corpse-like skin glistened in the white light of the glow stones.

Neither Tradan nor Venthan looked liked they were inclined to actually use their swords, so she slipped past them, brushed a spear thrust of the lead boggard aside with her off hand, and drove her sword through the creature's flabby neck.

She kicked it to pull her blade free, stopped the thrust of a second spear by slashing off its end. Tradan called for her to retreat. Useless ass. "Shine your lights in their eyes!"

Boggards were cowardly without overwhelming numbers, and her spirited defense sent those in the lead scrambling back toward the hall as those behind gibbered at her, squinting and shielding their bulbous eyes as Tradan obeyed her command.

A croaking voice from behind and below exhorted the boggards to attack.

"Retreat, Mirian, for goodness' sake!" Tradan apparently felt honor-bound to remain, but not quite brave enough to stand shoulder to shoulder.

A spear hurtled out of the darkness and she sidestepped. Four boggards crept forward, emboldened by their numbers, and she heard the scrabble of claws on stone as others clambered out of the pit.

"Jekka?" There were too many now. She blocked a spear thrust. "We're out of time!"

Three of the boggards gibbered and bounded forward.

One moment, she stood alone. The next, Jekka was beside her. With a swift slice he downed one boggard. As it fell, its bulbous eye split, he drove his spearpoint straight out the back of another's throat.

More boggards were already pressing from behind.

"Let's move!" Mirian said.

Tradan led the retreat down the hall and around the corner. Jekka dashed after, one pack over each shoulder. Mirian heard the boggards bounding in pursuit.

She and Jekka rounded the corner at full speed. "You get what you need?" she asked him.

"All the books. And the ship eyes, and the sculptures that seemed—" he paused as a spear clattered against the floor behind them "—interesting."

As they rounded another corner, they ran straight into the sphere of Ivrian's glow stone. The younger man waited tensely, wand at the ready.

"I thought I told you to stand guard at the front!"

"I heard sounds of fighting back here and—"

Did she have to think for all of them? "Get back there! Venthan, Jekka, with him! Tradan, stay!"

Her brave friend hurried off with Jekka and her cowardly brother-in-law remained, nervously fingering his glow stone.

"Lights off," she snapped. "Silence."

Tradan actually obeyed without protest.

There was no missing the sound of the boggard advance, the croaks and the slapping of broad feet.

With a word, Mirian shined her light directly into the eyes of their enemies. Only a second later, Tradan followed suit and the boggards threw up webbed gray hands to ward themselves.

Mirian and Tradan sprinted around the corner, on past a display case of fabrics. Behind came a frustrated gabbling noise. On they ran, corner after corner, and before long Mirian saw their friends standing in a pool of dim light, in the tomb's opening.

Mirian motioned them out. A low mist had risen in the greenery outside, concealing everything below her calves. She frowned. "Jekka, on point."

He hurried forward, staying low.

From up ahead came the sound of shouts, and a human scream.

"Now what's that about?" Tradan asked.

"Forward." Mirian ushered them ahead. Whatever was happening up there, they had to get away from the opening. The sun wouldn't keep the boggards back for long.

Jekka bounded into sight, waved them forward. "Stay low," he said softly. "And hurry. Boggards and pirates."

"Pirates?" Tradan whispered too loudly. "Why would there be pirates?"

Mirian ordered Ivrian to cover the rear, sent Jekka forward, and told the others to stay close. They hurried into the thick tree cover just as a loud crack of thunder sounded somewhere close at hand, followed almost immediately by gibbering cries of pain.

"That sounded like spellwork," Mirian said. "Someone has a sorcerer with them."

"Wizard, I think," Jekka said. "It's the woman from the ruins."

"From the ruins?" Mirian blinked for a moment. "What ruins?"

"The one who fought us in the ruins in the hills. She fell down a pit then. She was with the pirates."

Mirian's lips curled back into a dangerous scowl. "You mean Rajana?"

"I think so."

"Who's that?" Tradan asked.

"You don't want to meet her," Jeneta said quickly. "She's—"

Ivrian had been watching their rear, as ordered. He called a warning. "Boggards! Coming out of the tomb!"

Mirian spun and saw about two dozen of the things streaming from the tomb. Four in the front were blinking in the light, but the others fanned out as a large, hunched mottled-brown boggard pointed them forward.

They weren't alone.

More boggards erupted from the forest on their right, croaking war cries as they spotted Mirian's little group. Suddenly she was face to face with two of them, trading blows. The moment one went down another was there to take its place.

The next one dropped with its brain-pan half melted by a lance of green acid from Ivrian's wand, but those behind showed no sign of stopping. In moments, Mirian and Jekka were in the thick of it, broad forms on every side thrusting at them with wicked barbed spears, all the while gnashing pointed teeth.

She sent another down in a welter of blood, heard a male cry of pain.

"Help!" Venthan called. "Lord Tradan's been hit!"

There was no time to worry about that. Mirian knocked a spear aside with her free arm and slashed another foe across the leg. It dropped, warbling.

There were too damned many of them. She heard Ivrian's wand blasting, and Jeneta's battle cry, but couldn't see past the boggards lurching forward on three sides.

Suddenly the one on her left went down in a welter of blood, its skull split by a savage overhand slice.

Mirian blinked in astonishment—Ensara was there, flashing a grin at her before he had to dodge away as a pair of boggards closed on him. A column of pirates had advanced into the boggards, and the monsters turned to confront the new threat.

It was the only opening they were likely to get. She pivoted, motioned Venthan and Jeneta forward. They were supporting Tradan between them. No time now to see how serious his injuries were, though it was reassuring to see him able to walk.

"Ivrian, Jekka, on point! Get us clear!"

She motioned the others after them, then hurried into the trees, catching a last glimpse of Ensara next to the hulking pirate named Sarken as they traded blows with the boggards and dodged between trees.

Jekka guided them forward at a steady pace and soon they left the sounds of combat behind them. Belatedly, she wondered if she should have stayed to help Ensara. Surely he hadn't been there to help her, had he? Not if Rajana was there with him—and how was it those two knew each other?

She felt a strange lift knowing she hadn't killed him, then wondered if by abandoning him just now she'd finished the job. Yet how could she possibly have remained if Jekka were right and Rajana was with them?

There was no time to worry about that, not right now, and she forced her mind ahead as she caught up to her friends moving through the undergrowth. She wasn't able to get a good look at Tradan, but he seemed conscious. There was an awful lot of blood on the back of his shirt.

"Jeneta says I'll pull through just fine," he said over his shoulder, as though trying to reassure her.

That was a point in his favor. Mirian didn't expect her sister would like her to bring him back dead.

"He'll live." Jeneta tried to sound reassuring. "It was a nasty wound, but Iomedae gave me strength to heal the worst of it. I'll tend him again when we stop."

"And I pray we can stop soon," Venthan said, panting.

"Not happening." Mirian shook her head. "We can't slow down until we're safe."

"I was praying you wouldn't tell me that."

"As long as you're praying, pray that nothing's eaten our mounts and killed our guards, or we'll be carrying him even farther."

14

WOOD FOR THE BURNING
ENSARA

Very interesting." Rajana circled round the husk of the lizard man. She might have appreciated the room and its peculiar contents, but Ensara had given up concealing his distaste. The tomb and its grisly treasures needed burning. It wasn't so much that corpses disturbed him, for he'd looked on many a dead man in his day. It was just that these folks needed to be put to rest. Even the lizard man. It wasn't . . . seemly having their bodies lying about like that. Especially the way they were all propped. Like they were going to start up with living again the moment he turned his back, except with their bodies all rotted out. It made the hairs on the back of his neck rise just thinking about it.

Ensara wiped sweat from his brow. "I'm not sure you should take very long here," he said. "Those boggards we killed might have friends."

"Then we'll deal with them if they do, Captain. Although I appreciate the concern you show for my welfare."

"I'm certain you can manage things for yourself, m'lady." Ensara sketched a bow despite the fact the noblewoman wasn't looking at him. "I'm thinking about my men." Two had died, and three remained wounded, for Rajana maintained only a few healing spells.

"What sort of pirate are you?"

This came from deep-voiced Narsian, Rajana's bodyguard. Ensara had heard the man address his mistress on several occasions, but the fellow hadn't yet spoken to him. He didn't much care for the man's arch tone.

"We're surrounded by treasures," Narsian went on, his full lips widening in a mocking smile. "Surely you want to paw through them. Whatever the lady doesn't want is yours."

"He's a different sort of pirate, Narsian." Rajana peered at a strange tile mural upon the back of the throne that supported the lizard man's moldering corpse. "He values his men first and money second. You should appreciate a hireling who cares for his tools, don't you think?"

"Yes, m'lady," Narsian's voice registered complete agreement but his eyes showed disdain.

Somehow Rajana noticed. "Do you mock me, Narsian?"

"No, m'lady," he said quickly.

"I tolerate a certain amount of independence in those who work for me," she said, those cold dark eyes turning slowly to consider her bodyguard. "Their social and personal habits, no matter how . . . unorthodox, are none of my business so long as they don't interfere with my goals."

"Of course, m'lady," Narsian stammered with another bow.

Rajana stared at him, and he bowed more deeply. She then regarded Ensara and brushed a lock of dark hair away from her cheek. Not for the first time, he sensed she preened a little when in front of him, which he didn't understand. He knew he was handsome, but he'd done nothing to encourage her attentions. Who could tell about women, though. Maybe the lack of flirtation on his part was seen as a challenge.

"Feel free to express your concerns about security with me, Captain. I assure you I regard them with full consideration. I realize our position is not easily defensible and I will not loiter unnecessarily. However, there may be details here that Mirian Raas and her people missed. I require more time."

Ensara nodded.

"If you've no interest in the items here, perhaps you would feel more comfortable seeing to the perimeter."

"Yes, m'lady. If you're sure that you're safe."

"How very sweet. Do you hear that, Narsian? I remember when you were more solicitous."

"But m'lady, I remain your humble servant."

"Servant, yes. Humble, no."

"I shall endeavor to be more humble. I didn't mean to offend."

"See that you succeed. That is all, Captain." Rajana turned back to her studies.

Ensara stepped gratefully into the hall. By the light of a flickering torch held by a pirate, three more were busy heaving boggard bodies back into the pit the creatures had apparently emerged from, cheerfully hacking them into smaller pieces so they'd fit better.

Knowing boggards, they'd find this a tasty treat, but they'd also understand the message about what awaited them if they tried to venture out of it again.

Ensara stepped around them, then moved through the spiraling square of halls and passed where the dead men hung in semblances of life. He was nearing the exit when he saw Sarken walking toward him, bearing a lantern.

"What is it, Sarken?"

The first mate's mouth twitched. He looked over Ensara's shoulder, then at him. "I want to talk to you. Alone."

What was this about? "First tell me about the perimeter."

"I've got two men at each corner near the entrance, and two pairs farther on, watching the trail out. Each just in sight of the others. Just as you ordered."

Ensara nodded. "All right, Sarken. What's the problem?"

"You know damned well. I saw you, Cap'n."

"You *saw* me?" He repeated doubtfully, even though he knew exactly what Sarken was talking about.

"You had a chance to kill that Raas bitch, and you hit the boggard instead. What's wrong with you?"

His guts tightened every time he heard Sarken call her that. "I'm not sure you saw exactly what happened, Sarken."

"I damned well—"

"First thing, Rajana doesn't want Mirian dead before we can question her about what she found here." He was lying—Rajana had said nothing of the kind. "Second thing, I was getting ready to hit her with the flat of the blade when the boggard got in the way."

"That's not how I saw it."

"Are you questioning me, Sarken?"

"Maybe I am."

"Maybe you need to remember who's in command."

"I think you're going soft."

He rested his hand on his pommel. "You want to try me, Sarken, we'll see just how soft I am."

"That's not what I'm talking about. That bitch killed my brother—*your* sorcerer—and you save her? Where's your loyalty, Cap'n?"

"To my ship, and my men. And to the coin that keeps them afloat." Ensara raised a finger. "Right now, Lady Rajana wants Mirian Raas alive, and she's paying the coin. I don't know if you noticed or not, but she's one woman I mean to keep happy."

"Why, what charming sentiment."

He hadn't heard Rajana coming up behind him. She must have just rounded the corner, her bodyguard following.

She stopped in the circle of lantern light. "Is there a problem with your first mate, Captain?"

Sarken called to her. "Did you really tell the captain not to kill that bitch Raas?"

There was that word again. His fingers tightened on his pommel.

"Your captain has correctly inferred that the Raas woman remains of interest to me. Especially now. Until I am completely clear on what she has recovered, I may well need her alive."

"But you didn't tell him that," Sarken said.

"I didn't say that she did, Sarken," Ensara retorted.

"You just told me—"

"I told you she didn't want Mirian dead!"

"There you go, callin' her *Mirian* again. He's soft on her."

"No," Rajana said after a moment of contemplation. "He simply comes from a more cultured place than you, Sarken. Captain, do you need help with this man? Narsian would be happy—"

"No, m'lady," Ensara interrupted. "I don't need help with my crew. Sarken's a little . . . passionate about Mirian Raas."

"Because of your brother," Rajana said. "So I've heard." She stepped closer and considered Sarken dispassionately. "Don't forget that she killed my sister. Not through accident, like your sibling. No—yours she simply abandoned. Mine she shot in the face with her wand. So you see, I have little interest in her well-being. Except where it might serve me. And you," she added. "For by my recent scrying, I am almost certain she's on the cusp of a momentous discovery. One that we will reap the benefits from. All we need to do now," her eyes slid over to Ensara, "is follow her."

"Follow her where?" Sarken asked thickly.

"For now, back to her sister's mansion. It's remote and it's late at night, and they'll surely think the worst is behind them. Narsian, didn't you tell me it was made of wood?"

"Yes, m'lady."

"Wood burns so easily, doesn't it?" Rajana smiled.

Ensara cringed.

"What's wrong, Captain?"

What was wrong was that it was somebody's home, not some robber's roost or treasure vault. What was wrong was that he might be a pirate, but he was a gentleman, and gentlemen didn't go around burning down people's homes. What was wrong was that he didn't think he was going to be able to get himself, or Mirian Raas, out of this without coming to some kind of decision he wasn't going to like.

"I was just thinking about the logistics," he said. "Sarken, go in and pull our men back."

"Aye, Cap'n." Sarken said gruffly, then shouldered past Rajana and Narsian.

When he had passed the corner, Rajana addressed Ensara softly. "You should kill him. He's beneath you, and he'll drag you down."

"He's been a loyal mate."

"But is he still? Loyalty only matters if it's current." She stepped closer. "More and more you interest me, Captain. I sense depths in you that are quite curious. When our business arrangement is over, perhaps we'll discuss other matters."

There was no mistaking *that* look. He'd seen it in enough feminine eyes. She wanted him. And she was a lovely woman, no doubt about it. At least on the outside. The nearness of her set his heart speeding despite himself.

She must have sensed that, for she looked at him through lashes and smiled knowingly before turning abruptly away. "Come, Narsian."

She swept on, and there was no missing the dark look Narsian favored him with as he left.

Ensara followed. It seemed he had no other real choice in the matter.

15

THE COMPASS

MIRIAN

There was no further sign of either the boggards or the pirates, but that didn't keep Mirian from pushing her party to the limits of their endurance. She took point and set Jekka and Jeneta trailing, leaving Ivrian and Venthan to carry Tradan

It was a relief to find the sturdy horses right where they'd left them with their guards, unmolested by boggards or pirates, in the camp a mile and a half north of the ruins. Jeneta set her hands once more to Tradan and the resulting magics left him feeling more clear-eyed.

He even commented upon the eagerness of the horses, which had been stubborn on the trek south but were now utterly compliant.

"It's the mist," Tradan said. "They don't like the mist or darkness, where predators can hide. They're eager to get home."

That they were, moving at a fast clip through the jungle and out into the scrubland and finally onto the dirt track that led to the ven Goleman estate.

Charlyn held herself together when she saw her husband, but there was no missing her eyes, wide with concern, or the shocked look she gave Mirian before she helped Jeneta get her husband upstairs. Tradan babbled nervous reassurances the entire way, telling her how the injury looked worse than it was and going on about how brave her sister was. Mirian didn't think that was helping matters much, but she didn't volunteer anything. Once

Charlyn learned Tradan had a fever, she completely ignored Jeneta's assurances it would fade and angrily demanded Mirian do something about it.

Mirian hurried down the stairs with a vague plan for making some willow bark tea, and found Ivrian and Venthan waiting nervously. Each held a drinking jack, and the thought of putting foaming ale to her lips herself made her salivate.

"Is everything all right?" Ivrian asked

She nodded. "Jeneta's fine with wounds but can't deal with a fever, so Charlyn wants me to do something. I'm going to see about some tea brewing."

"We could ride to town for another healer," Venthan suggested. Apart from helping carry Tradan, it would be the most useful thing he'd yet done in Mirian's presence.

Ivrian quickly seized on the idea. "It shouldn't take too long. Particularly if Venthan knows where the best healers are." The writer pushed back a wave of hair and checked with Tradan's assistant, who nodded vigorously.

"I do."

Her instinct was to tell them not to bother. Tradan's fever was low, brought on by the wounds, and would swiftly break. But then she remembered the tight, strained expression on her sister's face. And suppose that Jeneta had missed something, or that Mirian herself was misjudging Tradan's condition? "All right," she said.

Mirian wasn't particularly eager to let either of them go, and was surprised when Ivrian passed the wand over. She took it and stared distractedly at the thing before trying to hand it back.

"You might need this more than me," she said.

Ivrian shook his head. "No. I'm worried the pirates will come back here. If they make it through those boggards." Ivrian took a deep swig from a mug, handed it back to Venthan. "Do you think the Mzali are working with them?"

"I think the boggards were just hungry. And we can hope that the Mzali aren't working with anyone else. Now hurry back, and be safe."

Once they were off, Mirian consulted with the new guard commander, who had eight on watch outside. She then went to check on Jekka.

Her blood brother had gathered all the book cones and some candles and set them on Tradan's desk, then taken a seat to inspect them. He'd shifted the chair so the back rose on his right, a preference of his. Jekka hated having to slide his tail through chair slats.

Mirian watched him from the doorway as he shifted frenetically among the cones, the candles sending flickering shadows against the walls. She wondered whether Jekka's hopes for his lost city were rising or falling. There'd been precious little time to talk.

He looked up after a time. "Your sister's mate is still healing? He will heal, I mean?"

"Yes." She didn't bother him with details. That kind of minutia always bored him. She gestured to the book cones. "What do we really have here, Jekka?"

"Almost everything, my sister." He sounded elated. "I've found the entryway. I know how to open the gate in the sea."

She came around the desk to join him as he brushed the surface of one of the cones with shaking fingers. "Reklaniss recorded the whole of the story, here. How the humans came on, and on. How he looked into the future and saw a land where all of his people were driven into the jungles or lay dead and forgotten, when his language no longer sounded in the air. So he fashioned a wall around the island of Kutnaar using the power of the tear. A colony must still live there."

That had happened a long, long time ago, but she didn't say that to him.

Jekka continued: "That wreck we found must have been on its way to Kutnaar when it foundered. It needs the jewels to open the gate. We can put the ones you found on the *Daughter of the Mist*."

"And then the gate will just open for us?" Mirian asked.

"It is a little more complex than that."

Of course it was. "How complex?"

"You can only get through at dawn on the days of the full moon."

Mirian performed swift mental calculations. Yes, they might just be able to make that.

"King Reklaniss didn't want Kutnaar to be found by just anyone who could locate the gemstones. Once through the gate, there is a maze of reefs and obstacles. Only someone with the chart and a special compass can find the way through it." Jekka's dexterous hands fluttered nervously. "Here on these cones is the ritual for installing the gemstones. Here on this cone is a description of the path through the maze of reefs. But I do not have the compass. It's focused on the island, not on the north. Do you think it might still be in the tomb of Reklaniss? That we missed it?

"I don't know, Jekka." She didn't like the idea of returning to the strange tomb Reklaniss had set up as his museum. "I wouldn't like to go back unless we've no other options."

"There could be one on the wrecked ship we found."

"There might," Mirian agreed, "but finding the wreck again is likely to be problematic, seeing as how I sent it careening along the . . ." She stopped in mid-sentence. "Ensara's alive!"

"Yes."

"He might be able to describe where the wreck settled."

"He might, but why would he help?"

Mirian still puzzled over the most recent encounter with the pirate; why he'd stalked her in league with her enemy, then struck down one of her enemies rather than her. Usually pirates' intentions were blatantly clear, but Ensara's behavior just didn't make sense.

"Easier to go back to the tomb," she decided.

At the shuffle of footsteps behind them, both turned with hands reaching for weapons.

But it was no enemy, only Tradan, leaning heavily against the door in a tan shirt and trousers, his hair combed back from his forehead. Jeneta stood watchful beside him, as if she expected him to crumple at any moment.

"Aren't you supposed to be in bed?" Mirian asked.

"I'm not that bad." Tradan forced a grin, though he looked ghastly pale. "And I couldn't wait to hear what Jekka had found."

"Everything we need, really," Mirian told him. "A chart. The magical stones that open the gate. The problem is that we need a specialized compass to show us exactly where the gate lies. A compass that apparently points only to Kutnaar."

"It's energies are attuned to the gate," Jekka added.

Tradan sagged a little in the doorframe.

Jeneta frowned, her voice tense with concern. "I told Lord ven Goleman he should stay in bed. Lady Charlyn is furious with him."

"That's the way of wives," Tradan said philosophically. "Would this compass happen to point northwest?"

"Only if you're southeast of the gate," Mirian said slowly. Of course, they were southwest of the gate now, if it really was in the Lizard Kings reefs. "Why do you ask?"

"I have a lizardfolk compass I found in the ruins," Tradan said. "I thought it was broken. Because it doesn't point north."

16

THE CATACOMBS

JEKKA

Charlyn, sister of his sister, met them as they exited the study, garbed now in a green robe she wore over a long white dressing gown. The ruby ring still glittered upon her hand. Jekka thought he detected anger in the set of her lips.

"You told me you would rest, Tradan," she said. "And then you sneak downstairs? Can't this wait until the morrow?"

"Nothing to worry about, poppet. Just going down to the vaults."

Charlyn turned to Mirian and Jekka.

Mirian sounded apologetic. "If you just tell me how to retrieve it, it probably *is* better if you rest."

"Nonsense. Besides, it's a bit of a maze down there. The old homestead's built over some ruins my family walled off for storage. And you needn't look like that, Mirian. It isn't some grim temple or anything. Nothing to worry about. But—it's dark and winding."

"I can't believe you're insisting on doing this now, Mirian," Charlyn said. "You see how he is."

"Perhaps we should wait until tomorrow," Mirian offered.

Jekka fairly burst with eagerness to find out whether the compass lay beneath the house. Did Charlyn not understand? "This is the future of my people, sister of my sister. If we find this compass, I will know whether or not my cousin and I are the last of our clan. I have waited long."

Charlyn's look softened and she exchanged a glance with Mirian.

"I'll go with them," Jeneta said quickly. "As long as your husband moves slowly, he should be all right."

"You see, pet, I'll be perfectly fine. I won't even strain myself. I'll walk slowly. Jekka—I wonder if you'd mind—let's keep the new items down in the vaults for now, shall we? The things Venthan was carrying in his pack? I store all the most important things below."

"Are you sure you can't simply tell them where to go?" Charlyn asked. "It won't take that long to draw a map."

He laughed shortly. "My dear, you simply worry too much. I have things in hand."

Charlyn frowned at him and her small chin rose in what was clearly anger before she whirled away.

"Ah, women, eh, Jekka?" He chuckled.

"Women what?" Jekka asked.

"Damn it, Tradan," Mirian snapped. "You're being an ass."

Jekka didn't understand why Tradan flushed suddenly. Was he angry, or ashamed?

"The woman's in love with you," Jeneta said. "And you just insult her?"

"I'm not really sure it's your business. Or yours, Mirian. You're suddenly watching out for her? After all these years?"

His sister jabbed a finger at Tradan. "I saved your butt today, Tradan. And Jeneta carried it for a couple of miles. Seems to me that earns us something."

Again Tradan flushed. He cleared his throat. "Well, let's get along then, shall we?"

It was Mirian who shouldered the pack, not Jekka, who, despite assurances that there was nothing to fear in the basement, took his weapons. He dearly wanted to read the rest of those book cones, but he would be back very soon.

The door to the family storage lay at the bottom of a set of old wooden stairs behind a door to what proved to be an underground larder off the kitchen. The door was a very sturdy construction of thick, aged oak, sealed with an extremely elaborate lock. Jekka, tilting his head, heard no less than four clicks when Tradan thrust in the key and turned it. Beyond lay a long hallway smelling of cool stone and dry earth. Tradan set the key back on his belt, lifted a lantern he'd brought with him, and started forward.

"People who aren't of the family don't usually get to come in here," he said. "Really, you're among the first." He laughed a little. "Although technically you're sort of family," he added with a glance at Mirian. "Just not of direct blood. Ah, you know what I mean."

"It's a special honor," Mirian said in a peculiar tone that set Tradan laughing nervously.

There was some sort of human social interaction underway that Jekka didn't quite follow.

As they headed into the wide corridor of fitted stone, Jekka noted the narrow branching corridors and wondered just how extensive the ruins were, and who had built them.

Jeneta, a pace behind Tradan, glanced at Jekka. "This must be exciting for you."

"I am excited, yes."

She hesitated a moment, then said: "I have prayed for you and your cousin, Jekka."

"That is kind of you." He didn't add that the gods no longer heeded the prayers of his people, for it didn't seem polite.

He was, on the whole, not given to contemplation of the future, for it had rarely presented him with anything particularly pleasant. Yet with the information in the study and the gems they could install upon their ship, he was nearly home. All he needed was the compass.

"Do you worry about how these lizardfolk will greet you when you turn up?" Jeneta asked. "Or us?"

He hissed slowly as they turned down a narrow stone corridor. That was a question he hadn't considered, and it merited thought. But he spotted a faint silvery light farther down the hall.

"Lord Tradan—what is that light?"

"Ah—nothing to worry about," Tradan answered. He'd stopped at a door on the left and handed off his lantern to Mirian to fumble with more keys. He steadied himself against the stone, and Jeneta hurried forward to check him.

"How *are* you planning to introduce us to your people, Jekka?" Mirian asked softly. "If they're still there, they aren't likely to welcome humans."

"I will make clear that you are my friends and family," Jekka answered, though suddenly his mind was turning over these unexamined risks. Suppose his folk were less accepting than he? If they were as skeptical of all humans as he had been only a few months ago, any that he brought with him would be in danger.

"To be frank," Tradan said as he rattled the keys, "I wonder if they're still there. I mean, wouldn't they have to come out sometime? If they're still there, surely we would have seen some evidence of them."

He got the key in the lock and bared his teeth in an odd smile toward Jekka. "No harm meant, of course, and I hope the best for you, but you must be prepared. It might be that they've died out."

"Tradan," Mirian said with a growl.

"You don't think he should be prepared?" Tradan asked her, then finished twisting the key in the lock and opened wide the door.

Tradan was right. He should be more prepared. Jekka resolved to give greater thought to what might lie ahead.

They stepped through into a musty stone chamber filled with wooden shelves, each heavy with carvings and book cones and statues and old pots. Tradan's light spilled haphazardly over any number of interesting items as he searched.

"Ah. Yes. The Kalabuta material is mostly centered here."

Jeneta held up her lantern and Jekka saw crabbed hand-writing on slips of paper propped beside even the tiniest fragment.

"Is this all your doing?" Mirian asked.

"Ah . . . no. I'm afraid the 'exploration' bug has been in the family for several generations now. Although it bit me harder than the others." Tradan cleared his throat. "Really, though, we've all just been dabblers compared to the Raas family."

"These," Jeneta said, indicating a dark wooden statue with a leering face that lay upon its side. "Are these the Hidden Ones?"

"Yes, yes. Avert your eyes!" Tradan chuckled. "The Kalabuta are very superstitious about that. Only sacred folk are supposed to see them."

"And you just have them rotting in your basement?" Mirian sounded surprised.

"Surely you don't believe any of that nonsense."

"There's a difference between belief and respect, don't you think?" Mirian asked.

Jeneta nodded.

"I don't know where you have room to complain terribly much. Your family loots and sells what it finds—"

"From the ocean floor," Mirian said, "and never sacred relics."

"Well, these are being preserved."

"In your basement?" Mirian asked. "For whom? If you want to preserve them, turn them over to the Pathfinders."

"Perhaps I will." Tradan moved to his left and the lantern light shone finally on an array of book cones and fragments from lizard-folk wall murals. Jekka bent close and saw that the writing praised the victories of a lizardfolk queen whose name he'd never heard. He briefly examined the side of a book cone and could make little sense of it—the subject appeared to be the preparation of fish for some sort of ceremony.

"Ah!" Tradan reached out with one slim hand and plucked a delicate steel object from the shelf.

It was no longer than Jekka's palm, and shaped roughly like a short, flattened arrow with a blunt point. Lines drawn into the tarnished surface suggested feathering.

A fraying string was tied through the crescent hole at its center. "Watch this," Tradan said, even as Jekka was trying to reach for it to inspect its small, precise lettering.

Tradan lifted the object by the thread, steadying the arrow so that it swayed only gradually, and within a few moments it had swung to the left. Tradan chuckled a little to himself. "Watch what happens when I try to point it to the north."

Jekka knew what would happen and was a little frustrated. Tradan had already stated the object was a compass, so it was hardly necessary to demonstrate its power. Jekka wanted to see what was written on its side.

"Hah!" Tradan said as the arrow swayed and settled again to the left, as if his watchers had doubted him. "It is a compass. A damned peculiar one, if you'll pardon me, but—"

"May I see it?" Jekka asked.

"Oh. Quite. Of course."

Tradan reluctantly passed it over and Jekka held it up to the lantern obligingly lifted by Jeneta.

"It's not actually a compass," Mirian said. "More like a gate location device."

"I suppose you're right," Tradan agreed.

Jekka focused on the lettering.

"What does it say?" Jeneta asked softly.

It took a little effort to translate the poetic sentiment of the old tongue into something approximating human language.

"'True and spear-straight lies the path to the city, so long as you bear eyes and sail with knowledge of the Kutnaar ridge . . . reefs,'" he corrected.

"So you have everything you need," Mirian said, smiling.

He studied her, sensing something amiss. A wariness? A sadness?

"Well, well!" Tradan looked as excited as though he'd personally invented the object himself. "So we'll be reuniting him with his lost people! Your writer friend should have a fine time with that. Although I hope he leaves me out of the whole thing."

Jekka, still a little stunned, turned the compass over in his hand and read the writing there. "I wish my brother were still here. I can hardly wait to show it to Kalina."

Mirian turned and looked toward the doorway.

"What is it?" Tradan asked.

"Someone's out there."

Jekka tested the air for scents as the others turned toward the door.

"Pet," Tradan called. "Is that you?"

Jekka heard a male cough, then a curse.

"Douse the lights," Mirian said suddenly. "Someone else is down here."

"But that can't be," Tradan protested.

"It is," Mirian insisted. "Douse the lights and get down! Jeneta, make sure he stays safe."

Jeneta nodded and drew her sword. "I'll protect him with my life."

"Let's hope it doesn't come to that," Mirian said, and blew out the lantern.

17

GUESTS OF THE HOUSE

IVRIAN

Ah, the vicissitudes of fortune! I had constantly been sepa-
rated from my friends when they experienced the most
harrowing of their adventures. I returned with a retiring
but experienced healer from Port Freedom, never knowing
that my friends were already in danger once more.

I wished I'd been at their side, the blood pounding
in my veins as I stood shoulder to shoulder fending off
the forces of darkness. What I had never wished was to
confront those forces alone, powerless to save either myself
or my allies.

—From *The City in the Mist*

As the carriage turned down the lane, the local healer, a bony colonial, shifted tensely. Ivrian had promised the fellow double what he would normally have asked for a nighttime call after Venthan blathered about pirates and boggards. Tradan's assistant didn't have much sense.

Right now Venthan was chattering on as if nothing at all were wrong. "I think what amazed me the most was that the adventure was just like something you would have written in a pamphlet! Will you be writing this one up?"

"Most likely." Ivrian answered. Venthan didn't seem to pick up on social cues like terse answers that hinted a conversation should conclude.

"What will you say about me?"

Ivrian was reminded suddenly of Kalina, who'd asked him the same thing. During the early portion of their expedition into the Kaava Lands, she'd been his only friend. Rajana's sister had condemned her to the arena, where she took the wound that killed her. It still seemed impossible to him that she had returned, brought back by the power of the gods, and remained alive and well in the safety of the Pathfinder lodge.

"I'm sorry. Did I say something wrong?"

Ivrian shook his head. "I was thinking about a friend of mine." He offered a smile. "I'll say that you were bookish but determined. Handsome," he added. He'd probably also say that he talked too much and was too self-involved, and that he might know how to hold a sword but not really how to handle one. Except he couldn't be that cruel in print.

"Handsome, eh?" Venthan smiled, and Ivrian felt it like a stab wound. People just didn't have any business doing that to him with a smile.

"I haven't decided what else I'll say," Ivrian added. *What the hell.* "Or whether I'll give you a love interest."

"A love interest?" Venthan's smile broadened. "Aren't I a minor character?"

"I'm not sure how 'minor' you'll turn out to be," Ivrian said. "Some things bear closer investigation. It comes down to timing."

"So the timing has to be right."

"Always." Ivrian liked the bright-eyed way Venthan looked at the world, but he didn't know if there was much more beyond that, or if there needed to be. It'd been a long time since he shared someone's bed.

On the other hand, Venthan's self-focus was liable to be an irritant really quickly. That shouldn't matter for a quick roll, but . . . Ivrian found himself strangely cautious. They really were a little more complicated than they used to seem.

The cart came to a stop and he heard the seat in front creak as the driver hopped down, and the crunch of his footsteps on the gravel as he opened the carriage door. Ivrian climbed down first to survey the surroundings. The healer followed, adjusting his round-brimmed cap. Venthan was babbling about how nice it would be to take a long, warm soak, but Ivrian was done flirting for the moment.

He started up the stairs, wondering why no one was posted on the porch stoop. Perhaps Mirian had pulled all the guards inside.

He knocked on the door.

It was yanked open even as there was a yelp of alarm from behind. Ivrian turned his head. Two burly forms had moved out from behind the large pots beside the stairs, and even in the darkness he made out the blades in their hands.

And before Ivrian was an ugly, bent-nosed man with a cutlass.

"Ho!" someone called behind him. "It's the writer!"

Ivrian wished he was as daring and skilled as a character in his stories, but with a naked cutlass at his throat, he just raised his empty hands.

"Smart lad," the pirate told him.

"Where's Mirian?"

"I was hoping you'd tell me," he said. "Who're these?"

"A healer, and Lord ven Goleman's assistant."

"Who's the healer for?"

Didn't they know? Ivrian thought quickly. Might Tradan and some of the others have escaped? "Just to tend to our wounds."

The pirate scowled at him.

"Get him out of the doorway," said a smoother voice, and Ivrian found himself facing a tall, olive-skinned man with sad eyes and a black mustache and chin beard. A frayed sense of grandeur clung to him, despite his threadbare appearance, like cobwebs in some fading mansion.

The man's eyes softened further as they met Ivrian's, which was more than a little curious. His voice, though, was hard as he turned to his subordinates. "Put the others under guard with the servants." Venthan, the carriage driver, and the healer were led away by four pirates, and Ivrian tried to wish Tradan's assistant courage. The look Venthan flashed back was one of bewilderment.

They closed the door behind them, and Ivrian was alone with the pirate he now guessed must be Captain Ensara. He wondered why the man's expression seemed genuinely friendly.

"So you're the one who wrote that little book," he said. "I rather liked it."

Normally Ivrian would have appreciated the compliment, but he was still looking for a chance to prove his bravery. "I didn't realize pirates could read."

Ensara's expression fell to such an extent Ivrian actually felt a little bad for the quip.

"No point in making us enemies, lad." He indicated Tradan's library with a sweep of his hand, deftly withdrawing Ivrian's sword as they stepped into the room.

The first thing he noticed pulled him up short. Rajana stood behind the library table. One of her hands was bare, the other in an opera glove, but both were surrounded by a nimbus of energy. In front of her lay a display of lizardfolk book cones, their gems glittering.

He tried not to stare at the limp form of Charlyn ven Goleman, lying at the foot of a smug, well-dressed man in black, intently binding her in an absurd number of ropes.

"You may leave us, Captain Ensara," Rajana instructed.

"Yes, m'lady."

Ensara gave him a last look that might have been one of pity, then closed the door behind him.

"So." The glow about Rajana's hands faded, and she lowered them. Now the primary source of light was the forest of candles set upright among the book cones. The light rendered her coldly beautiful, as though she were formed all of ivory. "It's the pamphleteer. Someone who might actually be able to give me answers. I'm afraid Mirian's sister passed out from my pain spell. She's not cut from quite the same cloth, is she?"

"She wouldn't know anything anyway."

"Ah, but you do." She lifted the twin to the wand Ivrian had passed off to Mirian. "I read what you said about my sister," Rajana went on. "And you give her more credit than she deserved. You have a certain facility with adjectives, but your prose is too—what is the word I used, Narsian?"

The big man in black looked up from Charlyn, and Ivrian paused in his own worries to wonder at the fellow's intent. He was still tying Mirian's sister with elaborate care, as though she were some sort of escape artist. He couldn't count the number of loops already wound about her calves.

"'Garish,' Countess." He paused for a moment, then seemed to realize he would not be called upon again and returned to his work, like some sort of human spider.

"What's he doing with Lady ven Goleman?"

"Narsian plans an experiment with the Raas woman, and I like to indulge him now and then."

"An experiment? She's innocent of—"

Rajana's voice was like a whip. "You will address me as *m'lady*. And I've not authorized you to ask questions."

Ivrian considered insulting her, but there really didn't seem to be a point. Not yet. He wanted to know what she was doing here.

"I am not circumspect, Lord Galanor. I see little need for prevarication. Through my scrying I know that you are close to finding a dragon's tear. I know that these objects here are a map and some kind of opening device." She tapped two large black gems that Ivrian had never seen before. No, he decided, they were a dark blue.

"I gather," the countess went on, "that Charlyn ven Goleman has little to no knowledge of them."

"She's doesn't know anything about it," Ivrian said. "She's had no part in any of this. I don't really understand—"

"I don't care if you understand. And you will address me appropriately."

That was rather absurd, really, given that they were both nobility, though he'd heard the Chelaxians sniffed at the idea of Sargavans remaining their equals.

Narsian spoke up behind him. "Do you wish me to deal with him, m'lady?"

"How kind. No, Narsian. I'll let you know if I need your help."

Rajana tapped the wand against her hand. "There's probably only one thing I can offer you that would cause you to give me the information I want. If I promise you life, you can trust that I will give it to you. Without trickery. Instead of burning you up with the house, I will cast a sleeping spell upon you and leave you in the carriage house."

"If you've been scrying us, what could you possibly want to know? M'lady." He hated himself for adding the last. Not because he was afraid . . . no, he admitted, he was definitely afraid. He stood a better chance of getting out of this alive if he didn't antagonize her. But he was also curious.

"It's not as though I can watch you all day long, every day. No one's that interesting, and no one has that much magical energy to burn. So I've missed a few things. Like where Mirian Raas is." Her eyes narrowed.

Ivrian didn't say anything.

"You aren't going to tell me, either?"

He wasn't sure what to say. If he admitted to not knowing, would she believe him? Without the use of a spell to verify, that is?

There was a rap on the door.

"Yes?"

It was Captain Ensara again, who advanced with one hand on the door latch and bowed in brief acknowledgment. "There's some sort of vault in the basement, m'lady. I've sent in some of the men."

"Not Sarken?"

"No, m'lady."

"Good. I *do* want her alive."

"Of course." Ensara bowed and closed the door.

Rajana considered Ivrian. "I don't think you were dissembling. I think you didn't actually know."

"Very true, m'lady."

"And I'm not entirely sure you'll still be of use to me," she said, swinging the wand negligently. Still, when she extended a glove hand, he was glad the wand wasn't pointed in his direction. At her whispered words, sleep rolled over him. He sank to the floor, wondering why it suddenly looked so comfortable and why anyone in the world would ever want a bed.

18

PEOPLE OF THE VAULT

MIRIAN

Gruff male voices muttered to one another as their footsteps scuffed the old stone, and lantern light shifted in the corridors from which Mirian and her group had come. The intruders spoke with the coastal accents of colonials, so she could be sure it wasn't the Mzali again. And if she'd had any doubt at all as to them being the pirates, they were quashed as she heard one of them curse Ensara for sending them down into this maze.

With only lights to judge their numbers by it was difficult to count them, but Mirian thought there were less than a half dozen, which were pretty good odds, considering she had the wand. More concerning was what might have happened upstairs. Clearly Tradan's local guard force was compromised, incompetent, outmatched, or dead. But then, she supposed a wizard of Rajana's power might have enough spells up her sleeve to quickly weaken the perimeter and exploit the damage.

Since the pirates were in the house, Charlyn was in danger. And they had probably taken Jekka's map and ship eyes, which meant Jekka's search for his homeland was in jeopardy.

Mirian motioned to Jekka. She knew his vision was better than hers, but she couldn't be sure he saw the hand signal to hold his action.

She aimed the wand and concentrated, her target not the man in the front, but the man at the back, one of the two holding lanterns. She whispered the activation word and the wand's tip glowed a fiendish emerald before a line of deadly energy streamed forth and took the poor sod in the wrist.

He screamed and dropped the lantern. It shattered and the light dimmed to nothing.

The other pirates erupted in alarm, and the remaining lantern-bearer naturally shined his light toward her.

"It's her—it's Raas!"

"Get her!"

She dropped to one knee, targeted the lantern-bearer's chest. He clutched at the wound, screaming as the acid ate through his shirt and then fingertips. His cries of pain rose shrilly as he sank. His lantern struck the floor and cracked. It lay on its side, still burning feebly. The pirates swiftly called a retreat, recognizing there was no safe way forward down the long corridor.

Or at least that's what she thought until she saw the floating bead of red energy that careened into the room where the pirates lay dying. Eyes wide, she sprinted and threw herself around a corner.

There was a terrific explosion behind her and a blast of heat, as though someone had just thrown open a blazing oven.

The screaming stopped but there came the nauseating smell of cooked flesh.

And then there was a woman's voice.

"Mirian Raas," it called. "I don't really think I need you anymore."

Mirian didn't answer. She knew from past experience that Rajana was deadly and capable.

"You *are* still alive back there, aren't you?"

She knew Jeneta and Tradan were safe, but she wondered if Jekka had managed to escape the flames. If he'd been wounded, he was remaining completely silent. She wondered morosely if she'd be able to detect the difference between the smell of cooked human flesh and cooked lizard flesh.

"I was thinking about trading you for your sister, but I've decided I don't really care. I've given your sister to one of my men. I've got your books and gems, and I'll get whatever else I need from your writer friend. But first I'm going to burn down this house and everyone else who's in it. What do you think of that?"

"I think," Mirian said, forcing calm into her voice, "you're making a mistake."

Rajana laughed. "Really."

"You might have the map and the seeing stones, but you don't have the gate compass."

"You're a poor liar, Mirian."

Tradan called out then, from deeper in the catacombs. His voice was hollow, weak. "I'll give you whatever you desire," he cried, "if you'll let my wife go free! She's not involved in any of this—"

"You have nothing I want!" Rajana called back.

Mirian spoke quickly. "The only safe way beyond the gate is with the compass. Why do you think I'm down here in the catacombs? I came here to get it out of storage!"

A long silence fell. The hand holding her wand rose reflectively, but she saw a brief flash of light—one of the glow stones going on and off—and glimpsed Jekka in a side corridor, signaling his presence to her. He must have found some connecting passage to retreat into. And if he could find a way, mightn't the pirates do the same?

"I don't need a compass," Rajana assured her, sounding quite satisfied. "I found one in the ruins. But thank you for the tip. Enjoy the burning."

Mirian retreated further, hoping Jekka would do the same. She banged her shin on the side of a warped plank table as she threw herself through an archway into another side room, cursing in pain at the same time as a titanic ball of fire exploded in the corridor outside. She heard Rajana laughing, and then a second explosion followed, for an instant transforming the entire hallway into a broiling furnace. Mirian averted her eyes. The heat even ten paces from the hallway was so intense it curled her eyebrows. She felt the pressure of the flame like a burning hand upon her neck.

The light faded, though it clung to the furniture now burning in the main hallway. Mirian clutched her wand, wondering if the wizard would be foolish enough to come in after them. She whispered a prayer to Desna.

Tradan shouted again. "Please, spare my wife! She's done nothing! Take me instead!"

Rajana's response was faint, as though she were far away. "If it's death you want—"

Mirian peered out from her hiding place to see Jeneta yanking on Tradan's arm in a frantic attempt to pull him to safety.

It did little good against the lightning blast that arced out from the dim recesses of the corridor. Even as Tradan fell backward, the lightning struck him.

The attack was followed by the sound of Rajana's laughter, then the unmistakable thud of the vault door being slammed.

Mirian moved her head, her neck stabbing with pain. She caught her breath, reached into one of her pouches for the brass tube that contained the potion of healing.

Her first thought was to down it, but she checked herself. She wasn't sure Jekka had brought any of his own gear, and Jeneta had probably used up most of her healing magic. If Tradan was still alive, he'd probably suffered more damage than Jeneta could handle. He'd need the potion.

She worked her way back to them and the storage room. The smell of seared stone, scorched mortar, and charred flesh hung rank in the air.

Jeneta bent over Tradan, calling in a loud, desperate voice upon the power of Iomedae. All Mirian could see of her brother-in-law were his legs, and she thought she should probably be glad for that. She'd seen a lot of death over the years, but she didn't want to see Tradan burned and mutilated.

Jekka emerged out of the gloom and handed her his own vial of healing potion. "I'm going to make sure they've gone," he said. "You look bad," he added to Mirian before sliding away.

"I don't know if I can keep him alive," Jeneta confessed, her face twisted in anguish.

Tradan's face didn't actually look bad, but his shirt was burned away, revealing blackened flesh. Smoke twisted from the charred wound and twisted toward the ceiling.

Wordless, Mirian handed over the vial and Jeneta unstoppered it. "I'm just not powerful enough," the young healer said. "My faith is strong, but . . ." She propped open Tradan's mouth and poured in the full draught. He stirred, fitfully.

"It's not enough," Jeneta said, whereupon Mirian passed down the vial Jekka had given her. Upon its application Tradan blinked and raised hands to feel his chest.

"By the gods. I thought I was finished." His voice was a hoarse croak.

"You were. Jeneta, can you take a look at me?"

"Yes. Turn. What are we going to do, Mirian? Do you think she's really going to kill Ivrian?"

"Not if we can help it."

Mirian's injuries were more in line with the young woman's skills, and after a whispered prayer and cool hands laid to her burning skin, most of the sting faded to minor irritation.

Tradan, naturally, was worried about his wife. "You heard that woman." He still sounded terribly weak. "We've got to save my wife."

"And Ivrian," Jeneta said, then added, "and your servants and guards. Is there some other way out?"

"There is," Tradan said. "Come on. We've got to hurry!" He pushed to his feet.

Jeneta rose and put an arm under his shoulder as he limped forward, her face grim with effort.

"Jekka," Mirian called.

After a few moments her blood brother returned to confirm the exit sealed, and they started after the others. Mirian was silent, stunned by the turn of events. Even if they got out of here, how was she going to rescue Charlyn and Ivrian?

Mirian wasn't given to blinding rages, but she burned with the urge to find Rajana and finish her properly. The wizard wasn't invulnerable, no matter her skill.

They were closing on that eerie, silver glow Jekka had asked about earlier.

Tradan and Jeneta stopped short at the end of the hall and were conversing now in low, urgent tones.

Mirian and Jekka joined them. "What's the hold up?"

"I didn't expect to come here," Tradan said. "I forgot the token."

"The token?" Mirian prompted.

"A magical symbol. My grandfather told me never to enter here unless I had the Moon Token."

"We can't exactly go back," she reminded him.

"This is an ancient crypt," Tradan said, his voice rising in panic.

Jeneta put a hand to his arm, her voice calm. "Is the way out through here?"

"It is." Tradan's head bobbed rapidly. "But there are wards, unless you wear the symbol. I don't know what to do!"

"You're sure this is the way out?"

"Yes." He nodded quickly. "It's a door in the wall over there. But I don't have the token—"

Mirian cut him off with a sour look. "Unless you can pull the token out of your backside, we're going to have to chance the wards. Jeneta, is there anything you can do about this?"

"I'll try," the priestess said hesitantly. "It depends upon what sort of wards they are. I can pray to Iomedae to protect us from evil."

"Do that, then."

"Yes, Mirian." The woman bowed her head then chanted in a clear, pretty voice. After a few moments, she nodded thoughtfully.

"Lead on, Tradan," Mirian said, and then, at his hesitance, "I'll walk right beside you."

Jekka still carried the glow stone in one hand, but it wasn't really necessary because of the round silvery glow in the midst of what proved an oval chamber, supported by arched pillars incised with crescent moons.

Apart from the superstructure, the space was crowded with statues of hooded, kneeling figures, their faces turned toward the orb radiating light in the chamber's center. Each leaned upon lifelike hands sculpted with palms facing down toward the floor.

As they neared the gleaming sphere, light fell upon the figures facing it from the other side and cold fear suddenly surged through Mirian's chest. Long gray hair escaped from some of the hoods, straggling down across dried and empty faces.

These were not statues, but bodies sheathed in plaster.

Mirian had no time to count their numbers, but guessed there must be forty or fifty of them, all bent around a glowing, pock-marked sphere set upon a flanged, head-high pillar.

A peculiar cracking noise rang through the empty space, as of porcelain being broken, or cement being chipped . . .

. . . or of the ancient dead pushing up from their positions of reverence in a rain of plaster.

Tradan gasped as the first of the figures rose and reached for them with clawlike fingers.

"Wards," Mirian said in disgust as she ripped her sword from its sheath. She brought the blade crashing down through one ghastly arm and cut half through a lurching figure on her right.

Dozens more tottered to their feet. Tradan had increased to a sprint, his goal apparently an archway twenty feet farther ahead.

Mirian evaded one grasping hand, shrugged off fingers that grabbed at her shoulder, and swung precisely to the right and left as though she were hacking away jungle foliage. One figure bent low as it came in so Mirian sheared off the top of its head, complete with dried fabric, scalp, and dusty skull, which clattered into fragments against the pitted floor.

Jekka lashed out with his staff, tripping the awkward dead and slicing through ancient leg bones.

"Be gone, foul ones!" Jeneta called with conviction, her voice certain and rich with power. Iomedae's symbol glowed in her hand. "Return to the sleep of ages! Cease this parody of life!

The shambling forms recoiled from her.

Mirian arrived at the door while Tradan fumbled at his keys. Jekka stood just behind, warding with his staff.

Jeneta came after. Only a few paces behind, more dark figures staggered on, reaching with skeletal arms.

"I . . ." Jeneta stammered. "I seem only to have affected the weaker ones."

Mirian tried to keep her voice level. "Tradan, you planning to open that door soon?"

"I may not have the key."

Mirian cursed, sheathed her sword, and pushed Tradan out of the way. She tore off her utility pouches and dug out her picks, all the time trying not to focus on the clack of long-dead feet against stone, the frightened breaths of her allies.

The trick to lockpicking was concentration and a steady hand—a little challenging with all the chaos behind her. How long would they be able to keep the dead things at bay? And what kind of madman would have allowed them to stay in his basement anyway?

Fortunately, the lock was a simple affair with two large tumblers and it took only a few moments of manipulation before she heard the proper click. The door swung outward.

Mirian grabbed her pack and, still holding the two picks in her other hand, shouted to her friends. "Come on!"

Jeneta was the first through, the symbol of Iomedae in one hand and the sword in the other.

Tradan followed. Jekka made a final sweep with his scythe blade, dropping one of the crowding forms by shearing off its ankle. The attack left him open from the side, and swift though he was, one of the dead women latched on to his left arm.

Mirian drew her cutlass and darted back out, sword slashing in a graceless overhand swing.

One blow cut through dried limbs, cloth, mummified skin, and bone. They smashed into the floor. Mirian grabbed Jekka by the shoulder and brutally snatched him back. As soon as they were through the archway Jeneta pulled the door shut. It slammed to with a click. The four of them then stood panting in the narrow hallway. Jeneta played her glowing symbol over the stone walls and they listened for their pursuers.

"They're scratching at the door," Jeneta said.

Mirian turned to Tradan, her glow stone shining on him. "You mean to tell me," she said, breathing heavily, "you slept in a house with those things in your *basement?*" The rough-hewn stones in the narrow hallway threw back her voice with a metallic ring.

Tradan's voice rose weakly in objection. "They're perfectly safe so long as you have the ward. They're sort of a family alarm system, if someone tries to break into the vaul—"

"That's insane," Mirian snapped.

Tradan sounded offended. "My great-great-grandfather swore to preserve the ancient sisters when he purchased this land from the natives. My family are not thieves," he went on proudly. "We keep our word."

"Table this for later. Is there anything past here to worry about?"

"No. An ancient tunnel that leads down near the river." His voice fell. "It was to be an escape tunnel . . . should anything ever happen to the family."

"Let's move then, and see what we can do."

They hurried ahead, Mirian leading. Wide stones formed walls and ceiling. The tunnel was so low that Jekka had to hunch.

Cobwebs filled the place, and puffs of dust rose with every step. As they progressed, Mirian swept the webs away with her cutlass. At one spot they reached a point where the right wall had fallen in, but there was enough room to press past the debris. The tunnel went on and on, and Mirian began to wonder if it might stretch for miles.

"How long is this tunnel?" she asked.

"I'm not sure." Tradan, twice injured and already exhausted, paused for breath after every word.

It was hard to gauge the time down there. Mirian reckoned it was at least a half hour before they arrived at an upward flight of stairs and she paused to brush away another mass of webbing. Beyond she heard the distinctive sound of a snake hiss, and her glow stone reflected upon the eyes of a large mamba coiled at the top of the steps.

Mambas were one of the most poisonous snakes on Golarion, as dangerous or more than any lurking horror, each bite capable of killing a full-grown human in minutes.

She brought her sword up by instinct, sidestepping and swinging wide.

She caught the thing on the end of its lunge, cutting it just a finger span on the back of its head. The head soared on to bounce off Jeneta's skirt and lie on the dirty stone, spasmodically biting the air again and again.

The headless corpse flailed wildly, tumbling down the stairs, and it was only then that Mirian felt a surge of adrenaline.

Jekka slipped past and took the steps himself. There was the sound of another strike into flesh, and then another.

"There were more," Jekka's voice came back, "but they're dead now."

She ignored the twitching bodies of the additional mambas and considered the hexagonal chamber with its weathered metal panels framed in dark stone. A ceiling buttressed with rusty metal stretched a few feet overhead.

Even as she looked for a key or a doorknob, Jekka latched hands upon a metal bar in front of him and pushed down. Mirian heard a soft clanging noise and the entire panel swung inward.

Air rushed in—clean air with the moist, warm tang of the jungle. A light shone in the distance, and it wasn't until she'd followed Jekka into the fresh air that she realized it was the moon shining on the dark river.

They'd emerged in a small circle of pillars on a knoll overlooking the southern end of Port Freedom. Their passage ended in the base of a statue of a woman with upraised arms.

Mirian reached back to help Tradan out. Jeneta followed, wiping sweat from her brow.

The scholar in her was curious as to whom the statue represented and how long it had stood there, for Mirian didn't recognize the blocky architectural style. But there were other, far more pressing matters. Tradan was in poor shape. And she and Jekka had a long trek ahead of them, and pirates to fight.

"Jeneta, get Tradan to town, and—"

"No," Tradan said, breathing heavily. "Can't abandon—"

"Get to town, and send guards. They'll come at your authority, won't they?"

Tradan nodded slowly. "But—"

"No buts. We can't do this on our own. Jekka, are you ready?"

"But there are only two of you!" Jeneta said. Her speech was pressured, nervous. "We've got to save Ivrian and Charlyn!"

Mirian laid a hand on the younger woman's shoulder. "And we will. But I need you to help Tradan get reinforcements."

Jeneta's jaw clenched, but she nodded.

With that, Mirian and her blood brother turned and started back for the jungle. They'd be lucky to get back in time at all. She hoped at least to be able to scout the area before reinforcements arrived. Much as she hurried, though, she was afraid her bloodline was going to lose another member this night, and that she'd be attending the funeral of another friend.

19

CHANGING PLANS
ENSARA

He hadn't really thought she'd burn the place down, but he had come to find out Rajana was a woman of her word. Ensara was just glad she had ordered the servants and the visiting healer into the barn where she'd put them under with a sleep spell. He liked to think that even his men would have balked at burning the servants alive, but he wasn't sure.

The men certainly seemed pleased with Rajana—they'd looted the great mansion, carting away silverware and gold idols and a small chest of Mirian's sister's jewelry.

He could hear them now talking about what they'd do with the money, but he was shaking his head in the entryway of the old farmhouse they'd taken shelter in, a few miles from the ven Goleman estate. It had all gone wrong.

Sarken came lurching down the hall and stopped, catching sight of him in the shadows. He advanced past the lantern they'd hung on a rusting hook in the wall. "Something wrong, Cap'n?"

"It's not clean, Sarken. We're pirates, not arsonists."

His first mate frowned at him and stepped closer. "How's this any different?"

"The city guard's going to come down on us. Hard." It was a weak answer. It wasn't even what he was thinking, so he couldn't be sure why he said it.

"I'd like to see any city guard who could stand up against Rajana's magic." Sarken's voice practically dripped contempt. "You've gone soft."

"No."

"You could have that fine piece right now, the way she looks at you. What's wrong with you?"

He felt the little devil of rage sitting on his shoulder. "As a general rule, I prefer not to bed down with vengeful folk who league with devils."

Sarken snorted. "You need to relax, Cap'n. The men are happy. We're living well." Sarken encompassed their dilapidated plantation house with a sweeping gesture of his hands.

He could hear several men laughing it up in the dining room on the other side of the wall. Overhead, meanwhile, he heard low voices, and a grunt.

"I hope they kick the shit out of that writer," Sarken said. "You think Rajana will let me have a turn with the woman when they're done questioning her?"

"I don't think I'll let you have a turn with her," Ensara said, coolly.

"That's too bad." Sarken smiled. "Say, are you in charge still? While we're on land, I mean? Or is it Rajana? I mean . . . this was all her idea. The idea that's getting us paid. It sure as seven hells wasn't your idea."

"You want to cross blades with me, Sarken?" Ensara's hand dropped to hilt.

"Naw, Cap'n." Sarken showed gapped teeth in a confident smile. "Not right now. I just think maybe you ought to do some thinking. Maybe your 'principles' don't add up to much, gold-wise. Or crew-wise. Or woman-wise."

Sarken swaggered off down the hall and ventured into the dining room. His arrival was met with a roar of pleasure.

While Sarken stood framed in the doorway, greeted like a conquering hero, Ensara fought down the urge to drive a knife into his back. Hardly gentlemanly.

"Bloody hell," he whispered.

Hand still to his blade, he started down the hall. Without really planning his steps, he started up the creaking stairs to the second floor. On reaching the landing his eyes strayed immediately to the closed door where he could hear the woman's voice, and the man's answer.

That, he knew, was where Rajana and her creepy assistant were treating with the writer and his friend. Ensara frowned as he passed, and came to a door farther down the hall, where one of his men sat against the wall beside it with arms crossed. He was carving his initials into the floor with a knife by the light of a rusty lantern.

"Go," he said.

Bolvik stood, yawned, scratched under one sleeveless, tattooed arm, then considered Ensara. "Whatcha doin', Captain? I thought you said the woman was off limits."

"None of your damn business," Ensara snapped. It was a fair question, and he didn't have a lie ready.

Bolvik didn't like that, but he moved off toward the stairs, frowning.

Ensara picked up his lantern, turned the doorknob, and pushed open the door.

At one time this might have been a finely appointed bedroom, with splendid wall hangings. No doubt there had been a large wardrobe and dresser. Certainly the old frame would have had a mattress on it, not just a pile of sheets over the sagging frame. And probably, though he couldn't be certain, there had never been a bound and gagged woman lying in its center.

He hadn't been there when Rajana's man carried her here. He'd kept far away. Now he saw that staying far away didn't really inoculate him against the evil, because he should have stopped this.

He'd heard the expression "bound hand and foot" but he'd always imagined that meant tied at the ankles and wrists. Charlyn ven Goleman was practically clothed in rope. She'd been caught in her night shift, and so the ropes began at her bare ankles and wrapped up to the back of her knees. There was a gap there, and then another mass of tightly coiled ropes about her thighs.

Her arms were likewise secured to her sides and, as though there were not already rope enough tying her in place, her wrists were bound behind her back and then secured to her ankles. She had been blindfolded with torn white cloth and gagged with the same.

At the sound of his entrance she shifted helplessly, the whites of her soles wriggling, her hands twitching. She mumbled a protest into her gag and her tumble of dark hair shook.

At the sound of his tread her mumbles increased and she struggled violently, shaking the frame and accomplishing nothing.

That tore it. No way was he going to let his honor be stained by this woman's suffering. Ensara retreated, closed the door behind him, and set the lantern on the floor. "Shh," he cautioned. "I'm not going to hurt you." That, he thought, might be exactly what a rapist would say, and he scowled at himself. "I'm here to free you. Stop making so much noise."

She went silent at that, and he withdrew his knife. Charlyn struggled uselessly in the bonds. He didn't see how Narsian could possibly have assaulted her while she was wrapped like this, so he might have saved her from the worst of her captor's plans.

"Hold steady," he instructed her, quietly. From the room across the hall he heard a masculine shout of pain.

Charlyn held her wrists stiff, straining to keep the rope taut as he sliced through, careful not to touch her skin. Strangely, Narsian hadn't taken her bejeweled ring. Ivrian then cut the first of the chest ropes.

One slice there and the rest of the chest ropes fell away. He took off her gag and blindfold, and she squinted at him in wary surprise.

"You're one of the pirates," she said weakly.

"To my shame."

"Why are you helping me?"

"Because," he said, moving down to her ankles, "you deserve far better, m'lady."

A few slices and she was free below as well. Charlyn moved quickly to the headboard away from him, the bed creaking loudly, and rubbed her wrists.

"You're all right now," Ensara told her. "We can get you out that window there," he said. "The gods know we've got plenty of rope—"

"What about the others?"

"The others?" Ensara repeated, stupidly. After a moment he understood. "I don't think there's any hope for your writer and his friend. And we didn't get anyone else. Including your husband," he added quickly, "and sister. "

"What about Jekka?"

"The lizard man?"

"Yes."

"They were in the basement. If there's another way out, they might be okay. Otherwise someone's going to have to dig them free . . ."

"Then we'd best hurry.

He reached past her for the ropes, ignoring that she flinched from him. In the rooms below, his men laughed at something. He was betraying them. And what was he going to do, after? Head to the ship? His ship? He supposed there were enough men left aboard to crew her, and others could be hired.

He was going to cut and run, and leave Sarken and these fools here. Tell the others things hadn't worked out . . .

"You let them burn down my home," she said, her voice shaking. "My home. And everything in it."

"I didn't have any way to stop them without being killed—" He fell silent as she choked down a sob and wiped at her eyes.

"Let's just focus on getting you out of here," he said, and with deft hands set to finding the longest strands of rope and tying them together.

"Where's Ivrian?"

Ensara shook his head. "They're questioning him."

"You've got to free Lord Galanor."

"No," Ensara said.

"No?"

He sighed as he reached for another rope and knotted it. "Look, I would if I could. But I can't. Rajana—she's a Chelish wizard. If you read Ivrian's story you know how powerful she is. She and her . . . well, the man who tied you up, are questioning him right now." Best to keep her mind off of that. He nodded toward the shuttered window. "That goes out the back. We'll just lower down on these ropes and then we can get down—"

"You're coming with me?"

"I can't stay here," Ensara answered morosely. He finished knotting the rope, then crept over protesting floorboards and opened the shutters. One creaked faintly, and some dust dropped into his hand. He peered into the darkness, searching for the sentries he'd posted. He didn't see any, though he knew damned well he'd set one in that crumbling outbuilding to the left. Odds were they'd be watching the perimeter, not the house, and that they wouldn't notice two figures in the darkness against the building.

But then, odds weren't in Ensara's favor these days.

Outside, the steamy darkness of the tropical night greeted them, along with the bleating of frogs and the chittering of insects.

Ensara's hands were clumsy with his mounting nerves. This was taking too long. If Rajana wandered in to investigate, or if she were alerted by Sarken . . . He tied the escape rope to the bedframe and lowered it carefully so it didn't thud against the aged siding.

Charlyn looked frightened but determined as she climbed over the sill and grasped the rope, wincing as she scraped her arm. Ensara cringed as her body bumped against the building's side, making a soft thud.

He heard footsteps in the corridor.

She was down and out of sight. Ensara blew out the lantern and, his heart pounding, scrambled after her. Rope climbing was second nature to an old salt like himself, and he was halfway down in seconds.

"Hey!"

Someone was shouting from the window directly overhead. Sarken?

He dropped the rest of the way, stumbled, and grabbed his hat as it tumbled into the long grasses.

He spotted Charlyn moving through the darkness with exaggerated care, probably because she had the soft feet of a noblewoman and the ground was covered with dense clumps of weeds and thick grass.

"Hey!" Sarken called out. "The bitch got loose! Sentries, wake your asses up!"

There was movement in the shadow of the outbuilding.

Ensara caught up to Charlyn and effortlessly lifted her in one arm. She let out an indignant cry and slapped at his back.

"Stop that," Ensara snapped, and jogged deeper into the darkness.

But it was too late; he heard footsteps behind. With the woman slung over his shoulder, he ran, cursing softly.

"Why didn't you get me some shoes?" Charlyn asked.

Where was he supposed to have gotten shoes? He didn't feel like telling her he was just sort of making this up as he went. It wasn't until he'd seen her lying there helpless that he'd decided enough was enough, which she'd probably think reflected just as badly on him as everything else he'd already said.

"No time," he told her, and hurried on, fully conscious of the noise he made as he crashed through the low plants. The road was just a little farther on, but he pulled up short to listen beside a thick baobab tree, setting her down.

Sounds of the nearby jungle echoed through the night. There was some kind of hooting bird or mammal, the insistent hum of insects . . . and the shouts of the pirates who followed.

"Do you know what you're doing?" Charlyn asked.

"I can't say as I do," he said, rather testily, "but I could do with a little less criticism, if you don't mind."

He scooped her back up, blundered and tripped in the roots of a bush, and they both tumbled.

She cursed colorfully, and the sounds of the chase grew closer.

"Hide over there," he said gruffly. "I'll try to even this out." He looked around. "Actually, get over there and make some noise."

She slid away and before long was shaking the boughs of a nearby bush.

"They're over this way!" shouted thin-voiced Neshmer.

Ensara waited, steel held in the shadow of a tree so no moonlight could silver it.

Neshmer's squat body crashed out of the bushes. The other sentry, crookbacked Perken, was a few steps behind. Ensara waited for them both to pass. Even as Perken called for Neshmer to go left, he came up behind. Perken was starting to turn when Ensara caught him in the head with the pommel of his cutlass. He lay moaning.

"Perken?" Neshmer said. "Perken?"

And then Ensara had a sword to the man's back.

"Just drop the blade, Neshmer, and—"

But Neshmer whirled and slashed at Ensara's head.

Ensara threw up his sword to block, got tangled in the lower limbs of a tree branch.

Luck was with him, though, for Neshmer's own cut lodged in the same limb, and as he struggled to free it Ensara ran him through.

"Sorry about that, lad." He hadn't wanted to kill him, but he hadn't had any choice.

There was the crash of more brush behind him, and he heard Sarken calling.

"Ensara, I know you're out here! I know you let her go, you bastard!"

"Keep making noise," Ensara suggested softly, hoping Charlyn was still nearby. He slid off into the brush, looking for a better angle of attack.

Sarken was hurrying through the jungle, making all kinds of racket. Ensara tensed, waiting . . .

And then he heard the snap of a branch behind him.

Reflexes born of a dozen battles set him moving to the side as he turned, and that was all that saved him, for Sarken's overhead blow whipped through the space where his head had been just moments before.

How the hell had Sarken gotten behind him so fast?

"I knew you'd gone soft," Sarken said. "You want a woman so bad you turn your back on your mates?" He thrust at Ensara, driving him back.

Ensara kept clear, wary of Sarken's greater strength.

"She's a fine looking piece," Sarken continued, "but you could have had Rajana."

"I could have drunk poison, too." He dodged another swipe. "And that's what she is. That's what all this is, Sarken. We're sailors. Not murderers. Not kidnappers—"

"We're pirates, you stupid bastard!" Sarken hacked through intervening brush and motioned back Belvic. "He's mine. Just like the captaincy."

It was goggle-eyed Belvic who'd been making all the racket. Sarken had been using him as a decoy just as Ensara had used Charlyn.

"You're working with dark powers."

"What do I care?" Sarken demanded. "We're going to be rich, you dumb shit. You and all your airs. I put up with them because you used to have style. It gave us a reputation, like."

Ensara parried a broad swing. Sarken's massive strength almost tore the weapon from his grasp.

Ensara backed away.

"You've know this was coming for a long time. Face it."

He was forced back and back again. He bumped up against a branch with his arm, then grabbed it with his left hand as he retreated, pulling it back like a great bow. He let go just as Sarken advanced.

The larger man cursed as the limb slapped into his shoulder and Ensara followed up.

But Sarken caught the thrust, locked the blade, then punched Ensara in the face with his off hand.

The captain spun away, tripped, fell flat on his back. His sword sailed off into the darkness.

He knew he needed to rise, but there didn't seem to be enough energy in his legs to move him, or enough air in his lungs to breathe. And what was that distant shouting?

He heard the smile in Sarken's voice as the mate loomed over him, a darker shadow against the black jungle. "Nice knowing you—"

A scuffling sound and then a heavy *thunk* interrupted the first mate. Sarken grunted. Another blow, and Ensara felt liquid splatter down on his face and shirt and knew it for blood.

Sarken sank. Still fighting to regain his breath, Ensara scrambled out of the way, eyes lighting on a slim figure.

Charlyn stood over Sarken's body holding a sword in two hands. She breathed heavily. "The other one ran off when I cut him in the side. I barely hit him."

"Belvic always was a coward," he said weakly. "Good thinking," he added.

He bent to reach for his sword, only to find a long, sharp spear at his throat.

20

NET OF FIRE

IVRIAN

They told him everyone was dead.

He had no illusions that they meant anything better for him, but they'd kept him alive so far and had gone to the trouble to tie him to the half-rotted chair. Venthan still moaned sluggishly in the other one. The countess had tried to make the poor fellow scream three separate times, but he'd shown more mettle than Ivrian expected.

"I don't actually enjoy inflicting pain, Lord Galanor," Rajana was saying. "I just like answers. The problem is that I didn't ready enough spells for asking questions. I was prepared for combat."

"That sounds inconvenient," Ivrian said.

Narsian slapped him, and he rocked back in his chair. The man grinned into his eyes.

"You will speak only when I require an answer," she ordered. "Is that clear?"

Ivrian waited a moment, looking back and forth between the sadist and the wizard.

"You may speak," Rajana said, helpfully.

"Your man has made that abundantly clear, m'lady."

"How very nice. Let's not labor under any false apprehensions, Lord Galanor. I trust the pain I've inflicted upon your associate has proved my point? There will be no mercy if you do not cooperate."

"I see."

"I read your hand-pressed assemblage of paper and ink. I think I give it too much credit to describe it as a book. You assign motives without precedent, you tell rather than show, and you present information without due research." She paused to put her hands behind her back. "You knew nothing of me, but you referred to me as 'an aging beauty, sinister and malicious.' I bear no one malice, Lord Galanor, not even you. Not even your late friend, Mirian Raas. Emotional investment in any particular person or object is a waste of time. If you had bothered with any research, you might have learned that about me."

"When it's reprinted, I'll add footnotes."

Narsian smacked him again.

"No, let him speak."

Ivrian wondered what he should say. He couldn't imagine that Mirian and Jekka were truly dead, no matter the assurances from Rajana that they and Jeneta and Tradan were buried beneath the burning mansion, and that Rajana had personally collapsed the egress to the vault with a titanic spell.

Ivrian either needed to keep Rajana talking long enough for Mirian to free herself and come for him, or somehow suggest to the wizard he was more valuable alive. The latter, he thought, might actually be harder than the former.

"I didn't realize I'd been captured by a literary critic," he said, "but I do apologize." The words were bitter in his mouth, especially with Venthan sagging in the chair under the lantern, bleeding from his nose and mouth.

Ivrian forced calm. "You have to understand the market for which you write. My market demands a certain . . ." had his hands been free he would have waved them in the air, "melodramatic flair. If my taking of artistic license offended you, it was hardly my intent."

"I know you cared not a whit for my feelings, and I don't need an apology. What I want to know is whether you know anything in particular about the cones, and the eyes. My guess is no, and that I already have everything I need, but I do like to be careful. I hardly 'race unconsidered with vengeance seething in my breast.'"

If she could so easily quote his words about her, it suggested to Ivrian that the words had struck home far more than the woman was willing to admit. And there, then, lay his salvation, for he knew nothing about the accursed cones or eyes—whatever they were.

"I detect," he said, "a natural facility for language in you, m'lady. And despite present circumstances, I can't help but be impressed with your ability for memorization."

"Memorization comes easily to those who apply themselves to the magical arts." Did he imagine that her tone had softened just a modicum after his praise?

"Do you write your own spells? Do you set words to paper under your own name?"

"M'lady," Narsian interrupted, "he's stalling."

Bastard.

Rajana snapped at her subordinate. "I know very well what he's doing. Lord Galanor, do you take me for a fool with your attempt to distract me? You think I would want writing advice from one such as you?"

He thought that she might, though she was unwilling to admit it. He laughed shortly. "I know what I write isn't work for the ages. I've been working on something more along those lines, though I've a feeling I won't live to finish it. But I can tell you that I've spent years studying my betters."

"Such as?"

"Well, first among all is Ailson Kindler. Her writing is suffused with dark lyricism that I can't even hope to emulate."

"Ailson Kindler," the countess sniffed, "gets the details right."

"Oh, yes."

"I am speaking. You can tell when she writes of the blood-hungry dead and the phantoms and necromantic objects that she has encountered them firsthand. Whereas in your work . . . even though I'm well aware you witnessed some of the events you describe, the whole might as well be invented, so poorly do you describe it."

"Ouch. Well, you know what they say about critics, Countess."

"I do not."

"A critic," Ivrian said, forced to paraphrase, and quickly, for he couldn't remember the precise wording, "is someone who arrives at a battle after its conclusion and kills all the wounded."

"You find yourself unfairly accused."

"To what standard should I be held? A work should be judged by its intended purpose. Attack me for writing poorly if you will, but don't say I wrote poor comedy when I crafted a tragedy. Don't attack me for lack of agricultural details in my sea epic."

"Oh, you're a victim, are you?" Rajana asked with mock sympathy. "You have a sad tale of woe? Well, Lord Galanor, so does everybody." Her teeth shone. "You're nothing special."

"I know that," he said, though he'd rather hoped he might be a little special.

"It's good that you have no pretensions as to your own place and value."

He wasn't sure he had much more he could say to keep her talking. "M'lady, if I tell you what you wish to know, is there anything you can promise me apart from a swift death? Or will even that be painful?"

"I have no interest in either your life or death." Rajana brought up one gloved hand. "Save that if you are allowed to live, you will no doubt one day write more drivel about me."

"With Mirian dead, there's no incentive," he said. "No one would want to hear about a failed expedition. What's the fun in that?"

"You're taking your comrade's death rather easily. I thought yours was 'a friendship forged in the fires of turmoil and sacrifice.' Dreadful."

"Everything's exaggerated for effect."

"So what do you know?"

"I know a lot of things."

She sighed. "Narsian, show him what I do to people who waste my time."

Her assistant grinned, then stepped over to Venthan and casually sliced his throat.

Ivrian cried out in disbelief as the man rocked in pain. Blood spattered and Venthan produced a horrifying wet choking noise as he wobbled in his seat, finally falling to one side, the chair coming with him so that both lay in an expanding pool of blood.

Narsian laughed.

"Gods—what . . . why would you—heal him, m'lady! I know you can heal him! I'll tell you whatever you want to know!"

"Tell me and I will heal him. Speak!"

"I . . ."

"He doesn't know anything, Countess," Narsian said. "Or he'd have given it up right now."

"Too bad for you, Lord Galanor."

Venthan still kicked feebly. Ivrian was more angry than frightened, even though he could guess he was next.

Suddenly the door slammed open and a huge pirate leaned in. "The woman's escaped!" he shouted. "And the captain's in on it!"

Narsian tensed. Rajana's eyes narrowed.

"Go get her," she said. "And him. But be careful you don't try to frame him, Sarken. I happen to value the captain. I will be able to tell if you lie."

"I'm not lying," the pirate declared. "I saw him running into the jungle!"

"I will retrieve them both," Narsian volunteered.

Rajana faced him. "I know you intended on making the woman your new project, but I think Sarken can handle matters."

She looked once more to Sarken. "Get some men and solve the problem. But bring the captain alive."

"And the woman," Narsian added quickly.

Rajana's expression soured and she kept her eyes upon the pirate. "You do as you wish."

"Right away, m'lady." Sarken closed the door and shouted to his men as he pounded down the stairs.

Venthan was still, but Ivrian had seen those who looked just as bad brought back by a powerful spell or healing draught. In vain he looked to his captors. How could he plead with them when drawing their attention would likely result in his own death?

Rajana's voice to Narsian was like an icy whip. "You don't give the orders here!"

"Yes, m'lady."

"This is the second time in as many days you've overstepped your bounds! I think I rewarded you too quickly. I think I forgave you too soon!"

"No, m'lady." He licked his lips.

"It shall be a long road before you have my trust once more." She turned her attention once more to Ivrian. "It's difficult to find good help. But then your late employer had that issue herself. A wiser woman would have used better guards. And she would surely have used a better promotional agent." She stared a moment longer at him, sighed with distaste, and turned wearily to her sadistic adjutant. "Narsian, he has nothing I need. Kill him."

Ivrian steeled himself as Narsian bowed his head to the wizard. He didn't think he'd be greeting his mother in the afterlife so soon, and hoped Mirian and Jekka wouldn't be there with her. His eyes drifted to Venthan's body, noticed that the chair had mostly collapsed with the dead man's fall.

A desperate hope . . . As Narsian advanced, Ivrian threw himself to the side.

He heard the chair splinter beneath him. He took the brunt of the fall on his shoulder but rolled, the chair disintegrating further, and he came up in a crouch, tied now by one hand to the chair back.

"Father of lies!" Rajana spun on Narsian. "I thought you, of all people, could tie a proper knot!"

Narsian snarled. He lunged at Ivrian, then whirled at the sound of smashing timbers. A dark figure crashed through the shutters and landed on his feet. Rajana spun in surprise, but couldn't stop what looked like a burning coal tossed from the fellow's hand. It expanded into a net of fire which wrapped Narsian. The bodyguard screamed as he was webbed in flame.

Rajana threw a fiery globe of her own, but the shirtless, muscular intruder caught the seed of the spell in a black gauntlet and crushed his fingers around it. Instead of an explosion, only smoke rolled forth.

Narsian dropped, setting the floor aflame as he rolled, shrieking.

Rajana backed through the door and bolted away. Her heels rattled on the stairs as she hurried down.

The stranger contemplated the now-silent, burning corpse. Ivrian lifted the shattered remnant of the chair like a club. He'd never before seen a native like the stranger, with white facial paint that suggested a skull. The intruder padded forward on powerful bare legs, reached down to touch the fire net. It immediately collapsed into a glowing coal, which fastened itself to the palm of the gauntlet. The intruder waved hands over the flame as though stroking an animal, and the fire subsided to tiny winking flames before vanishing in a puff of smoke. There was no sign it had ever been—apart from the ghastly corpse and blackened floor planks.

From below came screams, an explosion, the clank of sword against sword. The smell of burned human flesh was thick in Ivrian's nostrils.

Yet he said nothing, did nothing but eye the native sorcerer. The man wore only a kiltlike green tribal loincloth and the ebon gauntlet—apart from those and his face paint, he was naked, and completely sheathed in muscle.

"So the colonials fight among themselves," the stranger said in a slow, thoughtful voice. His accent chewed consonants. "I think you are of the salvagers, yes?"

"I work for Mirian Raas," Ivrian answered.

"And you have fire in you. That is good. What did you tell them?"

"Nothing," Ivrian said.

The glowing coal in that strange gauntlet flared, and the stranger's teeth showed in a grin. "Your thoughts agree with your words. You are braver than you look. Such loyalty to a woman not of your race."

"She's my friend."

Again his nostrils flared.

Ivrian wondered if this was the man behind the Mzali attacks. Surely there wasn't another group interested in their doings. Even if he guessed right he saw no reason to assume hostilities. "I definitely owe you my thanks." He bowed his head. "I am Ivrian Galanor. Who are you?"

"I am Telamba, servant of the Great Walkena. And you owe me no thanks. I mean to drive you and your kind into the sea, or send you burning down to the devils you worship."

"You have me confused with the Chelaxians. I'm no devil worshiper."

Telamba grunted. If he did have a thought -reading spell working, he would have found confirmation in Ivrian's answer.

"Speak truth to me and live, then, Sargavan. Tell me what you know of the dragon's tear, and tell me what it is the Chelish woman wanted."

21

THE OPEN WINDOW

JEKKA

Jekka heard Charlyn's cry just as he was poised to plunge his spear under the captain's chin.

"Don't!" She threw up a hand. "He saved me!"

The man beneath him locked eyes but was still, save for his strained breathing.

He heard the sizzle of Mirian's wand and a scream abruptly cut off with a gurgle only a few yards to the right and knew she had dealt with someone else.

A human hand touched his shoulder, and he recognized by scent it was Charlyn Raas, who also smelled of sweat and fear.

"He freed me from the house, and then fought this one to protect me." She waved vaguely at the dead man nearby. "Jekka, they told me you were dead. Are Tradan and Mirian alive?"

"Yes."

She choked back a sob. "Praise the gods! And they're all right? What about Jeneta? Where are they?"

"Mirian is nearby. Jeneta is with Tradan. He was wounded, but will recover. They are summoning soldiers."

"How badly hurt is he?"

But Jekka had communicated all that was necessary about wounds, and was more concerned about understanding what to do with the fellow below him.

"Why did you help her, human?" Jekka hoped there wouldn't be a lengthy explanation. He wasn't in the mood for complications.

"They were going to hurt her," he said. "And I didn't think that was . . . gentlemanly. Do you mind if I stand?"

"Yes," Jekka answered.

"Gentlemanly." Mirian emerged from the brush, her voice hard. "You worried about being gentlemanly?"

Charlyn embraced her sister even as the captain answered, his eyes flicking to Mirian before returning to the spearpoint.

"I am, believe it or not," he said. "Events spiraled out of my control. I decided to do something about it before it got . . . worse."

Mirian disentangled herself from her sister, whispering that Tradan was going to be fine and that they'd talk in a moment. She stepped to Jekka's side and dropped a glow stone. Ensara flinched as it landed near his foot. The thick foliage touched him with sharp, leafy shadows.

"Thanks to you," Mirian told the captain, "things have already gotten pretty bad."

Ensara actually sounded pained. "I know. And I'm sorry about that."

Jekka looked to Mirian for guidance.

She was frowning. "What the hell's going on back there? All the shouting?"

"I don't know," Ensara admitted. "That didn't happen until after your sister and I got out."

"What about Ivrian?" Mirian asked, her tone sharply mocking. "Did you feel gentlemanly about him as well?"

"Rajana had him. And yes, I did . . . but there was no way I could pull him out of there. Not when Rajana and her assistant had him."

Mirian let out a mild oath. "Is he still alive?"

"I think he was when I left. Believe me, I would have freed him if I could have."

"It would have been nice if you'd had your attack of conscience a few weeks back," Mirian snapped.

"Mirian," Charlyn said, "he really did save me. Don't kill him."

At that, Jekka pulled the spearpoint back. It did seem that he would be sparing the captain, but he wished still to show him a threat display. "What of the eyes, and the book?"

Ensara didn't answer for a moment.

"Speak, Captain!"

"I don't know anything about a book! I swear it."

"They would have been cones." Mirian's voice was steely with impatience. "Lizardfolk book cones."

"Oh! Yes, Rajana had those."

"And there were some big jewels," Mirian said.

"Sorry. I didn't see them."

Again Mirian cursed.

"What do you wish, Sister?" Jekka asked.

She was silent for only a moment. "We've got to get Ivrian out of there. I'm just trying to decide how far to trust Ensara. Not real damned far."

"He fought through his own men to get me free," Charlyn volunteered.

"Probably to save his own skin," Mirian suggested.

"And hers," Ensara pointed out. "This is awkward, Mirian—"

"We are *not* on a first name basis, Captain. And I'm glad it's awkward."

"Fair enough, Captain Raas," he said smoothly. He slowly lifted his hands and Jekka tensed until he saw that he showed empty palms. "I apologize. I sincerely regret my actions. I fully intended to partner with you, and to return your wand—"

"Save the apologies! If you know the ground around the place you're holding Ivrian, take me there, otherwise I'll leave you for the jungle."

"Mirian!" Charlyn sounded shocked.

"He led people to your house! They burned it down and tried to kill us!"

Ensara closed his eyes, wincing. "Sorry about that. Look, I'll take you back to the ruined plantation. Give me a sword, and I'll even fight at your side."

Mirian snorted. "Keep an eye on him, Jekka. Charlyn, for your own safety I think you'll have to come with us. I can't leave you in the jungle alone."

"I understand."

Jekka pulled back and watched Ensara climb to his feet. He saw the captain glance to where a bloody blade lay in the brush only a couple of feet from where he'd knelt, but he made no move to pick it up. Likely he carried a knife or three on his person, and Jekka expected Mirian to say something about that.

But she didn't. "We've wasted enough time. Jekka, if there's any sign this bastard is getting ready to turn on us, stick him. Charlyn, take that sword."

"If you think so," she said. Her voice seemed a little shaky.

Ensara described the layout of the old plantation as they moved through the jungle. He whispered, although with all the distant shouting Jekka was fairly sure they could have been as loud as they wanted.

It was an abandoned home, overgrown by the jungle. It had two floors and two outbuildings on the south side where guards had been posted as lookouts. Upon closer examination, Jekka smelled Mzali, and informed Mirian.

"What's this all about?" Mirian's teeth gleamed as she turned on Ensara. "You're working with the Mzali?"

"No," Ensara protested. "Rajana's only been working with us. No natives."

Jekka readied to stab him until Charlyn spoke up. "There were no Mzali before," she said. "Just pirates."

Jekka watched his sister, who seemed to be thinking. Finally she said: "I suppose we might be lucky. If the Mzali really aren't in league with your people, they won't be expecting an attack themselves. Especially if they've just killed a bunch of your men."

Mirian instructed Charlyn to stay put. "If we don't come back, you need to hide in a tree bole. Soldiers should be here soon, so stay put and don't try anything heroic."

"I'll help," Ensara said. "Give me a sword. I swear by Irgal's axe I'll come through for you, or die trying."

"An axe?" Jekka repeated.

Mirian's gaze was almost blank as she faced Ensara. "You're honestly telling me that you're Nirmathi."

"Aye."

"A pirate. From Nirmathas. It's landlocked," she explained to Jekka.

"I swear," the man insisted with great fervor. "I have never lied to you, Mir . . . Captain."

"You've done a whole helluva lot worse."

"What I mean is that I keep my pledge. And a Nirmathi pledge by Irgal's axe—"

"I know," Mirian cut him off.

Jekka would have liked to have heard the rest, but since this little ceremony seemed to satisfy Mirian, he supposed it should satisfy him as well. They would get more pertinent details later. Unlike a lot of humans, Mirian didn't waste time with verbal reassurances and the repetition of information. It was one of many things he appreciated about her.

"Take Charlyn's sword," she said, with the same tone she usually reserved for cursing. She passed over her machete to her sister, then pointed a finger at Ensara, her voice a deadly whisper. "Remember I'm watching you, and I can burn your head off with my wand."

"I know." Ensara sounded indifferent.

"Our goal is to get Ivrian out alive. I happen to blame you for his predicament so if you go down saving him I won't be too upset."

"Understood."

"Where was he being held?"

"In the upper story. Around on the other side. That window there . . . well, you can't see, but that's how I got us out. I dropped a rope over the side. It's probably still there."

"All right. That's our way in. First, though, the sentries. If we have to make a lot of commotion we do it on the way out."

A brief survey showed them four men roving on this side and two at the front of the house.

Jekka crept forward in the darkness. He'd been the chief warrior of his clan, and his step was softer than the wind. The tribesman on guard heard nothing, felt nothing, before Jekka laid a scaled hand over his chin and cut his throat with a human dagger. He lowered him to the ground, then dropped down to all fours and crawled.

As he reached the side of the house, he spotted the rope, and an additional sentry in the shadows of the back door, standing on an open, half-rotted porch.

His elimination wasn't part of the original tactical plan, but he clearly couldn't be left there. Jekka slid closer, sprinted two steps to build up speed, and used his staff to spring onto the porch and land behind the warrior.

The man started in surprise and grabbed Jekka's shoulder with one strong hand, but Jekka thumped him in the head with his staff, then drove the knife up through his chest. Jekka watched him kick as he died, gasping, and wondered if he, too, would meet his end like this someday.

But now was not the time for those reflections. He returned to his original goal.

The rope was just where Ensara had described. Jekka signaled to Mirian, then watched as she and Ensara dashed over.

He left his staff in the care of his sister and started up. An expert climber, he had no trouble locating footholds in the vine-encrusted siding, and in mere moments he was peering into the room beyond. A human would have seen only darkness, but his eyes perceived the gray and silver outlines of the rotted furniture, the knotted rope stretched from the sill to the bed, the darkness of the doorway and the faint light behind.

He scrambled silently through the window, crouched, listening, and thought he heard Ivrian's voice. Good. He didn't want the writer dead.

He leaned out the window and waved an arm, caught the staff that Mirian tossed, then advanced to the room's doorway as she started up.

He heard the babble of human voices, though he didn't understand their words. Two men were speaking low-voiced in a fast-flowing language he didn't recognize.

He peered round the corner.

And that was his undoing, for two powerfully built native humans were conversing just inside the doorway, and one faced him. As Jekka readied his spear, he felt the thump of Mirian setting foot into the room behind, but also saw a glowing red object floating in one of the stranger's hands as the man turned toward him.

22

QUESTIONS FROM A DEATH MASK

JEKKA

Is there anything you can do for Venthan?" Ivrian heard the desperation in his voice, hoped it didn't sound too much like begging. The tribal warrior was unlikely to respect that. "I'll gladly tell you anything you wish to know so long as you help him—"

Telamba cut him off. "This one?" Telamba looked at the body and spat. "He took money for information. And you would save him?"

"What do you mean?" Ivrian looked at the limp body.

"He told us you were coming."

At Ivrian's look, the man laughed. "You think I lie, colonial? Why would I bother? He's dead and beyond my power, even if I cared. Our shared enemy does not make us allies."

"It could," Ivrian suggested.

"Drop the club."

He did, and it dangled from the rope still tied to his wrist.

The stranger grunted. "Tell me of the woman."

Ivrian glanced once more at the limp body of Tradan's assistant. All right, maybe he was dead, and he'd sold out Ivrian and his friends for money. And this Telamba had sent people to try to kidnap or kill Ivrian and his friends.

Yet if Ivrian was to live, and he definitely planned on that, he would have to meet this newest obstacle without flinching.

He faced the fellow squarely. "She's a noble of Cheliax, and she's sinister and treacherous." It pleased him only a little to parrot the words he'd already written of her, because he knew they'd made her angry. "She wants the dragon's tear for her own."

"How many men does she have?"

"In the house? Maybe a dozen. But it doesn't matter, because she's probably magicked herself away with the treasures you seek. She just about has to have a teleportation spell if she survived the first time we met."

"So you have faced her before?"

"Yes. I thought she was rotting at the bottom of a well in the Fortress of Fangs."

"Hah! So she is the type who leaves her men?"

"Yes. She has more."

"Where? And where would she go?"

"Probably back to the ship she's using."

Telamba backstepped to the doorway and shouted down the stairs in a flowing, melodic language Ivrian had never heard before. Someone below answered in the same tongue, then could be heard pounding up the stairs. He stood just out of sight, conversing with Telamba.

After a brief exchange, Telamba returned his attention to Ivrian. "You are right. It is reported that the woman vanished after setting three of my men to sleep. When Chakan awakened my sleeping men, they said she had taken jewels and silver cones. Were any of these the tear?"

"Just signposts to finding the tear," he answered, then added: "Maps."

"Your thoughts ring true." Telamba eyed him. "But I do not sense fear."

"The only thing I'm afraid of is that I won't be able to avenge my friends."

"So you're a warrior."

"Something like that." In truth, he was simply weary, sad, and powerless. He didn't think he stood any chance against Telamba and there didn't really seem to be a point to not telling him what he wanted. "What about the other prisoner?" Ivrian asked. "A woman. Have you freed her?"

"My men have found no other prisoner. Where is she?"

"In the room next door."

Telamba shook his head. "There was nothing there but a rope hanging from the window."

Ivrian brightened.

"So you think she escaped? Who was she?"

"The sister to Mirian Raas. An innocent in all this," he added quickly.

Telamba grunted.

Ivrian wondered if he'd said too much. Would Telamba hunt after her now?

Apparently Telamba didn't care, for his questions returned again to the dragon's tear. "What do you plan with the stone? You honestly did not know of its power. So why do you want it?"

"We seek the stone so that my friend, the lizard man, can return to his people through a gate in the sea."

"Your words make no sense. What gate in the sea?"

"That's where the tear lies, on the other side of a gate, in the midst of a city of the lizardfolk. It will be hard going."

"I shall find a way. You are a strange man. You speak the truth to me and do not fear. You seek the stone, but not for yourself."

"Jekka is my friend."

"And you name a half-Bas'o and a frillback as friend, and do not lie."

"Why would I?"

Telamba's quiet regard was sinister under the white skull paint. Yet his words were not. "I begin to like you, Sargavan."

For all that Telamba said that, there was no outward change in his demeanor. And Ivrian remembered just how brutally the Mzali had struck against the guards at Tradan's home. Still, he decided to risk asking a question of his own. "How do you even know about the tear?"

"It was foretold by Walkena." With his free hand, Telamba made a cryptic sign over his chest. "The tears of a dragon shall rain upon the coast. He sent me to look into matters and find the way to the tear so that our people have its mastery. And so we watched and listened for word of it." He glanced contemptuously toward Venthan. "We have many agents among your people converted to our cause, although some worship only money."

Ivrian was about to inquire further, but Chakan, lingering in the doorway, said something to Telamba, who replied curtly in his own language.

Chakan shouted suddenly in alarm. Telamba raised his gauntleted hand as though directing it at something beyond, in the hallway.

It was the only chance Ivrian was likely to get. He flipped the chair leg, still tied to his arm, up into his hand and charged as the coal floated upward and began to glow.

Ivrian slammed the chair leg down at the native's head.

Telamba sidestepped, his concentration disrupted so that the coal dropped back to the glove. Ivrian caught sight of Jekka's rush as the lizard man drove his spear into Chakan and pushed the dying man toward Telamba. The man in the skull paint backed toward the window even as Ivrian swung again.

Ivrian clipped Telamba's chin and the native staggered.

Telamba recovered swiftly, threw himself backward through the window.

Ivrian reached the sill just a moment after the lizard man, and was stunned to see the native land on the ground below with ease. Telamba raised his gauntlet.

"Back!" Ivrian dragged Jekka out of the way moments before the flaming net exploded across the window frame. The old wood immediately caught fire.

From the doorway came the sound of a familiar voice.

"Are you two all right?" Mirian asked.

Ivrian turned, smiling in relief, and noticed for the first time that his wrist stung from where it was still knotted to his makeshift club.

Mirian's eyes swept down to Venthan and then over to the blackened corpse of Narsian, disappointment and disgust flitting briefly across her features.

"Rajana's got the cone and the eyes," Ivrian said.

"And where is she?"

"Fled. Teleported, probably, if the Mzali are to be believed. They said she vanished."

Mirian turned for the door. The burning net had disappeared from the window, probably sucked back to Telamba's gauntlet. Red flames wreathed the window.

"The Mzali have a sorcerer or something, with a fire net," Ivrian said as he followed them through the doorway. He stopped short, for he saw Captain Ensara holding the landing at the top of the stairs against two natives, parrying thrust after thrust of their spears with his cutlass. A third warrior was scrambling up behind them.

Jekka leapt effortlessly over the balustrade, landing atop the third man and spearing him through the throat in the same fluid movement. He ducked a spear cast from somewhere below, freed his weapon from the twitching body, then dashed out of sight. Someone screamed.

Mirian's wand blast tore through the throat of one of Ensara's opponents, rattling the other so thoroughly that Ensara slashed him nearly in half.

"Let's go," Ensara breathed.

Ivrian was all for moving, and he ran with them into the room across the hall. Footsteps pounded on the stairs, but it was Jekka, narrowly avoiding a pair of spears, one of which stood quivering in the top step.

"Since when have we been working with him?" Ivrian thumbed to Ensara.

But no one had time to answer. Ensara reached the window and waved the others to follow. "Come on, come on!"

Jekka went through first, disdaining what Ivrian now saw was a rope and merely taking to the sill one-handed before dropping over.

"Down you go," Mirian said, then stopped to hold the door against another Mzali.

"Go on, lad," Ensara told him. "We came back for you."

Ivrian took the rope even as Ensara waded into the crowding natives. He started down, discovered he was a little more unsteady than he realized, and lost his grip on the rope. He slid for a foot or two, which burned his palms like hellfire, then let go, landing flat on his back and slamming his head into the ground. His vision swam. As Jekka leaned over him, he could have sworn the lizard man had a halo of fire. Somewhere there was even the distant ringing of trumpets, as though a choir of heavenly lizard men were welcoming them to the afterlife. Then he passed through a sea of painful black streaks shot through with starlight, and consciousness left him.

23

THE EYES AT THE BOTTOM OF THE SEA

MIRIAN

Tradan's voice was sharp with anger. "Tell me again why this man isn't in custody."

Mirian's glance slid from the aristocrat standing by the bulkhead over to Charlyn, sitting demurely now on the cushioned bench under the wide gallery window of Tradan's boat. Mirian could get used to a stern cabin this size, though this wallowing river yacht wasn't built for swift service like the *Daughter*.

The sun had risen some hours ago and now glowed on the horizon, just visible over her sister's shoulder.

Mirian looked over to Ensara, sitting at the ship's table across from Jekka, and she wasn't sure she had a good answer. Because he'd risked his life for Charlyn and held the stairs against their attackers? Perhaps that was balanced against everything else he'd done, but it hardly wiped the slate clean.

Tradan's eyes blazed out from a face pale from exhaustion and injury. "If he knows where this shipwreck is, then by the gods, beat the coordinates out of him and haul him off to jail!"

"It's not that simple," Mirian countered. "First—" She paused to glance over at the somber, laconic-looking captain, sitting in his faded finery. His hat had been lost somewhere in the jungle, but he retained a stained white silk shirt and a torn pair of breeches stuck into worn, calf-length black boots. "—he's cooperating fully, so there's no need to threaten him."

Tradan sighed in agitation.

"And," Mirian continued, "Captain Ensara thinks he knows where the lizardfolk ship ended up, but only approximately. If his first guess is wrong I want him there for other educated guesses. We've got a limited window."

"The gate can open only on the dawns immediately before, during, and after the full moon," Jekka explained. "If we're to reach the gate, we must recover the eyes from the shipwreck. And captain Ensara knows where it lies."

Tradan shook his head and kept shaking it. He held on to Ensara's guilt the way a dog worries a cloth scrap ripped from an intruder. Mirian understood: Tradan's house was burned to the ground, his servants assaulted, his guards slain, his chief assistant murdered, and his wife abducted.

Tradan still wasn't satisfied. "Even if this pirate's right, you said the seas beyond the gate were a maze, and you needed the chart. Rajana has that."

"Jekka's memory's practically flawless. He thinks he can remember the book cone's chart well enough to guide us through the maze beyond the gate."

"*Practically*," Tradan repeated. "Mirian, haven't enough lives been lost? Even if you can find this wreck, and even if your . . . friend's memory is as good as you say, who's to say how the lizard-folk on the other side of the portal will greet you? You saw what they did to the humans in the tomb. They arranged them like museum exhibits."

"They will listen to me," Jekka promised.

"Will they?" Charlyn had been quiet until then. Her voice came very softly, but carried a quiet power. "Can you be *sure* of that, Jekka?"

"My people will give me right of speech," Jekka explained. "They will hear from me that the humans are my kin and allies."

"How long has it been since they walled themselves off?" Charlyn asked. "Five hundred years?"

"Closer to two thousand," Tradan corrected.

His wife might not have known the precise date of Kutnaar's founding, but she knew her nation's history. She faced Jekka, speaking slowly. "Five hundred years ago, the Chelish Empire ruled the waves. Now many of its vassal nations have broken away and the center is rotten to the core with devil worship. It doesn't take very long for customs to change a great deal. They may not agree to hear you at all."

Jekka remained unfazed. "In the human world, perhaps. My people's customs remain the same."

Charlyn's voice was weary. "You do realize you'll be risking the lives of your sister and your friends, don't you, Jekka? Their survival is completely dependent upon your memory to get them through the maze, and your speech to convince the lizardfolk beyond."

Jekka's tongue flicked out, but he did not speak.

"You're forgetting one thing," Ensara said quietly. Everyone looked to him in surprise. "If Rajana gets her hands on that dragon's tear, it's going to be bad news for Sargava. And anyone else, really. She has to be stopped."

Tradan's face flushed. "How *dare* you! How dare you offer advice on the security of our nation! You're the one who put her on our path!" Tradan lifted clenched fists and started forward.

Mirian grabbed his wrist and Tradan angrily shook her off.

"He just wants his ship back," Mirian reminded her brother-in-law.

Ensara shook his head sadly. "I think my ship's gone."

"Good," Tradan snapped.

"Be that as it may," Mirian said, "the captain has a point about Rajana."

"Rajana surely does not have the power to take the tear from an entire island of my people," Jekka asserted.

"If they're still there in force," Mirian said. "Suppose they're not, or that they have no wizards? She'd wreak havoc among them."

From outside came a tentative knock.

"Yes?" Tradan answered gruffly.

"The ship's boat has pulled up alongside, m'lord."

Mirian had sent a messenger back to the *Daughter of the Mist* rather than taking her wounded and exhausted team back through the maze of docks. After arranging for an outrageous fee to the Rivermen's Guild to use her own vehicle, the boat must have maneuvered through the marsh to where the wealthy had their flat-bottomed river vehicles docked.

Tradan turned, still frowning, to his guests. "It looks as though this debate has ended. If you're determined upon your fool course, I can only wish you my very best." He sighed, and his tone softened. "I wish there were more I could do." He pointed a shaking hand at Ensara. "I will tell you that you should not trust him any farther than you can throw him. And you should probably throw him into the sea."

"We'll be keeping a close watch," Mirian assured him.

Jekka moved toward the door, and Ensara followed slowly, perhaps because he'd been on his feet for more than twenty-four hours.

Mirian caught Jekka's eye. "See that Jeneta and Ivrian are up and moving."

"Yes."

Charlyn came forward to put a hand to Tradan's arm. "I'd like a moment alone with my sister."

"Of course, my heart." Tradan smiled tightly to her, waited for Jekka and Ensara to exit, then bowed his head politely to Mirian and stepped into the bright sunlight. He closed the door behind him. He was a pompous racist, but he really did seem to love her sister.

It had been a very long night, and between the lengthy conversation with the guards and the lengthy trip to the riverboat, Mirian estimated she'd gotten less than two hours of sleep.

"Mirian." Charlyn patted the cushion beside her and Mirian came and took a seat, feeling strangely like she were being invited for a chat with her mother, even though Charlyn bore no resemblance to the Bas'o artisan who'd captured her father's heart.

Her sister's throat worked silently before she spoke. "Mirian, my mother is ailing and may not have much time left. My uncle is dead, and my grandparents. Our father is dead, and our brother is dead, and my children lie in the family plot." Charlyn reached out and clasped her hand, squeezing her fingers tightly. "Apart from my mother you're the only blood relative left, and I barely know you. But I know now that I *want* to know you. You're brave and decisive and clear-headed—everything I would want my own daughter to be . . ." Charlyn paused, briefly closed her eyes, and Mirian felt something give a little inside her.

"Even if I knew nothing about you," Charlyn managed, "I could judge your character by the company you keep."

Mirian pressed the small, cool hand between her own. "I wish I'd reached out to you sooner."

"We can look forward, not back. That's what your brother, Jekka, told me. I like him, Mirian. Very much." Charlyn's eyes sought hers. "But be careful. He's so eager to find his people that he doesn't see he's already found his family."

Mirian smiled weakly. The shot had gone home. "I relate to that."

"You will be careful?"

"I'm always careful."

"So I've seen," Charlyn said seriously, then squeezed her hand a final time and released it. "I will pray for you."

Mirian bowed her head in acknowledgment. "And I'll take comfort from that."

Charlyn nodded slowly. There looked to be something more she wished to say, but she seemed hesitant.

"Is there something else?"

Charlyn let out a long, slow sigh. "I killed a man today. To save the pirate captain."

"I know."

"You know?"

"I wasn't sure you wanted to talk about it."

"I'm not sure I do." Charlyn's tone had grown strained. Mirian clutched her sister's hand again, accidentally brushing against the ruby stone she wore.

"He was an evil man," Charlyn said weakly. "I know it. I heard him asking if he could have me, when the other man was done, and he said . . ." Charlyn shook her head. "Why do I feel bad that I killed him?"

"Because you're a good person. You saved Ensara. And if you hadn't saved Ensara, Jekka wouldn't have a chance of finding his home."

"I suppose that's true."

"I don't think you'll ever have to face that kind of dilemma again." She patted her sister's hand and released it.

"But it wasn't a dilemma. I didn't even think about it. That's what bothers me. I think I wanted to kill him."

"He had it coming, didn't he?"

"Is that what a priest would say?"

"It depends on the priest."

Charlyn smiled ever so slightly.

"You did what you had to do, Charlyn. I'd have done the same."

She nodded slowly. "How do you get used to killing?"

"It's not something you get ever get used to, but you have to be able to get past it. He was a bad man, and you had no other choice."

She nodded slowly. "I wish . . ." she shook her head. "I wish lots of things, Mirian. Most of all I wish that you and Jekka will come back to me. Please be safe."

Mirian reached for her sister and pressed her tight. She breathed in her scent, as she always did when she embraced her mother, and wondered why she'd never done this before. She resolved to do it more in the future.

Charlyn walked her to the door and touched her hand a final time, and then she left the single, large cabin and moved on across the deck. Tradan she found in conversation with Jeneta beside the railing, which surprised her more than a little. She overheard them as she drew close.

Tradan was mid sentence "—be able to thank you properly for all that you did."

Jeneta's answer was quiet and little formal. "It was my duty, as a priestess—"

"You saved my life," he said. "And I shall be eternally grateful. If there's anything I can ever do for you, you have only to ask."

Jeneta nodded once as Tradan continued speaking to her. "I want you to know that I overheard some of what my, uh, former assistant was saying to you about the Mzali, and what you said to him."

"Yes?" Jeneta's tone was icy.

"You did a fine job putting him in his place." Tradan cleared his throat. "It seems through no fault of the present generation that we are stuck with one another, and perhaps there's a better way forward than at each others' throats."

"Or with one of us as the other's servant."

Tradan blinked at his. "Quite. Although I don't know how to turn that around."

Jeneta spoke with quiet confidence. "There are native scholars you might partner with, m'lord. Young minds from both cultures might be enriched from your sponsorship."

Mirian added: "But you couldn't swoop in and tell them everything they're doing's wrong and that your way's the right way."

Tradan put a protesting hand to his breast. "Mirian, I would never."

It seemed likely to Mirian he would, but she couldn't be entirely sure. Tradan looked back again to Jeneta. "I'll give what you've said some thought, young woman. There's a fellow in Kalabuto I might reach out to. A native, I mean. He's doing some interesting work."

"That would be a start," Jeneta said.

"I'll do it." Tradan flashed Jenete a smile and then patted her shoulder, as he might a child. Mirian stifled a groan. At least he was trying to exceed his limitations. It was going to be a long road.

Tradan moved to stand at Charlyn's side as Mirian and Jeneta climbed down into the boat, and they called a final farewell as Mirian waved.

Bald, dark-skinned Gombe grinned at her as she set her boot on the rower's bench. "Got your message, Cap'n! Pirates. Bloodthirsty natives with fire nets. And I see my cousin has kept everyone alive and is still looking her finest. Just like me."

Homely Gombe was ever ready to make fun of his own appearance. Mirian was happy to see him, but too tired to enjoy any jests. "Let's get underway."

"Aye, Cap'n. You heard her, lads."

With that, they pulled away from the expensive yacht that would be her sister's home until arrangements were settled upon for a new apartment. The mansion itself would be rebuilt eventually, but for now, for peace of mind, Charlyn and Tradan were staying in more familiar quarters.

"Smartly, boys," Gombe said. "We don't have all day."

There was a lot of traffic along the docks, and Mirian found herself searching the anchored boats and the barges of the rivermen for the faces of Telamba and Rajana. Absurd, she realized, to even think they would reveal themselves.

"The *Daughter*'s shipshape?" she asked Gombe.

"Assuredly, Captain. You haven't been gone *that* long!"

She supposed they hadn't been, although it felt like a lifetime. And gods, she was tired. Almost as tired as Ivrian still looked. He'd claimed that he heard angelic trumpets after he smacked his head during his rescue. The trumpet blasts had been the sound of cavalry sent from Port Freedom against the pirates.

As they headed into the reedy river channels, she leaned toward the writer. "How are you holding up?"

He smiled cheerfully back at her. "Just fine, Captain."

"You lie so well I almost believe you."

"Nothing a little rest won't cure." Ivrian's expressive face grew more somber and he brushed at the sleeve of his borrowed shirt. "There's something that's been troubling me, Mirian. Venthan informed on us."

"Did he?"

"The Mzali sorcerer, Telamba, refused to help him because he was their informer. I guess they used him but didn't respect him."

Mirian was so tired she almost told him that people reaped what they sowed, which wouldn't exactly have given Ivrian the solace he was after. "I suppose if he hadn't spied for them, the Mzali wouldn't have turned up, and then it would have been a lot harder extricating you alive."

"Huh. I guess you're right. Why do you think he did it?"

"There's no telling. They might have threatened him." Since the Port Freedom healers hadn't been able to revive him, even after Tradan donated generously to the local temple of Iomedae, she supposed they'd never know.

Gombe chattered a little, trying to raise their spirits, but sensing their mood, the second mate eventually lapsed into silence.

The hot sun on her face, the rhythmic creak of the oars, and the slap of the water was soothing. Mirian wanted, more than anything, to close her eyes and rest just as Ivrian decided to do. He sat low, his head lolling against Jeneta's thigh. The priestess smiled contentedly down at him, surreptitiously stroking his hair.

Mirian started. There was no missing the tender, protective look in the healer's eyes. In a sudden crash of insight she considered

Ivrian's chiseled chin and striking features, his flashy dress, and way with words. She recalled just how young the priestess truly was.

Mirian suppressed a groan. Seventeen was the perfect age to fall head over heels in love with the wrong person. How could Ivrian be letting her—

Mirian's thought died in midstream. Judging by the gentle rise and fall of Ivrian's chest, he wasn't letting her do anything. The writer was deep asleep.

Mirian would have to have a talk with her. Later, though. She was so tired.

It would have been so easy to lean back against the bench, but instead she held her breath from time to time, or rubbed her eyes, or hummed softly—any trick to stay conscious. Dozens of ships anchored at the makeshift moorings beyond the river's mouth, and as they passed, faces peered down from the decks and stern gallery windows. Who could say which among them might be leagued with Rajana or Telamba?

Rajana, at least, was probably already well away, but that didn't mean she might not have paid someone to make trouble for them. No, she realized, Rajana seemed to have thought them all dead. That's what Ivrian had told her, at least. She shook her head. That didn't mean she wouldn't take precautions.

Mirian was relieved when they final pulled up alongside the *Daughter*. She stiffened her back and feigned energy she lacked as she hurried up the ladder. Once upon the weather deck, she formally greeted Rendak. The sturdy first mate gave her a fierce hug before turning to help the others aboard.

Shortly thereafter, Ivrian had been set up in the tiny mate's cabin and Ensara had been introduced for a second time to the scowling Rendak. Jekka, Mirian and Ensara then went with the first mate to the cabin, where Mirian pulled out the precious undersea charts drawn from generations of salvaging.

Jekka watched, blinking rarely. Outside, Gombe could be heard getting the ship underway. They had no precise heading yet, but Mirian had given orders to sail north toward Smuggler's Shiv.

"Well?" Rendak growled.

Ensara wiped his eyes and stared down at the chart. "I've never seen one with sounding depths this precise. Not beyond the shallows."

"Generations of my family have been salvaging Desperation Bay. We've kept notes." Mirian tapped a light mark she'd drawn on the chart. "This is approximately where we found the wreck."

Ensara peered at the mark, then the numbers indicating nearby depths. Finally, he touched the paper with a grubby fingernail. "Here."

"Kellicam's Trench?"

Halfway between Smuggler's Shiv and the Kaava Peninsula a finger of deep ocean thrust into Desperation Bay—one of such dark depths that her family had never felt especially compelled to explore it. It was indicated as a thin slash across the chart, stretching west to east. Her great-grandmother's precise handwriting labeled it in several places as "unknown."

"You sure it's not this trench?" Mirian tapped an underwater sinkhole only a half league south.

Ensara rubbed his short beard and his dark eyes glinted mischievously. "Is that where you want it to be?"

"It's not as deep," Rendak said. "We've touched bottom there. Only Mirian—or someone else with the rings—could get to the bottom in Kellicam's Trench. Maybe. It's very, very deep."

"I'm not sure how deep the drop-off was," Ensara said. "The wreck was heading over when the three of us swam clear."

"And the creature was still aboard?" Jekka asked.

"It was still eating my men," Ensara answered grimly. "If it hadn't been distracted by its meal, the three of us could never have gotten out. Now, it might be in your sinkhole, because it was hard to know exactly where we came up. But I think . . ."he paused to drag his finger over to the trench, "that we were here." Again his eyes looked to Mirian's. "My ship was heading north by northeast when they heard us calling."

She nodded.

Ensara sounded more tentative. "Incidentally, why lead us down to be ambushed and then pull me out of the way?"

"I didn't know the monster was there," Mirian said.

A smile twitched at his mouth. "Really."

"I swear."

"So you really were going to strike a bargain with me," he mused.

"No—I was determined to find a way out. You'd threatened to sell my people into slavery."

The light in his eyes dimmed.

"What did you expect?" she asked.

"If you wanted a surprise, why did you save me?"

"I still haven't figured that out. Why'd you chop through that boggard instead of me?"

Ensara glanced over at Rendak, but found no welcome in either his gaze or the eyes of the lizard man. "I figured I'd made things bad enough for you already," he said. "I swear by the gods, Mirian—"

"Captain," she corrected.

"Captain," he said wearily. "I was going to send that wand back to you with a note of apology."

"Were you. Until someone offered you money for it?"

"It got complicated! I saved your sister!"

"After you helped burn down her house!"

"I didn't give those orders! That was Rajana. By that time she was in charge, and my first mate was planning mutiny because he saw me chop through that boggard who was coming for you!"

"So it's *my* fault you got in over your head?"

"I never said that!"

Rendak cleared his throat. "So, Captain, what's our heading?"

Mirian sighed and pulled herself together. "Kellicam's Trench. I hope you know what you're talking about, Ensara, because we don't have a lot of spare time."

"I just hope that thing isn't still on the ship," he said.

"I don't plan to go aboard. I just need access to the jewels set in the prow."

"You want me to put him in irons?" Rendak asked.

So far as she knew there were no irons on the ship. She guessed Rendak was being metaphorical. "No. He's as flagged as the rest of us. Get him some grub and then let him bed down. But he's to be kept under guard."

"You want me to waste manpower keeping a man watching him the whole time?"

"You've been able to trust me so far," Ensara said.

Mirian snorted in derision.

He turned up empty palms. "Look, what do you think I'll do? I want to stop Rajana as much as you."

"What about after?" Rendak asked him.

"I haven't figured that out yet."

Rendak's dark eyes fastened on Mirian. "What do we do with him then?"

"I guess I haven't figured that out yet myself. It depends upon how he comports himself."

"Right now I just want to comport myself to a hammock."

Mirian stared hard at Ensara. "Your word, as a gentleman . . ." She tried not to sound too mocking. ". . . that you'll not try anything?"

"My word," he said, with great, sad dignity, "on Irgal's axe."

Rendak rolled his eyes, but Mirian knew Ensara believed in his own pledge. "You heard me, Rendak. Feed him and bed him down. When he wakes, put him to work."

"You really think—"

"I'm too tired to think. Just do it. Don't wake me until we get there unless there's a sea monster or a pirate fleet bearing down on us."

"Aye, Captain. Come on, you scrub." He motioned Ensara after him.

Mirian rose on tired legs and made for her bunk. Jekka, though, still hadn't left. He'd remained strangely silent throughout the conference.

"Shouldn't you grab some sleep as well?" she suggested.

"Mirian." He stepped closer.

"Yes?" She paused at the bunk side, turned, and sat down on it to pull off her boots. Gods, a good wash would be fabulous. A bath would take too much energy, but a nice cold cup of water she could rub over her face would be wonderful. She guessed what he was after. "I wish we could stop and get Kalina, Jekka, but if we're to reach the island before Rajana we just don't have time."

"I know that. What if there's no one there?"

She dragged her mind away from thoughts of clean water. "You mean on your island? Kutnaar?"

"Yes."

"Why wouldn't they be there?"

"Why haven't they ever come back? Tradan asked that, and he is right. My people are curious. Wouldn't they have returned from time to time, to look around?"

"Maybe they have and they've been careful about it."

"Then why didn't they contact any of us?"

Why was he dragging this out? Wasn't he tired? "You said that your people were scattered. Maybe they came out from Kutnaar and couldn't find them."

"Yes," Jekka said, his voice trailing off slowly.

"Is there something else? Because if you take too much longer saying it, I'm liable to fall asleep sitting up."

"No, my sister."

He started to turn away, and she felt a little pang of guilt.

"I don't know what we'll find, Jekka. But we'll find it together, all right?"

"Yes."

Sleep enveloped her like a soft, hearth-warmed blanket on a chilly evening. She knew no dreams, only surprise when Rendak set a hand on her shoulder.

Light in the cabin was dim, but he held a lantern near his bearded face so she'd recognize him.

"We're at the anchor point," he said softly, "just shy of the drop coordinates. How are you feeling?"

She sat up, stifling a groan, and stretched. She felt dirty. She'd be in the water soon enough, but what she really wanted was a hot bath with perfumed soaps. "Awake," she said. "Any trouble?"

"Nothing. A little mist on the waters near the shore. Some storm clouds are scudding in from the south but they don't seem headed our way."

She nodded understanding. Rendak backed away to hang the lantern from the hook on a ceiling joist, and Mirian swung out of the bunk. "I suppose I'd best eat."

"We've got a fine oyster stew and some fair bread and cheese waiting your pleasure."

She set feet to the planks. "Thanks. You think we're doing the right thing trying to get through this gate, Rendak?"

"You mean do I think you're guiding us into the right thing?"

"Yes. Usually it's just you and me and Gombe taking the risks—"

"Now that's not true, Captain. We all take risks anytime we go to sea. There's no telling when a storm will drift down, or when a ship on the horizon will turn out to be a pirate. And besides, think of the payoff if we get through."

"Will there be a payoff, Rendak? Jekka thinks he can get us through the maze if we can get through the gate. All right, I trust his memory. But can he really keep us from getting killed outright by the other lizardfolk?"

"Those are fair questions. I'm glad I'm not the captain."

"Thanks," she said dryly. "I just can't help wondering if this is too big for us."

"Meaning?"

"Maybe we should turn this one over to the Custodian of Sargava. Let him send in a fleet."

Rendak grunted as he sat down beside her. "There's all kinds of problems with that, the first being you can just about guarantee you'd be starting a war, even with Jekka on board. The lizardfolk on the other side won't take kindly to a fleet, will they?"

"All right," she acceded grudgingly.

"Second, it'll take too long. We've got one night before the full moon, and you know that Chelish wizard's going to get there first. There's no way you could muster the Sargavan navy and get them into position before her—"

"We might—"

"—and you want to be the first." He grinned at her. "And you know what's best for Jekka. If this is his homeland, a place of safety for his people, do you really want the Sargavan fleet knowing how to get in and out?"

"No." And that brought up another worry. "What if there *is* no way out?"

"Now nothing that he found said that, did it?"

"What if he never wants to come back out?"

"Now we get to it." Rendak nodded slowly. "If it's a safe haven for him, why would he want to? I know your oath to him and all that . . . and I'm fond of him myself. He's good in a pinch. But when the time comes, you'll have to let him go."

"You sound like my father when my dog got old."

"Well, it's kind of like that, isn't it?

"Jekka's not a pet," she said sharply.

"No, but he's not human. And as much as he loves you—and I think he does, mind—he wants his own kind. And I don't just mean Kalina. Hell, how'd you feel, trapped in a swampland with your cousin and a bunch of lizardfolk? There'd be no men around, not even a good-looking pirate bastard like Ensara. There'd be no children. You'd never—"

She felt a flush touch her cheeks. "I get the analogy, Rendak."

"Well. There you go, then."

"So. We're doing it for glory."

"Right."

"For our nation."

"Right—can't risk that Chelish wench getting hold of that magical doodad."

"And for my brother. My brother, the lizard man."

"I've met a lot of humans I valued less."

She nodded, then decided to make a point. "I don't think Ensara's attractive, by the way."

"No?"

"He's handsome, but there's nothing there."

"I'm glad you made that clear." He smirked.

She wagged a finger at him. "Now you're mocking me. Just because someone's handsome doesn't mean I'm interested in them. Besides, I seem to remember you mooning over someone just a few days ago like a moonstruck boy."

"If you're referring to the astonishing Djenba, I was the soul of discretion."

She laughed.

"I was!" Rendak put a hand to his chest, as if wounded. "What a woman."

"All right, loverboy. Get me some of that oyster stew. And then it's time for a drop."

24

A FRIEND BELOW

MIRIAN

Rendak insisted upon joining the dive, even after Mirian reminded him it might be too deep for him to reach with just an air bottle.

"Jekka and I can keep watch above you," he said stubbornly.

And so he slipped overboard with Jekka and Mirian and Ivrian. If she'd let him, Gombe would have come along as well. Instead, she left him in command and had Jekka shoulder Gombe's air bottle so he wouldn't have to keep surfacing.

Ivrian still had dark circles beneath his eyes, but he assured her he was fit and ready. And, no matter that Gombe and Rendak were seasoned divers, next to her, Ivrian had the most experience working with the magic rings. With them, the writer would be the only one beside herself capable of diving deep.

The nighttime ocean again provided a magical light show. Schools of blue-and-green jellyfish pulsed as they drifted along, trailing strands of tentacles many times longer than their translucent bodies.

Mirian led them deeper and deeper, seeking the ocean floor. Once she saw the waving tendrils of seaweed stirred by a cool current, she diverted north, glow stone shining on her chest.

Rendak swam to her left, tube leading back to the air bottle in the pack on his shoulder, and beside him, Ivrian. Both men wore tight-fitting pants and short-sleeved shirts. Rendak carried a short spear and Ivrian, now that he wore the twin to Mirian's ring allowing free movement underwater, a sword. He carried his wand in a holster strapped to his hip.

Jekka swam on her right. She'd grown used to having him there, at her side. What would it be like without him?

The drop-off into the trench loomed suddenly out of the gloom, a yawning darkness that swallowed light. She hovered in the cool water. The glow stone only touched the coral and anemones along the closest edge. Tiny points of color gleamed below, like distant stars, but there was no knowing if these were luminous fish, or the lures of strange predators of the deep.

She led them east along the rim of the trench. She hoped to find a track left in the ocean floor by the shipwreck's passage, and they fanned out along the rim to seek it, each staying within ten feet of their nearest companion.

They almost missed the signs, as the ship had skipped along the bottom, sometimes touching, sometimes drifting. If they hadn't doubled back to look at the seafloor eighty feet back from the edge, they would never have discovered the path of chaos stretched through the sandy bottom.

Mirian shined her glow stone into the depths, but it didn't show her anything. The darkness was so intense the light fell off only five feet out.

How deep did the trench go? Beyond a certain level Jekka and Rendak could not accompany, since the pressure would be too great.

Mirian led them over the edge and down, taking care to keep a few feet clear of the wall. She played her light along the side, searching always for holes and crevices.

Jekka dove beside her, his own glow stone piercing the depths ahead. Ivrian followed, his magical fins glowing brilliantly like Mirian's. Rendak brought up the rear.

The lights each bore were a fragile, illusory comfort. There was always some worry with a salvage drop, but Mirian's was tripled in this enveloping darkness. She hadn't felt this kind of apprehension since her first dive, long years ago. And well did she remember her grandmother's warnings never to risk a deep dive, even if the family magics made it possible. There was too much, she'd warned, that lived in the deep dark and was fearless of humans.

They swam farther and farther down. Their light reflected from a pair of wide green eyes that quickly withdrew into a crevice. A curious bullnose shark swam near, attracted by the glow, but swam on when Jekka swished his tail threateningly.

Finally Rendak surged up to touch her calf. When she turned to look at him, he held his hand before his glow stone, signaling that he needed to rise. He'd reached his limit.

Mirian, protected as she was by the ring, felt only a hint of the pressure she knew must be compressing his chest. She pointed him up. Rendak grabbed Ivrian's shoulder, pointed at Mirian, then kicked up. He was warning the writer to keep an eye on her. Apparently he didn't think it necessary to do the same with Jekka.

Mirian checked in with her blood brother. The lizard man pulled his air tube into his narrow mouth, sucked in a gulp, then signaled his readiness.

How much deeper could he go?

They descended another ten feet, and then twenty before her light caught on something promising farther below—it looked like a tree shorn of leaves, standing canted away from the side of the trench. A ship's mast?

A few feet further down she confirmed it. She glanced at Jekka, then saw him signaling—he too had reached his limit.

She motioned for him to retreat, looked back overhead to the glimmer of light that was Rendak's glow stone, and pointed Jekka up toward him.

So it was up to her and Ivrian. Even with him swimming at her side, she felt honest fear. Except for the narrow circle of light, the darkness completely encompassed her. Anything might lie beyond her narrow range of vision.

She tried not to think about that. Focus on the task at hand, her father had told her.

The wreck's stern had scraped against rock that had torn the beautiful railing away. Mirian swam over the deck of the ship and the yawning mouth to the stairway where the devilfish had laired, and felt a chill entirely different from that of the cold water surrounding them. Still, she debated again about trying to remove the strange gear that had sent the ship on its underwater journey. Unlocking the secrets of that magical propulsion unit could advance naval technology by tremendous bounds . . . but that was not why they'd come. Not today.

Swimming toward the prow, she found the ship hadn't actually come to rest on the bottom, but was suspended on a projection of rock outthrust from the wall, its prow jutting over the darkness of the trench.

She carefully inspected the trench wall and found it blank. That didn't mean something might not be crawling or floating along five feet to her left or right, but it gave her the illusion of security. Certainly it would feel safer trying to pry out the eye on this side of the ship than while floating unprotected over the abyss. She touched Ivrian's shoulder, then indicated the darkness.

He gave her a thumbs-up and turned, sword at the ready, floating only a few feet away from her.

There was no trouble finding the gleam of the violet ship's eye, set high along the prow in the starboard side, for it reflected the brilliant white of her glow stone. She hoped that its different color didn't indicate a different function. Those they'd found in the tomb of Reklaniss were onyx.

Once she scraped the scum completely clear with her gloves, she saw the great gem was seated in a brass fitting bolted to the ship's dark hull. If she was merely after the gem itself, she could pry it free, but then she'd have to worry about constructing a makeshift holder. Better, then, to remove the entire assembly. She reached carefully into her pack of tools.

Even with Ivrian watching, she had the terrible sense something was creeping up from the dark void on her right. She ignored it and worked carefully with a small pry bar. The ancient bolts were anchored more securely in the old wood than she would ever have guessed. Just as the first came free, a flash from above her right shoulder set her heart pounding.

But it was Jekka, drifting down. He used hand signals to ask if they were all right. She signaled that she was, and then he quickly retreated.

With the first bolt clear, the bracket now hung down from the bow of the vessel. After a little more work the rest of the mounting popped free, and it was only her quick reflexes that kept it from drifting off to her right and into the abyss.

She stowed the gem in her pack and then, alert to the spread of darkness, swam to the port side of the prow and the other eye.

Ivrian swam just before her. His rings, like Mirian's, imbued him with glowing fins and gills, which illuminated the hull. He hung in the darkness like a beacon, constantly shifting his position to peer into the enveloping gloom.

She turned to the prow and worked quickly. In only a few moments she had the portside ship's eye partly free. She was finishing with the second and final bolt when something flashed in the corner of her vision. She jerked around to see Ivrian moving swiftly toward the ship.

No—he wasn't moving under his own power. A tentacle had dragged him up and out of sight.

Her blood chilled. The devilfish still prowled the wreck.

She shoved the second great jewel in her pack and swam after her friend.

As soon as she rose, a long, hook-lined tentacle swept streamed past her face, missing her ear by a cat's whisker. She found the creature's bulbous body rooted to the prow, where it crouched spiderlike, its baleful blue eyes glowing dully. How long had it been watching them? It must have swum up from the hold, alerted by her noisy work with the bolts.

So far as Mirian knew, devilfish normally grew no larger than horse-sized, but this thing must have been ancient, for it was half again as large, with ten-foot-long tentacles. Three were now wrapped around Ivrian. The creature drew him in even as he hacked with his sword. A tentacle snared his weapon arm, making it impossible for him to aim his wand. The creature rose up to reveal its pale underside. A beak emerged, clacking eagerly for Ivrian's flesh.

Revulsion and fear rose up so strongly within her. Every sense beat at her to swim fast and far away. She surprised herself when she kicked toward the thing.

The same tentacle that had struck toward her reached again, but this time it met her sword's edge. The limb withdrew in a billow of dark fluids and another shot toward her. Mirian felt the hooks of the tentacle bite into her leg. Pain like a dozen knives ripped at her calf and she lashed out, skinning a long, deep line of flesh off the rubbery tentacle.

The thing released her as though prodded by a hot poker. It relinquished Ivrian as well and squirted out a thick cloud of the blackest ink. This swiftly concealed everything, including the beast's glowing blue eyes and Ivrian's magics.

"Surface!" Mirian shouted, although she had little hope Ivrian could hear her. She kicked, hard, heart slamming her rib cage. At any moment she expected to feel those coils wrap her and pull her toward that rending beak.

In vain she searched for Ivrian and the beast even as she swam free of the murky cloud.

She swam up and up, looking for Ivrian. Hadn't he made it clear? *What if it had trapped him in the ink? What if he were dying right now, being devoured within that terrible cloud?* She slowed, peering at the billowing blacker darkness that hung within the depths.

The thing exploded out of the cloud, four tentacles lancing at her.

Mirian screamed as she brought up her sword, the sound dulled. She pivoted left and evaded one reaching tendril, but a second grabbed her arm. The hooks dug deep and she groaned even as a third grabbed the same leg as before. The beast dragged her toward the open beak and she brought her sword in line, gritting her teeth against the pain.

A green bolt of energy lashed past her and struck the creature's underside.

Ivrian had fired the wand at last.

The blazing green light bubbled and sizzled and smoked along the monster's skin even as Jekka's spear drove through the monster's body.

Still it wasn't finished. The arm about Mirian's leg tightened and her vision dimmed with the pain as she jabbed at the beak. She felt her weapon pierce flesh but was whipped around so quickly by a flailing tentacle that she couldn't see where she'd struck. Another green bolt struck the thing's body and then Rendak was beside her, his dark hair billowing behind him as he sliced at the tentacle holding her.

The creature released her at last, fleeing in a spasm of tentacles. The last she saw of the thing as it descended in the darkness was of a green glowing blotch of the acidic magic eating away at its side, four of its arms leaking blood.

They started up, keeping close, and Mirian was so startled it was all she could do to hold back and keep pace with the others. More than anything, she wanted to be out and away from the waters. She was in pain, yes, but it was blind, mortal fear that held her closest. Even knowing the devilfish was far too wounded to pursue them was no solace. She doubted she'd ever forget the way it had swept out of the black ink toward her, tentacles grasping while that beak gnashed hungrily . . .

It was then she noticed Rendak lagging. She turned her glow stone on him and saw he had one arm to his chest. Had he been hurt?

There didn't seem to be a scratch on him. Mirian's fears for herself suddenly vanished. Rendak had risen too quickly. Diving with air bottles was always a trick. Even an experienced salvager like Rendak could make a mistake, and mistakes down here could be fatal. If you didn't release enough air from your lungs as you swam up, pressure could build, and burst them.

Rendak moved only feebly as she and Jekka reached him, and he seemed very pale in the light of the glow stone. His lips moved, soundless.

They tipped him backward and kicked with him toward the surface. Mirian knew that if the air sucked in from the bottle at this high-pressure depth remained inside it would expand and kill him.

And so she did what normally would have been unthinkable—she opened his mouth and cocked back his head so that the air trapped would not explode his lungs as they swam higher. She just hoped it hadn't happened already.

Jekka kept watch as they swam on and up. Protected as she was by the ancient magics, she could sense the lessening pressures only feebly. With the waters so dark, it was hard to know for certain when they neared the surface. It seemed an impossibly long time. Rendak moved only feebly in her arms and then, more ominously, went still.

Finally, they broke the surface and breathed clean, cold air. The sky was dark above, and stars glittered through drifting clouds.

Ivrian surfaced beside her. "Is he all right?"

She was too busy digging the brass stopper out of her healing potion with her teeth to answer him. They hadn't had time to reequip, but she'd taken Gombe's on the dive.

Please stay with me, Rendak, she prayed. Jeneta could save him. She wasn't as skilled as old Tokello, but she could heal him . . .

She supported Rendak by his back and neck as Jekka's reptilian head broke the water nearby.

"I'll find the ship, Mirian," Jekka said.

She poured the potion down Rendak's throat. "Come on!" She urged. "Come on!"

But Rendak didn't move.

25

REVELATIONS

IVRIAN

Ivrian hated being helpless. As he stood in the captain's cabin, his mind turned without any great interest toward the things he should be doing. Making journal entries, for one. There were a lot of details to record. Yet it had grown harder to put a romantic slant upon anything. He was used to exaggeration and embellishment, but now that he was involved personally in the adventure, it was hard to justify placing himself in any kind of heroic role, especially in their latest series of encounters. All he'd done was manage to get himself captured or injured, although he supposed he'd been some help with that monster from the deep.

He'd not been as badly injured as Mirian supposed. Not nearly as badly as poor Rendak. Jeneta's finest ministrations had barely roused him, and the first mate was resting, pale and shrunken, on Mirian's cabin bunk. Mirian was medicating with a bottle of wine while consulting with a worn-looking Jeneta, who'd just finished helping them bandage their wounds. After all the care she'd administered to Rendak, she'd had no magical energies left to tend the savage injuries the tentacles had inflicted upon them.

"There's nothing more I can do," Jeneta said. "I must rest and pray before I can treat anyone else. I'm sorry," she added.

Mirian winced as she leaned forward to offer the younger woman the bottle of rum, but Jeneta shook her head. "That stuff leaves a sour taste in my mouth."

"Thank you," Mirian said.

"I wish I could have done more." Jeneta departed with a forlorn, backward glance at Ivrian, who forced a smile, hoping to encourage her.

She brightened and left.

Ivrian resumed pacing. His leg stung, but it hurt more when he sat still.

"You sure you don't want to sit down?" Mirian sounded irritated.

Before he could answer there was a rap on the door.

"Enter," Mirian said.

Gombe poked in his head, almost comically mournful. "How is he?"

"Alive. And sleeping."

Gombe stepped over to look down at his friend. He bowed his head, and after a moment Ivrian realized the second mate was praying quietly. He'd never heard the man express the remotest religious sentiment, even though his cousin and uncle were in the priesthood.

Gombe had left the door open, and a moment later Jekka slipped through, followed closely by Ensara.

"The panels are secured, my sister," Jekka said. "And this one said he's a master helmsman." He pointed his hand at Ensara.

Mirian glanced over to Rendak, then frowned. Ivrian had seen several of the crew man the helm over the months, though Rendak seemed to take it by default. He was certainly in no shape to do so tonight.

"A master, eh?" Mirian said. She stared, hard, then quaffed another drink.

"We should be underway," Jekka continued. "The others have a head start."

Jekka might not have many facial expressions, but Ivrian couldn't help noticing his frill was taut and red spots had appeared along his neck. Ensara looked like a man hoping for a stay of execution.

Mirian sighed. "All right, you damned pirate. Take the wheel and steer wherever Jekka guides you. Gombe, get us underway—every inch of canvas we can raise. There's still a chance we can beat the pirates there."

"Yes, Captain," the two men said at once. Ensara seemed to think better of adding more, and left on the heels of the second mate. He closed the door behind him.

"Wine, Jekka?" Mirian pushed the bottle across the table toward him.

His tongue slipped out, but he didn't advance. "What's wrong, my sister?"

"It's been a trying few days."

Jekka cocked his head to one side, then swiveled it over to the form huddled under the dark stern gallery window. He stepped over on his long, scaled feet and peered down at Rendak. "He will recover?"

"Probably."

Ivrian heard a sailor shout that the anchor was up, heard the rumble of feet on the deck as Gombe ordered sails spread.

Jekka stepped over to the table and took the proffered drink. He tipped it far back into his mouth, then set it down and stared unblinking at Mirian.

"Mirian," he said finally, "we should stop this quest. I will live with you, and be your brother. I wish no more of your clan that is not a clan to be endangered. I have seen a clan perish before. Kalina would agree with me. We will look elsewhere."

Ivrian smiled sadly. This wasn't what Jekka wanted, at all, but he had grown cognizant enough of human expressions to recognize Mirian's, and to guess why she was so upset.

"My friend," Mirian said stiffly. "My brother. It's no longer about what you wish. I'll be *damned* if I'm going to let Rajana get anywhere near that dragon's tear."

"My people won't let them take it."

"I'm going to do my damnedest to make sure your people don't ever have to see them," she said, though how she meant to accomplish that Ivrian couldn't guess. "We've risked too much now to end this."

"If that's your wish," Jekka said.

"Yes. Now go out there and keep your eye on Ensara."

"You don't trust him."

"Do you?"

"I don't think he plans to wreck us."

"No. And I don't think he has some clever plan for betraying us, either. But I still don't trust him, and neither should you."

"Of course." He lowered his head to her with a swift, birdlike bob, then exited. The door clicked shut behind him.

"Should I go?" Ivrian asked. "Do you need to rest?"

"I'll probably grab some shut-eye in Rendak's cabin," she said. "But there's one little thing." She sighed, pushed back in the chair, and stretched a leg. "These wounds still sting. I hope Jeneta can tend us one more time before we have to do anything else."

"Me too."

Mirian cleared her throat. "Have a seat."

Very strange. Ivrian pulled out the chair nearest her and sank into it, conscious now that the *Daughter of the Mist* was underway. He couldn't help thinking that if they'd invested in a larger ship, they wouldn't now be worried about running into Ensara's old pirate vessel. They'd have extra warriors and weapons aboard should it come down to combat.

Mirian's dark eyes were intent upon his. "We have a small problem that might interfere with the way the crew works, and you're involved."

"Me?" Ivrian's mind raced. "If it's that I didn't keep a sharp enough eye—"

"No," she said quickly. "You're an asset to the team. I'm talking about Jeneta."

He repeated her name, stupidly. "Jeneta? How am I—"

"She's in love with you. Or she thinks she is."

He chuckled in disbelief. "What makes you say that?"

"Because I've seen the way she tends you, and looks at you when she thinks you're not paying attention."

He blinked in astonishment. "But she's . . . I'm . . ."

"I know. She's very young."

"Well, yes. I mean, even if I were interested, she'd be too young, wouldn't she?"

"You only have five years on her."

"But can't she tell I'm not interested in women?"

Mirian smiled tiredly. "She's a lovestruck girl. She's probably more worried that you're rich and . . ." she hesitated, ". . . a colonial."

"Well." Ivrian couldn't think of anything more to say. It wasn't as if they actually spent that much time together. "I don't even know her that well. How could she be in love?"

"Look at it from her side. Everything she's seen of you has been impressive."

He laughed. "I've managed to get myself captured, and injured, and—"

"And you leap selflessly into danger, are cool under fire, are sharp-eyed enough to detect an ambush, and in a matter of months rose to become one of her most trusted friends. *And*," she added, "you've a way with words. That's always appealing, especially if you're successful at it. Throw in the mystique of you being from another culture, and—"

"—we might as well be doomed lovers from a stage play."

"Exactly."

"Except that I've no interest in her."

"Which feeds into many a young person's fantasy, doesn't it?"

Ivrian sighed and put a hand to his forehead. "That's definitely a problem." Ivrian massaged his forehead and looked down at where the bandage around his leg bulged under his leggings. "Should I speak to her when she wakes up?"

Mirian shook her head. "No. I'll handle that. I just think you should be aware of it so you don't accidentally encourage her."

"I wouldn't!"

"I know you wouldn't on purpose. But remember when you rested against her on the boat ride?"

"Gods," Ivrian groaned. "All right. Is there anything else?"

"Yes." She pushed the bottle toward him. "Help me finish this damned thing. I hate drinking alone."

26

THE VEIL

JEKKA

The simplest part of the task had been affixing the ancient metal plates to the ship's prow. The chief carpenter and bosun managed it in less than a quarter hour. Now Jekka stood near the helm, eyeing a dark horizon lit by flashes of lightning. A misty rain typical of the region was washing down, a cooling spray that left them a wind strong enough they crowded their masts with canvas.

"She handles well," Ensara said quietly. It was the first thing he'd said to Jekka since he'd taken the wheel.

He didn't know how to answer.

"She's got a narrow profile and sleek lines. Good for short, quick runs, I expect."

"Useful for outrunning pirates," Jekka said.

Ensara glanced at him.

"So . . . this fellow that's wounded. Mir— The captain's taking it pretty hard."

"He is like clan to her."

"That's too bad."

"He is first mate. Perhaps you understand."

"Ah. My first mate tried to kill me yesterday."

Jekka didn't care. "You can maintain the heading?"

"Aye. Everyone knows where the Lizard Kings reefs lie. So . . . is this fellow the captain's lover?"

Now Jekka glared at Ensara, and he felt his frill rise. Ensara seemed to understand what that meant, for Jekka smelled fear on him.

"Is that your business, pirate?"

"I don't guess it is—"

He hissed. "You wish to mate with Mirian?"

"I . . . I just wanted to be her friend. Maybe buy her a drink." He looked off at the lightning.

"If not for my sister's sister," Jekka told him, "I would have left you bleeding in the dirt. Spare me your words. We are not friends. We are not clan."

"Sail ho!" the bosun shouted.

"Where away?" Ensara called aloft.

The answer was swift in coming. "One point off starboard!"

There was a thump, the sound of footfalls, and the cabin door swung open. Mirian emerged onto the deck. "What ship?"

"Looked like a three-master, Captain," the bosun cried.

"On this heading," Ensara said, "it's got to be Rajana. On *my* ship."

"You may be right," Mirian said, and her eyes swept up to consider the masts. "Gombe! I want all reefed sails drawing full! I thought I made that clear!"

The second mate came running from somewhere aft.

"Yes, Captain. I was afraid we'd part a shroud—"

"We're not at gale strength," Mirian said. "The *Daughter*'s masts will hold. Shake the reefs! Full sail!"

"Aye, Cap'n. You heard her, lads! Slow and steady, though. One hand for yourself, one for the ship!"

The crew scrambled into the ratlines.

"She's a good ship, Captain," Ensara ventured. "I like how she handles."

"Who's left to manage your old ship, Ensara?" Mirian asked.

"The third mate. He's only fair, but my sailmaster's got a good head on his shoulders. They might be a little shorthanded, unless they picked up some more crew."

"Probably not," Mirian guessed. "They're in as much of a hurry as we are. You think there's any chance of us catching her?"

"We might," Ensara said. "She's overdue for careening. But her holds are empty. And she can fly a lot more canvas than the *Daughter*. Not to mention Rajana might throw spells to keep her moving."

"I don't think Rajana's that sort of wizard. Although you never know."

They followed the ship through the long hours, at first only seeing the *Marvel* as lightning slashed down, but then the squall blew out and the stars peeped out from behind the curtain of clouds, and they could see the *Marvel*'s outline as they slowly gained.

In the sky behind them still loomed a mass of dark clouds.

Finally, in the predawn light, the lookout reported sight of the reef chain known as the Lizard Kings. In ancient times, Jekka's forebears had carved huge images of lizardfolk into the towering rocks. Time and tide had worn them down and dulled the details, but the brooding heads still rose above the sea, and the coming dawn outlined their frilled silhouettes. So sharp were the rocks around them that ships usually gave them a wide berth. Not Ensara's vessel, though. It veered two points to port and headed straight on.

"They're going to tear out their keel, aren't they?" Ensara asked him.

Jekka hissed. He hoped they would. And yet, as he held the lizardfolk compass he saw that the *Marvel*'s heading was dead-on.

If the ship crashed, it meant there was no gate and everything had been for naught. And as much as he wanted to find the gate,

Jekka felt a strange sense of relief at the thought it might be closed. He couldn't explain why, even to himself.

Just as he thought the *Marvel* was done for, a blue-gray mist formed between two of the great stone images. Bright red lights blossomed in the cavities of their eye sockets.

"I'll be damned," Ensara breathed. "There's nothing back of that but sharp rocks."

"No," Jekka told him. "That is the Veil, raised by the sight of the old kings, who have given their return gaze to the ship. That is the gate in the sea, to the island of my people." He looked down to the compass, now glowing from within. "Mirian, they will reach there first."

"Sail ho!"

This time the call came from Caligan, upon the stern. As one, Ensara and Mirian called: "Where away?"

"Aft, two points to starboard," came the answer.

Mirian faced the man at the wheel, her voice low. "I'll thank you, Ensara, to let me answer the lookout aboard my ship."

"Apologies, Captain. Old habits." He tried a smile.

Jekka saw Mirian hurry aft, but he couldn't tear his eyes from the *Marvel* as its prow struck that line of blue mist. He fully expected to hear the gut-wrenching din of the ship smashing on the rocks that lay just beyond, and to see its stern swing and twist dizzily as it struck, but then the vessel passed beyond, as through a curtain.

And into another world. The world of his people.

27

INTO THE MIST

MIRIAN

She raised her spyglass and discovered a high three-master bearing down on them fast.

"How," she asked long-limbed Caligan, the sailmaster, "did you miss her? She had to be coming up on us for hours!"

"She came out of the squall behind us, Captain!"

Mirian steadied her arm with her other hand as she searched the deck. She didn't recognize the ship—it looked like a typical south-seas rig with Sargavan lines, but . . .

There, along the rail, stood a native warrior, his own glass winking at the dawn.

Mirian cursed. "It's the damned Mzali. He must have a sea witch!" She frowned. They might have to recruit one of their own from now on. Jeneta was a healer, not an elemental magic worker.

She studied the pursuer, then twisted round the spyglass to consider the lizard statues. The *Marvel* was gone, and the veil that had lifted between the two largest statues had vanished with it. Now there were only the great carved rocks and the reef that lay beyond them, jagged as shark's teeth in the dawn. And less than a quarter hour away, at their speed. The question was whether they'd arrive before their enemy caught them.

"Jekka." She stepped to her brother. "How long an opening do we have?"

"I don't understand."

"You told me we could only cross at dawn. How long is 'dawn'?"

"Until the sun stands a hand's height above the water."

That wasn't an especially precise guideline. It depended upon the size of the hand, not to mention the length of the arm. Mirian looked to Ensara. "You think we can reach those reefs before that?"

"Aye, just. If that other ship doesn't catch us. But if we're going in full speed, and the eyes don't work, we won't be able to turn. We'll break into kindling."

He was right. "I'd planned to ease in, but the best laid plans . . . Can you keep a steady hand?"

"Aye."

"I can't have you turning off—"

"I'm in till the end with you, Captain. I at least owe you that."

"Damned right you do," she said, though she regretted it a little. His did seem a steady hand, steadier at least than that of Gombe, who always preferred working aloft to the helm.

Ensara swung them a point to starboard. Just as Mirian opened her mouth to correct him, he steadied his hands on the wheel. He had an instinctive feel for the ship and its limitations.

For all that, she would still rather have had Rendak there.

"Cap'n," Caligan called from the stern, "those bastards are closing, fast!"

The sun had climbed halfway up over the distant spread of the Sargavan coast, a crescent of blinding crimson and gold.

The great statues of the Lizard Kings loomed like malevolent spectres, more than a dozen of them, their mouths wide as if they longed for a banquet of broken timber. Jekka stared once more at the compass, pointing unerringly between the two largest. She saw the spray on the rocks just beyond them.

There was no longer need for a spyglass, for their pursuer loomed huge only a few ship-lengths back. If the newcomer had ballistae, the *Daughter* was done for.

But then Mirian realized the ship probably had no intention of sinking them. It probably meant to close and ride through on their tail. How else could it get through without eyes on its prow?

"Ivrian!" she called, and soon the slim, well-dressed lord stood beside her. He still looked haggard and pale. "Take the wand and make things difficult for them. Aim for the waterline."

He grinned. "Aye, Cap'n."

She hoped the pursuers wouldn't be throwing any spells of their own. Hopefully their sea witch was busy keeping wind in the sails. Hopefully Telamba couldn't throw a flaming net several ship-lengths. But then, if they meant to ride through after them, they wouldn't be trying to sink the ship.

She hurried back to Ensara. He and the crew in the rigging stared as one at the great Lizard Kings and the reefs beyond them. "Steady as she goes, Ensara!"

"How close do I get before their eyes catch fire?" he asked Jekka.

The lizard man was so intent on his compass that he didn't hear him.

"Close as you have to," Mirian answered.

She looked back to the stern rail where Ivrian was leveling his wand. He fired once, twice. Emerald bolts struck their pursuer's planks above the foaming bow wake.

Then he changed his aim and blew a hole through the mainsail.

This provoked immediate shouting, for the fist-sized bolt of acid instantly ate a widening hole. The sail tore and sailors rushed to fight the flapping canvas. The ship fell back.

"Archers!" a voice screamed from the other ship, and a line of men converged upon the larger ship's foredeck. Mirian rushed back to consult with Ivrian, watching as the archers drew back on their bows.

Ivrian's eyes were wide. "Damn."

"Shoot first!" Mirian cried. There wasn't time to explain that archers were unlikely to aim well. Not only did they have to shoot around their own bowsprit, their ship and their target were constantly moving.

"Captain!" It was Ensara. "It's not working!"

One of the archers dropped, screaming, as Ivrian's shot went home. The archers looked more like mercenaries than natives. They scattered as Ivrian fired a second time. Telamba screamed at them to hold position.

Mirian might have grinned, except when she reached the wheel she saw Ensara was right. The *Daughter*'s prow slid closer and closer to the gap between the central statues. They were a ship-length out now. What if Jekka, in his eagerness, was wrong? What if they'd missed their window and the gateway wouldn't open because the sun was too high, or what if only one ship could pass through each day? They'd be smashed against the rocks.

Ensara gripped the wheel with white knuckles. Jekka stood stiff beside him.

"Maybe the eyes on our ship weren't placed right," Ensara said. "Did you polish them? Maybe they were out of magic."

"Shut up," Mirian snapped. "Steady as she goes."

There was no longer room to turn. The waves crashed against the titanic statues. Were they real giant lizards, they might have reached down to smash the ship.

"My sister," Jekka began.

And then the eyes in the great statues bloomed with scarlet light and a vast curtain of glowing blue mist spread before them.

A moment later, the bowsprit touched the Veil and passed through. Gombe and the front half of the ship vanished within. Mirian's jaw clenched as she suddenly knew an altogether different kind of fear. Suppose that it wasn't really a proper gate at all, but just a death trap?

"Are you ready, my sister?" Jekka asked her.

Mirian looked to Jekka just as the mist struck them. "I'm ready, my brother."

And they passed through.

28

ROUGH PASSAGE

MIRIAN

Shifting mist surrounded them on every side, alive with tendrils of glowing light so thick Mirian could barely see past the ship's rails. She shouted for sails to be reefed and men scrambled up the lines to ease the sails and drop their speed. "Gombe, drop a line and give me depth!"

"Captain," Ensara said, "the ship's sluggish."

"Explain," she snapped.

"It just doesn't feel right," he answered. "The wheel has too much play."

"Best figure it out, Ensara," Mirian said. "Jekka, did those books say anything about this mist?"

"It said a sea of mists lay beyond the Veil."

That's what he'd said earlier. Only now was she realizing she had assumed she knew what that meant.

She couldn't see Gombe, but there was no missing the worry in his voice as he called to her from the prow. "I don't think there's water down there, Captain! My line's not hitting anything—not water, not land beneath! We're sailing on the mist!"

Ensara's shocked look would have been comical if she hadn't felt the same way.

A pinnacle of rock rose along the port beam.

"Our first landmark," Jekka said. "Prepare to bear to port."

"How do I do that if we're floating on mist?" Ensara asked. "No wonder she feels weird!"

"Give it a shake and see how much play you have," Mirian suggested.

Ensara spun the wheel and the ship shifted slightly. So whatever was keeping them afloat at least responded a *little* like water. Another worry came to her. If that ship was right behind them, could it have made it through before the Veil closed?

"Ivrian," Mirian called back. "Did our pursuers come through with us?"

"I can't see them," the answer floated back. But then, he wouldn't be able to see far.

"Bear to port three degrees," Jekka said, and Mirian shouted for the crew to adjust the sails accordingly.

"Port, aye." Ensara turned the wheel and the ship heeled.

"Easy, easy," Mirian said.

"Sorry. Overcompensated for the extra play."

"Look to starboard," Jekka said.

An immense, round object the size of the *Daughter* materialized in the mist, resolving itself into a great lizardfolk head carved from green marble and studded with emeralds. The sailors marveled with one another.

"Eyes forward!" Mirian shouted.

"Another nears," Jekka said.

They came upon a second head, just as large, this one with open maw. It had been decorated with gold and glittering bits of stone that sparkled like glass. The slitted eyes of the thing were immense rubies.

They drifted past. One ship-length, two—

"Starboard five points," Jekka ordered. His voice was level, controlled, as if he had done this a hundred times. Mirian called to the crew to adjust sails once more.

"Starboard five points, aye," Ensara answered, and spun the wheel. The ship creaked, heeled, turned. "We're definitely not on waves. I'm not meeting much resistance at all."

"Just as long as we keep floating.

"Be warned," Jekka said. "We're about to hit the first of the three currents."

"All hands clap on!" Mirian shouted, and just in time, for the *Daughter* shuddered. The ship pitched forward, borne by unseen energies.

She heard Jekka counting quietly, methodically beside her, as though he had no care in the world. At eight he said, "Port twenty degrees!"

Ensara echoed the command, shifting the *Daughter*, and they blew past a reef that reached, clawlike, from starboard. A moment later they heard a rending crash, and a host of screams from somewhere aft.

"Ivrian?" Mirian called. Whatever that was sounded too far away for the *Daughter*.

"I think that was Telamba's ship," Ivrian called back.

Mirian found a tight-lipped smile on her face. The screams continued, as did the sound of smashing timbers.

The current seemed to have slowed. Nothing was visible but tendrils of mist glowing with green and blue energies. About them all was quiet save for a rising wind, like the wail of forgotten souls.

The ship lurched heavily to starboard. Mirian grabbed Jekka's arm to steady herself.

The ship rocked, battered by a surge from port.

"We are halfway," Jekka said to her questioning glance. "Ensara, ten points to starboard. We are approaching the inner circle and the last current."

Once again the pirate captain repeated Jekka's order. "Standing by."

"Gods preserve us!" Ivrian's plea mixed with colorful curses and even a series of male screams as the shattered hulk of a ship tumbled end over end in the mist directly aft, borne by some errant current in the swirling mist.

"Starboard!" Mirian cried.

Ensara scrambled with the wheel. What Mirian had taken for a ship was but the front third of one, shattered, trailing broken timber and bits of line. Incredibly, living men clung to the wreckage.

"Straighten us out," Jekka cried. "We can't miss the next current—"

"If I straighten us, we'll hit them!" Ensara objected.

"If we don't, we'll sail off course!"

"You heard him, man!" Mirian ordered

Ensara groaned, swung the wheel as the hulk tumbled past their port side. "I think we might just ma—"

The ship shivered as the wreck brushed their port rail. The *Daughter* lurched further to starboard.

A figure leapt from the heaving deck before it was swept away. He landed in a crouch beside the rail and immediately stood. He was tall, muscular, and dressed in an emerald loincloth, his dark face painted with the white lines of a skull. He raised his gloved hand. From Ivrian's description, she knew him immediately for Telamba.

Mirian ripped her cutlass free and charged him.

Her blade caught in Telamba's gauntlet before the red glow in its center spread. Her strike broke the spell but didn't cut the glove or even the warrior, though it forced him back. He snarled into her face.

"We're clear!" Gombe shouted from the prow, and suddenly they burst into bright daylight. The ship's deck heeled dangerously. Mirian couldn't help lurching away from Telamba, who steadied himself at the rail.

"No," Jekka cried. "Port, Ensara! Port!"

"She's not answering!"

"It's too soon!" Jekka shouted. "We're supposed to turn port—"

Mirian caught only a brief impression of what lay ahead: a vast wall of glowing mist circling beyond a tiny island covered in thick greenery and red-leafed trees. Ancient domed buildings poked up through a forest canopy. A ship rested peacefully against a long, narrow dock.

And the ocean lay sixty feet below the prow.

Telamba flipped himself backward and overboard, arcing over the water with beautiful form. She couldn't see if or how he landed.

For a second the *Daughter* hung half out of the mist, above the waves. Ensara struggled vainly with the wheel.

"Hold for your lives!" Mirian screamed. "Brace for impact!" She sheathed her cutlass and grabbed the rail. The crew shouted in fear, and the *Daughter* dropped.

Mirian's stomach dropped with it. There was a seemingly endless moment of expectation as time unspooled.

The jolt tore Mirian from the rail and flipped her onto the planking. Her breath was knocked away and waves tumbled over the deck. Someone up front let out a moan of pain and the ship rocked and lurched. A huge hunk of timber cracked. The bowsprit? The forward mast?

Her eyes raked the vessel's prow. "Jeneta, see to the wounded! Gombe, check for damage!"

She climbed to her feet to survey the damage even as the second mate reported that the spritsails were gone by the board.

"Cut 'em loose," Mirian ordered, and found her spyglass. She scanned first for Telamba, but found no sign of him. Then she turned her attention to the ship at the dock a half league off and was stunned to see Ensara's vessel there. How had it arrived so far in advance of them?

She made out a handful of figures along her rail, pointing at them.

She stepped over to Ensara. He wiped blood from his face but doggedly manned his post.

With any luck the majority of the pirate crew would be ashore, which would give them the advantage of numbers.

"Furl the sails, and bring us in alongside," Mirian said. "Caligan, grab every spare hand, arm them, and line the starboard rail!"

"Aye, Cap'n."

Ensara steered the *Daughter* toward the crescent-shaped harbor. Great stone walls, overgrown with vines, trailed from a vast complex of domed buildings of various widths. Her first thought was that the lizardfolk had incorporated the very jungle into their city, as they had with the water in the settlement she'd visited with Jekka and his clan only a few months before.

But judging from the damage roots and vines had done to the stonework, this had gone untended for centuries. She looked to Jekka, saw his mouth opening, saw his frill rise, fall, rise again. His color darkened.

"I don't . . . what has happened, my sister?"

Were he human she would have clutched his shoulder. All she could do was slowly shake her head.

The city's greatest buildings rose to multistoried, balconied heights draped in red-and-green plant growth. Long tongues of stone extended into the sea.

Mirian made a speaking trumpet with her hands as they closed on Ensara's ship. "Ahoy, *Marvel*! Surrender and stand by for boarding!"

The sailors on deck crowded together in hurried conference. One of them pointed repeatedly toward the men with swords ranged along the *Daughter*'s rail.

Finally one waved a white cloth over his head and stepped to the rail. "We surrender!" He quickly slung the cloth around in a circle.

"Throw down your arms," Mirian called, "and step back!"

She and Jekka led the way over, followed by most of their crew, with the exception of Ensara, Gombe, and Ivrian, the latter keeping watch with his wand.

A thorough search of the vessel turned up only a dozen frightened sailors. Their bosun was the highest-ranking crew member left aboard.

"Where's everyone else?" Mirian demanded.

"Up there." The pockmarked man pointed to the central hill in the city, and the domed temple atop it. The bosun supplied more details. "The wizard woman went in a day and a half ago."

"A day and a half?" Mirian wondered if the man was drunk. "You're yanking my chain."

"I swear by Besmara's sweet tits," the fellow said. "We don't want any trouble. We didn't want to go into the city after the first men didn't come back, but . . . the woman went to investigate with more of us." The fellow licked his lips. "They didn't come back either. We haven't left the ship since."

"It is said that time flows differently here," Jekka explained. "But I thought it was metaphorical."

He might have mentioned that part earlier. But then, maybe both of them had been misunderstanding the text on the cones. Was there anything else they had missed? "Jekka, what do you think's up there?"

Her brother tasted the air with his tongue. "The mother temple. A sacred place."

The domes were gilt with icons of silver and gold lizardfolk, glimmering in the sunlight. Mirian wondered at the red and blue and green lights that glinted along the heights of some, then guessed they were gemstones reflecting sunlight.

She considered the dome, then the fearful pirates. Deadly wizard, maddened pirates, a murderous Mzali sorcerer, even an army of lizardfolk—all those she had anticipated. Not a mysterious temple that swallowed all who entered.

In short order, she set a party to securing the pirate ship, leaving their sailors under guard. When she called for volunteers to go ashore, all but a handful of her sailors raised hands, no matter the threat of the pirates' tales. She selected Harse, the second-best swordsman, wishing she could spare Caligan, the sailmaster, who'd once been a fencing instructor. But they needed the ship ready for departure, in case they had to flee for their lives.

Jekka, Jeneta, and Ivrian she took without hesitation. But when she saw another hand thrust up, she hesitated.

"You need me," Ensara said. "There's a chance I can talk sense into my crew on the hill. Especially if they're trapped or in some kind of danger. The last thing we need is more people trying to kill us."

"So long as you're not one of them."

"Captain, I think I've proven myself by now."

He'd proven steady during that weird trip through a sea of mist. And he'd risked everything to save her sister. Ensara had been honest so far, and if he spoke the truth, he might be useful. He might yet plan some elaborate bid to get his ship back, she supposed. But she was tired of trying to predict people's motives. "All right, Ensara. Gombe, see that he gets a sword."

29

BEYOND THE GATE
JEKKA

He had allowed himself to become distracted by hope, and the truth had crept up to drive in a blow so deep he still reeled.

He had looked on ruined lizardfolk cities in the past; but those he had known to be ruined before he reached them. He'd foolishly thought this one would be different, and now the reality of his people's fate was like the taste of dust.

His sister in blood and their companions seemed to know his mood. Perhaps they had enough empathy despite a vast gulf of understanding that lay between them that none dared speak of it. They talked only of keeping their eyes sharp, and of looking for tracks.

Ivrian remarked to Mirian that if anyone had made it through the gate before this, they'd have chipped out the huge silver letters scrolled upon the city's domed heights, and dug out the jewels ornamenting the graceful statues of forgotten lizardfolk that lined the boulevard.

Jekka lowered his inner lids and squinted. It was easier that way to imagine the city in the long ago. The trees and plants thriving now among the paving stones might easily have been gardens.

Mirian walked two paces to his right, brow furrowed in a faraway look, cutlass in hand. Ivrian was on his left, sword in one hand, wand in the other. Behind them were Jeneta and Ensara, followed by Gombe, and Harse, who could be heard nervously asking if Gombe thought there were angry lizardfolk watching them.

"No, Harse," Gombe answered quietly. He and Ivrian brought up the rear.

"Then why haven't the pirates come back to their ship?" Harse pressed on.

"I can't say," Ivrian said soberly, "but I don't think it's lizardfolk."

Jekka tasted the sweet, warm tropical scents in the air and found none of his people. No lizardfolk had walked this city in centuries.

He'd been an idiot to believe this would end any other way. The humans were too numerous. They hunted too surely, bred too quickly. Once his people had arrogantly assumed the humans were a resource to be exploited, then a threat that could be contained.

From some mistakes there was no recovery.

The city was alive with the cries of tropical birds and the shrill calls of monkeys as well as the repetitious croaking of frogs. Blue and green vines clotted the high, oval windows.

Jekka had never walked these streets, but it felt more like home than any human settlement he'd ever visited. It was arranged in a proper, organized manner and the colored marble and decorative touches worked into the buildings thrilled him. Here was true craftsmanship, not the shoddy human semblance of it. Art and function blended seamlessly as one.

Mirian crouched suddenly beside clumpy spoor and scanned the brush on the right. Sure enough, there were a series of splayed, three-toed tracks about the size of a lizard man's foot. But these were from no intelligent creature.

"*D'vaak*," he told her, adding, "the pack hunters."

"This is fresh," she said.

Jekka nodded his head once. "Within the last few hours." The heaviness in his heart had rendered speech difficult, but he heard himself address his companions, sounding calm. Some part of him still cared, or pretended to. "Stay very sharp, friends. They like the ambush, and they must be close."

"You think they're what killed the pirates?" Harse asked.

"They certainly could have. We can hope so," Jekka added, "for then they would not need to feast for some time."

He ventured to the boulevard's overgrown edge of bushes as he tasted the air again and again.

It had been a long while since he'd hunted d'vaak, for they, too, were being driven from the wilds by humans. Not that he felt any particular sympathy for the beasts.

He hissed softly, recalling his last hunt with his father and uncle and the striped d'vaak he'd slain. She had been large and powerful, and his hunting of her had become been part of his song. He had not heard that song for a year or more. He did not expect to hear it again. What point was there to sing a song of praise to oneself, or to hear it from a single relative?

"Close ranks," Mirian commanded. "I wish that witch didn't have our other wand."

"Technically," Jeneta said, "she's not a witch."

"I think she's going for more of a behavioral descriptor," Gombe suggested.

"Their first attack's always a lure," Mirian told her group carefully, and Jekka nodded agreement. His sister always knew exactly what to say. "If we all turn to attack one or two, then the others hit from the flank. So, if something obvious leaps out, only the two nearest should handle it. The rest should form a circle. Am I clear?"

"Clear," the humans answered.

They continued their walk along the dead boulevard as it sloped gradually toward the glistening marble dome and its shining letters. In the far distance, the mists towered into the sky, an ever-swirling wall from which a whistling wail rose to the cloudless azure sky.

"How big are these d'vaak things?" Ensara asked. "What are we looking for?"

"They're a little taller than a man," Mirian answered, "with sort of a crocodile mouth and huge claws. They've got the same claws on their feet. They're swift and can leap as well."

"Fabulous," Ensara muttered.

"But they taste like chicken," Gombe added, which set Ivrian to making a noise that meant he felt amused.

"Any scent of our 'friends'?" Mirian asked Jekka.

There was, and he should have said as much. He had to pay more attention to the now, and distance himself from sorrow. "A faint one, Sister. They continued for the hill."

He saw Mirian's dark eyes narrow as she stared up toward the steps. "If they've posted sentries, there's no missing us."

She was right. They were walking straight up the boulevard. Yet Jekka detected no human watchers.

"What do you think happened to the lizardfolk?" Ensara asked quietly. "It couldn't have been war, not with that weird gate protecting the city."

"I don't know," Jekka answered simply. "It wasn't humans, or the place would be looted." He was repeating information Gombe had already said. He must truly be distracted.

"And where are we, really? We're not inside the reefs. Is this truly some sort of pocket dimension?"

"That's what the cones suggested," Mirian answered. "Although the cones haven't been entirely clear."

"On starboard!" Gombe shouted.

He heard the rattling growl of the d'vaak on his right, but Jekka whipped left. He sought the hunter he knew would be stalking from the other direction.

He'd predicted accurately. From behind a statue broken off at the shoulder came another d'vaak, silent, a fit young female with a scaly hide covered in ochre feathers.

It charged on its back legs, front arms thrust forward, mouth open to reveal blade-like teeth.

Jekka danced in, swung, and caught the scythe end of his blade in the meat of the creature's right leg.

That slowed the d'vaak's charge, enough that Ivrian had time to blast its chest with his wand.

Jekka almost pitied the creature as it collapsed, kicking and clamping its mouth open and closed.

But there were three others yet to contend with—the one now engaged with Ensara and Gombe, who barely kept it at bay with their cutlasses, and the two who'd run toward Jeneta and Harse.

Ensara's wild swings forced a horned male back; Jeneta jabbed another with her longsword, her blade already slick with blood. Ivrian didn't seem to be doing anything but standing there, which wasn't like him at all, but there was no time to contemplate his choices.

Jekka raced to Jeneta's side, swinging at the creature's head.

He connected just above the eye, which set it roaring. He saw the tail lash, the hint of a crouch, knew it gathered to spring.

"Down, Jeneta!" he yelled. She threw herself to the left, but not far enough. As the monster leapt, he saw it tilting the claws on its feet to land on her chest and throat.

He swung desperately, caught one of those outstretched limbs in midair with his blade staff. He sliced six inches from the creature's foot and sent the claws and flesh and blood splattering over the weedy cobblestones.

Jeneta contorted frantically but still the thing landed across her lower back. She cried out more from startlement than injury, for the d'vaak struggled to stand on one good foot. A brutal cutlass swipe from Ivrian tore through half its trunk.

Jeneta turned and finished it with a solid slice to the back of its neck. It was still a long time dying.

Jekka quickly surveyed the rest of the melee. Harse and Gombe had driven theirs off. Mirian had made short work of the other, and the one Ivrian had blasted twitched where it had dropped, smoking.

"Are you all right?" Mirian asked Jeneta.

"It's a scratch," she said, though blood streamed down her arm and back. She closed her eyes, lips moving silently.

"Will the other one come back?" Harse asked Jekka.

"I don't think so. They're not stupid animals. We killed its pack. The survivor will have to fend for itself and seek smaller prey. It will see us as one large animal, not to be trifled with."

He wasn't sure why he had added so much additional information. He felt oddly separate from himself. Distant, almost, as if he were processing everything at two levels: one where he functioned at the side of his friends, another where he grieved for all that his people had lost—all that might have been for him and his cousin.

He was dimly aware of Mirian and Ensara talking, him responding, her checking with the others.

"There's something up there," Ivrian said, his voice strained and faint.

Everyone stared at him, but Ivrian's gaze was focused far beyond the temple.

"What did you see?" Mirian asked.

"I felt it," Ivrian shook his head. "There's a . . . presence up there, and it's aware of us. It's powerful."

"I didn't know you were a magic-user, lad," Ensara said.

"He's better than me with the wand," Mirian said. "He has some kind of natural affinity, but he's untrained, and this kind of thing is new. What are you sensing, Ivrian? Is it Rajana?"

Again he shook his head. "No. I don't even think it's human."

"How do you know?"

Ivrian's brow furrowed. "I just . . . *know.*"

"Maybe someone's using the dragon's tear," Jeneta suggested.

The other humans stared at her.

"If one of our enemies has figured out how to use it," Mirian said, "we're going to be in a lot of trouble. All right, Ivrian, you keep us posted if you sense anything else, okay?"

"Aye, Captain."

Another few minutes saw them to the weed-choked stairs below the central dome. Ensara ran his hand along the edge of the banister, half hidden and cracked by yellow lichen. Each post was a unique lizardfolk warrior.

The pirate's voice was quiet with awe as he took in the long length of the stair. "This must have taken years to craft."

"Generations," Jekka answered. "It might have been an extended family, all devoted to their profession."

"That's amazing." Ensara's gaze remained fixed sideways upon the carvings as they advanced.

"Your people sure love their art," Gombe said.

"Yes."

"You sensing anything else, Ivrian?" Mirian asked.

The writer didn't answer right away. "No—I mean, there's something there, but it's not attacking us. It's just waiting."

Mirian frowned. "This is the way the pirates went." She waved a hand vaguely at the stairs. Jekka had seen the tracks as well. There was no missing the damaged vine and weed growth from the passage of at least a dozen travelers.

She advanced at a crouch up the stairs to just below the top step, then looked over its edge.

Jekka glanced behind. The ships bobbed toylike in the harbor, and the Veil churned beyond them, still a whirling mass of blue fog.

"Something's moving inside the temple," Mirian said.

"What is it?" Gombe asked her.

"Listen."

"Sounds like scuffling," Gombe said after a moment.

"It sounds wrong," Ensara said.

Jekka strained for some hint of the noises himself, and heard an irregular clumping noise, as though someone were staggering and dragging something behind them.

"What do you mean *wrong*? Gombe asked.

"Like someone limping," Ensara said. "And it's damned peculiar if they're trying to be sneaky."

"Maybe they're trying to distract us," Ivrian suggested.

"Then it's working." Mirian glanced at her followers. "Are you ready for this? Something's up there. It may not be sailors."

"We're with you," Gombe said grimly.

"Keep your wits sharp and sword in hand." Mirian put extra force into a final warning. "Stay together."

Jekka raced to join her as she started forward. They passed a fountain choked with reeds and grass and a single sturdy bluewood tree. As Jekka trod over the pavement, he perceived silver and gold symbols through the detritus of leaves, soil, and grass. He could read only portions of the letters, and no complete words, but he could guess the gist of the message. They approached the Hall of Eternity and Communion, the heart of the city, where high ones would have met for council. No humans could have walked these steps, on pain of death. Jekka appreciated the irony that he preceded his human sister to guard her from danger, whereas an ancestor would have slain her the moment she set foot here.

He advanced quietly under the portico shading the dead fountain, his feet brushing the weeds with a faint whisper. He stopped behind a blue marble column studded with gemstones and curling glyphs proclaiming the glory of the city and the wisdom of its people, asking for the blessing of the Great Mother.

Like all his people's requests, it seemed to have fallen on deaf ears.

Mirian reached the other side of the doorway and motioned for the others to halt a moment while she peered around the corner. Jekka looked with her.

The hall consisted of one immense, circular chamber, its floor formed of concentric rings, each tier lower than the last.

An army of lizardfolk sat in the stone chairs arranged on every tier but the lowest. Jekka searched for signs of life, but found only empty eyes staring from dried-out bodies. It was as if they had all perished the moment after they took their seats, which was preposterous. Presumably someone had placed them here after death.

Yet there was movement, human movement. Two dozen men in sailor garb twitched upon the floor of the lowest ring. A few moaned softly. Jekka didn't smell blood, nor detect other signs of injury. There, closer to the narrow altar in the center of that lowest floor, lay Rajana, in spasm like the others.

"What's wrong with them?" Mirian whispered.

"I don't know." Jekka suspected poison, then stared at the silvery teardrop resting upon the altar.

It seemed almost to be staring back. "That is what Ivrian senses," he said.

"The dragon's tear?"

"I don't know." His tread soft, his staff ready, Jekka moved forward. Something silver rested under the folded hands of each lizardfolk corpse. A tiny globe.

One pirate was pulling himself along with his hands and drooling, his gaze vacant. Clearly the humans were no longer any sort of threat. Had the tear lashed out against them?

"Stay back, Sister," Jekka warned.

"They must have tried to use the tear," Ivrian said. "And something went wrong."

"Then we'll keep our hands off," Mirian said.

There was another troubling matter apart from the peculiar behavior of the humans. Scavengers should have eaten the dead bodies long before they had the chance to dry out. The hall was open—why had wildlife not entered? There were no bird nests, or spiderwebs, or even the little blue anoles that were to be found everywhere in the tropics. Not even vegetation had rooted its way into the chamber.

Jekka heard Ensara muttering in awe at the jewels set in the walls.

"We should leave," Jekka said, even as the tear glowed with silvery power.

He hissed. That light exploded, sweeping out in a ring. He threw himself at Mirian, to shield her, then the energies touched him and he plummeted headlong into dreamless sleep.

Jekka woke in the same chamber. As he opened his eyes, he realized little time had passed, for the light conditions had not changed. Mirian lay unmoving beside him.

"Please accept my apologies, Lord." Ivrian spoke in the language of Jekka's people, his pronunciation impossibly flawless. Jekka's head swiveled, his eyes widening in curiosity.

About Jekka lay the rest of the expedition—Ensara, Gombe, Jeneta, Harse. Mirian. All breathed shallowly.

Ivrian stood at Jekka's feet, his stance stiff and unnatural. Strangest of all, a mist of shifting colors, identical to that surrounding the island, filled his eye sockets, some of it drifting free as he lowered his head. "To facilitate the capture of the humans you have presented, I was forced to render you unconscious as well. I hope that you will accept my apology."

Jekka tasted the air about Ivrian again. He still breathed, but his scent was wrong.

He no longer smelled human.

Jekka grasped his blade staff and climbed to his feet.

"I am grateful that you responded," Ivrian said. "You were so long in coming that, did I live the true life, I would have despaired. Why didn't you bring folk from the Shadakarn?"

The Shadakarn? There had once been a powerful rival clan by that name. They had long since perished in battle with humans.

It was a strain to recall the proper phrasing and pronunciation. "They sleep with the Great Mother. Those I brought with me, are they—"

Ivrian interrupted him. "All the Shadakarn sleep the eternal?"

"All."

"Is that why you brought humans? I will use them if I must. What of the Kavanakaar or the Saraen?"

"A few of the Saraen remain, deep within the jungle."

"Then we will take these vessels and use them to capture the Saraen so we may wear them."

Vessels? Jekka sensed that the thing in Ivrian did not mean ships. This entity, whatever it was, meant to put the spirits of the lizardfolk into lizardfolk from enemy clans.

Jekka drew himself up straight. He would see to freeing his sister, but that would require the proper formalities. "What manner of guardian are you?"

"Forgive me, Lord. So long has it been since I spoke with living beings that I have forgotten decorum. I am known as Senakka, the Guardian of Destinies. I see by the markings upon your weapon and robe that you are a lord of the Karshnaar."

"I am Jekka Eran Sulotai sar Karshnaar."

"The founders will be honored that so great a lord answered their summons."

Jekka hissed while he considered his course of action. "You have occupied the body of Ivrian?"

"I have assumed control of this vessel, yes. I shall relinquish it soon to bestow upon one of the founders."

"Is the human dead?"

"He is in submission to my will."

So Ivrian lived yet. That at least was good news. "It is you who maintain this building?"

"Yes, Lord. Likewise am I responsible for the life force of those beneath my charge."

"I confess a lack of understanding of this matter. What are you?" Was Jekka expected to know these things, and would he be under suspicion if he did not?

"I am a sorcerous construct," Senakka answered, "crafted by the great Reklaniss. I maintain the Veil that shields the island from its enemies. I safeguard the spirits of the last lords so that I may place them in new vessels."

"What happened to the lords?"

"Was not all this stated in your summons?"

Summons? Jekka knew of no summons. His gaze returned to his sister. It pained him to see her lying so still. It was a great struggle to force composure. "Many years have passed. Your summons is remembered imperfectly."

"The last lords feared the humans still would come, for word reached from the outside world that their powers grew. And thus my charges took refuge within their globes so that I might restore them after reinforcements arrived. Word was sent to our cousins for help in this battle. Is this not why you came?"

So this guardian had watched over these spirits for . . . eons, waiting for saviors who never arrived. If word had ever reached those who could have helped, they had not returned. He wondered if that lizardfolk ship they'd found had been one of those lost vessels.

"How many do you require?" Jekka asked.

"Two hundred and four."

Jekka considered the orbs resting in the laps of the corpses. Could there really be that many lizardfolk lords awaiting revival?

What would it be like to converse not just with members of his own clan, but ancestors who understood the great secrets of the past?

He breathed deep and scented the arena, his view taking in the strange condition of the humans below. "What has happened to them?"

"I do not understand your question."

"Have you attacked the humans?"

"I have placed the high lords of our people within them, as I will do with the humans you have brought me."

"No," Jekka said, "you must not."

"I require more vessels, Lord, not fewer. Why do you forbid me?"

"This one is my sister. Most of these others are my friends."

Ivrian's head cocked. "Now it is I who do not understand."

"Your understanding is not required. You have my leave to take the one known as Ensara, but the consciousness of the others is to be restored. The female is my sworn sister and of my adopted clan."

"I shall have to consider your request."

"You shall consider it carefully. It is in my power to return with more vessels, thus you would be wise to seek my pleasure."

"I shall do as you ask." Ivrian extended a hand. Mist sprayed from his fingertips, touched Mirian cheek, and then his sister's eyes flickered open.

Jekka helped her to her feet.

Senakka spoke on with Ivrian's voice. "If these others are not of your clan, I will have to ignore your request. I shall begin preparations for the first transference." Ivrian turned and walked stiffly down between the rows of mummified figures.

"What's happening?" Mirian asked. "What's wrong with Ivrian?"

It was unpleasant to speak a human language again; he had to struggle to convey meaning quickly, and the words came clumsily.

"Ivrian's body is being controlled by a sorcerous guardian. It's readying to transfer spirits from some of those seated here into the bodies of our companions. But something's wrong."

He didn't understand Mirian's expression, but knew she studied him intently. "Do you have a plan?"

"I'm still working on that. Senakka," he called.

Ivrian pivoted as though he were on a crank.

"There's something wrong," Jekka said. "Do you not see what the lords are doing?"

"The lords planned to take the vessels of those who were presented to them. Thus has it transpired. They do with them as they will."

"There's nothing left of your great lords," Jekka said, realization coming to him as he spoke. "How long have they been confined to the orbs their fingers clutch? Four or five hundred cycles? A thousand cycles? They are mad, Senakka. Look, they do nothing but drool."

"Is that not what they wish to do?"

"I don't think so. They would converse, and walk."

Ivrian turned. Mist continued to drift from his eye sockets as he looked up at Jekka. "There is something to what you say."

Jekka moved down toward Ivrian. "Was there any contact between them? Or are they each alone within their orbs?"

"Each is alone. It is safer that way—one orb might fail, but not all of them."

Jekka's head swayed in sorrow. "Their safety has doomed them. They have been driven mad by isolation. Didn't you monitor their well-being?"

"They are safe, within their orbs," Senakka said. "So long as my magic functions."

"Safe within a prison from which there was no escape. Can you sense their life forces, Senakka? Can you commune with their spirits?"

Ivrian ceased movement.

Mirian had started down after him. "What's happening?" she asked. Naturally, she couldn't understand their speech.

Senakka replied. "You are correct." Ivrian's mist-filled eye sockets turned once more to Jekka. "I lack understanding of this matter. The magic in each is intact, yet when I call out to the spirits, no one answers." He lowered his head, bobbed it twice. "They did not tell me that they could not endure."

Jekka supposed that the lizardfolk, for all their wisdom, had not guessed they would remain so long in stasis.

"You must give the human bodies back," Jekka said. "You have no use for them. I do."

"I can return this one and awaken these new humans."

"Do so."

"It shall be as you say, Lord. Likewise, I will turn the city over to you as well. It is yours."

"The city is yours, Senakka."

"No." Ivrian swayed his head and shoulders, a lizardfolk gesture of remorse. "My purpose was to safeguard the entities and that is no longer possible. My task is complete. Farewell, Jekka Eran Sulotai sar Karshnaar. To you and your descendants I leave the city."

And as suddenly as a candle is snuffed, the mist drifted from his eyes. Ivrian collapsed limply.

Jekka heard a great roaring of wind and his head snapped around to the doorway. He sprinted up the steps past Mirian.

He reached the height of the stairs, looked through the archway and down across the city's roofs to the dock where the ships were still lashed to the pier. He saw exactly what he had feared.

The Veil, with no magic to support it, had collapsed. It now rolled in a vast, thousand-foot wave of mist toward the city.

30

THE STORM
IN THE TEMPLE

JEKKA

While Jekka dashed up, Mirian sprinted for the dais and the silver, tear-shaped stone glistening at its height.

The pirates groaned and shifted, struggling to sit upright. Rajana, though, swung up her head and met Mirian's eyes. There was no mistaking that gaze for madness.

"The Veil!" Jekka called from the archway at the top of the stairs. "It's collapsing!

From outside rose a rumble like a mighty storm, the frightened cries of distant animals, and the alarm calls of birds.

Rajana pulled herself up the dais. Mirian was starting for her when she caught a flash of movement in an archway above.

Telamba had stepped through an open archway, and the red coal burned in his palm.

"It comes!" Jekka cried.

Mist spewed in through every archway, propelled by shrieking wind. The swirling mists were somehow buoyant, tossing objects and beings as it reached them. Jekka was sent tumbling through the air like a leaf, and then the dead lizardfolk whirled up in a ghastly, gravity-defying dance.

Mirian was flung into a row of brittle corpses, felt her elbow crunch into a dried chest. Her hand smashed into a chair back. A clawed hand struck her face and she fought down panic . . . but the things were not alive. Only the wind granted them movement.

The glowing mist buffeted and howled. Somewhere she heard Ensara calling to grab the pillars.

"Jekka!" Mirian cried.

There was no answer. She searched the floor. There, through the curtain of mist and rolling debris, she spotted Rajana. The wizard had pulled herself up the dais and grasped at the tear.

Mirian grabbed her knife, aimed, and threw, but the wind carried the weapon far off target. She rose, cursing, and pulled out her cutlass.

The wild wind buffeted her as she advanced. Something swam crazily past to her left—a headless lizardfolk corpse.

A monstrous crash of stone shook the floor.

"The dome's caving in!" Jeneta screamed from somewhere to the left.

Through a gap in the mist overhead she spied an immense crack shooting along the dome, widening.

Mirian had lost sight of Telamba. There was no missing Rajana lifting the tear and waving her hand across it with a look of elation. It was only a brief one, for a net of fire soared out of the mist. Instead of wrapping her, it defined a protective shield of energy that surrounded the woman. The fiery red of the net burned with increased vigor even as Rajana's shield glowed an eerie yellow. Half hidden within, Rajana shouted something.

As the mists thinned Mirian spotted Telamba striding past a hunk of stone. Much as he needed to go down, she wasn't about to attack him, for fear his own attack against Rajana would fail if his concentration was shattered. And she couldn't reach Rajana beneath the net.

She spotted Jeneta helping a dazed-looking Ivrian to his feet. Ensara veered past a cluster of broken seats and ran toward Mirian. She lost sight of him as masonry crashed down, stirring so much dust she couldn't see if he'd leapt clear.

The ground shook, and Mirian threw herself to the side as a gargantuan hunk of stone slammed into six rows of stone chairs to her left. Chips of stone flew into the wild currents. A sliver slashed her neck. By the time she struggled to her feet, both the net and the shield seemed to have failed. Telamba raised his gauntleted hand toward Rajana.

Pirates formerly allied with Rajana raced wild-eyed past her. One of them screamed as another hunk of the dome fell. It raised a cloud of dust that soared into the mad winds still coursing through the room.

Telamba sent an arc of burning red lightning toward Rajana, but she blocked the attack with a curtain of misty silver energy.

She was drawing on the power of the dragon's tear, and grinning as she did so.

Damn it.

Ivrian pushed away from Jeneta and lurched in from the upper ring. Rajana, startled by the sudden movement, spun and raised a glowing hand, ready to defend herself. It was the only opening Mirian expected she'd get, and she charged.

The spellcaster whirled, mouthed a spell and lifted a hand to shield herself—the same one she'd lifted months before. Except this time fingers of glowing mist were there in place of the ones Mirian had sliced away. They held back the blade as Mirian brought it down.

A wicked, curved knife fashioned from shining light formed in Rajana's other hand. She punched it toward Mirian's chest.

Mirian sidestepped. The dagger skimmed through her shirt and into her left shoulder with a cold so intense it burned. Mirian gasped in agony and staggered back even as a muscular shape dashed past her.

Telamba. Snarling, he raised a short, curved blade. Before he could swing it home, a coruscating blast of energy hurtled from Rajana's palm. It lifted him bodily and tossed him away like detritus.

Smiling, Rajana drifted backward above the floor, caressed by a rippling blue cloak of energy.

Mirian sprinted after, reaching Rajana as she soared through the archway and out to the walkway that circled the temple. Hearing her footfalls, Rajana turned, smiling wickedly, the dragon's tear a silvery-white glow in her hands.

Mirian slashed at her but the Chelaxian laughed and flew a foot backward into the air.

The mist swirled and whipped and flashed beyond Rajana, occasionally flowing low enough to reveal straining treetops or the heights of domed buildings.

"There's nothing you can do now!" Rajana told her. "I am a goddess! Kneel to me, Mirian! Kneel to me and beg for me to spare you!"

There, low in the bushes just to Rajana's left, something crept along on its belly within the rolling mist—Jekka, with his sword staff. He must have escaped through one of the archways.

Mirian had to buy just a little more time. "If I kneel," she said slowly, "will you spare my people?"

Rajana laughed. It was a strained sound, as though she were unaccustomed to it. "I may, or may not. I haven't decided whether I shall be a benevolent goddess. It will depend upon my mood. And my mood will depend upon how those beneath me comport—"

Jekka's spearpoint emerged from Rajana's chest and she dropped to her knees with a groan. But she was not yet done. Her fingers splayed and mist lashed up like whips to strike the lizard man. They wrapped his limbs and twisted them, flung him broken into the side of the building.

Mirian swung hard and sliced deep into Rajana's right arm. She cried out and the dragon's tear soared off into the mist.

Yet still Rajana had life within her. She struggled to one knee as Mirian raised her sword. Her eyes burned with hatred. "Before I die, I shall take—"

With her first stroke, Mirian cut halfway through the woman's neck. The second sent her head rolling away into the mist. Rajana's body collapsed with a sickening thump.

Mirian dashed to Jekka's side.

Her brother was worse than she'd feared. He struggled to rise on one arm. The other was twisted and broken.

"I can't feel my legs," he told her. His speech was slurred, and Mirian now saw a slim chip of stone embedded in his forehead. Blood trickled down the side of his face, delineating scales usually too small to notice

She gasped, reached for him. She knew he didn't like to be touched, but she grabbed his hand.

"Do not worry, my sister," Jekka said softly. "I hoped to go to my people. Now I will."

"Not you ..." Mirian gripped his cool reptilian flesh in her hands.

"When you have your children," Jekka said, "you will tell them of your brother?"

"Oh yes." Mirian's eyes burned with tears. "Jeneta! Damn you, Jeneta! Get over here!" But had the healer even survived the collapse of the dome? And even if she had, these wounds were beyond her skill.

There were footfalls from behind Jekka, but it wasn't Jeneta. She looked past her dying brother to find Ensara panting there, Ivrian leaning heavily against him. The writer's hand was raised and she stared in sudden shock as the dragon's tear floated through the air and into his palm.

She'd known Ivrian had some natural magical aptitude, given the ease with which he'd used the magic wand, but for him to command this level of power . . .

Ivrian's eyes filled once more with mist.

The teardrop settled into Ivrian's hand and he looked down, his face like a theater mask of tragedy. He raised his hand and a coil of mist rose. This time, though, it touched Jekka gently, like the caressing hand of a lover. It brushed his forehead, lingering there, and the stone splinter faded in glowing sparkles. The mist then shifted to wrap Jekka's torso and arm.

Her blood brother's glazed expression cleared and he sat up, flexing a perfectly shaped arm that had been a bent and devastated wreck only moments before. Mirian, at a loss for words, gaped in joy, helping Jekka to stand. She looked to Ivrian, but the writer had turned to consider the mist across the face of the sea, and the reefs that loomed behind it. The light of Golarion's sun streamed down, setting the rubies embedded in the distant lizard heads aflame. The mist clung to the buildings and trees that swept down toward the ocean, concealing much but revealing tracts of jungle or pavement as it slowly shifted.

Mirian laughed in joy. She clapped Jekka's shoulder, then threw herself at him and held him close.

"Ivrian!" Ensara cried.

Mirian spun.

The pirate captain supported the young miracle worker, now slumped and limp.

Mirian released Jekka and hurried forward. "Is he all right?"

Ensara bent his head to Ivrian's face. "He's breathing."

Mirian bent to examine Ivrian's as well, and saw that his slowly blinking eyes were normal now, or at least free of sorcery, for he didn't look like he could focus. She lowered him to the stones, now almost clear of mist, and heard a sharp intake of breath and scrabble of sandals as Jeneta sank down beside him.

Mirian started to ask where she'd been, then saw that her left arm was caked in blood, and that her cheek was swollen. "I think he'll be fine. What about you?"

"I took a tumble. I'm all right." She knelt beside the writer, her eyes huge with worry.

"Check him over," Mirian ordered, although Jeneta obviously was planning to do just that. She really was going to have to be told . . . but not just now.

Mirian stepped away, her eyes shifting briefly to Rajana's motionless corpse.

Ensara drew up beside her, nodding at Ivrian as Jeneta pressed hands to the white ruffled shirt wrapped about the writer's chest. "You think he'll be all right?"

"Are you a praying man, Ensara?" So far as she knew, Ivrian hadn't been physically harmed. But he'd had that sorcerous thing inside of him, and he'd wielded vast magical energies. Who was to say how fine he'd really be? She could only hope.

With concerted effort she shifted her attention to Ensara. "What happened to your men in the dome?"

Ensara's expression darkened. "Some of them got out. A lot of them didn't. The gods must have meant me to survive." He wiped blood from his brow. "Maybe they needed me to guide Ivrian up here so he could save Jekka."

"Who knows what the gods want," Jekka said. "I think, sometimes, that they laugh at us. But I thank you for bringing Ivrian."

Ensara nodded wearily. "I heard Mirian calling. I couldn't see Jeneta, but Ivrian said he thought he could help, so . . ." His voice trailed off as Jeneta sat back on her heels.

"Jeneta," Mirian called, "is he going to make it?"

"He seems all right, just exhausted."

The mist was dissipating at last, burned away by the warming rays of the sun. Here and there little pools of it still lay among the ruins like gray shadows. And she could see sailors on the decks of the ships.

Ensara bent to examine the dragon's tear, but refrained from touching it. Mirian sank down on one knee beside him.

A significant fracture showed along the artifact's base and trailed along almost to the point. She wondered if that had happened through overuse, or when it had been dropped.

"That thing's a blessing and a menace," Ensara said. "I see why Rajana and Telamba wanted it so bad."

"Now I see why everyone wants it," Mirian replied.

31

THE MUSIC OF THE TEAR
IVRIAN

The lizardfolk were everywhere. Small green ones danced in lines. Four aquamarine ones sat around what looked like a flaming pie, and a huge frilled fellow with red and yellow spots tapped the shoulder of another seated on a flying blueberry. It was all very strange until Ivrian blinked again and he understood he was looking at a wall. The lizardfolk weren't moving; he was. Or at least he felt like he was moving. He rolled from his side to his back.

He lay looking at a small domed ceiling gilt with more lizardfolk and their writing and hundreds upon hundreds of emeralds. None of the lizardfolk were actually dancing around food; they were pictograms carved amid a field of embedded gems.

Suddenly Telamba bent over him, the white skull painted on his face half washed away by sweat, his cheek splotchy with a purple bruise. His eyes bored into Ivrian's own.

"You live," Telamba said softly.

Ivrian tried to convey that he was as surprised as Telamba, but his voice came out in a mumble. Now that he thought about it, how had Telamba come through? He thought he'd seen him killed.

"I managed to escape," Telamba said.

He still must be reading my thoughts.

"I am, Ivrian." Telamba's voice was low. "And do not fear, for now. I did not come to kill you. You are tied now to the tear in a way no human has been before. My god tells me you may be the one meant to wield it."

Ivrian felt as though his wielding of it had been entirely up to chance.

"Chance, or fate? Or both, because of your character? You name a Bas'o as your sister and a lizard as your brother. You are no ordinary foreigner." He loomed suddenly closer. "Know this, Sargavan." Telamba's voice was a dangerous whisper. "I shall be watching. If you wield the tear against us, Great Walkena himself shall turn his wrath upon you!"

Ivrian started to protest that he'd never wield the tear against anyone, that he was through with it, but his vision swam, and the lizardfolk on the ceiling danced once more, and he fell into slumber until another voice spoke beside him.

"You're awake!"

It was only then he recalled a persistent shaking of his shoulder. Had his conversation with Telamba been a dream?

He looked up into the shining eyes of Kalina, her colors bright. She crouched beside him

Ivrian smiled easily. "We found the city," he said. And then he felt bad, because, of course, Kalina and Jekka could not have been hoping for an abandoned ruin filled only with the dead. He was too tired to think straight.

"Jekka and Mirian have told me all about it," Kalina said. "And I've made discoveries myself—"

Kalina was interrupted by a young woman's voice, one vibrant with pleasure.

"I knew you would come 'round," Jeneta's voice declared. "The Custodian is here, and he'll want to see you."

"The Custodian?" Ivrian asked. Did she mean the ruler of Sargava? Maybe he was still hallucinating.

He heard the click of sandals on stone and then Jeneta passed in front of his view and toward an open archway through which sunlight leaked.

Ivrian took stock of his surroundings. He appeared to be lying on a cot—no, an entire bedframe—set up in what was surely some portion of the lost city of Kutnaar. A gray coverlet draped across his body.

"You are truly all right, Ivrian?" Kalina asked. "I poked you again and again, but you didn't move."

"I told you not to poke him," Jeneta said, sweeping closer. She blushed as Ivrian studied her face and for a moment he wondered why.

"Oh," he said. *Right.* "Thank you for tending me," he said, for he had a vague memory of her looming over him again and again, sometimes with a cooling hand and sometimes with a cloth. He hoped she hadn't been bathing him. Surely Mirian wouldn't have been letting her do that.

As he heard voices drawing closer, consciousness returned with greater sharpness and some of Jeneta's words registered more fully. The Sargavan Custodian? What was Ivrian wearing?

He looked under the coverlet, discovered he was garbed in a tan overshirt and black shorts. Ghastly, really. He tried to sit up, because he'd caught sight of his sea chest over there on the right . . . But he was too woozy to rise, and collapsed back against the pillow just as the Custodian emerged from behind the curtain held open by a curtsying Jeneta.

Baron Utilinus was a tall, handsome man clad in expertly tailored brown pants and matching vest. A starched white shirt with ruffled sleeves stretched over his muscular chest. He offered a smile, though there was no missing the concern in his eyes. Mirian trailed after, alongside an unfamiliar woman and two soldiers.

"Ah, Lord Galanor!" the baron said. "No, don't try to rise. I was told you've been asleep for most of the last two days."

"He's been very weak," Jeneta added.

"But I woke him," Kalina reported.

"And I see that you've been under very good care."

"Um," said Ivrian, wishing there was something more he could think of, but he was utterly perplexed. "Thank you, Baron." Should he admit he wasn't sure what was going on? And then another thought occurred to him. "Is Jekka all right? What about the rest of the sailors?"

"Everyone is fine." Mirian smiled. "Thanks to you."

"Jekka and Kalina have been made the lord and lady of Kutnaar," Jeneta volunteered brightly.

The baron chuckled good-naturedly. "It's their city, after all. And a scholar's dream. Not that there aren't some other uses for it as well, of course. Sargava can use the gems built into the city, make no mistake. But I've pledged to the Pathfinders that we'll leave everything else intact."

He bent down and patted Ivrian's shoulder. "Earlier this year I learned you had hidden depths, but I never guessed you were a spellcaster."

"Um," Ivrian repeated, wondering where his eloquence had fled. "Neither did I, Baron. Speaking of which . . . where's the dragon's tear?" Had Telamba taken it? Or had that visit been a hallucination?

"Safe." It was the unfamiliar woman who'd lingered silently behind the baron. Her dark eyes were alight with fierce intelligence. She was a thin, broad-nosed woman with umber skin, clothed in a simple green dress.

"Forgive me," the baron said. "This is Elgia Matanis, my magical advisor. Your artifact has quite a crack in it."

"Wielding it again may be dangerous," Elgia said. "Using it while damaged may be what injured you."

Ivrian shook his head. He didn't think so. And he smiled at the thought of the raw, animal vitality that had shaken him to his very core the moment he touched the power at the tear's center.

"I have some questions about the tear, if you're strong enough," Elgia said. "For instance, what techniques did you use to attune yourself to its power?"

"I don't know. It just . . . called to me." He put a hand to his head. He could still feel it, somewhere far away, like a distant melody borne on the wind. He turned his head, trying to seek it out.

"Baron." There was a warning tone in Jeneta's voice. "He's still very weak."

"I just woke him," Kalina added helpfully.

"Yes," the baron said. "Of course. Ivrian, Sargava is grateful to you for your service and sacrifice. We'll talk more when you're better rested."

Ivrian nodded distractedly, for the words were drowning out the sound of the dragon's tear.

Its music was very, very lovely, and he wished to hear.

32

HOMECOMING

JEKKA

The sun stained sky and water alike a burning scarlet as it sank, casting a shimmering pillar across the waves.

The moon was but a sliver to the east, glittering above soldiers of Sargava standing sentry in the ruins of his people. Over the last few days, four camps had sprung up and nearly half of Sargava's small fleet had been deployed to protect the tiny island that had suddenly appeared just outside its sea lanes.

Much had transpired, but Jekka, who had long since ceased to brood upon the past, didn't dwell on it. He did, however, permit himself to look toward the future just a little as a slim schooner slid into place at the end of a quay already thick with ships. He walked along the old stones as the gangplank was lowered, so that he was there when Charlyn descended in the company of the ship's captain and two sailors.

The captain eyed Jekka a little dubiously, but Charlyn halted immediately and smiled at him.

"It is good to see you, brother to my sister," she said in her high, clear voice.

"And it's a pleasure to be again in your presence, sister to my sister."

The captain cleared his throat and touched his hat brim. "What shall we do with your dunnage, ma'am?"

"My dunnage?"

"Her mate—I mean, husband—is stationed in the tents in the cleared section near the end of the quay," Jekka said. "Ask the sentries on duty."

"You're one of them famous frillbacks, aren'tcha?" one of the sailors said, pointing.

"He is a lizard man," Charlyn corrected, with all the icy disdain of the nobility, "and my kin, so you will address him with respect."

"I didn't mean nothin', m'lady," the sailor said, touching his head where a cap would have lain.

"Get on," the captain growled, then touched his hat to the lady. He nodded once to Jekka and moved on ahead of them.

Charlyn extended her arm to Jekka, elbow pointed, and after a moment he understood that he was supposed to take it. He touched it and started to lead her on.

She laughed. "No, Jekka, like this." And she slid his arm through hers. "A gentleman walks a lady on his arm."

"I am a gentleman now?"

"You have a new medal now, don't you, as one of the land-holders of Kutnaar?"

Jekka looked down at his chest where the two ribbons that led to his medals crossed. "I do."

"That makes you a gentleman," she said, "though it's all in the way a man, or male, in your case, presents himself. Did you like meeting the Custodian?"

"I had met him before," Jekka said as they walked up the quay. "He is wise."

"Praise be that it's so. And he is generous."

Jekka nodded, though he wasn't entirely sure why everyone was so impressed that the baron had granted titleship of the island to himself and Kalina, which meant a percentage of all treasures found upon the isle. It had been granted to him by the dying construct. But then, perhaps other humans were just as skeptical about the honor of their kind as he himself had been.

A less far-minded ruler would have set immediately to whole-sale looting, but the baron had sent in scholars, Pathfinders, and historians, along with artists, to record the appearance of the works, magicians to search for magical secrets, and soldiers to protect from more dangers. It was a project, the baron had told him, likely to last at least a generation, and the conversations had involved the imbibing of sweet wine and the awarding of another medal, which Jekka had rather liked.

If it was not the outcome he had wanted, he at least was content.

"Mirian wrote that your cousin found something in her researches. She didn't say what it was, but she sounded excited."

"Ah, yes. Kalina thinks there are other gates where we might find cities of our people. The text was . . . badly rendered? I'm not sure how you would say it. But with a little work, we might find them yet."

Charlyn smiled. "That's wonderful news, then!"

Jekka's head bobbed in imitation of a human nod. He still didn't think he quite managed that right. "Yes," he said. "There's no telling what we'll find, though. Or if we'll need another dragon's tear. The Custodian said the one Ivrian had is dangerous to use again. It's cracked."

They'd arrived at the end of the quay.

"It's good that you still have a chance," Charlyn said. "I'm looking forward to meeting your cousin."

"Yes. You will like her. Your husband is working up near the great dome. They've found a chamber that's very interesting to him. Do you wish me to take you there?"

"Perhaps. I'd like you to give me a tour. Perhaps tomorrow. I'd hoped to speak with Mirian this evening."

"As she has hoped to speak with you.".

They passed the sentries and moved on toward the road leading up to the ruins of the great dome. The entire way was lighted with paper lanterns now, and soldiers were stationed every twenty feet or so. They didn't look happy about it, and Jekka had been given to understand they'd prefer to keep all exploration to the daytime, but the explorers were too fascinated to stop. They were all working long shifts.

Jekka and Charlyn started up the stairs. By lantern light two artists were setting down the intricate carvings to paper. They and some bored-looking soldiers made way for them.

"And Ivrian?" Charlyn asked. "How is he?"

"He's recovering," Jekka said.

She felt Charlyn's eyes upon him. "You didn't really answer."

"It's because I'm not sure how to describe his health. He's not quite the same. Jeneta monitors him, of course. I think she wishes to become his mate."

Charlyn laughed lightly.

They neared the head of the stairs, where there was another cluster of lights. Here, under one long portico, Mirian and her salvage team had erected their own tents, and she now descended, arms spread. Gombe rose from the table, setting aside a napkin, and Jekka oversaw the greetings. Mirian thanked him and stepped away with her sister.

"We saved you some wine," Gombe said.

That pleased him. "That was kind of you."

"Did you ever think you'd own your own city?" Gombe encompassed the city with a sweep of his arm.

"No." Jekka stared down at the row of lights. Despite the squads of scholars, vast sections of the ruins remained unexplored and dark, and he found himself trying to imagine what it would have been like to breach the Veil and find living lizardfolk.

Gombe clapped him on the shoulder and he just managed not to raise his frill, because he understood this as a friendly gesture. The human grinned at him and offered him wine in a bottle. Rendak climbed up from his own chair and raised a glass.

"Here's to our friend," Rendak said, "Lord Jekka of Kutnaar."

And they drank together.

Jekka lowered the bottle, looked at the smiling bearded man. "I wish my brother might have lived to stand here beside us. He would have been very happy here." He stared out at the city, imagining what that might have been like.

Gombe cleared his throat. "You're a celebrity now. People will be clamoring for Ivrian to get the story written so they can learn all the behind-the-scenes details."

"Right you are," Rendak said.

"There's not much to it." Jekka sipped only lightly as he looked out across the darkened streets. "It's about someone who risked the lives of his friends to seek out a family that was already dead." He turned to him. "But it's also a story of friendship."

"It's a heroic adventure," Rendak said. "With you as the star. All it needs is a little romance." He cleared his throat. Jekka wasn't sure, but he had a feeling Rendak now regretted his words.

"He was speaking metaphorically," Gombe said. "A hero tale always has a romance in it, but all we've got is a rich snob with a pretty wife and a pretty cleric swooning for a fop." Gombe sighed at that.

"I see," said Jekka, because he thought that was what he was supposed to say.

Once more he suffered the hand of a human as Gombe tightly squeezed his shoulder. "We'll find some more of your folk out there, Jekka. I know we will."

Now he understood. Gombe, talking of him as the hero, thought he should have found a mate by the end of the adventure, and felt badly for bringing it up.

"Let us have more wine. Among my people, we tell the stories of our ancestors by the nights. Do your people do that?"

"Sometimes," Rendak answered.

"Sometimes we trade stories about stupid things we've done." Gombe grinned. "Like that time Rendak bought that goat to get in with that pretty Mulaa girl."

"Hey!" Rendak objected.

"A goat?" Jekka asked. "What was funny about the goat?"

"The way it happened," Gombe said, "was like this . . ."

And Jekka sat back and listened as his human friend spun his tale, under the stars.

33

A Drink
Between Friends

Mirian

She sat with her sister on the highest stair in the city, just outside the ruin of the great dome.

Charlyn patted her knee. "It's lovely. It's amazing."

"It is, isn't it?"

"I could never have done what you've done with your life," Charlyn was saying. "The adventure. The constant danger."

"I don't know," Mirian countered. "It seems to me you've held up pretty well."

Her sister looked sidelong at her. "Do you think we'd have been close if we'd grown up together?"

Mirian doubted that. There were more than fifteen years between them. "There's no point worrying about it, is there? But we can try now. Tradan's going to be busy here for a long time and I'll be working with him. I'm sure he'd be glad for any extra help."

Charlyn laughed. "Do you mean me, helping in the ruins?"

"You can't tell me this place doesn't fascinate you."

"It does," Charlyn admitted. "But it's sad as well. I think about poor Jekka. How closely related is he to his cousin? Could they marry?"

"He hasn't mentioned it, and I haven't brought it up." Despite their closeness, it seemed an extremely sensitive topic.

"I quite like him," Charlyn said. "I see now why you welcomed him into your family."

"For a long time," Mirian said haltingly, "I thought the only way I could have a family was by gathering folk around me I liked. Blood ties aren't always what they're cracked up to be. But I was wrong to casually dismiss them so easily."

Charlyn squeezed her knee. Mirian wondered where she'd picked up the habit. It wasn't something their father had ever done. "Maybe I should have tried harder," Charlyn said softly. "But father was so bitter over the divorce. It was much easier to stay away from him. And it seemed as though we were busy with our separate lives."

There was a burst of laughter from off to the left; Mirian recognized Gombe's deep-throated chuckle and heard him say something about a bucket of yellow paint and a goat and realized he was telling the story of the goat and the stowaway ham and the pretty harlot. Rendak's voice sputtered with mock indignation.

"Maybe we can try again," Mirian said.

"I'd like that."

"There you are," said a familiar voice. Mirian and Charlyn both turned and Ensara stopped short. He lifted a curiously long-necked bottle.

"Ah—Lady ven Goleman. I didn't know. That is . . ." He cleared his throat.

"You're looking for Mirian, I take it?" Charlyn rose gracefully.

Ensara bowed. "Yes, m'lady. I didn't mean to intrude."

"That's quite all right." Charlyn looked down at Mirian, watching her carefully to try to gauge her feelings.

Unfortunately, Mirian wasn't quite sure of them herself. She was happy things were off on a better tack with her sister than they'd ever been, but she still wasn't entirely sure what to say to her, and she honestly didn't know what to think of Ensara.

Charlyn nodded to Ensara. "I was just leaving to ask a man about a goat," she said.

"A goat?" Ensara asked.

But Charlyn didn't explain. "I'll see you in the morning, Sister," she said. "And I'll talk with Tradan about assistance." With that she turned and proceeded around the curving walkway toward the sound of Gombe's laughter.

Ensara glanced after her, then down at Mirian. Apparently deciding that further inquiry might be impolite, he raised the bottle. "I brought this for you."

He handed her the bottle and set his hands to his hips as he contemplated the setting sun. "I'm not sure I could get tired of this view."

Mirian inspected the gift, stunning blue glass with a tapered, curving neck. Lizardfolk work. "Wine?" She raised an eyebrow. Anything in that bottle would have given up the ghost centuries before.

"Oh, it's vinegar now, I'm sure. But the bottle's lovely. I found it in a house near the docks." Ensara sank down beside her, hands on his knees. He reached inside his vest and pulled out a flask, uncapped it. "Here's something we can actually drink." He took a long swig and passed it on.

"Is this the quiet drink you told me you've been after?"

He sighed a little. "It's not what I pictured, no. But then, nothing's been what I planned for a long, long time." He spoke slowly as she put her lips to the flask. "See, I talked myself into thinking that if I drew the line in one place I was a gentleman. But I kept letting other people move the line for me."

She tasted the lukewarm metal, then felt the warm burn of a smooth rum. "That's not bad." She passed it over.

He indicated the docks with a nod of his chin. "I bought it off one of the officers the Custodian brought with him. It's not what I planned, but—"

"What did you plan?"

He laughed shortly and leaned back against the stairs. "More like a daydream than a plan. You have to actually work for a plan, you know?" He read her silence as a prompting. "I figured we'd be sitting on a balcony in Eleder, overlooking the harbor, at sunset. The ships would be in, and the sky would be lit up with stars, and there'd be folks done up in proper garb catering to us. And you and I could just sit and talk."

"Just talk?"

He nodded. "Aye. About whatever you'd like."

"What I'd like," she said, "is some spiced Thuvian ale." She took the flask back and took another bolt.

Ensara laughed. "Well, Captain, you can probably buy yourself a shipful with your percentage of this particular find. Can't say as I've ever shared a drink with such a wealthy woman."

"I didn't know wealthy women felt this tired. Or sad."

"It's the way of things, isn't it?" Ensara stared out at the sea. "Life rolls on. Sometimes it takes your mates, sometimes it takes your fortune. And sometimes it drops little treasures in your lap. Like that sunset there. Even if I didn't have pearls as big as my thumb in every pocket, I'd be rich tonight. I've got a fine drink and a fine view, and fine company. That's something I'll not be forgetting."

"So you've been at the Custodian's treasures?"

"Jekka let me have them," he said, defensively. "In payment for my help. I told him he didn't need to do that, but he said he thought I needed it."

She hadn't meant to suggest he'd stolen it, so she gentled her voice: "Do you have plans for that money?"

"I've been thinking on that. You spend so much time just working on ways to get it, it's hard to know what you do when it's finally in your hands. Buy a really fine ship? Settle down on land somewhere? I don't know. What about you?"

"I've been wondering that myself." She set elbows on the stairs behind her. "This is a salvager's dream. My crew and I may never need to dive again. And I'm pretty sure the baron would knight every one of us if I asked him. I probably will," she said with a smile.

"But what do you want to do?"

"Later I'm going to see if I can help Jekka and Kalina find survivors of their clan. They have a few more leads. For now, I'm going to spend some time exploring these ruins with my family and my friends."

Ensara nodded slowly. "Captain," he said very softly, "is it too forward of me to ask if you number me among them?"

She decided her answer as she spoke it. "You may call me Mirian."

About the Author

Howard Andrew Jones is the author of three previous Pathfinder Tales novels—*Plague of Shadows*, *Stalking the Beast*, and *Beyond the Pool of Stars*—as well as the short stories "The Walkers from the Crypt" and "Bells for the Dead" (both available for free at **paizo.com**). In addition, he's written the creator-owned novels *The Desert of Souls*, *The Bones of the Old Ones*, and the forthcoming *For the Killing of Kings*, as well as a collection of short stories, *The Waters of Eternity*. His books have been honored on the Kirkus New and Notable Science Fiction list and the Locus Recommended Reading List, and *The Desert of Souls* was number four on Barnes & Noble's Best Fantasy Releases of 2011, as well as a finalist for the prestigious Compton Crook Award for Best First Novel.

When not helping run his small family farm or spending time with his wife and children, Howard has worked variously as a TV cameraman, a book editor, a recycling consultant, and a college writing instructor. He was instrumental in the rebirth of interest in Harold Lamb's historical fiction, and has assembled and edited eight collections of Lamb's work. He serves as the Managing Editor of *Black Gate* magazine and blogs regularly at **blackgate.com** as well as at **howardandrewjones.com**.

ACKNOWLEDGMENTS

I'm indebted again to Rich Howard for providing me with a wealth of details about diving, and am especially grateful to the long and careful manuscript critique of my friend Chris Jackson. He steered me into far safer and more accurate waters, not just with maritime matters, but character and motivation as well. If there remain technical inaccuracies as regards to seafaring or diving, the fault is mine alone! I would once again like to thank James Sutter for encouraging and supporting this tropical adventure, and bow in respect to Christopher Paul Carey for well-considered editorial direction and numerous tweaks that improved the story.

GLOSSARY

All Pathfinder Tales novels are set in the rich and vibrant world of the Pathfinder campaign setting. Below are explanations of several key terms used in this book. For more information on the world of Golarion and the strange monsters, people, and deities that make it their home, see *The Inner Sea World Guide*, or dive into the game and begin playing your own adventures with the *Pathfinder Roleplaying Game Core Rulebook* or the *Pathfinder Roleplaying Game Beginner Box*, all available at **paizo.com**. Those interested in learning more about Sargava specifically should check out *Pathfinder Player Companion: Sargava, The Lost Colony*, or explore it themselves in the Serpent's Skull Adventure Path.

Avistan: The continent north of the Inner Sea, on which Cheliax and many other nations lie.

Avistani: Of or related to the continent of Avistan.

Bandu Hills: Mountain range in central Sargava.

Bas'o: Nomadic tribe native to Sargava, known for its skilled warriors and hunters.

Boggards: Froglike humanoids that live in swamps and often attack other sentient races.

Chelaxian: Someone from Cheliax, either ethnically or by legal citizenship.

Cheliax: A powerful devil-worshiping nation located in south-western Avistan, of which Sargava was formerly a colony.

Chelish: Of or relating to the nation of Cheliax.

Colonial: Sargavan slang term for a Sargavan citizen of Chelish heritage, or anyone in Sargava's primarily light-skinned ruling caste.

Crown's End: Sargavan port city north of Eleder, known for its corruption and rampant smuggling activity.

Custodian: Alternative formal title of the Baron of Sargava, the nation's ruler.

Desna: Good-natured goddess of dreams, stars, travelers, and luck.

Desperation Bay: Large bay around which Sargava wraps.

Devils: Fiendish occupants of Hell who seek to corrupt mortals in order to claim their souls.

Druids: Those who revere nature and draw magical power from the boundless energy of the natural world (sometimes called the Green Faith, or the Green).

Eleder: Capital of Sargava and thriving port city specializing in shipping raw resources north to more powerful nations.

Free Captains: The leaders of the Shackles' legendary pirate bands, paid by Sargava's government to keep Cheliax from retaking Sargava.

Garund: Continent south of the Inner Sea, renowned for its deserts and jungles, upon which Sargava lies.

Halflings: Race of humanoids known for their tiny stature, deft hands, and mischievous personalities.

Ijo: Coastal tribe of native Sargavans known for their skill with boats and fishing.

Inheritor: Iomedae.

Inner Sea: The vast inland sea whose northern continent, Avistan, and southern continent, Garund, as well as the seas and nearby lands, are the primary focus of the Pathfinder campaign setting.

Iomedae: Goddess of valor, rulership, justice, and honor, who in life helped lead the Shining Crusade before attaining godhood.

Kaava Lands: Jungle-covered peninsula north of Desperation Bay.

Kalabuta: Of or related to Kalabuto; a citizen of Kalabuto.

Kalabuto: Ancient Sargavan jungle city now inhabited primarily by native Sargavans and ruled by a small cadre of colonials.

Laughing Jungle: Jungle in southern Sargava.

Lizardfolk: Ancient and tribal race of intelligent reptilian humanoids; often viewed as backward by humans.

Mulaa: Prominent tribe of native Sargavans known for their farming and ranching.

Mwangi: Of or pertaining to the Mwangi Expanse; someone from that region. "Mwangi" as an ethnicity is a catch-all term created by northern humans to describe the wide variety of cultures found in central Garund.

Mwangi Expanse: A sweltering jungle region found in central Garund.

Mzali: Massive temple-city located south of the Screaming Jungle and east of Kalabuto. Its xenophobic inhabitants, also called Mzali, worship the Child-God Walkena and seek to drive all nonnatives from the Mwangi Expanse.

Native: Sargavan slang term for the nation's indigenous peoples.

Nirmathas: Fledgling forest nation in central Avistan that is constantly at war with its former rulers.

Nirmathi: Of or pertaining to Nirmathas; a citizen of Nirmathas.

Oubinga River: Major river in the Kaava Lands.

Pathfinder: A member of the Pathfinder Society.

Pathfinder Lodge: Meeting house where Pathfinder Society members can buy provisions and swap stories.

Pathfinder Society: Organization of traveling scholars and adventurers who seek to document the world's wonders.

Pharasma: The goddess of birth, death, and prophecy, who judges mortal souls after their deaths and sends them on to the appropriate afterlife; also known as the Lady of Graves.

Rivermen's Guild: Powerful monopolistic guild based in Port Freedom that controls river travel in the region.

Sargava: Former Chelish colony which successfully won its independence, and maintains it through an expensive arrangement with the piratical Free Captains of the Shackles.

Sargavan: Of or related to Sargava; a citizen of Sargava.

Scrying: Using magic to view something from a distance.

Sea Devil: Intelligent and predatory aquatic race with a resemblance to the sharks they adore.

Sea Drake: Breed of lesser aquatic dragon capable of breathing devastating electrical attacks, but still less intelligent and powerful than a true dragon.

Shackles: Chaotic pirate isles northwest of Sargava, ruled by the Free Captains.

Shelyn: The goddess of beauty, art, love, and music.

Smuggler's Shiv: Dangerous island in Desperation Bay known for both its smuggling activity and the many monsters that inhabit its wilds.

Sorcerer: Someone who casts spells through natural ability rather than faith or study.

Taldane: The common trade language of the Inner Sea region.

Venture-Captain: A rank in the Pathfinder Society above that of a standard field agent, in charge of organizing expeditions and directing and assisting lesser agents.

Walkena: The mysterious leader of Mzali, also known as the Child-God, who ruthlessly seeks to drive all nonnatives from the Mwangi Expanse.

Wand: A sticklike magic item imbued with the ability to cast a specific spell repeatedly.

Wizard: Someone who casts spells through careful study and rigorous scientific methods rather than faith or innate talent, recording the necessary incantations in a spellbook.

Turn the page for a sneak peek at

GEARS OF FAITH

by Gabrielle Harbowy

Available April 2017

2

WELCOMING COMMITTEE

ZAE

Veena Heliu, the Precentor Martial for Magic, was often described as fiery for reasons that had nothing to do with her red hair. She was deep in an argument when they arrived, her raised voice audible from the other end of a long marble hallway. Pages wearing indoor boots of soft leather shuffled past silently, carrying scrolls in secure tubes and not making eye contact with Zae or each other. Keren, in contrast, had the conspicuous jingle and clank of armor to accompany her every step.

Zae couldn't distinguish Veena's distant words through their echoes, and she was almost disappointed when the yelling cut off abruptly upon their approach, replaced with the sibilant hisses of angry whispers. From the set of Keren's jaw, this wasn't normal; Zae surmised that whatever the source of the buzz Keren had mentioned, it had not been resolved overnight.

Zae had never been inside Vigil's Crusader War College, but Keren's father had taught here, and his children had grown up within Castle Overwatch's walls. Zae and Appleslayer followed as Keren led the way with the familiarity of muscle memory rather than recent experience. She tried a couple times to make conversation, but Keren's face was drawn tight and Zae left her to her own thoughts.

"Keren Rhinn! Right on time." Most people towered over Zae—she was used to that—but she suspected Veena Heliu could tower over people even taller than the sorcerer herself. She radiated such power and certainty that the air was alive with it. Zae looked around, but saw no one else; whomever Veena had been arguing with had left, if they'd ever been physically present at all.

"Reporting as summoned," Keren answered, stopping sharply at a respectful distance. Veena was a half-elf, and though she was not Keren's true aunt, Keren had referred to her as "Auntie Veena" on the walk over. There was no sign of that informality on Keren's part now. "This is Sister Zae, Cleric of Brigh."

The Precentor nodded curtly toward Zae, then surveyed Appleslayer, who stood alert at attention in his polished saddle. "And this is your mount, ready for his combat training." More often than not, the people Zae encountered were surprised to see dogs in such a role, but Heliu's life revolved around the art of war and the duty of defense. Her lack of surprise was no surprise. A note of approval hung in her voice, which might or might not have been Zae's hopeful imagination.

Appleslayer's plumed tail twitched back and forth once in a single, uncertain wag.

Heliu held out her hands, one toward each of them. "Are you ready?"

Keren hesitated.

"Speak freely, Crusader."

Keren cleared her throat. "Excuse me, ma'am, but I'd requested to be briefed on the reason for the fast transport."

"I didn't receive orders to brief you. I'm afraid your request's been denied from higher up."

Zae looked between the two women. Keren always accepted command decisions even when they left her conflicted—and Zae knew when she was conflicted, because the bottled-in frustration came out in the safety of their home—but Zae had also seen Keren's "Can't we work around this?" face enough to recognize it now.

"Well, thank you all the same," Zae said to defuse the silence. "I would be excited to spend weeks on a boat, but I'm sure Keren's glad to be getting to where we're going."

"Quite so," Heliu answered. "I'll be taking you into a park— it's discreet, quiet, and no one pays much attention to how many people are wandering around there. I must return immediately to my duties, so I won't be able to direct you to the Seventh Church myself, but someone from the church will be there to meet us."

They both took Heliu's offered hands, and Zae and Keren each buried their free hands in Appleslayer's fur. The sensation was slight—just an odd weightlessness in Zae's stomach, and then it was over. Her feet were now on grass. Where they had left at noon, they arrived in a place where the sun was noticeably lower in the afternoon sky. A copse of trees made an almost accidental clearing that would be difficult to stumble upon by chance. In different circumstances, it would have been a perfect spot for a moonlit tryst.

Zae checked herself and her companions. No limbs seemed to be out of place. Appleslayer whuffed softly under his breath, and Zae shook her head. "No exploring for now. Stay close."

When they stepped around the corner and into the larger park, they found an expanse of lush green meadow dotted with people lounging in twos and threes. In front of them, sitting on a stone bench with a small leather-bound book in her hands, was a woman dressed in the robes of an Iomedaean.

"I leave you to it." Veena nodded toward the initiate, and exchanged quiet words with Keren. Zae was too distracted studying her surroundings to pay attention.

The initiate stood and tucked the book away into the folds of her robes as Zae and her companions approached, greeting them with a warm smile. Roughly the same age as Darrin's aunt Estrelle, she had straight honey-brown hair and a particular intensity Zae had often seen in people who were strongly devoted to their gods.

"Welcome," the woman said to them, gaze lingering on the white and gold of Keren's armor. "You must be our new arrivals from Lastwall."

"That we are." Keren held up her left palm in greeting, showing the priestess the sword-mark there. Zae and Keren both bore the shield on their right palms. While Zae had her odd gear-shaped birthmark on her left hand, Keren had received the sword-mark of Iomedae on that palm to identify her as a Vigilant defender of Lastwall. "Crusader Keren Rhinn, and this is Sister Zae. Thank you for meeting us. We're pleased to be in Absalom."

"My name is Kala, initiate of Iomedae. It's a pleasure to be of service to the Knights of Ozem, especially in these trying times. Shall we?" Kala gestured to the path.

They walked along a quiet wooded trail at an unrushed pace that surprised Zae, considering how hasty their departure from Vigil had been once all the gears were in motion. Kala addressed Keren while Zae and Appleslayer followed behind. Keren stole a look over her shoulder, her eyebrows drawn in momentary concern, but Zae smiled assuringly in response. She didn't feel slighted. If her organization had greeted them, Zae would have expected the attention to be hers, but it was a pleasant day, with a breeze stirring the tops of the trees, and she was content to walk with her dog, enjoy the weather, and muse about what studying at the Clockwork Cathedral would be like.

"What's the name of this place?" Keren asked.

"Oh! I should be a better guide. I'm sorry. It's always so exciting to meet new people. This is the . . . well, the Greenery Park. We'll be heading west into the center of Absalom from here. It's the best route at this time of day."

Her hesitation sounded like embarrassment, so Zae said, "City planners are strange creatures. Seems like a redundant name for a park, doesn't it? Does the temple have you on guide duty often?"

"Oh, not often. Well, not until recently. All these servants of Iomedae flocking into the city. I do quite enjoy meeting new members of the order. Not *new* new, I mean, intending no offense to your possibly extensive and decorated service, but new to me."

They followed a wide carriage road out of the park and entered the bustle of a city headed toward evening. "These trying times, you mentioned?" Keren asked.

"Are those . . . camels?" Zae blurted at the same time. While there were a few horses and donkeys to be seen, camels seemed to be the customary beast of burden and transport here. Zae had never seen a camel in person before, and something about them struck her oddly. Maybe it was the spindlyness of their legs, or the long, questing necks, but they just didn't look like they'd been assembled according to an optimal design. Appleslayer stopped in the middle of the road, sniffing the air, and took a few steps toward a narrow side street, whining under his breath.

Zae followed him and peered down the street. She saw an aged pub sign creaking over a narrow doorway, and a shadowed dead end piled with rubbish beyond. She snapped her fingers by her thigh. "Come on, Apple. I know the camels stink, but I need you to stay close."

The dog whined once more, grumbled under his breath, and trotted back to Zae's side. She rubbed between his ears. "Good boy. I know it's all really interesting, but we need to keep up with Keren."

When Zae returned with Appleslayer at her side, Kala was still describing the various troubles the city was facing. Keren, who had never lived in any city but Vigil, listened patiently while the initiate rambled. Zae, who had spent time in several cities, knew the issues to be most generic. Sewers not keeping up with rising population; crime in the poorer districts; too much distrust of certain officials and too much trust of others. Meanwhile, there was no mistaking their passage across some invisible border into the next district to the west—buildings were suddenly closer together and more people crowded the streets, all with different destinations. A knot of chaos resulted, which for Zae manifested as a sea of knees and thighs. She noticed armor, leather and metal; women in soft breeches or simple dresses with minimal ornamentation; and very few shoes that had seen a brush or cloth in recent memory. These were commoners by and large, with a few servants shopping for their masters, and a few lawkeepers maintaining order or soldiers doing their own errands. Hopping up into Appleslayer's saddle— and then, while stopped at a corner, standing atop the saddle with Keren's arm for balance—Zae caught a glimpse of the peaks of market stall tents.

"What's this place?" Zae asked.

"Ah, this? This is the Gold District."

A passing servant with a broad basket at her hip bumped into Kala and looked at her askance. "It's the Coins, actually," she said, and then moved on.

Kala cleared her throat, ignoring the imposition, but Zae exchanged a glance with Keren. A translation error, perhaps, though Kala didn't have any particular foreign accent that Zae could place. "Whatever you call it, it's the trade quarter, if you will. Anything can be bought and sold here, at any time of day or night. Is there something like it where you come from? Lastwall, wasn't it? They never tell me anything about the arrivals, just when to be at the meeting point."

The constant questions were having an effect on Keren's bearing, though Zae knew no one else would have noticed the weight of them on her armored shoulders. "Have you always studied here in Absalom?" she asked, redirecting the initiate.

"Oh, I've only arrived recently, myself. It's the home of so many miracles, you know. Legendary for its concentration of relics, too. I've heard that practically everything of religious significance probably finds its way here eventually. Have you heard that?"

"I hadn't, actually."

"Well, apparently it's true. The Pathfinder Society has its head-quarters here, and securing relics is one of the many things they do. And there are so many museums! Both public and private collections. This truly is where antiquities are traded and where history lives."

"Speaking of living history, are you taking us directly to the church, or to our lodgings first?" Keren asked. The row houses here weren't exactly crumbling, but they looked like drunken old men in the small hours, propping each other up as they stumbled home from a tavern. It would be interesting to stay in one of them, Zae thought. She imagined them smelling of booze on the inside and swaying slightly around last call.

"Oh, to your lodgings of course, so that you can freshen up before you present yourselves to the church. You'll be staying just west of here, in the Foreign Quarter, where most of the city's guest housing is. I brought you this way because it's just so important to know where the markets are in a new city, don't you think?" Kala returned her attention to Keren. "Everything can be bought and sold in the Coins."

Keren nodded. "As you said. It's very good to know; you have our thanks."

Kala pressed her point. "Everything."

"Indeed, Priestess."

"So, if you were searching for someone who'd stolen some-thing, perhaps to sell it, this might be where you would look. Wouldn't you say?"

Zae knew the expression that went with that particular uncomfortable shift of Keren's shoulders. For a moment, she made the same face, herself. "I daresay you know the city far better than we, Priestess." Keren was only that formal when she was choosing her words carefully. "Surely a city this large has many crevices for people who don't want to be found."

"Yes, surely. But where are they sending *you* to look?"

"Look for what?" Zae asked, nudging Apple to keep up. Kala didn't spare her a glance.

"It's all right." Kala shifted closer to Keren. "I know why you're really here. I so desperately want to help, but I'm a new initiate so they've got me just escorting the seasoned ones in. I don't get to see any adventure for myself. Take a little pity on me and let me live vicariously through your mission. The other groups have all told me where they're being sent . . ."

"I didn't think it was exactly secret," Keren said, and Kala's posture straightened expectantly. "My mission is to train at the Tempering Hall. I'll be deepening my understanding of my faith, studying the Acts of Iomedae, and—"

Kala waved her graceful hand. "There's no need for such pretense."

"Pretense?"

"Your cover story is practiced to perfection. It's completely believable. But I mean your *actual* mission, of course. The . . . artifact. You know."

"I'm sure I don't," Keren said. "Perhaps you've confused us with another traveling party."

Kala smiled a smile that was just on the forced side of amusement. "Anyway, it doesn't matter. Tell me, in—Lastwall, did you say?—is torture a part of your training?"

"The giving or the enduring?" Keren's voice was just a notch too tight to be joking. Kala tossed her head back and laughed.

"Oh, you're lovely. The enduring, of course."

Keren stiffened again, and Appleslayer's muscles tightened and bunched under Zae's saddle. He knew how to read Keren's body language as well as Zae herself did, or perhaps she was simply giving off a sudden scent of wariness.

"Yes, yes, you're very loyal. I can see why they chose you." She turned a corner, leading them down a narrow alley that ended at a crumbling wall. "But unfortunately, that loyalty means you're of little use to me. I've given you plenty of chances to answer me freely, but those answers will be carved out of you if need be. No one can hold out against torture forever." Four shadows dropped from the low roofs on either side of the alley. "This is your last chance."

Zae blinked. At times like this, when the course of events took a turn she wasn't expecting, she felt like a clock that had just started to run down and would be fine again after a bit of winding. While it was a relief to see that, once again, Appleslayer's wary instincts had been correct, Zae felt strangely betrayed.

Three men and a woman in leather armor and shrouding hoods moved forward, weapons drawn, to converge on them. Rather, to converge on Keren. She had the big sword, and she had held Kala's attention. Zae and Appleslayer had not registered as a threat. This was something Zae could use to her advantage; she retreated a few steps and dropped her hand to her side, palm back, signaling Appleslayer to wait. She called upon Brigh to bless her allies, and saw courage surge through Keren and the dog.

Keren drew her greatsword up into a parry, deflecting an attacker's sword with a clang of angry metal. "I don't know what you think I have, but I swear to you I don't have it. We're just here to train."

"Unlikely," Kala said, drawing a sword from the folds of her robe. "We've been waiting for the Knights of Ozem to get involved. How convenient that they always arrive at the same place. So. Lead us to the artifact and we'll spare you. Defy us and we'll kill you both, and the next knights they send after you, and the next."

Zae curled her hand into a fist; Apple, recognizing the word-less command, sprang forth with teeth bared.

"Tezryn—behind you!" one of the attackers shouted, and the priestess turned. She slashed at Appleslayer with her sword, but the dog sprang out of range. He circled and made a lunge for Kala's calf. The dog had enough sheer bulk to throw an unprepared opponent off balance and enough herding instinct to shuttle enemies toward Keren's blade, but Kala sidestepped, raising her sword to parry Keren's attack. No matter how many times Apple engaged in combat, Zae was always fascinated to see him employ the same leaping and bounding maneuvers that were trademarks of his breed's energetic play.

Zae ticked over the spells she had prepared that morning, without having known that she would be teleported to Absalom or dropped into the middle of an alley brawl. She now knew several things about their guide: not only was she not a priestess of Iomedae, but if her first instinct was to strike out with a blade rather than a spell, then she likely wasn't a priestess of any god at all. Meanwhile, something odd was tickling at her senses, something about the way the rest of them moved that wasn't quite right.

Kala—Tezryn?—dodged Keren's next attack, but that put her right in the path of Appleslayer's teeth. He latched onto her hamstring, jerking his head from side to side. Keren neatly sliced the back of her other leg, bringing her down, and then turned her attention to the closest attacker, matching him swing for swing.

Appleslayer released his prey and turned toward one of the other shadowy figures, a fury of sharp teeth and strong paws, nimbly ducking swords and unarmed swipes. He'd come in behind an enemy to keep it turning and distracted, and then Keren would take it down with one fierce swing. He and Keren fought as one, seamlessly aiding each other with each foe. While Apple's emotional devotion was to Zae, he was equally loyal to Keren. She had trained him well, and their rapport was a beautiful, fluid dance that just happened to result in a certain amount of blood.

But this time, it didn't. Keren sliced a man's arm clean off, and it fell twitching without the trademark arterial gush. Zae cursed herself for not realizing it sooner, and called upon Brigh to bring down her holy wrath upon the attackers. The maimed man fell, and the others cringed and staggered at the sudden assault of light. Though remarkably whole, they were not alive. And neither was their leader. She had struggled to her knees at the periphery of the fight, but she cried out and curled herself into a tight ball under the assault of power.

Appleslayer and Keren tore through the attackers one by one. Their blows rang against Keren's shield. When all of them were on the ground, Zae finished them with another surge of holy power. The priestess, however, had worked her way to her feet somehow, and was stumbling toward the mouth of the alley. In a fluid movement, Keren unstrapped her shield and threw it like a skipping stone. It scuttled across the cobbled street and cut Tezryn's wounded legs out from under her, sending her sprawling. When Keren pushed the leader onto her back, she was glassy-eyed but snarling.

Keren reversed her grip and held her sword over Kala's throat, two-handed. "What do you want from us? Tell me!" Her hands were steady and the swordpoint didn't waver, but Zae knew her well enough to hear the hurt in her voice.

When the mock-priestess only grinned at her with bloody teeth, Keren brought the blade down with such force that it struck all the way through the woman's throat and impacted the pavement beneath. The priestess gurgled, and was still.

Zae started to call Appleslayer back to her, but the dog was approaching Keren, so she held her tongue. He sniffed at the knight, tail low, pacing around her like an anxious child while she checked the other attackers to make sure they were dead. Now that they were still, peeking into their hoods showed skin stretched tight over starved cheeks, and the teeth within their open mouths were longer than they should have been.

Kala was dead without a doubt, but that didn't put Zae at ease. She pressed her fingers to the guide's forehead, then brought them to her own nose. The scent was faint, but it held notes of rosemary and clean linen. "Undead, and disguising it," Zae said. "Unguent of revivification, I think. The timelessness salve wouldn't be this fresh. And she's not anyone's priestess. She concealed both her appearance and her aura." Beneath the vestments, she wore the same leather armor as the others.

"Are you sure she wasn't just alive and evil?"

"Positive. I called Brigh's light down upon the undead, not the living."

"So the others . . . ?"

"Probably not under her thrall, but likely she told them where to go for a good feast. None of them bit you, did they?"

Keren shook her head. "Apple bit one of them, though. Should we be worried about that?"

"I don't know. I don't think so, but better to be safe than dog food. Would you mind making sure they don't get back up while I take care of him?"

Keren pushed up to her feet, but Zae motioned for Apple to stay with her. She reached a hand out for the dog, who sniffed cautiously at her fingers. They still smelled of the ointment, Zae realized. She wiped her hand on her coat and gave him her other hand instead, whispering to Brigh and sharing a soft, warming light from her fingertips through Apple's fur. "He's fine."

"Which means that our real welcoming party . . ." Keren and Zae exchanged a long look.

Zae mounted up on Appleslayer's saddle while Keren took the vestments of Iomedae from Tezryn's corpse and reshouldered their supplies. "Apple, that alley you were curious about. Can you lead us back there? Retrace our steps. Good dog!"

As they hurried away, Zae took a quick glance back over her shoulder. Figures were already emerging from the shadows and creeping toward the corpses. Zae had seen squatters and street gangs scavenge what they could from the dead in the seedier quarters of other cities. It felt a little strange to her, knowing that it was happening, but it worked in her favor; there would likely be little left for the attackers' masters to find.

In the alley with the pub sign, Apple's nose led them through a heap of rubbish to the dead end and a broken, upturned crate, underneath which was bundle of bloodied rags that had once been fine cloth; it must have been the victim's underdress. Keren cursed and turned away, but Apple stayed by Zae's side while she peeled the stiffening fabric away. There was little flesh to be found. Small scavengers hovered, drawn by the blood and determined to find a scrap to eat.

"Get, you!" she heard Keren shout, followed by a scattering of refuse and a scuffle of many tiny feet. Half a dozen rats scampered out of range of Keren's sword, but didn't flee from sight, unwilling to give up the chance of a meal. Keren crouched over the cloth, her expression set and cold.

Mirian Raas comes from a long line of salvagers—adventurers who use magic to dive for sunken ships off the coast of tropical Sargava. With her father dead and her family in debt, Mirian has no choice but to take over his last job: a dangerous expedition into deep jungle pools, helping a tribe of lizardfolk reclaim the lost treasures of their people. Yet this isn't any ordinary dive, as the same colonial government that looks down on Mirian for her half-native heritage has an interest in the treasure, and the survival of the entire nation may depend on the outcome.

From critically acclaimed author Howard Andrew Jones comes an adventure of sunken cities and jungle exploration, set in the award-winning world of the Pathfinder Roleplaying Game.

Beyond the Pool of Stars print edition: $14.99
ISBN: 978-0-7653-7453-0

Beyond the Pool of Stars ebook edition:
ISBN: 978-1-4668-4265-6

PATHFINDER TALES

Beyond the Pool of Stars

A NOVEL BY Howard Andrew Jones

Daryus Gaunt used to be a crusader, battling to protect civilization from the demons of the Worldwound, before a battlefield mutiny forced him to flee or be executed. Pathfinder Shiera Tristane is an adventuring scholar obsessed with making the next big archaeological discovery. When a talking weasel reveals that a sinister witch is close to uncovering a long-lost temple deep within the Worldwound, the two adventurers are drawn into the demon-haunted lands in order to stop him from releasing an ancient evil. Now both fame and redemption may be at hand . . . if they can survive.

From *New York Times* bestselling author Richard A. Knaak comes a novel of exploration, betrayal, and deadly magic, set in the award-winning world of the Pathfinder Roleplaying Game.

Reaper's Eye print edition: $14.99
ISBN: 978-0-7653-8436-2

Reaper's Eye ebook edition:
ISBN: 978-0-7653-8437-9

PATHFINDER TALES

REAPER'S EYE

A NOVEL BY Richard A. Knaak

Shaia "Shy" Ratani used to be a member of the most powerful thieves' guild in Taldor—right up until she cheated her colleagues by taking the money and running. The frontier city of Yanmass seems like a perfect place to lie low, until a job solving a noble's murder reveals an invading centaur army ready to burn the place to the ground. Of course, Shy could stop that from happening, but doing so would reveal her presence to the former friends who now want her dead. Add in a holier-than-thou patron with the literal blood of angels in her veins, and Shy quickly remembers why she swore off doing good deeds in the first place . . .

From critically acclaimed fantasy author Sam Sykes comes a darkly comic tale of intrigue, assassination, and the perils of friendship, all set in the award-winning world of the Pathfinder Roleplaying Game.

Shy Knives **print edition: $14.99**
ISBN: 978-0-7653-8435-5

Shy Knives **ebook edition:**
ISBN: 978-0-7653-8434-8

PATHFINDER
TALES

Shy Knives

A NOVEL BY Sam Sykes

Once a notorious pirate, Jendara has at last returned to the cold northern isles of her birth, ready to settle down and raise her young son. Yet when a mysterious tsunami wracks her island's shore, she and her fearless crew must sail out to explore the strange island that's risen from the sea floor. No sooner have they delved into the lost island's alien structures than they find themselves competing with a monstrous cult eager to complete a dark ritual in those dripping halls. For something beyond all mortal comprehension has been dreaming on the sea floor. And it's begun to wake up . . .

From Hugo Award winner Wendy N. Wagner comes a sword-swinging adventure in the tradition of H. P. Lovecraft, set in the award-winning world of the Pathfinder Roleplaying Game.

Starspawn **print edition: $14.99**
ISBN: 978-0-7653-8433-1

Starspawn **ebook edition:**
ISBN: 978-0-7653-8432-4

PATHFINDER
TALES

STARSPAWN

A NOVEL BY Wendy N. Wagner

When caught stealing in the crusader nation of Lastwall, veteran con man Rodrick and his talking sword Hrym expect to weasel or fight their way out of punishment. Instead, they find themselves ensnared by powerful magic, and given a choice: serve the cause of justice as part of a covert team of similarly bound villains—or die horribly. Together with their criminal cohorts, Rodrick and Hrym settle in to their new job of defending the innocent, only to discover that being a secret government operative is even more dangerous than a life of crime.

From Hugo Award winner Tim Pratt comes a tale of reluctant heroes and plausible deniability, set in the award-winning world of the Pathfinder Roleplaying Game.

Liar's Bargain print edition: $14.99
ISBN: 978-0-7653-8431-7

Liar's Bargain ebook edition:
ISBN: 978-0-7653-8430-0

PATHFINDER TALES

LIAR'S BARGAIN

A NOVEL BY Tim Pratt

The Hellknights are a brutal organization of warriors and spellcasters dedicated to maintaining law and order at any cost. For devil-blooded Jheraal, a veteran Hellknight investigator, even the harshest methods are justified if it means building a better world for her daughter. Yet things get personal when a serial killer starts targeting hellspawn like Jheraal and her child, somehow magically removing their hearts and trapping the victims in a state halfway between life and death. With other Hellknights implicated in the crime, Jheraal has no choice but to join forces with a noble paladin and a dangerously cunning diabolist to defeat an ancient enemy for whom even death is no deterrent.

From celebrated dark fantasy author Liane Merciel comes an adventure of love, murder, and grudges from beyond the grave, set in the award-winning world of the Pathfinder Roleplaying Game.

Hellknight print edition: $14.99
ISBN: 978-0-7653-7548-3

Hellknight ebook edition:
ISBN: 978-1-4668-4735-4

HELLKNIGHT

A NOVEL BY

Liane Merciel

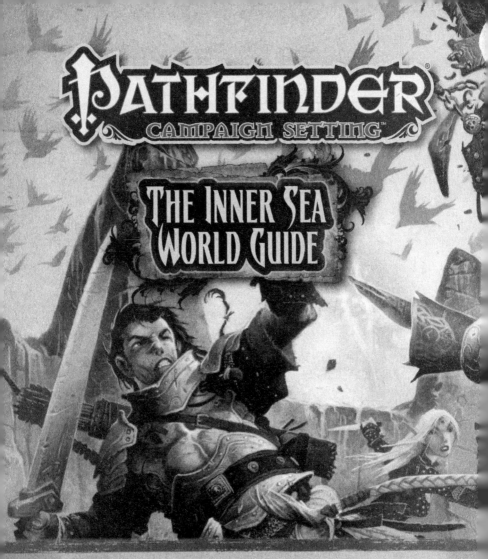

PATHFINDER
CAMPAIGN SETTING

THE INNER SEA WORLD GUIDE

You've delved into the Pathfinder campaign setting with Pathfinder Tales novels—now take your adventures even further! *The Inner Sea World Guide* is a full-color, 320-page hardcover guide featuring everything you need to know about the exciting world of Pathfinder: overviews of every major nation, religion, race, and adventure location around the Inner Sea, plus a giant poster map! Read it as a travelogue, or use it to flesh out your roleplaying game—it's your world now!

EXPLORE YOUR WORLD!

paizo.com